Kensington Books by Patrice McDonough:

Murder by Lamplight

A Slash of Emerald

A SLASH OF EMERALD

PATRICE McDONOUGH

KENSINGTON
PUBLISHING CORP.

kensingtonbooks.com

KENSINGTON BOOKS are published by

Kensington Publishing Corp.
900 Third Ave.
New York, NY 10022

Copyright © 2025 by Patrice McDonough

All Kensington titles, imprints, and distributed lines are available at special quantity discounts for bulk purchases for sales promotion, premiums, fund-raising, educational, or institutional use. Special book excerpts or customized printings can also be created to fit specific needs. For details, write or phone the office of the Kensington Special Sales Manager: Attn. Special Sales Department. Kensington Publishing Corp., 900 Third Ave., New York, NY 10022. Phone: 1-800-221-2647.

KENSINGTON and the K with book logo Reg. US Pat. & TM Off.

Library of Congress Control Number: 2024946552

ISBN: 978-1-4967-4639-9
First Kensington Hardcover Edition: March 2025

ISBN: 978-1-4967-4641-2 (ebook)

10 9 8 7 6 5 4 3 2 1

Printed in the United States of America

To Michael McDonough, the father who inspired a love of history in his children

The Color of the Grave is Green . . .
—Emily Dickinson

Annie O'Neill peered into the January mist and thought, *Why didn't I hail a cab?*

She had a crown for the fare, but the coin's solid weight in her pocket meant she would make her rent that week with shillings to spare. The girl pulled her woolen shawl tight to her neck, scant protection against the clammy cold that crept from the river.

Birdcage Walk by St. James's Park was a lonely stretch on any evening. That night, the shrubs and trees loomed from a wall of fog, taking solid shape only as she drew closer and passed them. Annie crossed the road to put them at a distance. Once she reached Fleet Street, she could hop an omnibus and ride the route for sixpence.

The mist veiled the visual world but sharpened the sounds around her: a cat's angry screech, the hoot of an owl . . . and then footfalls. Boot leather tapped and scraped behind her. Annie glanced over her shoulder, peered into the gray void, and shivered. She picked up her pace. At the corner, she stopped to listen. The follower still trailed her, and the footsteps were louder now. Then she thought of the girls: the shopgirls who'd disappeared, one by one, without a trace. Annie pulled her skirts away from her ankles and ran.

Two figures darted from an alley and blocked her path. A man grabbed Annie's wrist when she backed away, pulling her close, panting gin and stale tobacco in her face.

"What's your hurry, luv? The night's young."

CHAPTER 1

January 1867

Dr. Julia Lewis eyed the morning's post and a stack of earlier unanswered letters.

Her recent wrestling match with a killer and plunge into Regent's Canal had kept the postman busy. Most of her friends and acquaintances—and a surprising number of strangers—had written to wish her well.

Over the past few days, letters of a different sort had arrived at her grandfather's Finsbury Circus town house. A small item in the *Sunday Telegraph* had mentioned Julia's addition to the list of Scotland Yard's medical examiners, the first woman to be named.

One writer asked, "Have you learned nothing from your ordeal? Women belong in the domestic sphere as God intended. Remember, only the quick work of the men of Scotland Yard saved you from drowning."

Julia tossed the letter aside. *As if I need reminding.* On that fog-shrouded day, the killer meant for her to die. Instead, she'd been granted a second chance.

Julia abandoned her pen and pushed back the chestnut strands that had fallen from her hairpins. Her fingertips brushed the bandage on her neck. Had the knife slashed an inch to the left, her story would have had a different ending. She'd been lucky.

Restless, Julia drifted around the drawing room, taking in the blue-and-white tiles surrounding the fireplace and the light spilling between starched, white curtains. But domesticity wasn't the life she'd chosen, and two weeks of empty mornings and afternoon naps had bored her silly. It was past time she returned to her medical clinic in Whitechapel.

If some think that's unnatural, to hell with them.

Julia looked up with curiosity and relief at a knock. Muffled voices and footsteps followed.

Mrs. Ogilvie opened the door. "Inspector Tennant is here to see you, Doctor Julie."

The housekeeper stood back, and the tall, dark-haired detective with the erect bearing of a former army officer entered the room.

"Richard," Julia said, smiling. She glanced at the clock on the mantel. "Not yet noon. It's much too early for a social call." Her eyes dropped. "And you've held on to your hat. Does Scotland Yard beckon so soon?"

"Quite right. I see you haven't lost a step."

"This is a pleasure."

"I hope you'll still think so after we talk."

"Hmm . . . sounds ominous." Julia patted the armrest of a chair by the fireplace and sat in its twin.

Tennant settled in and fixed her with his grave and steady gaze. "How are you?"

"Recovered." She touched the bandage.

"Do you feel ready to—"

"More than ready."

"I wonder if your grandfather agrees."

"My only ailment is acute boredom." Julia waved around the room. "All this quiet is driving me batty."

"Let me see . . . two weeks caged in the house. I imagine Mrs. Ogilvie and the rest of the staff share the feeling."

"Itching for Monday when they'll finally see the back of me."

"Who's been in charge in Whitechapel?"

"Nurse Clemmie. But on paper, Gregory Barnes, a young doctor from the London Hospital. He's filling in at the clinic, thanks to Uncle Max."

"Doctor Maximilian Franklin to the rescue."

Julia smiled. "Useful when the hospital's chairman is your godfather. Doctor Barnes will stay on at the clinic, working two nights a week and every other Saturday."

"Something of a breather for you. Much earned, I'll add."

"Thank you." She sat back and looked at him over tented fingers. "Now tell me. What do you want me to do that I won't like?"

"I sought you out because . . . well, to be frank, the services of a female doctor would be useful."

"Sounds promising so far."

"Last night, a constable took a young woman into custody near St. James's Park. He spotted her walking alone on Bird-cage Walk and talking to a pair of privates from the Wellington Barracks. So, she was—"

"Let me guess. The copper arrested her under the Contagious Diseases Acts."

"Correct."

"And you want me to perform a forced medical examination on her?"

"An examination required by law."

"Because the law presumes any unaccompanied female

walking near an army barracks is a prostitute, most likely a diseased one."

Julia stood abruptly, her chair legs scraping the parquet floor. She crossed to the window and pushed the curtain aside. A wrought-iron fence edged her front garden, enclosing it from the foot traffic beyond. Sunlight caught the gilded pickets, a golden barricade pointing skyward. Anger radiated like a burn.

"Would any constable question *my* right to walk Finsbury Circus at dusk?"

Tennant stood. "Of course not, but—"

Julia dropped the curtain and turned. "But working women hurrying home in the evening? That's another story."

"Julia, don't pretend you don't understand the problem. Venereal illnesses are epidemic in the army. Parliament has raised questions about the readiness of our forces."

"And passes laws that omit the forced examination of males."

Tennant sighed. "Must we make this another argument about the many ways the world treats men and women unequally?"

"When Scotland Yard hires its first female copper, and they arrest the male partners of the women they exploit, then I'll stop arguing with you."

"Doctor Lewis, a job needs to be done. Will you do it?"

"I . . . I don't think I can be a party to it."

"For God's sake, Julia."

She threw out a hand. "I'm not the only one who thinks forced examinations are medical rape. I signed a petition to repeal the wretched acts. How can I—"

"You can stand on a soapbox on Hyde Park Corner, picket Parliament, or write to the queen, for all I care."

"But—"

"If you don't examine this young woman, the divisional inspector will call in a doctor who will. He may be less considerate of the girl's feelings than you. Is that what you want?"

"Of course not." Julia dropped onto her desk chair. She plucked a pencil from the desktop and tapped it distractedly on the blotter.

"The girl had a crown and six shillings in her pocket. It's quite a sum for a hatmaker from Aldgate. She claims she works part-time as an artist's model and was heading home to her bed." Tennant shrugged. "She may be lying, but I'm inclined to believe her."

Julia looked up. "Why did they call you? Prostitution is too commonplace a crime to involve the Detective Department."

"I was at the station house on another matter. When I suggested a female doctor, the divisional inspector's first response was . . . let's say he wasn't keen."

"You surprise me."

"If you want to know, he questioned your credentials. And he's impatient to get the girl out of his station house. So, the longer we argue—"

"I'll do it, Richard." Julia stood. "Of course I will. The poor girl . . . where is she?"

"King Street police station."

"Julia half smiled. "Shall I bring my medical registry certificate to convince this inspector person?"

"Division Inspector Evans, and documents won't be necessary."

"I'll get my bag. My Aunt Caroline expects me for tea, so I'll take a cab from King Street to Sussex Terrace when we're finished."

Tennant smiled faintly. "We won't keep Lady Aldridge waiting. I wouldn't dare." He put his hand out and stopped Julia before she went through the door. "She's young, and she looked frightened. Her name is Annie O'Neill."

Mary Allingham was late. Her bonnet's sapphire ribbons streamed behind her as she flew along the paths by the boating lake of Regent's Park. She was tall, fair, light on her feet, and waved to the Regent's Park groundskeeper who'd doffed his cap. Mary felt as sunny as the cloudless afternoon.

And why not? Mary knew she was singularly blessed. Although she'd lost her parents while still in the cradle, she'd come of age with a generous income and an older brother too amiable and indolent to check her independence. At twenty-three, she was clever enough to understand her good fortune and sensible enough not to let it go to her head. Men lost *theirs* in her company, something she'd understood since she was fifteen. But to Mary, her golden good looks were like her money, invested in the funds at five percent: not an object of pride or vanity but an asset she'd be a fool to deny.

The groundskeeper returned to his work. Mary watched him lift and drop his iron mallet with a resounding crack. Birds flocked to the water he'd freed from the ice. She stopped at the end of a path, shielding her eyes from the low January sun, tracking a swan's graceful flight and landing. Each beating wing rose to form a perfect V, the bird gliding until its webbed feet skimmed the ice, sliding to a stop.

Fifty yards from shore, about twenty stick-wielding men chased and passed a slippery disk. One hockey player followed the puck to the pond's edge, digging in his blades to stop, nearly colliding with the mallet-wielding groundskeeper. When the skater stepped back to push off, his boot broke through. He pulled out his foot, shook off the water, and skated away. Mary caught the parkkeeper's eye and smiled. He gave her a salute and resumed breaking the ice at the lake's edge.

Mary picked up her pace and spotted her sister-in-law standing by a bench along the south shore. She was easy to find. Louisa was as tall as Mary but more amply shaped and held herself like a queen. Her abundant auburn hair spread like wings under her cobalt hat, gathering at the back in a braided chignon at the nape of her neck. When she turned her head to peer down the pathway, her hair caught fire in the slanting sunlight. Mary smiled at Louisa's indifference to the admiring glance of a passing gentleman.

"Here I am," Mary called, coming from the opposite direction.

"You're late, my dear," Louisa said, sounding worried.

"Sorry, sorry, sorry."

Mary dropped her skates and sat. She looked across the lake, distracted by the winter landscape. She was a painter and had an artist's eye for nature's beauties. Mary's fingers itched for a pencil to sketch a birch tree's curling white bark and capture winter-bare branches like black lace against the sky.

Louisa eyed her sister-in-law. "Have you changed your mind?"

Mary smiled at her hopeful tone. "Not at all." She bent and fiddled with her skates.

"My dear, suppose you fall?"

"I wore my best lace petticoat just in case my skirts fly." She scanned the skaters. "I don't see Charles. Has he grown bored already and given up?"

Her brother's recent enthusiasm for the sport surprised Mary. He'd rarely done anything more strenuous than amble through a picture gallery. But Charles, being Charles, had no objection to her company that afternoon.

Mary spotted her tall brother etching lazy figure eights into the ice. Charles looked up and waved. Then, in a burst of energy, he tossed the end of his scarlet scarf over his shoulder and skated to the lake's edge, turning the inside of his blade into the ice, sending flakes flying. He doffed his fawn houndstooth cap in a sweeping bow.

"Ladies, no applause, please."

"You've been practicing," Mary said.

"And you're late—but what else is new?"

"Does your business partner know you're playing truant?"

"Allingham and Allen can do without me for a day." Charles turned to Louisa. "My dear, I hope you're not dissuading Mary from skating today."

Louisa swept her muff across the lake. "I don't see a single lady out on the ice."

"Lady?" Charles stretched out the word, raising his voice in a comical question. "You expect our Mary to do the ladylike thing?" A grin split the fair hairs of his trim beard and mustache. "I have the answer." He edged up the incline sideways and grabbed his wife's hand. "Come, my dear, you must set the precedent. Slide along with me. Never mind your boots. I'll hold you up."

"No, Charles. Certainly not." Louisa tried to back away.

He laughed and pulled her to him, holding her for a moment. Then he kissed her, released her, and regained the ice, skating away. Louisa looked pink, but a smile played on her lips, and her dark eyes shone.

Charles called to his sister over his shoulder, "Don't be all day."

Mary fitted her skates over her boots and adjusted the straps. Then she pulled on her mittens, stood, and swayed. She clutched at Louisa's arm for temporary support, took a step, and her right skate fell off. She refastened it. It slipped off a second time, followed by the left.

"My dear, they simply don't fit." Louisa looked over her shoulder at the rental kiosk. "Can you exchange them for another pair?"

Mary gathered them up and dumped them on the bench. "They were the smallest size they had. That prig of a clerk will be happy to see me back, tail between my legs. 'We don't carry skates for ladies, madam.' I wanted to throw them at him."

Mary looked out at the crowd on the lake. Then she dropped on the bench in defeat and leaned over to retie a bootlace that had come undone.

"Don't you get sick of it, Lou?" Mary said, tugging at the lace. "Everything women can't do—the blank busyness of our days. We're never allowed to stretch or look around. The world slaps blinders on us and sends us down a narrow path."

"You manage to go your way well enough," Louisa said.

Mary looked up, surprised, feeling the sting in the remark.

Louisa moved Mary's skates and sat next to her. More mildly, she said, "Besides, once you're married, and you have your own house and a husband to look after—"

"And become nothing but a broodmare. Good for spawning his heirs."

Too late, Mary wanted to bite back her words. For ten years, her sister-in-law had tried and failed to carry a pregnancy to term. Her third miscarriage in the fall had brought Mary home from Paris. She wondered if Louisa's heart would always beat for a child or if the yearning would die away.

Mary contemplated her sister-in-law behind lowered lids. It had been more than ten years since Charles had fiddled with the focus of his opera glasses and brought dark-eyed, flame-haired Louisa Upton into view. He claimed he never heard another note of the performance.

Is Charles happy with his prize? Mary wondered. Louisa didn't share the family passion for art and had little to add when the conversation turned to painting. As the years passed, her brother had less and less to say to his wife. Yet Louisa was an intelligent woman who was widely read and fluent in French. Mary envied her skill while she was living in Paris. Her sister-in-law should have married into a family of novelists, not painters.

Louisa's great tragedy was the empty nursery, but Mary didn't think it mattered much to Charles. None, one, or a brood of ten, it was all the same to her amiable brother. He was impossible to disappoint or provoke.

And yet . . .

Since Mary's return from Paris, she'd sensed something amiss with her brother. She looked up and sought his figure on the lake. Charles circled, retracing the same small loop, his hands clasped in the small of his back. Even from a distance, Mary saw his change in mood. It was as if the noonday sun had vanished in an eclipse. She read dejection in the slope of his shoulders, his bowed head, his gaze fixed on the ice.

"Lou . . . is something wrong with Charles?"

Louisa gripped her hand. "You've noticed it, too?"

"What's troubling him?"

"I wish I knew. Charles is away most evenings, dining at that club of his. And it's been months since he—" Louisa flushed and looked away.

Oh dear, Mary thought. She was trying to think of something to say when a splintering crack shot across the park.

Louisa gasped. "What was that?"

The sun-splashed afternoon collapsed in a confusion of shouts and screams.

Tennant held the door, and Julia entered the police station ahead of him. She felt as if a photographer had set off his flash powder, freezing an image in place. A pair of constables fell silent and stared. The sergeant perched on a high stool behind the duty desk halted over his ledger, pen poised. Julia straightened her spine and approached a wiry, hatchet-faced man in a police inspector's tunic. He frowned at his open pocket watch.

Tennant said, "Inspector Evans, this is Doctor Lewis."

He snapped the case shut and nodded. "Let's get this over with."

Thirty minutes later, Evans stood aside as a constable led the teary Annie O'Neill back to a holding cell. Tennant closed an oak door marked PRISONERS ONLY behind her.

Evans folded his arms and looked at Julia. "Well, Doctor?"

"Well, Inspector . . . I've just examined London's only virgin prostitute." Julia turned her back and finished rolling a set of instruments into a linen cloth.

Evans swallowed. His Adam's apple bobbed over his stiff collar. "You're sure?"

"Quite sure. Annie O'Neill is virgo intacta and certainly free of venereal disease." Julia stowed the bundle in her medical bag and snapped it shut. "Annie O'Neill is no more a streetwalker than I."

"Given the circumstances, we—"

"She said she'd been sitting for an artist. An inquiry at the studio would have spared her this ordeal."

The ruddy-faced duty sergeant snorted from behind his desk. "What would that have told us? Dropping her knickers for art? Bollocks. These models are no better than—"

"Better than what, Sergeant?"

"Everyone knows what they get up to, and that's a fact."

Julia's hand itched to slap the sneer off his face. "Annie O'Neill hasn't 'gotten up to' much. That's a fact, too."

At least Inspector Evans looked chastened. "The entrance to the Cockpit Steps leads to an alley that's notorious for . . . fleeting encounters."

"Just what the soldiers had in mind, no doubt," Julia said. "But Annie was simply exercising her right as a British subject to walk along a pavement."

"Rights," the sergeant spat out the word. "She knows the law," he snapped. "Or she should."

"Annie informed the policeman that the soldiers harassed her. She told them to 'hop it,' but the constable arrested *her*, not them."

The sergeant crossed his arms. "Lady, do you think we believe every fairy tale floated by a tart?"

"It's *Doctor*, and Annie O'Neill isn't a tart, is she, *Sergeant?*"

Tennant followed a fuming Julia out the door to King Street and waited with her for a cab. He cleared his throat. "I'm sorry, Julia. I wouldn't tolerate such impudence from my subordinate."

"The girl deserves an apology, not me. I doubt one will be forthcoming."

"I'll stay until they release Miss O'Neill and see that she gets home safely to her flat in Aldgate."

A cab slowed at the inspector's signal and stopped. Tennant opened the hansom's doors and stood back for Julia. He said to the cabbie, "Sussex Terrace, number . . ." Tennant looked at Julia. "What is Lady Aldridge's street number?"

"Twenty-four," she said, taking her seat.

Tennant closed the doors, and the hansom jerked forward.

Pandemonium had shattered the placid afternoon at Regent's Park.

It rose in a tumult of terror and despair: the screams of onlookers at the water's edge, the desperate cries for help from the lake, the rescuers' commands to "give way, let us through," and the shouted names of loved ones sinking beneath the surface.

Within minutes, the skaters near the shore had made it to safety, but over a hundred souls farther out had plunged into the water. Then the rush of skaters from the center pitched scores of additional people into the lake. Desperate victims clung to the edges of ice floes. Others threw themselves flat onto larger sections and waved frantically for rescue.

The Humane Society's icemen went to work immediately. They flung ropes to desperate men bobbing in the water. They rammed wheeled ladders between the chunks of ice and rolled them in as far as they could. Several icemen braved the water, pulling skaters to safety, buoyed by their cork life belts. Others recruited bystanders to help carry skiffs from the boathouse by the lake's western shore. They launched them with difficulty, oarlocks clanking, bows dinging ice blocks, progress blocked by the jagged floes.

Within twenty minutes, many had saved themselves. Bystanders had pulled out the skaters within easy reach, but scores still struggled in the water.

Knots of onlookers kept watch from the shore over selected victims. From time to time, a moaning wail went up as the skater in their sights slipped from a floe and vanished. When a top-hatted gentleman sank under the water, someone cried, "Look, he's gone, poor soul." Only his hat remained floating on the surface.

An old barrow-woman wrapped in tattered shawls rocked on the ground, keening, her basket of bright oranges at her side. "Jack, Jack," she moaned. "Dear God, will no one save him?" Her husband was beyond help. The onlookers watched the old chestnut seller slip off the edge of a floe. His wheeled, coal-fired brazier tumbled in after him, sinking amid the hissing steam.

Mary and Louisa stood among the desperate, watching loved ones struggle to survive. Charles was up to his neck in freezing water, clinging to a section of ice about thirty yards from them.

Louisa sobbed, "Charles, Charles." She clutched her sister-in-law's arm. "Mary, what can we do?"

Nearby, an exhausted iceman stumbled up the bank and fell to his knees. Someone untangled the rope that bound him to the man he'd saved. Then two others took the sodden, freezing pair away to the Humane Society's tent to be warmed.

Mary rushed forward and seized the discarded coil. She raised its looped end over her head.

"Twenty pounds to anyone willing to rescue that man in the deerstalker cap." She pointed to her struggling brother. "And two pounds each to the first three men who'll volunteer to pull them in."

A burly man shrugged off his jacket, grabbed the other end of the rope, and tossed it to his friend. Mary handed him the looped coil; he slipped it over his head and shoulders. Another man broke from the crowd, spit into hands the size of boxing gloves, and grasped the line with his meaty fists.

Julia knew something was wrong the moment her cab turned into Sussex Terrace.

Crowds streamed across the Outer Circle roadway, heading toward the park. When her rattling hansom stopped at her aunt's town house, Julia heard a muted din rumbling in the distance. Her aunt's front door opened while she paid off the cabbie, and the butler and footman struggled down the steps holding the handles of a large wicker basket.

"What's happening?"

"The ice in the park," the butler said. "It was rotten and gave way. Hundreds of skaters fell into the lake. Lady Aldridge is sending blankets and warm clothing."

Julia's Aunt Caroline appeared in the doorway. "And there's a call for doctors, my dear."

Julia and her aunt's servants rushed to the swamped relief station. The Humane Society had equipped it to treat the minor accidents that washed up on any given day. But that afternoon, the catastrophe surged like a tsunami, overwhelming its resources.

As Julia arrived, a soaked, shivering man pushed through the canvas flap and headed for the brazier. A burly laborer followed, backing through the opening, holding an unconscious skater under his armpits. His partner supported the victim's legs. Julia pointed to an empty cot. "Strip off his coat and lay him on his stomach."

A flame-haired woman of about thirty, visibly distraught, clutched the hand of a younger woman. "He'll be all right, won't he, Mary?"

"Of course he will." The fair-haired girl caught Julia's eye, looking less confident than she sounded.

"Perhaps if your companion took that seat," Julia said, smiling reassuringly, and nodded at a chair. Then she leaned over the bearded skater. She judged him to be a fit man in his early thirties, and that was all to the good. Julia applied her stethoscope and listened. "His lungs are clear, and he's breathing without difficulty."

"Oh, thank God," the older woman said with a shuddery sigh.

"And his color is good." Julia straightened up. "Let's make him more comfortable, shall we?" With the fair-haired girl's help, she stripped off his sodden socks and tugged on dry ones from her aunt's basket. Then Julia covered him with a blanket.

"May I have another?" The young woman nodded at the pile of blankets. "That shivering gentleman by the fire saved my brother." Julia handed her a blanket, and the girl draped it over the man's shoulders.

The older woman dragged her chair close to the cot. She raked tangled curls from the man's brow and stroked his cheek, murmuring, "Charles. Dear, dear Charles." The frost that clung to his fair beard and mustache had melted in the warm tent. She used her handkerchief to trace slow rings around his mouth and nose. Then she pushed it into her pocket and covered his hand with hers.

The girl touched Julia's arm. "Thank you for your help, Miss . . ."

"Doctor Lewis. Julia Lewis."

"I'm Mary Allingham, and that's my sister-in-law, Louisa Allingham. Doctor, may we take my brother home? The men who rescued Charles are waiting to carry him to our carriage. Unless you don't think . . ."

Julia smiled. "Oh, I think he can spend the night in his bed. Best place for him."

Louisa looked up. "His hands, his fingers. Doctor, is frost-bite . . ."

"There's no sign of it, Mrs. Allingham."

"Thank heaven for that," Mary said. "Charles writes articles for journals. He's an art critic."

"That's one less worry," Julia said. "Your brother's ordeal exhausted him. Dry him off, build up the fire, and watch for respiratory distress. Are you comfortable looking after him?"

"Louisa trained as a nurse, hoping to serve in the Crimea," Mary explained. "She'll take care of him."

Julia put her hand on Mary's arm. "Should you need assistance, please call for me at any hour. A note to number seventeen Finsbury Circus will find me."

"Thank you, Doctor. Will you come to us tomorrow morning? See how Charles is faring?"

She smiled and said, "Of course."

"We're in Kensington, near the Horticultural Society's gardens." Mary produced a calling card, scribbled her address, and gave it to Julia. Then she supervised her brother's removal by stretcher. The sodden man at the brazier handed Julia the borrowed blanket and followed the Allinghams out the door.

"Gone to collect his twenty quid."

Julia turned to the speaker. He was one of the Humane Society's icemen, still wearing his cork life belt. "What do you mean?"

"Saw it happen. That lass offered the chap twenty pounds to save her brother."

For the next two hours, Julia treated and released a score of skating victims and sent others by ambulance wagon to the hospital. She also pronounced several young men dead. Attendants removed their bodies to the Marylebone Workhouse to await identification by loved ones.

Sometime after six o'clock, Julia hesitated. She held a blanket at the shoulders of a dead young officer. The two pips on his tunic told her he was an army lieutenant. *Not a day over thirty.* She'd noticed his wedding ring. *A young husband. Perhaps a father?* Pity washed over her.

A rumbling bass behind her asked, "This is what you call resting, Julia?"

She turned around. "Grandfather. How did you—"

"Your aunt sent a message. Ogilvie is waiting with the carriage."

Dr. Andrew Lewis had removed his bowler, and his silver hair glinted in the lamplight. Julia was a tall woman, and her grandfather had grown more stooped over the years. Their eyes met nearly on the level. Julia held his gaze and said, "I had to do what I could, Grandfather."

He touched her cheek. "I know, my dear. I know." Then he looked down at the contorted face of the dead lieutenant. "A terrible last memory for whoever identifies the body."

"Yes," Julia said, thinking of the young wife. She wiped the froth from the lieutenant's mouth and wished she could do the same to the ghastly smile on his frozen lips. Her hand trembled as she drew the blanket over his purple face. Her grandfather put his arm around her, closed his hand over hers, and squeezed. She looked at him, knowing they were two minds with one thought. *Two weeks ago, Grandfather might have been looking at me.* Until that moment, she'd been too busy to think about her close call at Regent's Canal.

Julia spoke with the Humane Society's surgeon, then linked arms with her grandfather and opened the tent's flap.

"On the way in, I had a word with the police officer in

charge," Dr. Lewis said. "They've suspended the search until tomorrow."

The light had left the lake hours earlier. As Julia's eyes adjusted to the dark, she saw two icemen drag the last boat ashore. Scattered, mournful watchers remained, but most had gone home. The treacherous ice had frozen over, trapping the missing.

The grim recovery of the final victims would wait until morning.

CHAPTER 2

The morning after the skating tragedy, Julia hailed a cab and gave the driver the Allinghams' address.

He pushed his hat brim with his whip handle and scratched his head. "Marlborough Mews?"

For a moment, Julia thought she'd done something extraordinary. *Have I stumped a London cabbie?*

"Just off Kensington Road, miss?"

"That sounds right. Blenheim Lodge. It's near the Royal Horticultural Society's gardens."

On the way, they passed streets of terraced town houses with columned porticos as white and regular as perfect teeth. When the cab turned right into the mews, it stopped in front of an older residence. Blenheim Lodge, a red-bricked, ivy-covered mansion, was set back from the road in a broad, tree-covered lot.

Julia paid off the cabbie and paused, looking up at the house. The door opened, and Mary Allingham appeared, her tall figure framed in the doorway. She'd tied her long, fair hair to the side. It spilled across her shoulder like a pony's tail. Her apple-green "artistic dress" fell like a column from the bodice with simple lines and an absence of voluminous underskirts. It was an unfussy style that Julia also favored.

"You found us, Doctor. I've been on the lookout."

Julia smiled up at her. "You caught me admiring the house. It's quite different in style from the rest of the neighborhood."

"Blenheim Lodge is a good century older. Why it's called a 'lodge' escapes me. It sounds so rustic and cottage-like."

"Perhaps it's the trees," Julia said.

"A horticultural chap said the ancient yew in the back is a thousand years old."

"Heavens." Julia smiled. "Here before William the Conqueror."

She mounted the steps. Up close, Julia detected signs of strain in Mary's face: purple smudges under her eyes and tension around her mouth. "Before I ask about your brother, how are you?" Mary frowned, and worry lines etched around her eyes.

"No need to fret about me."

"But I do worry. Yesterday . . ." Julia shook her head. "It was a hellish day. I'm wondering, did you sleep?"

Mary bit her lower lip and shook her head. "I was exhausted. But when I went to bed, sleep wouldn't come. Only sounds and images—the cries and screams. And those bodies."

"It will stay with you, but time . . . well, it requires patience, but time will bring relief. Still, we can do something about the sleeplessness now. I'll leave you a mild bromide powder to take tonight."

"Thank you, Doctor. It's what didn't happen to Charles but *might* have happened. That's what haunts me. The thought goes around like a nightmare carousel." Mary shook herself and stood back from the door. "Please come in."

"How is Mister Allingham this morning?"

"I looked in a few minutes ago. He was breathing easily, and Louisa said he slept peacefully through the night."

"Good signs, all of them." Julia smiled. "Just what a doctor wants to hear."

"It's Lou who worries me now. Last night, she bustled his valet and me out of his bedroom and insisted on caring for Charles herself. This morning, she seems ... stunned is the word. When I took her hand, it felt like marble."

"The ordeal has caught up with her. I wouldn't worry too much. Still, would you like me to look in on her?"

Mary shook her head. "She's sleeping now."

"Then we'll let her rest."

They crossed a red-and-gold Turkish carpet that covered the marquetry floor of the two-story entrance hall. Curved archways framed the entrances to the upstairs east- and west-wing hallways. Art was everywhere, oil and watercolor portraits and landscapes.

At the top of the stairs, Mary turned right into the east corridor and stopped at the last door. "You can ring if there is anything you need. Alfred is the footman."

Julia jiggled the handle of her medical bag. "I have everything, I think."

"I'll let you get on with it. I'll be in the studio. Will you meet me there?"

"Your studio?"

"I'm a painter. Turn left at the bottom of the stairs. French doors in the drawing room will take you out to the terrace. The studio is to the left at the back of the garden."

"I'll find you there in a half hour or so."

Julia watched Miss Allingham stride away. Mary had called herself a painter, as Julia would say, "I'm a doctor."

An unusual young woman.

Forty minutes later, Julia descended the staircase and followed Mary's directions to the back garden. She faced two brick-and-stone buildings, one ivy-covered, its south wall pierced by four sets of oak doors wide enough to admit two carriages.

The other, clearly Mary's studio, had large, south-facing windows. Julia rounded a flagstone path to the studio's entrance and halted in shock in front of the door's smashed panels. She took a few steps, and glass crunched under her feet. Inside the studio, a tall, gray-haired man in a coachman's caped coat and a young constable writing on a notepad faced Mary. She stood amid the tangle of toppled easels and scattered sketches, looking dazed.

Good God, Julia thought. *What hellish timing for the poor girl.*

The constable looked up from his notepad. "You have rooms above the stables, Mister Taylor?"

The coachman nodded. "A noise roused me in the night."

"What time was that?"

"Late," Taylor said. "Past midnight. I circled the house with a lantern, checking the doors and windows. Saw naught to worry me."

He righted an overturned easel and set a damaged painting on it. A large emerald W marred the picture's center, and the intruder had sliced the canvas from corner to corner, cutting through the subject's face and cascading auburn curls.

"I'll see about repairing the window, Miss Mary," Taylor said. The coachman passed Julia, touching the brim of his cap.

Julia stepped across the threshold. "I'm so sorry."

Mary raised her hands and dropped them, her shoulders sagging. Then she turned back to the policeman. "Are we nearly finished?"

"Just a few more questions, Miss Allingham. Have you or your servants noticed any strangers in the neighborhood?"

"I haven't, but you might ask our housekeeper, Mrs. Drew."

He made a note of the name. "No quarrels with tradesmen? No one else with a grudge against you or your family?"

Mary's gaze slid to the damaged painting. A few seconds ticked by before she shook her head. The constable looked surprisingly young, barely out of the schoolroom. His tunic's collar seemed too large for his neck, as if he planned to grow into it. *There's something Mary's not saying,* Julia thought. A more seasoned copper would have spotted her hesitation.

The policeman closed his notepad and strapped on his helmet. "Thank you, Miss Allingham. I'd like to speak to the housekeeper before I leave."

While Julia waited for Mary to return, she studied a large, undamaged painting leaning against the wall. In the foreground, an auburn-haired woman reclined on a green velvet settee, her left arm stretched across the backrest. The subject sat in profile, dressed in creamy lace and pearls, the high collar of her gown skimming her earlobe.

Crunching glass announced Mary's return. "It's called *Repose,* of all things." She laughed hollowly. "I'd been brooding over it, so it was upstairs in my bedroom."

"Thank goodness for that. It's striking."

"Mister Taylor carried it down for me this morning. That's when we found . . ." Mary buried her face in her hands, shaking.

Julia plucked a wrap from its peg and draped it across Mary's shoulders. "Come. Let's sit." She led her to a pair of chairs.

"I'm sorry to be so feeble," Mary said, pulling a handkerchief from her pocket and wiping her eyes.

"Feeble? No. All this after yesterday?" Julia smiled. "At least on that score I have some good news. Your brother's pulse, temperature, and reflexes are all normal. His color is good, and his lungs are clear. He was quite proud of himself when he walked the length of the hallway and back, showing no signs of dizziness or excessive fatigue."

"Thank God."

"Mister Allingham asked for his wife. He became quite agitated when I explained she was resting after nursing him all night. He was calmer when I left him, but you may want your brother's doctor to examine him, too."

"Is there still some danger?"

"I've no reason to think so, but I'm afraid my examination wasn't as thorough as I wished." Julia smiled. "Your brother clutched his nightshirt like a bashful maiden when I tried to unbutton it."

"Oh, for heaven's sake."

"Not an unusual reaction, I assure you. All in all, he's a lucky man."

"As am I." Mary shuddered and drew the wrap tighter. "I would have been out on the ice, too, but for a pair of balky skates. That's another thought that keeps me awake."

"This should help you." Julia removed a small envelope from her medical bag. "Dissolve this powder in water and drink it shortly before you retire. May I return tomorrow morning? One last visit to assure myself that all is well?"

"Yes, please. That's kind of you."

"Now, what would you like to do? Wait until tomorrow to deal with the studio?"

Mary shook her head. "The thought of someone here, touching my things, pulling out a knife . . . the hatefulness of it. The sooner it's cleared away, the better."

"That sounds sensible." Julia clapped her hands on the chair armrest and stood. She asked, "Shall we get started?"

They spent the next twenty minutes picking up scattered paint tubes, canvases, and drawings. Mary shuffled through the sketches and looked up. "That's odd. I just realized that several drawings are missing. Studies of Margot Miller. She's the sitter in the damaged painting."

"An art-loving thief?" Julia won a wan smile as Mary bundled the remaining sketches into a folder.

Julia spotted an oozing, emerald paint tube, evidently the source of the slash across the canvas. She picked it up with her handkerchief and read the label.

"Paris Green." She looked at Mary. "Are you careful with

this? It contains a shocking quantity of arsenic. Medical journals have traced several deaths to its use."

"Good Lord, I had no idea. I grind cakes of the stuff and mix it when I watercolor sketch."

"Be sure to wear a cloth over your nose and mouth when you prepare it. And gloves." Julia dropped the tube in the box with the other paints. "I think that's the lot."

Mary nodded absently, staring at her damaged canvas, ripped and marred by the emerald W. She drew her finger along the tear and hugged herself.

"It's a pity," Julia said sadly. "Is the painting beyond repair?"

"I wasn't happy with it, so it's not worth salvaging. Thank God I'd sent three paintings away for framing. Next month, I'm showing them at the SFA exhibition in Mayfair. That's the Society of Female Artists."

"I wonder why the intruder painted a W across the picture before slashing it." Julia watched Mary closely as she answered.

Mary grimaced. "I can make a guess. Something someone sent in an anonymous letter. I've received two."

"Forgive me, but you didn't mention that to the policeman."

"The letters accused me of improper relations with my art teacher. Ridiculous, of course. The man is forty years my senior." Mary frowned. "Still, there's also . . ."

Julia waited. Then she asked, "There's something else?"

"Nothing. It's nothing. W for whore. That's what the letter writer called me."

That evening, Julia came down for dinner and found her grandfather and great-aunt conferring by the library fireplace, silvery heads together. Dr. Andrew Lewis and her Aunt Caroline looked up from their leather armchairs and exchanged guilty glances.

Julia chose a glass from the drinks cabinet and picked up

the sherry decanter. "You may as well tell me," she said as she poured. "You look like a pair of children caught with forbidden sweets."

Her grandfather cleared his throat. "Your aunt and I were, ah, debating the wisdom of—"

"Consigning this week's *Illustrated London News* to the fire before you saw it."

Lady Aldridge rarely had difficulty reaching the point and presented her cheek to Julia for a kiss. Her aunt shimmered in the firelight, all silvery elegance from her head to the metallic threads in her brocaded gown. Even seated, she looked tall and indomitable.

Dr. Lewis held the journal up and chuckled. "Your favorite reporter wrote the lead article."

"Johnny Osborne." Julia sat facing her relatives. "Who is he libeling this week?"

"My dear niece, you must admit he played fair with you."

"I agree," Dr. Lewis said. "Those articles about your ordeal were spot on. This week, Osborne's going after the army over venereal infections among the ranks."

Julia sipped and shrugged. "That's hardly news. There must be something else that you don't want me to read."

"His solution will incense you," her aunt said. "And I had hoped to have a peaceful drink before dinner."

"Let me guess. He suggests doubling down on the horrid laws and rounding up every female within shouting distance of a soldier."

Her grandfather smiled. "Something like that."

Julia sighed and leaned back with her elbows on the armrest. "I've expended enough anger on the subject—some of it unfairly aimed at Richard. I wish Johnny Osborne would investigate the skating disaster instead."

"Over forty souls, gone," her Aunt Caroline said. "You believe the tragedy was avoidable?"

"Yes, with proper procedures for judging the soundness of the ice."

Dr. Lewis asked, "How did you find Mister Allingham this morning?"

"Recovered, with no ill effects." Julia looked into her sherry and frowned. "It's his sister who worries me."

Lady Aldridge asked, "Was she injured as well?"

Julia explained the break-in at the studio. "And there's something else. A poison pen has sent Mary Allingham offensive letters."

Her Aunt Caroline shrugged in disgust "How repugnant."

"And embarrassing," Dr. Lewis said. "Which is why victims rarely report such letters to the police."

"Speaking of the police, have you apologized to Richard if you've treated him unfairly?"

Julia smiled a bit guiltily. "Not yet, Aunt, but I shall."

"Don't tarry, my dear," Dr. Lewis said. "I look at you and think, what might have been, but for Richard. I'm his debtor until the end of my days." In a steadier voice, he said, "He's an impressive young man. Scotland Yard should recruit more men of his caliber."

"There aren't many such men . . . available." Lady Aldridge sipped. She caught her niece's glance over her glass's rim and held it.

Julia knew full well the meaning behind her aunt's remark. Not long ago and in that room, they'd discussed matrimony— the impossibility of marriage, from Julia's perspective, and her belief in Richard's indifference. Aunt Caroline disagreed, claiming an elderly aunt's "fine eye" for observing and keen insight into matters of the heart. Julia doubted it.

"And what of Miss Allingham?" Andrew Lewis asked. "You said she worries you."

"There's something she's not saying about . . ."

"About what?" her grandfather asked.

"The letters," Julia sighed. "Today wasn't the day to press her, but I return tomorrow. I'm hoping she'll confide in me."

The following morning, Blenheim Lodge's footman opened the French doors to the patio. Once again, Julia followed the path in search of Mary. The studio door's windows had been replaced, and all traces of yesterday's break-in were gone. She found the artist sitting in front of her painting, feet up and arms wrapped around her legs.

Julia said, "Still thinking about *Repose*? You said you'd been brooding over it. Can you tell me why?"

"I can't decide if it's too subtle or crushingly obvious."

"Show me."

"No," Mary said, smiling. "You tell me."

Julia looked again. The elegant woman in the sitting room gazed over her shoulder through a large window enclosed by an iron grille. Claret drapes opened like a stage curtain, revealing details of the busy streetscape beyond. Striding, top-hatted men walked the street. One gestured for a cab, the sunlight glinting on the silver knob of his walking stick. Off to the side, a nanny gripped a little girl's hand. She pulled away, eyeing two boys in knee pants tossing a ball.

"It's two worlds," Julia said, nodding at the canvas. "You might have called it *Captivity* instead of *Repose*."

Mary laughed and said, "Full marks for you."

Julia turned to her with a wide smile. "Even the caged canary looks longingly out the window. Is the subject also the woman in the damaged painting?"

"Yes, Margot Miller. She's much in demand."

A maid with a coffee tray appeared at the door and carried it to the table next to Mary's chair. She bobbed a curtsy and withdrew.

Mary unfolded her legs and eyed the tray with a wry smile. "Two years on my own in Paris, and I've adjusted quite well to being waited on, hand and foot. I'm not sure what it says about my character."

Julia sat across from her. "Do you miss France?"

Mary poured their coffees and sat back, stirring and contemplating. "I miss the freedom. And I miss the evenings on my own when the city empties into its boulevards, and Parisians stroll the sidewalks. I'd find a table and sketch the passersby until the light failed."

"Unusual—an English girl alone in a foreign city. It must have been hard to give up Montmartre and the Louvre."

"Lou persuaded Charles to build this studio to lure me back. I would have come home anyway. Louisa . . . well, she suffered another miscarriage, and Charles was worried about her."

"I'm sorry."

"Louisa longs for motherhood. It breaks my heart to see her disappointed again. I often wonder . . ."

Julia waited.

"I think I told you Louisa hoped to nurse in the Crimea?"

"Yes, I remember."

"Well, her father was a doctor. Charles said Dr. Upton let Louisa train because he never thought she'd finish the course. Then her father refused to let her sail with Miss Nightingale and the other nurses."

"That seems particularly cruel."

"She nursed him to the end and keeps his doctor's bag and portrait in her room like a shrine. Poor Louisa."

"She did a wonderful favor for you with this studio." Julia looked around, her eyes resting on the damaged canvas. "Have you heard anything from the police?"

"Nothing yet."

"About those letters . . . should you have mentioned them to that constable?"

"Lou would faint if the accusations about my teacher wound up in a police report."

"And now this," Julia said. "It's possible the break-in and letters are connected."

"I've wondered about that." Mary bit her lip. "I should tell the police, but there are others involved."

Julia took a sip of coffee and waited for Mary to continue.

"A few painter friends received letters, too. One told me a man had followed her model and accosted the girl on the pavement outside the studio."

"That sounds serious enough to report."

"Oh, and a young milliner who models for us got a letter accusing her of posing in the nude and consorting with prostitutes. All lies, but the writer threatened to tell her employers." Mary shook her head. "Why extort a poor hatmaker like Annie O'Neill?"

Julia had taken a sip and nearly choked on her coffee. "Annie O'Neill?" She set her saucer and cup on the table. "Good Lord, poor Annie."

"You know her?"

"Yes, she's a patient." *How extraordinary,* Julia thought. *More trouble for the girl.*

Mary shrugged. "It doesn't make sense. She has next to nothing."

"So many victims . . . perhaps that's a reason to speak to the police. You might talk to one I know at Scotland Yard, Inspector Richard Tennant."

"He's the officer who . . . I'm sorry. I read about your ordeal in the newspapers, of course. He was the policeman in the case."

"Yes." Julia looked away. "I underestimated the danger to me. I scoffed at it, and that was a mistake."

"I'm not sure. . . ."

Julia gripped Mary's hand. "Talk to the other women. Try to convince them to come forward. Then talk to Richard Tennant."

*   *   *

Julia spent a quiet Sunday afternoon stretched on the library's settee, absorbed in the *Sunday Telegraph*. A sudden thrum of rain against the library's windowpanes pulled her attention from the newspaper to the gray outdoors. It had taken three weeks, but a foggy day or a dark winter afternoon no longer triggered a spasm of clamping fear. Julia folded the paper, curled on her side, and closed her eyes.

"Damn," she muttered at the sound of a knock. She swung her feet to the floor, felt for her slippers, and stood.

A minute later, Mrs. Ogilvie opened the door. "Inspector Tennant." The housekeeper stood back.

"Richard." She met him, smiling, her hand outstretched. "Sit. Grandfather is upstairs napping and will be sorry to have missed you."

"How is he?"

"Heart trouble is . . . unpredictable, but he's well enough." Julia smiled. "Mostly thanks to you for fishing me out of that canal." She put her hand on the whiskey decanter.

Tennant shook his head. "I have two reports to finish."

"Working on Sunday?"

"You keep adding to my caseload."

"Ah. Mary consulted you after all."

"I've just come from the house and wanted to tell you we'd spoken."

"I suppose . . . well, I imagine poison pens aren't usually the province of the Detective Department. Thank you for seeing her."

"They're dangerous all the same. And the physical attacks . . . they're unusual. One or the other, not both, assuming they're connected."

"Attacks?" Julia said. "There have been others?"

"Paddy O'Malley remembered an earlier report." Tennant shook his head, smiling. "The man's an elephant."

"More like an amiable grizzly bear."

"It's Sergeant O'Malley, by the way. His promotion came through."

Julia smiled. "I'm glad of it. What did he recall?"

"Last week, someone vandalized the French Gallery on Pall Mall. Splashed a can of emerald-green paint over the front steps and smeared the whole word—not just a W—across the double doors."

"Why that particular word there?"

"The featured artist this month is Jane Benham Hay."

Julia grimaced. "A female artist."

"I circulated a notice to all divisional inspectors with galleries on their turfs, asking them to be alert to possible threats."

"Mary mentioned an exhibit by women artists in February. Somewhere in Mayfair."

"I'll speak to the divisional inspector there."

"Richard . . . did Mary mention the letters sent to other women artists in her circle?"

"Yes. And, oddly, Annie O'Neill. The little hatmaker turned up again."

"I know. I must say, I was shocked."

"And something else surfaced. Another artist's model vanished about a year ago. She is one of three missing shopgirls from Cheapside."

"Good Lord," Julia said. "What's been done to find them?"

"Little, I'm afraid. Unfortunately, Chief Inspector Clark assigned the cases to a pair of our less energetic officers."

Julia shook her head. "Mary made a good point. Why torment a hatmaker with little money to spare?"

"The note sent to Annie concerned a former roommate, an artist's model named Margaret Miller, called Margot."

"That name rings a bell. . . . She was the model in Mary Allingham's paintings."

Tennant smiled. "Annie explained that Margot is spelled the French way 'with a silent T stuck on the end' just to be fancy."

"But why write to Annie about Margot Miller?"

"The writer called the old roommate a prostitute and said Annie must be a 'slag' as well if she associates with her. I've sent O'Malley to track down Miss Miller." Tennant looked out the window. "It's getting late, and my unfinished reports beckon. And you return to work tomorrow, too."

"Yes, back to the clinic at last. Richard . . . about that business at the station house with Annie O'Neill."

"Yes?"

"I took my anger out on you. And to spare Annie, you'd taken the trouble to call me in. I'm sorry."

"It's odd. . . ."

Julia smiled. "An apology from me?"

"I meant our encountering Annie again. Coppers are trained to be wary of coincidences."

"Well, coincidence or not, I'm glad the matter is in your hands."

"As it happens, I'm acquainted with Mary's sister-in-law, Louisa Allingham. Or was."

"Really?"

"A lifetime ago, before I left for the Crimea. When she was still Louisa Upton." He smiled faintly. "Another coincidence."

Was it wistfulness Julia heard? And there was a soft expression in his eyes.

"Miss Allingham would do well to listen to Louisa," Tennant said. "Charles Allingham was surprisingly offhand about the vandalism and letters. The fellow strikes me as feckless. Louisa and I urged Mary to take precautions. To lock her studio for one thing and not walk about the city unchaperoned."

"I hope Mary listens to you. She struck me as someone not keen to take advice, however well-intentioned."

"Indeed?" Tennant's smile flickered. "There's a lot of that going around."

"Very amusing."

"In the end, I had Miss Allingham's attention. I inspected the grounds of Blenheim Lodge and found discarded shells and a crumpled packet. Someone stood among the yews, eating chestnuts and scoring the bark of a tree. Waiting and watching the house."

Julia's stomach fluttered, and she looked away. A month ago, she'd dismissed the inspector's concern for her as male coddling. But now . . . *Another watcher in the dark. Waiting with a knife.* She looked up and found his gray eyes fixed on her.

As if he read her mind, Tennant said, "That slash across her painting worries me."

CHAPTER 3

At three in the morning, a young copper on the late January graveyard beat fought a jaw-breaking yawn. He stamped his boots to keep the blood flowing and made his way along Horseferry Road, shining his bull's-eye lantern through fence pickets for something to do.

His head jerked at the clattering racket of a speeding carriage. A four-wheeler flew toward Lambeth Bridge with lamps dimmed and shades drawn. The driver, a dark mass in the coachman's seat, cracked his whip as he neared the bridge, but his horses balked, wanting no part of the steep approach. The driver regained control with difficulty and turned the carriage east.

Change of plan, the copper thought. *Heading to Westminster Bridge.*

Instead, the carriage slowed and stopped. Doors opened and slammed. Then the coach rumbled off, out of sight by the time the constable reached the end of the road. He trained his lantern on something at the curb and walked toward a bundle where the carriage had stopped. The constable pulled at the cord, and the bag opened.

A cascade of copper curls tumbled out.

Sergeant O'Malley's bulk filled Inspector Tennant's doorway.

"A copper found a girl in a sack near Lambeth Bridge who fits the description of our missing shopgirl. The chief is giving it to us instead of that pair of slackers."

Tennant sat back in his chair. "You surprise me."

"We've 'pissed away' too many hours with 'letter-writing bollocks,' says he, and 'balmy' female artists." O'Malley grinned under his bushy mustache. "Time we did some real work."

"Where have they taken the body?"

O'Malley's smile faded. "To the mortuary on Horseferry Road. They're describing her as young, with flame-colored hair on her, like the last missing lass."

"Send a message to Doctor Lewis with my . . . you know the drill, Sergeant."

"With your compliments," O'Malley said. "And would she meet us on Horseferry Road?"

"That's the ticket."

Tennant and O'Malley waited inside the mortuary for Julia to arrive.

The inspector asked, "What about Annie's old roommate? Did you find Margot Miller at her flat in Chelsea?"

"That I did." O'Malley chuckled. "She's a fine one. I'm thinking it'll take more than a letter to frighten Margot—with or without a T."

"Hmm . . . from a room with Annie O'Neill in Aldgate to a flat in Chelsea. Margot Miller is rising in the world."

"She had two notes sent to her, printed in capital letters like the lady artists. Margot said she tossed them both in the fire.

She laughed, saying they were off the mark, implying that other accusations might not be."

They turned at the sound of a slight commotion. A young constable had stopped Julia at the vestibule's entrance.

"That's far enough, miss," he said testily, "The public is not allowed in this facility."

O'Malley rolled his eyes. "We're used to her, but he'll not be expecting a lady doctor."

Julia had fished a note from her pocket when O'Malley called out, "That's all right, son. Let Doctor Lewis through. She's here for the postmortem."

"Thank you, Sergeant," Julia said as she passed the wide-eyed young copper.

Tennant said, "As usual, you're a nine days' wonder, Doctor."

"Thank you for not saying 'circus sideshow,' Inspector."

Tennant opened a door. "The victim is through here."

He ushered her into a tiny but well-lit examining room. A sack still covered most of the girl's body, but coppery hair spilled from the opening, and purple bruises stained the left side of her face.

"Tossed from a carriage like yesterday's rubbish," Sergeant O'Malley said.

Julia pulled on a vulcanized rubber glove and slit the sack with a scalpel, exposing the dead girl's torso. Julia cut away her emerald wrap and held it up. Moths stitched in gold caught the light and sparkled against the bright green.

"A glittering shroud," Julia said. "There's blood spatter across the right shoulder."

The doctor moved the girl's head and found the probable cause of death. A blow had caved in her right temple. Julia cut away the girl's silk chemise.

Tennant fingered the rough sacking. "Impossible to trace the bag, I'm afraid. Seamen use them to stow their belongings. They're two a penny down in the docklands."

"They tossed her far from the quays of Limehouse and Poplar," O'Malley said.

"Her undergarment is silk," Julia said. "An expensive chemise for a shopgirl."

Julia found no other fatal wounds, but dark bruises stained the victim's right shoulder and upper arm.

Something gleamed in the bright light of the hanging oil lamp. Julia reached under the girl's neck, pulled out a snapped silver chain, and held it to the light. "Tangled in her hair," she said.

The sergeant moved deftly for a big man. He circled the table, retrieved the sack, and folded it back inch by inch until he found a shiny object caught in the seam. Julia slit the canvas, releasing a silver oval.

She held it up. "I see a field of stars surrounding the letter M and a cross."

"'Tis what's called a miraculous medal," O'Malley said. "In honor of the Virgin Mary. She'll be on the other side of it."

Julia turned it over. "Yes."

The sergeant crossed himself. "She could be Frances Riley, called Franny, one of the missing shopgirls. We sent for the landlady who reported her missing.

"She should be here soon." Tennant had cleared his throat, but his words still came out ragged. The light from the cramped room's glowing lamp shrank, and his head spun.

"Perhaps the landlady has arrived," Julia said. "Why don't you and the sergeant let me finish up, and I'll prepare the body for identification."

Julia had noted and ignored the inspector's pallor; she'd seen it before. Despite the cold of the room, a layer of sweat had covered his forehead, and he breathed raggedly. *What is it?* she wondered when the door closed behind him. *Not the body.*

He'd seen many in his line of work. Julia returned her attention to the corpse and completed the autopsy.

An hour later, a teary Mrs. Murphy arrived to identify Franny Riley. When Julia pulled the sheet down to the shoulders, Mrs. Murphy made a convulsive cry and pulled back. For Julia, the worst moment of any postmortem was that instant of recognition. Hope died in the eyes not slowly but swiftly, like shutters clapped close. Then came the wait. Julia stood by patiently and helplessly for Mrs. Murphy's goodbyes. She leaned over the body and caressed the girl's cheek, sobbing quietly.

After Mrs. Murphy left, Julia said, "Those weren't the tears of a landlady."

O'Malley nodded. "She left the girl's room as it was, praying she'd return. 'Tis lucky for us if there's something to find. Someone else would have crated her things and rented the room of a girl who'd vanished."

Julia drew a sheet over the girl's head and turned down the oil lamp's burner. She bowed her head as Paddy O'Malley crossed himself and whispered a Hail Mary before they left.

In the corridor, Tennant asked, "Can you determine the cause of death?"

"A probable beating. A right-handed assailant inflicted the facial injuries on the left side. But the fatal wound crushed the bones of her *right* temple."

"Two attackers," Tennant said.

"Perhaps. I found fresh bruising on her upper right arm and shoulder. She may have fallen to the ground after being struck, hitting her head on something solid."

The inspector asked, "Did you find other injuries?"

"Yes." Julia took a breath. "There were fading bruises on her thighs and extensive vaginal tearing."

"Evidence of rape," Tennant said.

Julia nodded and tried to steady her voice. "The poor girl

had been brutally used." She looked up and saw Tennant's eyes on her.

"Fading marks," he said. "How long before they disappear?"

"Severe bruising can take several weeks to heal, as would the tearing."

"Consistent with the timeline of her disappearance three weeks ago?"

"Yes. There's . . . there's something dreadful in that." Julia looked away. "A swift act, terrible and brutal, is bad enough. But three weeks of torment . . ."

O'Malley looked at the religious medal in his hand. "Where was the poor lass all that time?"

In the afternoon, Tennant and O'Malley met Mrs. Murphy at her shop on Silver Street in Soho. The grocer's widow still ran the business and lived comfortably in rooms above the shop. She ushered Tennant and O'Malley into a sitting room filled with evidence of her Catholic faith: a crucifix on the wall, a statue of Mary flanked by a pair of candles, and rosary beads in a dish by her rocking chair.

"Franny's parents left Ireland in the forties and rented my basement flat," Mrs. Murphy said. "Fleeing the hunger, only to be caught by cholera in '54. That last terrible day, they'd left Franny with me to run errands on Broad Street and stopped at the pump for water. By nightfall, they were dead."

O'Malley said, "No harm came to you and the lass?"

"Thank the Lord, I draw my water from the Warwick Street pump. It's nearer the shop. Poor little Franny . . . only eight with no family left."

"You offered her a home," Tennant said.

Mrs. Murphy's eyes were bright with tears. "God didn't bless me with children, but the Good Lord sent me Franny instead."

"You were a mother to her," O'Malley said. "'Tis sorry I am for your loss."

"She always called me Mrs. Murphy, but I felt like her mam."

"The sergeant who interviewed you three weeks ago . . ." Tennant watched her eyes narrow. "His notes don't tell us much."

Her expression hardened. "Franny was a good girl for all that fella hinted otherwise. And him . . ." She waved around the room. "Sneering at my statues the way some Protestants do. I'm begging your pardon, Inspector, but I didn't like the man."

"We're not sneering, Mrs. Murphy," O'Malley said. "Doesn't my sister have that same Virgin Mary in her bedroom?" He reached into his pocket and pulled out his beads. "Blessed by His Holiness, they were." He kissed the cross and put them away. "Now, what can you tell us that the other fella didn't bother to ask?"

"I didn't see her the morning she left. I was busy in the shop. But the night before, Franny said she might be late because a new girl at the store had invited her home for supper. That other sergeant didn't believe me. I could see what he was thinking. He thought she'd run off with some man."

"I believe she worked as a dressmaker's assistant at Harvey Nicols and Company," Tennant said. "Is that right?"

"Three years, now."

"Did she mention the name of the new girl who invited her?"

Mrs. Murphy shook her head. "I was so glad of the invitation. Franny's closest friend married and moved to Canada a year ago, and she missed her."

"She had no other near acquaintances?" Tennant said.

"She walked to Mass with the Callahan girls. Sweet things they are, but I doubt they'll tell you much. Franny hadn't much in common with them."

"Just the same, we'd like their names and addresses."

"Franny was a lovely lass," O'Malley said. "She must have had admirers."

"Oh, she had plenty of them. 'I'm in no hurry,' she'd say to me. Taking her time to look about."

"Are you recalling anything out of the ordinary?" O'Malley said. "Something that has you wondering?"

She frowned, considering. "She was working extra hours at Harvey Nicols, on and off."

"Starting when?" Tennant asked.

"Last summer. It was strange not to have her sitting across from me in the evening, and I worried. But she was grateful for the extra money, and they sent her home in a cab."

Tennant stood. "I'd like to see her bedroom, if I may."

Mrs. Murphy led them to a bright, comfortable chamber. If the room knew Franny's secrets, it kept them close. Tennant found only two things of interest: a drawing and some letters. The girl had pinned a pencil sketch of herself to the wall above her dressing table. Someone had signed it with the initials WQ.

"It's a good likeness of Franny," Mrs. Murphy said.

"May I borrow it?"

Mrs. Murphy unpinned it and smiled at the picture. "An artist in Hyde Park drew it."

"And we need to read the letters from her friend in Canada," Tennant said. "I will return them, of course."

At the door, Mrs. Murphy said, "Franny's best dress was missing from her wardrobe, but I wasn't telling the other sergeant that."

The interview with the Callahan girls was as unproductive as the landlady predicted.

Tennant pulled out his watch. "I think we can make it to Harvey Nicols before its doors close." He flagged a cab and directed the driver to Knightsbridge and Sloan Street. They settled in, and he shuffled through the letters, handing half to O'Malley.

"Let's start with late spring before Franny begins to work longer hours."

They rattled along reading until O'Malley broke the silence. "Here's something, now. Listen to this from June of last year. *'He sounds like a charmer—and the money is almost too good to be true. That should make you think twice.'*"

"The offensive sergeant may have been right," Tennant said. "There was a man in the picture. A charmer with money to throw around."

Several letters from the summer included tantalizing references. *"I'm glad I turned out to be a nervous Nelly,"* Tennant read. "And this one: *It seems to be going well.*"

"If only the girl would say what 'it' is all about," O'Malley grumbled.

"I'll cable the Toronto Police tomorrow and have them track the friend down."

The cab pulled up to Harvey Nicols thirty minutes before closing time. Tennant passed Franny's picture to his sergeant. "Show it to the man behind that newspaper kiosk and chat up the doorman. I'll see what they can tell me inside."

The store manager and the ladies' dress department supervisor were cooperative and polite, but they had little to say about Franny aside from her skill as a needlewoman. Tennant's question about her working hours puzzled them. They hadn't asked her to stay late and never sent their help home by cab. When the inspector asked to see the recently employed girl who worked with Franny, they looked blank.

"A new girl?" the store manager said. "We haven't added to our female staff in over a year, Inspector."

"Was Miss Riley friendly with any of the gentlemen who work here?"

The manager turned frosty. "We at Harvey Nicols discourage fraternizing among the staff."

"May I speak to the other seamstresses you employ?"

"Of course, Inspector."

Tennant sighed when the supervisor led him to a pair of ladies thirty years Franny's senior. He guessed they were unlikely confidants, and he was right.

Outside, O'Malley waited while the doorman helped a lady into a carriage. The man pocketed a coin and whistled his way back to the sergeant. The doorman remembered the Saturday evening Franny left the store and never returned. She usually caught an omnibus heading east on Knightsbridge. That afternoon, she turned west and walked down Brompton Road.

"She was easy on the eyes," he said, "and a pleasant, well-spoken young lady." He scratched his head under the sweatband of the hat. "Now that I think about it . . . when I turned back from a customer to look for her, she was gone. I remember thinking she must have hailed a cab or gotten into a carriage."

Tennant joined O'Malley on the pavement.

"'Discourages fraternizing,' does he?" The sergeant snorted on hearing the manager's remarks. "The law discourages many a thing, and here we are, chasing down criminals every day."

"Nothing from the doorman?"

"Walking a different way on the last night, says he." O'Malley explained the girl's changed route. "We haven't learned much after a day's work."

"We know that Franny lied to Mrs. Murphy about her plans and how she earned her extra money. She walked down one of London's busier roads in her best dress and headed toward Chelsea. Then she vanished."

"Until weeks later, we found the poor lass in a sack."

* * *

Mary Allingham felt a prickling sensation at the back of her neck. She didn't look around. Artists like Mary often sketched in the South Kensington Museum, and visitors stopped to watch. An observer wasn't unusual, but a critique was.

Someone with a pronounced Irish lilt said, "Those Muses, now. I'm thinking you've made them look too . . . amused."

Mary twisted around on the bench. A tall man with an unruly head of curly black hair looked down at her.

"You're mistaken. And they're not the Muses. They're *The Three Graces.*" She pointed her chalk at Antonio Canova's sculpture in the hall's center.

"A quibble." He set his paint box down and circled the statue. Blue tints from a shaft of sunlight shone in his jet-black hair. "Sure, it wouldn't be gentlemanly of me to say your Graces aren't graceful."

Mary eyed him slowly, tracking his scuffed boots, unbuttoned corduroy jacket, paint-smeared cuff, and loosely knotted necktie. He looked aggressively shabby.

"Gentlemanly?" Mary lifted a brow. "Hardly."

He smiled, his eyes glinting. *More green than blue,* Mary decided, *with flecks of gold.* Their expression irritated her.

The man glanced at her paint box. "M. Allingham . . . that wouldn't be Mrs. Charles Allingham, would it?"

"It wouldn't." She held up her ringless left hand. "For an artist, you're not very observant. Charles is my brother."

"An understandable error. Didn't I hear that Mrs. Allingham is the loveliest woman in all of London?"

Mary sighed and replaced her pastel chalks in their box. "It's rather late. I must be going, ah . . . sir."

"And where are my manners, now? Allow me to introduce myself." He dragged an oatmeal tweed cap from his back pocket, tugged it over his dark curls, and swept it off again. "William

Sheridan Quain, at your service, of Ballykilmuckeridge Downs, County Offaly, Ireland."

Mary blinked; he grinned. "Sure, the English like an Irishman who comes from a place with a comical name, so I oblige them. Truth be told, I'm from Waterford, like the glass. William Sheridan Quain. Will to my friends."

Mary picked up her paint box. "You must excuse me, I'm late." She crossed the foyer, walked through the doors, and down the steps.

Quain followed and looked around. "Where is your carriage?"

"I'm walking."

"To Blenheim Lodge on your own? Without a maid?"

Mary stopped. "How do you know where—"

"Didn't your brother invite me over to show him my work? Didn't he spend a few quid on some watercolors of mine? And you, away, studying in Paris? Sure, I can't let you go off on your own."

"You needn't concern yourself, Mister Quain. I cut through the gardens where there are many strollers about."

"If it's determined you are, I'll let you go. But I'll be watching you until you reach the gate."

As she approached the garden entrance, Mary thought, *I won't look back.*

When she looked over her shoulder, Will Quain waved his cap.

An hour after dinner, Mary tapped on the study door. "Am I interrupting?"

Charles shook his head. He'd laid his pen and spectacles atop a sheet of pristine paper. His glass and the whiskey decanter sat at his right elbow, its level down by several inches.

"Trouble getting your article started?"

Charles grunted a reply, tossed his drink, and poured another. He looked drawn and thin, with smudgy half-moons hanging under his eyes.

"Take a pew," Charles said. After she seated herself, he leaned on his elbow, chin in his hand. "What can I do for my lovely sister?"

"A forward Irishman accosted me at the museum today. William Quain claimed to know you. He said you'd bought some sketches from him."

"Quain . . . yes . . . 'musing fellow. Talented painter." Charles reached into the bottom drawer, pulled out a leather folder, and opened it. "This one's quite good."

Quain had painted a country scene, capturing the distant fields in quick strokes of every shade of green. He'd rendered the stream in daubs of purple, cobalt, teal, and Prussian blue. In the distance, wisps of whitish smoke roughly sketched curled from the chimney of a fieldstone cottage.

"He's spent time in France," Mary said.

"Quain's had a rough go of it. Fools at the Royal Academy schools rejected him."

Mary pulled two more pictures from the portfolio. The first was a watercolor of a woman's head and shoulders; the second showed her in full figure, standing at her washstand. Arms raised, eyes closed, she toweled dry a waterfall of coppery curls. A dressing gown of emerald silk lay tossed on the rumpled sheets of the bed behind her. The scene was intimate, the pose sensual. The model had never looked lovelier.

"Margot Miller," Mary said.

"Yes." He drained his glass and stared into it.

"May I take away the Irish landscape? I'd like to study it."

"Take the lot." He swept the sketches into the folder and pushed it across the desk. "On the wrong tack . . . too close to the wind. I warned him. . . ."

"Warned who? Charles, what's wrong? Is it the business? Talk to me."

"No . . . nothing to talk about." He placed his palms on the desk and pushed himself up. He tottered, and Mary thought he would topple forward. Then he steadied himself. "Nothing a change of scene won't cure. Leaving in the morning for Wales. David Cox wants my 'pinion on some landscapes he's painted."

"Louisa said nothing about a trip."

Charles weaved to his dressing room door and leaned against the frame. "Doesn't know yet. I'll speak to her in the morning."

"Will you be here for the women's exhibition? It opens in a week. A review by the eminent Charles Allingham . . ." She smiled. "We could use the attention."

"I'll be back. 'Night, m' dear."

The door clicked as he shut himself inside his small dressing chamber, a room with a single, narrow bed.

He'd been sleeping there for weeks.

CHAPTER 4

A week had passed since the discovery of Franny's body, and Tennant had little to report to Chief Inspector Clark.

Sergeant O'Malley busied himself with the canvass near Harvey Nicols, showing the sketch of Franny Riley to the cabbies and shopkeepers along Brompton Road. The street was a stretch of the leg, and O'Malley understood the doorman's surprise. How had Franny vanished from his sight? There was no turnoff before Knightsbridge.

A sudden gust snatched O'Malley's bowler, sending it tumbling into the gutter. He retrieved it and brushed the crown with his sleeve as Inspector Tennant pulled up in a hansom.

"We've had a message from the Mayfair station," he said. "There's trouble at the women's art exhibition."

O'Malley climbed into the cab and settled in. "The chief won't be happy we're back to the 'balmy' lady artists."

"I've been thinking about that drawing of Franny. It looks expert to me—not a sketch dashed off by a street artist. The girl was doing something to earn those extra shillings."

"Sitting for painters, you're thinking?"

"Let's not forget that a model for one of Miss Allingham's painter friends vanished a year ago. If Franny was modeling . . ."

" 'Tis all connected and maybe not balmy after all."

The cab dropped the inspector and his sergeant at a Mayfair address on Oxford Street. A police wagon pulled up behind them, and two constables from the Yard joined the local officers already at the scene.

"For the love of God," O'Malley muttered. "What are we having here?"

A sallow-faced man with a gray-streaked, ginger beard had padlocked his left wrist to the entrance railing. Dark, deep-set eyes flashed beneath bristling brows, and loose flesh hung from the sharp-etched cheekbones in his triangular face. Wintry gusts flapped the folds of his black coat like crow's wings as he spewed Scripture and waved a Bible over his head. A younger, dark-haired companion in a shabby black suit wielded a cane, blocking the bottom of the gallery steps.

A banner hung above the door: SOCIETY OF FEMALE ARTISTS WINTER EXHIBITION, 8 FEBRUARY–16 MARCH 1867.

The Mayfair constables stood between the two men and a group of women huddled on the cold pavement. Tennant spotted Miss Allingham and the two artist friends he'd interviewed about the anonymous letters.

"Delilahs," the old man shouted. "Salomes, Jezebels, and whores of Babylon, ye stagger down a crooked path. Proverbs warns us. Do not go near the door of her house." He pointed his Bible at the women. "For the weapons of our warfare are not of the flesh but have divine power to destroy strongholds."

"Let's break up the party, shall we?" Tennant called over to one of the constables. "Turn out the old fellow's pockets. Find the padlock key and liberate the gentleman from the railing."

O'Malley said, "I'll crack on with the boy-o at the bottom of the steps. Maybe the lad has it on him."

"Check his clothing and boots for traces of green paint."

O'Malley clapped a young policeman on the shoulders. "Come along, son. Let's have a bit of conversation with the creature."

The sergeant approached the boy and said mildly, "I'll have that stick, my lad." When he refused to hand it over, O'Malley twisted the cane from his hand. "Now, what are you and the old fella on about?"

The young man refused to answer, crossing his arms mulishly and digging his hands deep into his armpits. The towering sergeant leaned in and asked for the key. O'Malley stood six-foot-two, weighed fifteen stone, and rarely had to ask twice. Sullenly, the young man fished in his trouser pocket and produced it. He extended his arms at the sergeant's command and turned up his palms for inspection. Satisfied, O'Malley handed him to a pair of constables, who marched the boy to the police wagon.

O'Malley flipped the key in the air and handed it to the inspector.

Tennant asked, "Any paint on him, Paddy?"

"Not a speck."

Tennant unlocked the older man's chains and relieved him of his Bible. Inside the front cover, he found an inked name: Josiah Miller.

"Mister Miller, you will be charged with trespass and other offenses against public order. Sergeant O'Malley and these officers will escort you to the police wagon."

"They are the guilty ones," the old man shouted, pointing at the women artists. "The first book of John, chapter three. Sin is lawlessness. Nakedness . . ." He jabbed his finger repeatedly at the door. "That nakedness must be torn from the walls. Eve covered herself before the Lord. In Isaiah, chapter — "

O'Malley slammed the door of the wagon and returned to Tennant.

"The young fella's name is Micah Miller. Says the old holy

Joe is his dad. Miller, now." O'Malley smoothed the ends of his springy mustache. "I wonder. . . ."

"Inspector, may we have a word?"

Tennant turned to face Mary Allingham and her artist friends, Laura Herford and Barbara Bodichon. Petite, dressed in black from hat to boots, Miss Herford seemed as tightly furled as her umbrella. She'd glared at the intruders like a disapproving schoolmistress. The towering Madame Bodichon, her red-gold hair spilling from her bonnet, looked amused by the spectacle.

"Miss Herford has something to tell you, Inspector."

"I've seen the younger man before," Laura Herford said. "Last week, he accosted my model on the pavement outside my house. Shouting drew me to the window."

"You're certain about your identification?"

"It's his ears, Inspector. Pointed and quite distinctive, and those thick, slanted brows. I thought he'd make a marvelous Mephistopheles. Once Margot was safely inside, I sketched him from the window."

"Do you still have that drawing?"

"Why, yes."

"I'd like to send a constable around to borrow it. This afternoon if it's convenient."

O'Malley coughed. "Sir?"

The inspector turned. "Sergeant?"

"I have a question for Miss Herford. That model, now. Would it be Margot Miller you're talking about?"

Miss Herford looked surprised. "That's right, Sergeant. Full marks to you."

"The old preacher's name is Josiah Miller," O'Malley said. "There's many a Miller 'round and about. Still, the old fella has that ginger hair on him, and Margot's is bright as a new penny."

"It's worth looking into," Tennant said. "Are you ladies aware that this is the second attack on an exhibit?"

Laura nodded. "The French Gallery. The London art world is a small one."

"One of us sneezes, and we all catch colds." Madame Bodichon tightened her collar against the wind. "Speaking of which, may Laura open the doors, Inspector? I'm freezing."

"Of course. One last question. Did a girl named Frances Riley—Franny Riley—sit for any of you?"

"I don't know her," Mary said. "Barbara?" Madame Bodichon shook her head.

"I've not heard the name," Laura said, "and I know most models working in London. Who is she, Inspector?"

"A shopgirl who went missing. I'm sorry to say we found her beaten to death."

"My God. Could it be . . . ?" Laura's hand flew to her mouth.

"Yes, Miss Herford?"

"I was thinking about my model who vanished and what may have happened to her."

The police court's benches had filled with the day's haul of prostitutes, petty thieves, and drunk-and-disorderly charges.

The magistrate was about to release the Millers with a caution when his clerk coughed and murmured, "Inspector Tennant . . . a suspicion of more serious charges . . . additional inquiries." The judge changed course and held the pair for further questioning.

Two guards hustled the Millers out the door and back to the station's holding cells.

Tennant said, "We'll let them contemplate their sins, but we've got to connect the Millers somehow with the gallery and studio attacks."

O'Malley grunted. "I sent a constable to Miss Herford's house to borrow that drawing of young Micah," O'Malley said. "Witnesses to show it to are thin on the ground, I'm thinking."

"It's a long shot, but someone near the French Gallery may have spotted him. Or one of the barrow boys along Kensington Road may remember the man who bought a bag of chestnuts late at night."

"Ah, the watcher from the trees at the Allingham estate. But can you see either of these creatures writing those letters?"

Tennant shook his head. "We have parts of a puzzle that don't fit."

"And what about himself?" O'Malley asked. "Will the chief inspector be approving of all the time we're spending on this?"

"Probably not. But there's something, Paddy. Something is simmering. Nothing yet from our colleagues in Canada?"

"Not a word. There's sure to be some man in the picture. Mrs. Murphy was like a mother to Franny, but young girls don't tell their mams everything."

"I asked her Canadian friend in my cable. If there was a man, Franny may have confided in her. Meanwhile, let's head to the Millers' address in Poplar. See what a search turns up."

When Tennant and O'Malley got off the omnibus, the signs and scents of the nearby river surrounded them. Herring gulls wheeled across the sky, gliding low, drifting below the rooflines, calling out with mewing wails. They turned a corner and came face-to-face with the brick ramparts guarding the perimeter of Poplar's East India Docks. The smells of tar, tobacco, and the spices of the East—cinnamon and cloves—scented the air.

They passed the entrance just as a steam whistle shrieked. A foreman with a face like cracked leather and a sandpaper voice rasped out names from a muster book. Coins changed hands, and the laborers trudged out the gate.

"Backbreaking labor at fourpence an hour," O'Malley grumbled as they walked past.

"Not work for the faint of heart or shoulder."

"Up with the sun tomorrow, they'll be. Waving and shouting their names at the calling foreman, hoping to get on his list to work another day."

Tennant glanced at O'Malley, taking in his broad-shouldered bulk. "Did you ever work the docks, Paddy?"

"My dad shifted coal on Dublin's quays until the work gave out. He was a wreck of a man in the end. Sure, they'll work a fella to death if they can, these shippers. No, I made my way in the boxing ring before the Yard took me on." O'Malley flexed his gloved fingers in the cold.

The inspector remembered the broken knuckles on his sergeant's hands. Tennant had his own old injuries and shifted his weight from an aching leg. "Where's that address, Paddy?"

"There."

They crossed Barking Road and stopped at a corner building. It housed a busy pub, and next to it, a fading sign read MILLER AND SON, COOPERS. Tennant fitted the key he'd taken from its owner, and the door swung in.

Bins lined the back from wall to wall. Four half-trussed kegs waited, their flayed staves spreading like flower petals. Oddly, someone had stacked about thirty wooden chairs against the right-hand wall.

After a look around, Tennant said, "Nothing here." He opened the door to the living quarters in the back. They started with the smaller bedroom, Micah's chamber.

Tennant said, "Let's see what's under his bed."

"My knees are killing me." O'Malley lowered himself to the floor. "But rank has its privileges."

The sergeant dragged a battered suitcase from under the bed, unstrapped the lid, and pulled out a smudged, unsealed envelope, dumping it on the bed. He added dog-eared copies of the *Illustrated London News*, several sketches, and two books to the pile.

Tennant opened the envelope and shuffled through the contents. He handed it to O'Malley.

The sergeant gave a low whistle. "The naughty boy-o. What they call French postcards. Not the sort you'd send to your mam."

"What's in those sketches, Paddy?"

O'Malley thumbed through a set of charcoal drawings and handed them to Tennant.

"Well, well," Tennant said, turning them over. "Mary Allingham's missing drawings from the studio break-in. She signed them with her initials."

"That nails young Micah to the wall. And what's this? Pictures of Margot Miller, naked as the day she was born. Mother of God, the creature is keeping his sister under his bed with his stash of naughty postcards."

"And those books?"

"A copy of the ladies' exhibition catalog, with Margot Miller on the front. And a book called *The New Sprees of London.*" O'Malley flipped through the pages. "'Tis a guide to the city's bawdy houses."

"Keep Mary's sketches and the catalog," Tennant said. "Return the other items to the box. We're done here."

They returned to the workshop's main room and found their entry had drawn attention. A man in a barman's apron slouched against the doorframe. His face was as rough and wrinkled as a walnut, and he'd pushed up his shirtsleeves, revealing bulging arms covered with nautical tattoos.

"Alf Bailey," he said. "Owner of the East Indiaman next door. The finest pub in Poplar."

Tennant identified himself and Sergeant O'Malley as Metropolitan Police officers and asked about the Millers.

"Old Josiah's gone barmy over religion. Mind you, the cooperage is still a going concern—the docks eat barrels for breakfast, lunch, and dinner. Still, there's more yammering and less hammering nowadays."

"Meaning?"

"Every Sunday morning and Wednesday night, the blighter clears out his workshop and fills it with God-botherers, preaching and hymning all day and evening long."

Tennant said, "That explains the chairs in the workshop. The sign says 'Miller and Son.' What can you tell us about Micah Miller?"

"The boy . . ." Bailey narrowed his eyes. "The lad came into the family when Josiah married his second missus. She's dead, too. Still, the old blighter gave the boy his surname. Micah Miller—he's a strange one. Quiet. Always watching."

"So, Margot Miller isn't his sister," Tennant said.

"Margot? Oh, you mean Peggy Miller, that was. Not blood, and a good thing, too, with him always drooling after her. She's a looker, that Peggy Miller, whatever she's calling herself nowadays."

"Did she look back?" Tennant asked.

"Nah . . . but the young sod could hardly help himself. He was mad jealous if anyone eyed her. And that was just about everyone, all the time."

"We questioned the old preacher about Margot Miller," O'Malley said. "He denied having a daughter."

"Dead to him, Josiah said, ever since she started dropping her knickers for those artists."

"I'm seeing how old holy Joe wouldn't like that."

"Nor the stepbrother, I'd wager," the pubkeeper said. "Then there's her bloke, Arnie Stackpole. He's a seaman back after a twelve-month on the China seas. She'll be dead to him, too, once he finds her."

Tennant said, "And why would that be?"

"Rumor has it she's . . ." Bailey traced a mound over his belly.

"Up the pole," O'Malley said. "And himself away for a year?"

Bailey nodded. "Heard he's back and hunting for her."

It had been a long day. Late in the afternoon, Tennant halted in the vestibule of the Whitechapel Clinic. He'd been on his feet since morning, and his leg ached. He longed for a whiskey and his comfortable chair, but Julia had sent a message asking to see him, and she wasn't one to waste his time.

Tennant pushed open the inner door, and two familiar sensations struck him. First was the calm of the well-managed clinic and its contrast with the gritty, chaotic world outside its doors. And lingering in the air was the sharp scent of carbolic soap. He spotted Julia's head nurse at the end of the hallway, buttoning her blue wool cape. Gray threaded Nurse Clemmie's dark hair. She wore it pulled back and tucked under her cap. The middle-aged nurse cut a trim and deceptively slight figure: Tennant had watched her shift male patients twice her size with surprising ease. It was the first time he'd seen her since the day he'd burst through the clinic doors looking for Julia, only to find that the killer had lured her away.

"Good evening, Inspector. Doctor Lewis is in the men's ward."

"With the doctor back, are things settling into their normal routine?"

"Normal may take some time. I still see him waiting for her in the corridor. Smiling. Sipping that last cup of tea." She opened the door to Julia's office. "I'll tell the doctor you're here."

The inspector understood. The gut-wrenching drive through the fog, the knife at Julia's throat, the plunge into the canal's dark waters: those memories had become new nightmares for him. Lately, they had replaced the dreams that recurred more than a decade after the end of the Crimean War.

Tennant took a seat and eased his leg.

Julia didn't keep him waiting long. She touched his shoulder as he rose. "Don't get up." She settled in behind her desk. "You look tired. It could have waited until tomorrow."

"Days have a habit of getting away from me. But you look as if you could do another shift, and here it is, nearly six o'clock."

That was another reason he'd come that evening: he wanted to see how Julia fared in full harness. *Who am I kidding?* he thought. *Any excuse to call.*

"Sitting has made me realize I'm ready to sink into a chair and share a sherry with my grandfather." She smiled. "Or something a little stronger."

Julia leaned forward and plucked a pencil from the beaker on her desk and tapped it. He'd noticed her habit of fiddling with one when she was thinking. Tennant waited for her to make up her mind. Sitting reminded him how tired he was, too. He stifled a yawn.

"To be honest—" Julia stopped. "I'm not sure . . ."

"Not sure of what?"

"That there's anything much you can do. Still, given everything that's happened, you should know that the little hatmaker came to see me today. Annie O'Neill."

"Indeed?"

"I'd given her my card at the police station. She lives nearby on Aldgate High Street."

"Yes, I know."

"She'd dislocated her shoulder, cut her left cheek, and had a deeper gash on her forearm that needed stitches. Annie said she slipped on the steps, but I suspect someone may be to blame."

"What made you think she lied?"

Julia raised her forearm. "The slashing wound might have been a defensive injury."

"Consistent with someone threatening her with a knife?"

"Possibly. And Annie had welt marks here." Julia gripped her left arm just above her wrist. "As if someone grabbed her and twisted. Someone right-handed, most likely."

"You're convinced she suffered a physical assault?"

"After Franny Riley . . . two girls who worked for shops. I'm worried about Annie."

"Did you mention Franny to her?"

"Yes. Annie didn't know her. She became agitated when I asked if someone had attacked her, but she insisted it wasn't so." Julia sighed. "I doubt she'll tell you a different story."

"Probably not."

"Let me try again before you question her. I told Annie I would visit her in a few days to check on her bandages."

Tennant considered. "Very well. See if you can win her confidence."

"Annie seemed afraid of someone or something."

"We know who broke into Miss Allingham's studio, by the way. We found her missing sketches."

"Who is he?"

"Micah Miller, the stepbrother of Margot Miller. I have an artist's drawing of him to show to witnesses. It's an excellent likeness. Artists make good witnesses."

"It's their habit of observation, I expect."

"Something they share with doctors."

Julia rolled the pencil between her fingers. "It's fraught for females, this matter of looking," she said at last. "A bold, direct gaze is thought to be 'unladylike.' I expect that's half the problem for female artists." She looked up. "What?"

Tennant shook his head. "Nothing. I'm sure you're right."

"Hmm. Something I said amused you, but never mind. I see you're choosing to be your usual sphinxlike self."

"Sphinxlike? I'm an open book."

Julia laughed. "Oh, yes. One written in hieroglyphics perhaps."

Tennant had smiled because he remembered his early impressions of Julia. She'd met his gaze directly and spoken candidly about the sexual mutilation of the corpse she'd examined. At first, he'd found it unsettling.

"It's only a hunch, but I asked the women artists if Franny Riley had modeled for them. They said no."

Julia looked at him curiously. "What makes you think it?"

"Someone quite expert sketched her picture."

"Mary's invited me to the exhibit's preview tomorrow."

"Then you'll meet Miss Herford, the artist who drew Micah Miller. She sent a note with the sketch, recalling another attack several weeks ago. Someone ransacked the printing workshop at the Victoria Press."

"What's the connection?"

"They printed the catalog for the women's art exhibit. Miss Faithfull, the director, dismissed it as harassment directed at her female compositors and proofreaders. It seems their gentlemen colleagues in the printing world do not welcome them."

"You surprise me," Julia said dryly.

"We found an exhibit catalog in Micah Miller's bedroom. It had 'Property of the Victoria Press' stamped on the title page. It's the copy stolen from the window display. We'll charge him with the attacks on the printshop and Miss Allingham's studio."

"Do you know what drove him?"

"Jealousy and obsession over his stepsister, Margot Miller. She's in the painting on the catalog's cover."

"And she posed for Mary's picture—the damaged one."

Tennant nodded. "Micah doesn't want to share Margot with the world."

"What will happen to him?"

He shrugged. "Prisons are crowded. A guilty plea will bring fines for damages and a suspended sentence. And a warning to stop stalking his stepsister."

"Margot Miller . . . Annie's vicious letter about her, the catalog cover, and Mary's vandalized painting—all Margot."

"The drawings Micah stole from Miss Allingham were of Margot as well."

"At every turn, you come back to her."

"It seems so." Tennant eyed her cape and medical bag. After a moment's hesitation, he said, "If you're leaving . . . shall we share a cab? I can drop you off at Finsbury Circus and continue to Russell Square. It's no trouble. That is . . ." He felt oddly tongue-tied, and he cursed himself for behaving like an awkward schoolboy.

"Delighted." Julia stood and picked up her hat. "But on one condition. That we talk of anything or anyone except Margot Miller."

Tennant held her cape for her. "Agreed."

CHAPTER 5

Charles Allingham circled the gallery and returned to where he began his tour of the women's exhibition: his sister's picture, *The Three Graces*. He stroked the fair hairs of his Vandyke as Mary and Julia joined him.

Two Graces turned their heads to gaze at the bold-eyed, auburn-haired woman in the picture's center. Undraped, she looked directly at the viewer, a languid hand covering herself below, the other trailing a lily seductively along her cheek.

Allingham tucked away his spectacles. "'And from her eyes, desire—the melter of limbs—trickles down when she looks.'" He answered Julia's curious glance. "Hesiod's description of the Graces."

Mary took his arm. "Showing off your classical education, Brother?"

"Showing off your marvelous technique, Sister?"

They are a golden pair, Julia thought. *Tall and fair and gleaming.*

"Not to mention yards and yards of female flesh," Allingham said. "No wonder that old zealot frothed at the mouth."

"Not the response I sought, believe me."

"Still, that Grace in the center could walk out of the frame and strike a man dead." Allingham lifted his sister's hand to his lips. "My dear, I envy your talent."

"You're wasting yours, Charles," Barbara Bodichon said, arm in arm with Louisa Allingham. "Exert yourself. Pick up a brush again."

"My dear Madame Bodichon, I'm content to be a painter in words and a promoter of art—a writer, critic, and publisher. All the real talent is on the female side of our family."

"I say you're just lazy," Barbara said.

Allingham tucked his notepad and pencil away. "Rest assured, ladies, my article in the *Art Journal* will be fulsome in praise of your genius."

"*You* have a genius for nonsense, that much I know," Barbara said.

Louisa Allingham smiled at Julia and asked, "Tell me, Doctor Lewis, do you understand as little of art as I? Mary and Charles despair of me, I'm afraid."

"Well, I know what appeals to me," Julia said.

Louisa nodded. "As do I. But I'm afraid that answer is never good enough for my husband or sister-in-law. One must have complicated explanations for one's admiration."

Julia stopped in front of a landscape. "This one, for instance. It's quite different from the others. The rough brushstrokes aren't as polished. Yet, it's beautiful."

"I call it *Down the Rushy Glen*," Mary said from behind them. "This is how painters in Paris see the world. Nature as it looks in the fleeting instant. How it changes with shifts of light, the time of day, and the density of the air."

"Mary and her beloved Paris," Louisa said. "Everything is better in France."

"Ah . . . that's because it's true."

Charles stepped back, appraising the picture. "You're right to withhold it from the Royal Academy exhibition. The RA jurors would send it back and tell you to submit it next year—when it's finished."

"Oh dear," Louisa murmured to Julia. "That's just what I was thinking."

Charles laughed, "My dear, you must stick to poetry—although I find much of it as perplexing as you find painting."

"No, Barbara. No one knows her."

Julia glanced over her shoulder at the speaker. Laura Herford had joined their group. She and Barbara made a mismatched pair. Golden-haired Madame Bodichon towered over the dark, petite Laura Herford.

"I've asked everyone I know about this murdered girl," Miss Herford said.

"Murder." Julia heard the shudder in Barbara's voice. "Horrible."

"Yes, poor girl. This Franny Riley is a mystery."

The mirth and color drained from Charles Allingham's face. He froze and then swayed. Mary pointed to a detail in her painting and had Louisa's attention; conversation absorbed Laura and Barbara. Only Julia noticed Allingham's reaction.

"I . . . I'm sorry, my dear," Charles said abruptly. "Mary, I must leave—I've just recollected an appointment. Meeting a chap at the Reform Club."

"Charles, no." Louisa took his arm and drew him aside. "The caterers are setting up the luncheon—a celebration for Mary and her friends."

Gently, he removed her hand and said, "Forgive me, Mary. I'll hand out your exhibit announcements at my club."

"But . . ."

"Keep the carriage, Louisa. I'll take a cab. Ladies. My love." He bowed and kissed his wife's hand. Then he turned on his heels and walked rapidly away.

After a moment, Julia said, "It's a shame your husband had to leave early, as must I. But I'm happy Mister Allingham seems well."

Louisa looked at her blankly.

"After his ordeal."

"Oh . . . yes. Thank you, Doctor. Charles is quite himself again."

Mary spun around. "How can you say that, Lou? Charles is *not* himself. He's changed. Changeable and distracted. How he runs that publishing business . . ."

"Allingham and Son, the publishers?" Julia asked. "Is that his firm?"

"Allingham and Allen, now." Mary turned away. "Much good those announcement cards will do. The Royal Academy draws a flood to our trickle. If only the RA would showcase more women artists."

Barbara flicked her hand impatiently. "Ladies, we must stop whining about the unfairness of it all and get on with it. Bombard the RA with our best work until the ramparts fall."

"Here, here," Julia said.

Madame Bodichon eyed her appraisingly. "My husband is a physician. Where did you go to medical school? Not in Britain, I know."

"Philadelphia. Then I wiggled through a loophole to get on our medical register."

"How?"

"Parliament opened the door to graduates of foreign medical schools, forgetting that some of us are female."

"That's the tactic," Barbara said, brandishing her umbrella like a sword. "We'll hoist them with their own petards! Find all the chinks in their armor and exploit them to the hilt."

Julia consulted her watch. "I'm sorry to miss luncheon, but I'll be late for the clinic if I delay much longer."

Mary walked her to the door. "Thank you for coming this morning—and suggesting I speak to Inspector Tennant." She laughed lightly and said, "His appearance at the house worked on Louisa like a tonic. She's less fretful about the letters and less worried about me. She and the inspector are old friends, it seems."

"Yes, he mentioned it."

"Her confidence in 'dear Richard' seems boundless."

"It's well placed. Now, I must go." Julia said, offering her hand. "Thank you for a delightful morning."

Julia flagged a cab on Oxford Street and settled in for the ride to Whitechapel Clinic, wondering about Tennant and Louisa. They must have known each other well for the casual use of their Christian names to linger. But it wasn't Louisa Allingham who occupied her thoughts for most of the ride. It was Louisa's husband. The look on his face was as good as a confession.

Charles Allingham knew Franny Riley.

At three o'clock, Scotland Yard's duty sergeant flagged down Inspector Tennant and his sergeant as they crossed the lobby. He held up a note.

A porter from Doctor Lewis's clinic left this about three hours ago."

Tennant tore the envelope and read. "Well, well. We've got something, Paddy."

"What's the doctor have to say?"

"She's found someone who knew Franny Riley. Charles Allingham." Tennant crumpled the note. "Let's find him."

Julia's note said Allingham had left the gallery for the Reform Club. The inspector knew the club and its doorman well. Tennant's father had been a member before his fall from grace in a financial scandal. Like many exclusive gentlemen's clubs, the Reform stood on Pall Mall, a short walk from Scotland Yard.

"Mother of God," O'Malley muttered as they approached the three-story structure built of gleaming limestone in the grand palazzo style.

Tennant smiled as he spotted the uniformed doorman at the top of the steps. "Good to see you, Hal."

"Captain Tennant," the doorman said, using the inspector's army rank. "It's been a while, sir. I was sorry to hear about Mr. Tennant's passing."

"Thank you." Tennant produced his Scotland Yard warrant card.

The club doorman was too well-trained to signal surprise at Tennant's change of career. He said, "How can I help you, Inspector?"

But Hal couldn't assist. Charles Allingham was not a member, and no one of his name or description had sought entry. The doorman had been on duty all day.

As they crossed Pall Mall, O'Malley asked, "Could the doctor have mixed up the club's name?"

"I doubt it." Tennant looked at his watch. "What do you say, Paddy? East to Allingham and Allen or west to the man's house in Kensington?"

" 'Tis late in the day. We're like as not to miss him at the office."

Tennant nodded. The gas lamps atop the Reform Club's balustrade glowed dimly in the dusk. "You head home, Paddy. I'll take a cab to Blenheim Lodge and catch him before he sits down to dinner."

But the footman informed Tennant that Mr. Allingham was dining out. As for the "ladies of the house," Mrs. Allingham was resting, and "Miss Mary" had not yet returned from the gallery.

"Where is Mister Allingham dining?"

"The Reform Club, I believe, sir."

"No, he's not. I just came from there," Tennant said. "I want to speak to his coachman."

But the driver couldn't help him. Allingham had walked to Kensington Road to pick up a cab. *The man could be anywhere in London,* Tennant thought. He scribbled a brief note on the back of his card asking Allingham to delay his departure for the office in the morning. The inspector had a few questions.

"Please deliver this to Mister Allingham when he returns this evening."

The inspector thought, *No need to worry the man's wife or sister. At least, not yet.*

The following morning, Tennant and O'Malley arrived by cab at Blenheim Lodge just as a police wagon exited the drive. A pair of constables stood at the front door.

"Bloke topped himself," one young copper told O'Malley.

Tennant spun around after paying the cabbie. "Who are you talking about?"

"The master of the house. Charles Allingham."

"Mother of God," O'Malley muttered, shaken. "You're sure of that?"

The constable jerked his thumb over his shoulder. "Sergeant Armstrong is upstairs now, sorting it."

"Wait," Tennant shouted at the cabbie driving away. "Paddy, hand me your notebook." He scribbled, tore out a page, and gave one of the constables the message and a half crown. "I'll clear it with your sergeant. Take the cab and deliver this to Doctor Julia Lewis—*Julia* Lewis, mind you. Her address is on the note."

"Hell and damnation," Tennant said through clenched teeth as they mounted the staircase. "I should have tracked him down last night."

"Neither of us could guess at this." O'Malley crossed himself. "The man was in the wind and could have been anywhere."

"I should have parked myself in Allingham's foyer and waited."

Tennant and O'Malley found the Kensington sergeant in Allingham's upstairs study. The wiry, sandy-haired Armstrong listened gray-faced as the inspector told him he'd commandeered one of the sergeant's men. Tennant knew from experience that sorting the aftermath of a suicide was a grim business.

"I know the Yard had an interest in Allingham. Found your card in the man's pocket. What's it about, sir?"

"We're tracing persons who knew a murder victim," Tennant said.

"Was Allingham a suspect?"

"A possible witness. What is the cause of death?"

"Looks like suicide," Armstrong said. "Arsenic poisoning, most like. We found him sprawled face down here." He walked over to a door. "It opens into his dressing room."

Charles Allingham had died in his well-appointed gentleman's study, stretched across a burgundy-and-gold Turkish carpet. The police had removed the body, but evidence of the tragedy remained. A whiskey decanter, its contents tinted an odd color, sat on the mahogany desk. An overturned glass had spilled a few ounces onto a blotter, staining some papers green. Beside it, an envelope held the remains of an emerald powder; some of it had spilled across the desk.

Armstrong said, "He mixed it into his whiskey decanter and drank it off, poor blighter. When we turned him over, we found green stains on his lips, chin, and shirt front."

"Who pronounced him dead?"

"Doctor Scott, the family physician. He said a block of that green powder could kill off half of Kensington High Street. Artists use it to mix paint."

Tennant guessed the answer but asked, "Do you know the source?"

"The sister's studio, most like. A painter, she says. Struck near dumb when she saw the stuff and then shaking all over. I asked her to have a squint at her supply, and she thought some of it was gone." Armstrong ran his hands through his sandy hair. "Jesus. Questioning a suicide's family is hell."

" 'Tis the worst of the job," O'Malley said. "Tell me, was the paint Allingham used called Paris Green?"

Armstrong's eyebrows shot up. "That's right, Sarge." "We've seen it before."

"We'll test the stomach contents and whiskey to be sure," Armstrong said. "Doctor Scott is on our medical list, so I've asked him to do the postmortem."

"He'll perform the Marsh test?" Tennant said.

Armstrong nodded. "There's not much doubt it's suicide by arsenic poisoning, but the test will nail it down."

"He couldn't drink that green muck by accident," O'Malley said.

Armstrong nodded. "Murder's out of the question. No one could have slipped that stuff into his drink without his noticing the color."

"Where can I find the doctor?" Tennant asked.

"Preston Scott is one of these Harley Street blokes." Sergeant Armstrong scribbled an address and gave it to Tennant. "The doctor played chess with Allingham once a week. Last night was the last time."

"What did the doctor say about the dead man's state of mind?"

"Scott saw nothing amiss with his friend. The old chap seemed quite shaken by the suicide."

"Did Allingham leave a note?"

"We haven't found one."

"Sir?" O'Malley looked up from a leather portfolio on Allingham's desk. "No suicide note, but there's this—open on his desk." He handed Tennant a picture from a set of artists' prints.

Green smudges stained the white border. Its caption read *Chatterton (1856) by Henry Wallis.* The painting showed an ashen-faced young man sprawled across a bed with his arm hanging over the side. A vial had slipped from his hand to the floor.

"Allingham had death on his mind, by the looks of it," O'Malley said.

"It appears so," Tennant said. "Who found the body?"

"The footman," Armstrong said. "He brought the man his morning tea and found him on the floor. Allingham had been sleeping in here."

He opened the door to a small chamber. Inside was a narrow bed, the covers folded back but unrumpled.

Tennant asked, "Was that his usual practice?"

"When he worked late, his sister said." Armstrong closed the door.

The inspector circled the study. The *Chatterton* artist had draped his suicide artfully across a bed. But Charles Allingham had staggered from his desk, vomiting, the traces of his agony spewed across the floor.

"Death by arsenic isn't an easy end," Tennant said.

Armstrong grunted. "Made a pig's ear of it."

"Any surprises, Armstrong? Anything puzzling?"

"A couple of things, sir. The locked bottom drawer in that chest seems dodgy to me. Nothing else is under lock and key. The victim's desk and all the other cupboards are open to the world."

"And the key?"

"Missing."

"What's the second thing?"

"It looks like he burned something. Papers, most like."

"Show me," Tennant said.

Armstrong crossed the room and squatted. He pulled a pencil from his pocket and poked around in the cold fireplace. "There's quite a pile of fallen ash in the grate."

O'Malley leaned over for a closer look. As he straightened, he spotted a white triangle between the legs of the fire-iron stand. He drew out a torn scrap of paper with the tip of his boot and picked it up. All that remained was the start of a sentence, written in block capital letters in black ink: DON'T THINK I WON'T TEL

"That partial last letter might be an L," O'Malley said, handing the fragment to the inspector. "Probably 'Don't think I won't tell.' Are we looking at blackmail?"

"It's a possible motive for suicide," Tennant said.

"The same poison pen who's been tormenting the lady artists."

"It's a theory, Paddy." Tennant sized up the cabinet, inspecting its lock. "What's been done to locate the key?"

"We checked Allingham's pockets and his desk," Armstrong said. "I asked his valet about it, Rawlings by name. We'll get nothing out of that bugger. These 'gentlemen's gentlemen' shut their mouths tighter than oysters."

"I'd like a word with him."

Armstrong said to the constable at the door, "Bring Rawlings in."

If the presence of Scotland Yard at a suicide surprised the valet, he didn't show it. Rawlings didn't blink when Tennant identified himself.

"Sleek" was the word that came to Tennant's mind. Rawlings was a trim man of above-average height who had slicked back his dark hair with Macassar oil that gave off the citrusy scent of bergamot. His neat mustache mostly hid a mildly disfiguring harelip. The inspector was an expert at sizing up the cut of a man's clothing, and Rawlings was an unusually well-tailored servant.

The valet answered Tennant's queries about his background and the length of his service with the careful diction of someone who's worked hard to remove any trace of his class or place of origin. Tennant turned his questions to Allingham.

"Did you notice any changes in your employer's demeanor?"

"He seemed distracted," Rawlings said. "But nothing to show he was . . ." The man swallowed. "Nothing that made me think he had this on his mind."

"You were the last to see him alive, so—"

"I beg your pardon, sir. After Doctor Scott and Mister Allen left last evening, Mister Allingham didn't ring for me."

"Mister Allen?"

"My employer's business partner. He returned with Mister Allingham shortly before Doctor Scott arrived, around eight. That was the last I saw of him. I had laid out the master's night things earlier and turned down his bed."

"Was that usual? To finish your duties so early in the evening?"

"Mister Allingham often worked late or went out to his club. When he did, and on the evenings that he played chess, he went to bed unassisted."

"Thank you, Mister Rawlings. That will be all for now."

After the servant withdrew, Armstrong said, "So Doctor Scott and Allingham's business partner were the last to see him alive."

"Possibly," Tennant said. "What about his wife and sister?"

"Allingham retreated to the study with his guests. The ladies didn't see him again."

One by one, Armstrong brought in the servants. All had retired for the evening shortly after Mr. Allingham returned. All except Alfred: only the footman saw his employer later that night.

Charles Allingham had escorted his guests downstairs and

locked the door behind them. Before returning upstairs, he asked Alfred to pour a glass of port from the bottle in the dining room. The footman brought it to him, and Allingham tossed it off and asked for another. Then his employer asked him to check the first-floor windows and wished him good night. Allingham climbed the stairs unsteadily, and Alfred watched him until he turned into the hallway. The footman heard the study door close behind him.

Tennant asked Alfred about the missing key. He, like the other servants, knew nothing about it.

After Alfred left, Tennant said, "I don't know about you, Sergeant Armstrong, but I grow more and more curious about that key."

"If it doesn't turn up, we'll have to force the chest open."

Tennant nodded. "Let's have one more look around."

Her coachman drove Julia and the Kensington constable back to Blenheim Lodge. Aside from the policeman at the door, nothing seemed unusual. Julia reached for the doorknocker and changed her mind. She asked the constable, "Is it unlocked?" When he nodded, she entered.

Julia stood for a moment, listening. The door to the morning room stood ajar, and a fire crackled in the grate, so she tapped and went in. It took her a moment to locate Mary. A still, alabaster-faced girl hugging her knees stared from the window seat with red-rimmed eyes. Then she shook herself and swung her feet to the carpet.

"Doctor, forgive me. I didn't know you were here."

"Inspector Tennant sent for me." Julia took her hand. "My dear, I'm so sorry." Mary's icy fingers felt as though they might snap at the slightest pressure. "You're cold. Come away from the window."

Julia led Mary to a chair by the fire. The girl smoothed the white painter's smock that covered her dress and sat. "I'm sorry to receive you like this."

"No matter."

"I'd gotten an early start in the studio. Then they came for me. An accident, they said. But he . . . he used my paint." Mary shuddered and wrapped her arms around herself. "He used my Paris Green to . . ."

"I'm sorry," Julia said gently.

Tears welled. Mary blinked and turned her face away. "I had no idea about the arsenic until you told me," she said, her voice shaking. "When I mentioned it to Charles, he said Louisa—oh." Her hand flew to her mouth.

"What did your brother say?"

"It was only a joke. A silly joke. Charles told me to lock it away. That Louisa was so fed up with his moods, she might add it to the absinthe I brought home from France. Good God, I can't believe it." Mary closed her eyes. "But he hadn't been the same since . . ."

"Since his accident?"

"Before that. Since I returned from Paris in the autumn. After the accident, he'd grown moodier still."

"Mary, I'd like to take your pulse and listen to your heart. May I?"

The girl stared at Julia, hollow-eyed. Finally, she nodded.

Julia took her wrist and timed the beats on her pocket watch. Then she took the stethoscope from her bag and asked Mary to remove her smock and unbutton the top of her dress. Julia listened, satisfied with what she heard.

"I'll leave you with a mild sleeping draught. You can decide if you need it." She closed her case. "Shall I check on your sister-in-law?"

"Doctor Scott was here and left something to help her sleep." Mary leaned on her elbow, looking into the fire. "Doctor Scott . . . Charles had some nagging ailments. Sleeplessness. His eyes were giving him trouble, and Scott thought spectacles might relieve his headaches."

"Was he taking anything for them?"

Mary shrugged. "I don't know. I know nothing. Nothing about Charles's pain. Nothing about what drove him. Nothing." With each repetition of the word, Mary struck the flat of her hand against the armrest. "Oh, God," she cried, her voice breaking. "How could I not know?" She covered her face with her hands, sobbing.

Julia kneeled by her chair and put her arm around the girl's shaking shoulder and let her cry.

"I'm sorry. I'm so sorry." Mary tried to get up. "I must check on Lou."

"If Louisa is asleep, it's better to let her be."

Mary slumped back in her chair and fished in her pocket. "I never have a handkerchief when I need one."

Julia gave Mary hers and sat across from her. It was all so familiar: the shock and confusion, the regrets and recriminations. *Six years . . . nearly seven.*

"Mary?" She waited for the girl to meet her eyes. "I want to tell you something. Something I know from bitter experience. When someone you love takes their life, your mind searches in circles for reasons. And you blame yourself for not seeing the signs."

"Yes . . ."

"You'll feel many things that aren't your fault."

"I asked Charles if business matters were troubling him. He denied it, but I had a sense the answer was yes. Perhaps I only wish it were true. An easy answer."

A knock at the front door sounded loud in the silence of the household.

Mary stood, brushing her cheeks. "This may be Cyril. Mister Eastlake is our family solicitor. I sent the coachman with a message about Charles."

A trim man of average height in early middle age entered the room. He had close-cropped graying hair and a neatly trimmed mustache. He wore a dark frock coat, stiff upturned collar, and conservatively patterned necktie, the uniform of his profession. Everything about him telegraphed the solidity, competence, and discretion of a perfect family retainer.

"Mary, my dear." Eastlake took her hand. "Such an appalling tragedy. How is Louisa?"

"She's . . . she's resting. Cyril." Mary turned away. "This is Doctor Julia Lewis."

Eastlake blinked. "Doctor?"

"I treated Mister Allingham after his skating accident."

"*You* treated him?" The man looked shocked. "Not Doctor Scott?"

"He wasn't at Regent's Park. I was. I treated Mister Allingham at the scene."

"Oh. Well, I imagine he consulted Doctor Scott later. Have you seen Louisa, Doctor Lewis? How is Mrs. Allingham?"

Before Julia answered, Inspector Tennant entered the room. He offered Mary his condolences, and she introduced him to Mister Eastlake.

Julia saw the wheels turn in the lawyer's eyes. Yet, he didn't ask the obvious question: What was a detective from the Metropolitan Police doing at the scene of a suicide? *A patient man,* Julia thought, *who waits for information to come to him.*

"Cyril, can you—" Mary jumped when the sitting room door flew open, and the handle cracked against a bookcase.

"I'm sorry," Louisa Allingham said from the doorway. She looked at her black-gloved palm and said, "The doorknob slipped from my grasp."

Louisa looked beautiful and bereft in a jet-black widow's

frock, her face a pale mask above its high dark collar. Eastlake crossed the room. He caught up her hand and cradled it before raising it to his lips.

"Louisa, my dear."

Slowly, she lifted her gaze to his face. "It's a terrible mistake. Charles . . . he wouldn't. Cyril, you knew him. He could never . . . It must be an accident." Louisa pulled her hand away and let it drop.

Eastlake put his arm around her shoulder. "My dear, we're looking into it. Leave it to Mary and me. You should be resting." He looked at Julia. "Doctor Lewis, will you insist?"

Julia nodded to Mary. She slipped her arm around her sister-in-law's waist. "Come, Lou," she said gently.

Louisa looked at Tennant. "Richard . . . Richard, you will help us, won't you? Find the truth about Charles?"

"Of course," he said.

"Thank you," Louisa said, smiling tremulously. Mary led her away.

The weak and the strong, Julia thought. All sympathy and concern flowed toward Louisa Allingham. *It's natural for the widow. But Mary . . .* Julia shook her head. *Mary looks gutted.*

As soon as the door closed, Eastlake turned to the inspector. "I suppose there's little doubt."

"He drank a glass of whiskey laced with powdered green paint."

"Paint?"

"Arsenic is an ingredient in Paris Green," Julia said.

"It's a vivid emerald," Tennant added, "so it's unlikely he ingested the tinted liquid by mistake."

Eastlake looked stricken. "It's unfathomable, Inspector. Charles was the last man who would — "

"How well did you know the deceased? Were you friends as well?"

"More social acquaintances, I'd say. Our interests were rather different." Eastlake smoothed his mustache, squaring his shoulders. "When it comes to art, I'm rather a Philistine, I'm afraid." Julia thought he sounded proud, not apologetic.

"I'd like to speak to some of his friends and acquaintances," Tennant said. "Rawlings mentioned he belonged to a club. Which one?"

"That vulgar new one. The Topkapi Club on East Pall Mall."

"I've seen it. I had a drink at the Atheneum and noticed the club's unusual façade."

"Indeed?"

Julia heard his surprise and suppressed a smile when Eastlake registered Tennant's regimental tie and well-cut suit. *He's wondering about a copper who drinks at the Atheneum and dresses like a toff.*

Tennant said, "Reports suggest that Mister Allingham was worried of late. Did business concerns weigh on him?"

"Quite the reverse, I'd say." Eastlake cleared his throat. "Mind you, I'd have given a different answer five years ago. But after Charles took Sidney Allen into partnership, the ship righted itself."

The door opened, and Mary entered with Sergeant O'Malley. "I persuaded Louisa to rest," she said.

Eastlake took her hand. "This must be hell for poor Louisa. Appalling. She's not strong. Not like you, my dear. If there is anything I can do, you must tell me."

"Of course," Mary said. She withdrew her hand and returned to her seat by the fireplace.

O'Malley said, "Sir, we've searched for the key, but we haven't got eyes on it. Miss Allingham doesn't know its whereabouts. Perhaps Mister Eastlake?"

The lawyer looked blankly at O'Malley. "What key?"

"To the chest of drawers in Mister Allingham's study," Tennant said. "Any idea, sir?"

"None, I'm afraid."

"Then Sergeant Armstrong will have to force it," O'Malley said.

"I insist he calls for a locksmith," the lawyer said. "There is no need to inflict unnecessary damage on top of everything else."

"Very well." Tennant nodded to O'Malley. "The sergeant will see to it."

Eastlake cleared his throat. "Inspector, is there a reason Scotland Yard is involved?"

Took him long enough, Julia thought.

"Evidence of blackmail has come to light. In a case that ends in suicide, extortion could lead to a charge of manslaughter."

"Blackmail? Absurd." Eastlake threw out his chest. "I insist on being present when you open that locked drawer."

Tennant looked at Mary. "Miss Allingham, is that your wish?"

She nodded.

Julia checked her watch and gathered her things. "Mary, I must leave. But you should follow Mrs. Allingham's example and rest. I'll stop back in a few days, shall I?"

"Yes. Please do." She started to rise, so Julia touched her shoulder to stop her. She leaned over and kissed her cheek.

Tennant said, "I'll see Doctor Lewis out."

At the front door, he said, "Thank you for coming. By the time I arrived, Armstrong had assigned Allingham's postmortem to Doctor Scott. But I thought the ladies could use your support." He cleared his throat. "Tell me, did you look in on Louisa?"

"No. Doctor Scott treated Mrs. Allingham this morning. Mary said she was sleeping."

"First, her father—Louisa was very dependent on him." Tennant shook his head. "Now this."

"You're concerned for her, of course. I'm worried about Mary. She lost her only sibling. The supposed 'strong ones' are often overlooked."

"Yes, I'm sure you're right." He looked up the staircase. "I must get back."

He seemed hardly to have heard her. "Richard, don't let Mary fall through the cracks."

Julia watched him climb. Again, she thought about the power of the weak . . . and their attraction for the strong.

CHAPTER 6

Mary closed the sitting room door behind Eastlake, thinking, *Thank God.* If she had to listen to another minute of his hand-wringing over Louisa . . .

She leaned her forehead against the doorframe. *That's unkind of me.* But there was time enough to worry about her sister-in-law. Just then, all Mary could think about was Charles. She crossed the hall to the stairs, changed her mind, and left through the front door, making her way around the side of the house. She passed the yew tree. Its twisting beauty had always captivated her, and she'd sketched it more times than there were days in a year. That morning, she shivered as she passed it, thinking of the man who had lurked among the branches, watching.

Mary rummaged for her key at the studio door before finding she'd left it unlocked after the hurried summons to the house. Nothing and everything had changed. The coals still burned in the grate. Light streamed in from the south-facing windows. Her pencils were where she had left them, next to the sketches on her drawing table. All was the same, except the cake of Paris Green paint was gone. The police had taken it away.

Mary slid a folder from the shelf and opened a portfolio labeled CHARLES. Smiles and tears warred as she turned over sketch after sketch. Weeping won, tears brimming and streaking her cheeks. She came to the last picture, a watercolor sketch she'd done shortly before leaving for Paris. There he was, a white-suited Charles in a summer straw hat, arms crossed, leaning against a low-hanging branch, smiling in a garden she'd painted using Paris Green.

Mary threw the sketch on the coals. Instantly, she regretted it and tried to snatch it back, singeing her fingers. Mary watched the flames eat from the edges, blackening, curling, and finally consuming the image. Then she turned away with choking sobs.

Upstairs in Charles Allingham's study, the locksmith sat back on his heels and grunted.

"Ha. Gotcha, you bugger." He slid the bottom drawer open an inch and looked up. "There you go, gents. Bob's your uncle."

"Leave the drawer as it is," Eastlake said. "The police will open it."

"Right you are." The locksmith collected his picks and wires and sprung to his feet with the ease of an acrobat.

"Record time, Bert," Armstrong said.

He polished his nails on his sleeve. "You coppers are lucky I never went in for housebreaking." The locksmith held up his fingers and wiggled them. "In and out, and nobody's the wiser." He picked up his tool bag. "Cheers, gents. Hope you find what you're after."

After the door closed, Tennant said, "All right, Paddy. Let's see what's in that bottom drawer."

O'Malley eased it open. It contained a stack of oversized portfolios, each nearly as wide as the drawer, six in all. O'Malley handed them to Tennant, who laid them on the desk, untied their ribbons, and opened a collection of erotic paintings and sketches.

The pictures in the first folder looked vaguely familiar to Tennant, painted in the style of Renaissance masters. *Pleasure Gardens*, the second folder, depicted Asian women singly and in pairs, "entertaining" men in garden settings. Voyeurs watching lovers and women bathing filled the third. In the fourth folder, all the figures were males engaged in acts of sodomy. The fifth group was the darkest: scenes of captivity, flagellation, and sexual domination.

"The quality of the illustrations is striking," Tennant said. "They're a far cry from the usual thing we see. This is artful smut."

Eastlake said, "Surely a gentleman's . . . private art collection can remain just that. The Obscene Publications Act applies only to the distribution of salacious materials. This is England, sir, where a man's personal pleasures are his affair."

O'Malley handed Tennant the last folder. It contained images of women, alone or in pairs. Some of the girls seemed barely out of the schoolroom. In one picture, Margot Miller stretched out on a white sofa, one arm thrown over her head and a hand between her legs. A second girl reached for the paddle at her feet.

Halfway through the folder, Tennant stopped. "Paddy, look at these." Tennant spread three pictures on the desk.

O'Malley bent over the first two. "Franny Riley. She was posing for artists, just like you guessed."

"I never guessed this. Look at the last one." Margot Miller was the subject, and the artist had painted a green wrap thrown carelessly across the bed.

"Sweet Jesus," O'Malley muttered. " 'Tis a match for the one we found around Franny. Glittery green with moths stitched into it."

"Franny?" Eastlake said. "Who's Franny? Who in blazes are you talking about?"

"The murder victim in our investigation," Tennant said. "Last week, someone dumped Frances Riley near Lambeth Bridge. And today, I found her pictures in Charles Allingham's 'art' collection. The green dressing gown is identical to the one we found wrapped around Miss Riley's body."

"And there's this, sir." O'Malley handed the inspector an unsealed envelope.

Tennant unfolded a sheet of creamy writing paper. "It's a list of letters and numbers. AG: 10, RJK: 10, WQ . . ." Tennant looked up. "WQ—does that pair ring a bell, Paddy?"

"The initials on the sketch of Franny we had off Mrs. Murphy."

Sergeant Armstrong scratched his head. "What do you reckon? Lists of initials and payments?"

"Highly speculative," Eastlake said. "I see nothing to interest the police."

"Highly suggestive." Tennant folded the paper. "And I find I'm interested all the same."

The lawyer drew himself up. "I don't see on what basis—"

"This is an active police inquiry, Mister Eastlake. It involves murder, poison-pen letters, possible extortion, and now a suicide."

Eastlake opened his mouth and then closed it again.

"Gather up the folders, Sergeant O'Malley," Tennant said.

Eastlake sighed. "I don't know what I'll say to the ladies of the household."

"That's for you to decide . . . for the moment."

Eastlake's eyes popped. "Surely, you'll leave them out of this!"

"I have no desire to cause unnecessary distress," Tennant

said. "But investigations often uncover secrets that cannot stay hidden. Even from the ladies of a house."

"But . . ."

Tennant nodded to O'Malley. They left Eastlake in the study, struggling to formulate a reply.

While Sergeant O'Malley headed to Doctor Scott's Harley Street office, Inspector Tennant sought out Sidney Allen, Charles Allingham's business partner.

The cabbie dropped Tennant at Amen Corner at the end of Paternoster Row, the heart of London's publishing industry. The row curved like a narrow canyon, fronted by soot-stained, three-story buildings turned dusky from the coal smoke belching from neighborhood chimneys. Tennant spotted a familiar figure on the crowded pavement: Charles Allingham's manservant. Rawlings closed the street door of an office building and strode rapidly away, weaving around walkers, turning left at the first corner.

Tennant followed, passing a door with a discreet brass plate announcing the offices of Allingham and Allen. The inspector trailed Rawlings through Queen's Head Passage and stopped. Just ahead, the man had halted under the sign for Dolly's Chop and Ale House, stepping aside for a departing patron. Then Rawlings ducked through the door.

Tennant passed the pub, keeping some pedestrians between him and the window. He glanced inside. Allingham's manservant stood at the bar, chatting with the man who pulled a pint for him.

The inspector circled back to the offices of Allingham and Allen. A secretary in the outer office greeted Tennant pleasantly and politely. When the inspector gave his name and rank and asked to see the company director, the man stiffened, and his gaze darted to an inner door. He disappeared into an office and returned a minute later.

"Mister Allen will see you, sir." He stepped aside to let the inspector pass.

Allen was a ruddy-faced, middle-aged man of average height, solidly built but running to fat. Pale blue eyes peered from under dark, spiky brows, and wispy, gray-flecked hair receded from his forehead.

"You're here about Charles Allingham," Allen said with a pronounced north-of-England accent. "A terrible business. Inexplicable."

"Mister Rawlings brought you the news?"

Allen's eyes flickered. "Aye. That's right."

"I thought I saw him exiting the premises a few minutes ago."

"Mary—Miss Allingham—sent him along. Thoughtful of her, considering what those poor lasses must be suffering."

He offered Tennant a seat and sat behind his desk. The inspector let a short silence stretch out. Allen was a twitchy sort, not from unease, Tennant guessed, but from boundless energy. He drummed his fingers against the desk, fiddled with his watchchain, and swiveled in his desk chair.

Not a patient man, Tennant thought. *But willing to wait me out.*

"I've spoken with Mister Eastlake," the inspector said. "He tells me that you came to the rescue of a foundering firm. May I ask why?"

Allen shot Tennant an alert look. Then he hooked his thumbs in his waistcoat pockets and leaned back in his chair. "It suited me to play the white knight."

"For practical reasons . . . or something else?"

"You've probably sized me up already, Inspector. I'm not what you'd call a clubbable bloke." He laughed mirthlessly. "Too much of the North, aye man?" He shrugged. "I could barely pass muster—it was a close run even for the Topkapi Club."

"You are a member as well?"

"Thanks to Charles Allingham. Charlie was a gent. Not a snob about things, you understand, but summat old school and all. You know the drill." He pointed a stubby finger at Tennant's red-and-blue regimental necktie. "Grenadier Guards?"

"Yes."

"Officer?"

"Captain."

"Thought as much. The right schools, an elite regiment, they open doors."

"There's no denying it."

"Well, Charlie provided the class, and I . . ." Allen dug his fist into a trouser pocket, pulled out a shilling, and flipped it. "I supplied the brass. And in a world where men play dirty? An ambitious bloke gets down in the muck. But that wasn't for Charlie."

"A tidy arrangement."

Allen cocked his thumb at the window behind him. "An old family firm with a proper address on the row? Neighbors with Longmans, Whittakers, and the like? That's worth more than pounds sterling. We moved into the fine art market, and you'd be surprised at the profit margin in art books, catalogs, and prints."

"I probably would."

Allen grinned. "You'd be a proper doyle to lose money at it. Charlie had the connections. All he needed was the brass." He rocked in his chair, his chest swelling. "We've never looked back."

"Given the firm's health, Mister Allingham's suicide seems unconnected to business reversals."

Allen flicked a dismissal. "The company is Bank-of-England sound. Charlie's death had naught to do with the firm."

"Then your dinner with him last night was . . . what? Simply routine?"

Allen hitched his shoulders uneasily. "We had a difference of opinion to iron out, I'll not deny it. Sometimes Charlie has . . ." He swallowed. "He had a rubbish idea for a book. About some new French painters that no one's heard of. Old Charlie could be a stubborn bastard at odd times."

"How did you end it?"

"Charlie sort of . . . threw in the towel, sudden-like. 'Doesn't matter,' he said, 'have it your own way.' Heard him say that a hundred times when he'd grown tired or bored with something. Like the air went out of the balloon."

"And you played out your disagreement in front of Doctor Scott?"

"All over by the time the old bugger showed up at the house. But Charlie wasn't in the mood for chess. What of it?"

"Who left first?"

"We had a drink, made an early night of it, and left together. Charlie saw us to the front door, and we went our separate ways."

"I have a final question about your last meeting. Did Mister Allingham seem unusually despondent?"

Allen looked down at his desk and frowned. "Aye. Like he was carrying a hundredweight on his back."

Tennant left Allen's building, walked east along the row, and turned right on Old Change Street, heading toward the river.

As he passed St. Paul's, the setting sun honeyed the pale stone of the cathedral's façade, turning it golden. Winter afternoons were short, but Tennant had put in a long day, and his leg ached. He turned toward the river and winced when his boot twisted on the uneven cobbles. On the other side of the Thames, scudding clouds dragged bands of rain in his direction. He'd be caught in a downpour if he waited for an omnibus, so he shifted his weight to ease his leg and flagged a cab.

"Where to, guvnor?"

Tennant nearly told the cabbie to take him home to Blooms-bury. Instead, he clapped the hansom doors closed and told the driver, "Scotland Yard."

No matter, he thought. Lately, his house on Russell Square, a comfortable chair, and a glass of whiskey by the fireside con-tented him less. He'd begun to picture Julia there, sipping a sherry, sitting across from him, the flickering firelight gilding her chestnut hair. He pictured her in other rooms and imagined what it would be like to wake and see her hair spread across a pillow. Tennant hadn't longed for someone so intensely since his broken engagement to Isobel. A lucky escape, he'd come to realize.

But Julia . . . *She's so self-sufficient, damn it.* He could dream all he liked, but that was as far as it would go. It didn't stop his pulse racing at the thought of her in his bed.

The inspector sighed and returned his mind to the case, won-dering if he'd wasted his time with Allen. *He's a bit of a rogue.* But was he an out-and-out scoundrel involved in a blackmail scheme? Tennant had no reason to think so.

Still, the inspector thought the interview had been revealing. For one thing, there was that difference of opinion over Alling-ham's state of mind. The doctor had told Sergeant Armstrong that all had been well with his friend. Yet, Allen saw a despon-dent Allingham. Tennant thought about things unsaid. A clever man could take great care to monitor his disclosures. But the inspector had learned to listen for the unspoken. Allen hadn't asked him why a copper from the Met's detective department was investigating a suicide.

Tennant arrived at the Yard after six. He found two reports and a cable from Canada on his desk and snatched up the long-awaited message. Franny's friend said a man named "Charles," who published art books, had asked her to pose for some artists.

Tennant cursed the bad luck of timing. Had the cable arrived two days earlier, Allingham would still have been alive for questioning. He picked up O'Malley's report. It confirmed Allen's statement that he and the doctor left Allingham's study together. And as for the man's general health, O'Malley quoted Dr. Scott: "Charles Allingham was a superb specimen of British manhood."

The sergeant had attached a note to the official report: *Ticked the old fella off by asking about Allingham's health. A ship's surgeon in the Royal Navy, he was, and the man barked at me like I was a common swabby. Not happy that a copper thick as a plank questioned his report.*

The second report confirmed the cause of death: the Marsh test found arsenic in Allingham's stomach and the whiskey decanter.

All the evidence pointed to suicide by arsenic poisoning.

Julia passed the newspaper across the breakfast table to her grandfather.

The death notice in *The Times* read, *Suddenly, at home, Charles Frederick Allingham of Blenheim Lodge, Kensington, survived by his wife, Louisa Alice (née Upton), and his sister, Mary Margaret Allingham. The funeral and interment are private.*

Dr. Andrew Lewis lowered the paper. "Tragic."

"The coroner's jury is meeting this morning," Julia said.

"Not much doubt about the verdict." Her grandfather shook his head sadly. "Death by his hand."

Julia pushed away her unfinished dish of scrambled eggs. "Charles Allingham was young, well-off, and handsome. He had a beautiful wife and an affectionate sister."

"Outward blessings don't always add up to a happy life, my dear."

"But after Regent's Park . . . Grandfather, he'd been given a second chance at life. Others weren't as lucky." Julia thought of the young lieutenant she'd pronounced dead at the lake. "It's such a waste."

"Doctor Julie?" The housekeeper handed her a letter. "Miss Allingham's coachman is waiting for an answer."

Julia unfolded the black-bordered note and read it to her grandfather.

"*A confounding anonymous letter arrived in yesterday's post. In the day's confusion and distress, we overlooked it until this morning. I'd be most grateful for your advice if you have a free hour before you leave for your clinic.*"

"Strange," her grandfather said. "Have you any patients this morning?"

"Mrs. Oates is bringing Timmy in at ten to have his cast removed. Do you think you could—"

"Of course, my dear."

"Thank you." Julia got up and gave her grandfather a quick hug. "Mrs. Ogilvie, please tell Miss Allingham's coachman that I'll be down in five minutes."

A day after the death, the trappings of death had wrapped Blenheim Lodge in gloom. Servants had lowered the shades and drawn the draperies, and the house presented a closed face to the world. Someone had covered the brass knocker in black crepe, and Julia's rap sounded blunt and dead against the oak panel. A footman wearing a black armband opened the door.

"Miss Mary is upstairs, Doctor."

The thick carpet muffled Julia's footfalls as she crossed the silent hall. The servant's murmured withdrawal, the click of a closing door, and a ticking grandfather's clock were all she heard, sounds one would never notice in the ordinary bustle of a busy household.

"Doctor Lewis." Mary stood on the landing.

She came down the staircase, her face a pale oval above the

high neck of her black frock. She held a letter, a white rectangle against her dark dress.

"Thank you for coming, Doctor."

"Did you sleep?"

"Yes. But this morning, I feel numb. And every so often, I flame with fury at Charles." Mary blinked at her tears. "And now this anonymous letter. It looks very like the two sent to me."

She handed Julia the envelope. Someone had addressed it to Mrs. Charles Allingham in printed capital letters at the Kensington address. She pulled out the note and read the message. HE WAS WARNED. TELL HIM THAT. IT'S HIGH TIME YOU KNEW. MEET ME AT THE MAZE WITH TWENTY QUID OR THE WORLD WILL HEAR ABOUT IT.

Julia looked up. "The maze?"

"I suppose he means the one here in Kensington, in the horticultural gardens. It's a twenty-minute walk from our house."

"The note says three o'clock on the sixteenth. That's today." Julia looked at the grandfather clock. "Five hours from now."

Mary bit her lip. "I know."

"You must go to the police."

"Louisa . . . she's vacillating, and I don't want to go over her head. I thought, someone else. Someone whose opinion she respects. You might convince her to call them in." Mary gripped Julia's hand. "Please, will you come upstairs and speak to her?"

"Of course." Julia shook it and smiled. "But whatever your sister-in-law feels, you must inform the police."

"Yes. I understand."

Julia followed Mary up the stairs to a silent hallway. She knocked on the door to Louisa's bedroom and opened it.

"Lou?"

Julia followed Mary into a dimly lit chamber with drawn curtains. They found Louisa asleep in a chair she'd pulled close to the fireplace. Someone sensitive to mourning traditions had covered the mirror over her dressing table with a dark cloth. While Mary bent over Louisa, Julia looked around. A revolving barrel-shaped table held poetry collections: Shakespeare's sonnets and the works of Milton, Donne, and Wordsworth. Louisa had novels in French by Victor Hugo, Alexandre Dumas, and Gustave Flaubert. She had set aside a medical journal she'd been reading: an early February edition of *The Lancet*.

Portraits flanked the fireplace with Charles Allingham's picture on the right and an elderly gentleman on the left. *Louisa's father*, Julia thought. He wore a black frock coat, heavy watch chain, and snowy cravat, a uniform typical of prosperous doctors of his generation. He sat in a deeply carved mahogany chair with his left hand gripping the end of the armrest. In his right fist, he held an old-fashioned stethoscope at his breast like a scepter of high office. The top of a two-tiered table to the side of his portrait displayed a brass watch stand and gold-cased timepiece. The lower shelf held a well-worn, black medical bag.

A daughter's shrine, Julia thought.

"Louisa," Mary touched her sister-in-law's arm. "Doctor Lewis is here to see you."

Mrs. Allingham stirred and opened her eyes. She raised her black-gloved hand and pushed aside strands of her auburn hair. While Mary's mourning dress had drained her complexion, Louisa's high color and bright hair shone vividly against her widow's black. Julia noted the pinpoint pupils and thought, *Laudanum*. It was a powerful opiate prescribed too often by well-meaning doctors.

Louisa nodded at Julia's words of condolence. Then she turned away and fixed her gaze on the fire, her index finger worrying the oval mourning brooch pinned to her gown. Round and round, she traced its outer edge, a ring of black onyx stones. The firelight caught a lock of white hair under the glass in its center.

"Mrs. Allingham, this letter Mary showed me. Asking you for money is—"

Louisa roused herself suddenly, leaning forward, eyes glittering. "He must pay!" Then she fell back in her seat. "The rigid satisfaction . . ."

Julia looked at Mary, who made a helpless shrug. Then she knelt by her sister-in-law's chair. "Dearest Louisa, we must inform the authorities—not our local Kensington police. Perhaps if we called in Inspector Tennant—"

"Richard . . . Of course." Louisa clutched her mourning brooch. "Send for Richard. He'll know what to do. If you'll excuse me, I'll close my eyes until he arrives."

Mary and Inspector Tennant came downstairs from Louisa's room an hour later.

Julia looked at the hall clock. "I must leave for the clinic. Is there anything else I can do before I go?"

"Thank you, Doctor," Mary said. "Louisa seems calmer now that the problem is in the inspector's hands."

Tennant said, "The question is, will the letter-writer show himself?"

"My sister-in-law is in no condition to meet this man, Inspector."

"Of course not," he said.

She frowned, biting her lip. "But I'm about Louisa's height. Hatted and heavily veiled, no one will spot the difference."

"You're proposing yourself as bait?" Julia said. "Forgive me, but I think that's foolhardy."

"It may be our best chance to catch this man," Tennant said.

Julia stared at him. "Catching criminals is your responsibility. Miss Allingham is no more fit for the task than her sister-in-law."

"The risks are manageable."

"But you admit they exist."

"We'll surround her with a ring of plainclothes policemen."

"You don't know the depth of this man's anger or desperation. If it's too dangerous for Louisa, it's equally risky for Mary. But you're willing to gamble with *her* life? Surely, Mrs. Allingham would argue against it."

"Allow me to do my job, Doctor."

"Inspector, I respect our separate roles, but I'm speaking as a doctor. Mary has just endured a devastating loss. She suggests herself as bait, but my medical advice is not to accept her offer."

Tennant turned to her. "What do you say, Miss Allingham?"

Mary said, "I must do this for Charles."

Julia sighed and picked up her medical bag. "Then there is nothing more I can say."

Tennant said, "I'll fetch a cab."

"Thank you, but don't trouble yourself," Julia said. "I'll pick one up at the cabstand on Kensington Road."

Hours later, the Allingham carriage left Blenheim Lodge carrying a single, veiled passenger.

It rolled to a stop on Queen's Gate Road near the garden's southwest gate. Mary entered the grounds and spotted an unoccupied bench near the entrance to the maze. She sat and pretended to read. Minutes passed, and Mary looked up. Only a few visitors remained in the last hour of daylight; she knew some were policemen.

Minutes ticked by, but only strolling couples and nursemaids with children passed her bench. The wind picked up, and clouds rolled in, hurrying the sunset. Mary's heart lurched when a mustachioed man in a bowler hat emerged from the maze. He tugged the brim lower over his eyes and headed toward her. Mary held her breath. Then a little boy burst from the hedge's gap, grabbed the man's hand, and dragged him away. She closed her eyes and exhaled.

Finally, when Mary heard church bells ring the hour, she followed Tennant's instructions and returned to the carriage.

Back at the house, a dejected Mary removed her hat and veil. "Why didn't he show himself, Inspector?"

"The note's wording indicates that he sent it before your brother's death. Perhaps the news reached him."

"And frightened him off, you mean?"

"It's possible. Blackmail coupled with a charge of manslaughter raises the stakes considerably."

"Blackmail. Inspector, do you have any idea what . . ."

Tennant hesitated and hoped she hadn't noticed. "Absent the letter, we can't be certain. Whoever he is, he may have calculated that the risk of coming forward was too great."

Mary dropped into a chair. "Then he may retreat into the shadows and never show his face."

"I'm sorry, Miss Allingham."

Mary leaned her right elbow on the armrest and rubbed her temple. "I don't understand any of it." She looked up. "Did you speak to Mister Allen? *Was* Charles worried about the business?"

"Your brother's partner and Mister Eastlake say the firm is sound."

"Then, I'm at a loss. Charles . . . a suicide. I cannot fathom it."

The following morning, Tennant showed O'Malley the note sent to Mrs. Allingham.

"The writing is consistent with the scrap from Allingham's office. What do you make of it, Paddy?"

"Things not adding up . . . when one-plus-one isn't making two. All this writing to the artists. What's the motive in it? Are we thinking it's malice or money?"

"As far as we know, Mrs. Allingham's is the only letter that quotes a figure."

"And the others are a mix of truth and lies," O'Malley said. "Take Madame Bodichon, for instance. Him calling her a bastard. Yes, she was born on the wrong side of the blanket, but she doesn't give a toss who's the wiser for it."

"No possibility for profit there."

"Margot Miller is up the pole, and who knows the father's name. But a prostitute? And there's Miss Allingham."

"The affair with her aged Paris art teacher seems wholly fictitious," Tennant said. "And Annie O'Neill's letter threatened to tell her employer she modeled without clothing."

"A lie, poor lass. Just what she's refusing to do."

"And why blackmail a poor hatmaker? Any profit from the threat seems limited."

"A few bob at most," O'Malley said. "What did you make of the two other lady artists that Madame Bodichon put us on to?"

"One found the charge of an affair with her female model amusing. 'I'm a happily married woman with four children and a painting career,' she told me. 'I have neither the time nor the energy for a liaison with anyone.'"

O'Malley grinned. "Has the ring of truth to it, that does. And the other one?"

"She refused to name the threat, but the lady assured me the letter contained no suggestion of blackmail."

"Burned, like the rest of them?"

"Yes, damn it. If the letters don't make sense, are they a blind for something else?"

Tennant spun his chair and walked to the window. Cold air from a frigid blast leaked under the warped frame. A white blanket had dropped in the night, and a section of snow slid from the roof and fell with a whoosh past his window. Below in the street, churning carts and soot from countless coal fires had turned the snow the color of wet ash.

Tennant pulled down the shade. "I'll send a constable around to show Franny's sketch to all the women artists. Miss Allingham said she didn't know her, but someone else might recognize her."

"Maybe Margot Miller knew the lass. Let's show it to her. They both turned up in Allingham's naughty paintings."

"But not in the same ones. Let's start again, Paddy. Reread the interviews and go through our case notes."

"Something may leap out if we crack on with it."

While Tennant and O'Malley reviewed the case, Julia dodged the heavy foot traffic on Aldgate High Street in search of Annie O'Neill's address.

The cold wind sent people hurrying with their shoulders hunched and heads down, grunting the odd "sorry mate" as they collided. Finally, Julia spotted Annie's number. She followed the railing at the edge of the pavement. At the gate, she looked down. Three steps led to a basement entrance.

The door opened, and a woman carrying a hatbox exited the flat. She turned around, her full, emerald skirt swinging, filling the narrow space.

"Don't be a dolt, Annie. That priest of yours won't pay the rent."

The woman closed the door, raised her cape's black fur collar, and climbed the steps. Slanting sunlight caught and flamed her auburn hair. She gave Julia a curious stare and turned right on Aldgate High Street. She recognized the woman at once from Mary's painting: Margot Miller.

Julia descended and knocked. Within seconds, Annie yanked open the door. "I'll not be changing my—oh." A hand flew to her mouth. "I'm sorry, Doctor. I thought . . ." She pulled the door wider. "Will you come in out of the cold?"

Annie stood back and invited Julia into a combination sitting room and workroom. Tables held the tools and materials of the milliner's trade: thimbles and scissors, fabric swatches, feathers, bows, and yards of ribbon.

"Your basement rooms are much brighter than I expected."

"Light from the front comes in all the morning long." Annie pointed to the side windows. "With the street crossing to the west and nothing to block it, light streams in of an afternoon as well."

"The perfect space for your work."

" 'Tis that. My Aunt Maggie, God rest her soul, found it. She brought me over from Dublin and taught me all she knew. A wonder she was, that one." Annie smiled. "Learned her trade in Paris, France, if you can believe it."

"She went far afield."

"Daddy said his little sister had the soul of a Traveller. Black Maggie, he called her. She had the raven hair on her, just like a gypsy."

Julia eyed the girl's dark curls and said, "You favor her, Annie."

"Daddy was always saying so. She was a champion, my aunt. A woman on her own and making me think I could do the same."

"You had what many women lack. Someone to model."

"A woman needs a skill. Aunt Mags was always telling me that. Something to sell besides a pretty face and the rest of her."

"Indeed, she does."

"That's what the likes of some I know are peddling," Annie said. "One I could mention has a brain to go with it. . . . It'll get her in trouble one of these days."

"Shall we have that plaster off your cheek?"

Annie sat down and raised her face. She paired dark hair and brows with bright blue eyes and pale skin. A scattering of light freckles dusted her cheeks. It was a combination common among the Irish. In Annie, the mixture was magical. *No wonder artists seek her out,* Julia thought.

As the doctor peeled the bandage away, she asked, "Do you work for one hat shop in particular?"

"Wheatlands' in Cheapside is where most of my hats go. But that one . . ." She cocked her thumb at a lady's bowler, its band trimmed with flowers and dragonflies. "That one is for the dressmaker upstairs. 'Tis the fifth I've made for him this month."

"It's an unusual style for women." Julia trimmed the new bandage and applied the plaster. "There, that should do it. But you'll have to return to my office to have those stitches out of your arm. Let me look."

"Daft, I'm thinking," Annie said, pushing up her sleeve. "Strange to be wearing a fella's hat, but it's all the rage. My friend Margot was after me to make her one."

"Do you mean Margot Miller? I thought I passed her leaving your flat."

"You'll be knowing her?"

"I've seen Miss Allingham's painting of her. She's striking."

Annie frowned. "That was Margot, all right, picking up her bowler. She was my roommate until a year ago and poses for the lady artists as well as for . . ." She turned away. "I often have a brew-up this time of the day. Will you take a cup, Doctor?"

"Thank you. I know Margot is a sought-after model. Is she a hatmaker as well?"

Annie shook her head. "She worked for Wheatlands', running orders for girls who sew by the piece. Knows all the shop lasses along Bow Lane. But that was a year ago, now."

While Annie spooned tea into the pot, Julia asked, "Do you miss her company?"

"'Tis quiet of an evening, I'll say that. But she might be back."

"Oh?"

Annie cocked her thumb over her shoulder. "Isn't she paying rent on my back bedroom? 'My insurance policy,' says she. In case her fancy man tosses her out, I'm thinking."

Annie sat, poured the tea, and fiddled with her teaspoon.

"The lady artists . . . they're never asking me to do more than I'm willing. But Margot, now. She says I'm an eegit not to strip off for the men. Saying I'd get twice what I'm earning now."

"That must be tempting."

"That's looking for trouble."

Julia nodded. "You're right to resist pressure. It often ends in regret when you don't."

"That one, she's never one for regrets."

Julia returned her cup to its saucer. "Annie . . ."

"Yes, Doctor?"

"Your injuries. Are you sure you won't speak to the police?"

"I slipped and fell. Let that be an end to it."

A minute later, Annie stood and picked up their cups. Her hands shook slightly, the spoons rattling in the saucers as she carried the tea things to a washbowl. The doctor took the hint and gathered her gloves and medical bag.

Julia left certain that Annie O'Neill was hiding something—and that she was afraid.

CHAPTER 7

Julia's annoyance with Tennant lingered two weeks after the maze misadventure, but other pressing problems vied for attention.

For one thing, Julia's private practice continued to languish, disappointing after her grandfather's retirement. Most of his patients had transferred to her Uncle Max rather than sign on with her. Too many recalled the girl who played in her grandfather's back garden. They couldn't fathom the woman who'd placed first in her medical school class.

The police had called her in twice to examine women held under the Contagious Diseases Acts. Julia diagnosed one woman with a case of secondary-stage syphilis and left her with a tube of mercury ointment. The other was a widow and mother of three who showed no signs of the disease. Desperate and deprived of her male breadwinner, the woman had little choice but to take to the streets.

Julia believed that most readers of *The Times* or *The Telegraph* would be surprised by the number of women who worked as occasional prostitutes. They sold themselves on weeks when taking in washing or doing piecework sewing didn't cover the rent. Women who would be "respectable" if they could afford it. Women who'd stay home at night with their children if their day jobs put food on the table, clothed their children, and kept a roof over their heads; women whose husbands had bought it, scarpered, or had been thrown in the nick. Women like the widow Julia had examined.

She rolled a pencil between her forefinger and thumb. *What do people see?* That desperate widow she'd examined . . . *she was a hopeful bride and mother, once upon a time.*

It had been two weeks since Julia had spoken to Tennant. Perhaps she'd overstepped, but she still questioned his decision to send Mary to the maze. He'd criticized Julia's recklessness on their last case. *Why has he thrown caution away now?*

She wondered about Tennant and Louisa Allingham. How close had their relationship been? Had his eagerness to serve her interests clouded his judgment? *And what business is it of mine anyway?* He could do what he liked; console the helpless widow for all she cared.

Julia felt restless and distracted. And she was curious about the Franny Riley investigation. For all her annoyance, she missed their . . . *What? Partnership? Friendship?* She sighed and returned to the clinic's night report. *Concentrate.* She started again at the top of the page and read until a knock interrupted her. Julia smiled when she saw O'Malley filling her doorway.

"Sorry to be disturbing you, Doctor."

"Not at all, Sergeant." She put the report down. "Will you sit?"

He shook his head. "I'm behind my time after coming from your place in Finsbury Circus. The inspector sends his compliments, and can you come at once?"

"Where?"

"To Kensington and the gardens with the maze."

"Again? Now, look here." Julia pushed back her chair. "If the inspector is using Miss Allingham a second time to—"

"A parkkeeper found Margot Miller dead in the shrubbery. Someone slashed her throat."

The curious had lined up four deep at the Queen's Gate entrance to the horticultural gardens, kept back by a cordon of constables.

"Stand aside, now," Sergeant O'Malley said. "Make way for the doctor." He signaled a pair of coppers to clear a path for Julia.

"Doctor?" Someone laughed. "Makes a change, doesn't it, mate?"

Julia edged through the crowd, murmuring, "Excuse me."

Inside the gardens, Inspector Tennant and a police sergeant holding his helmet stood at the entrance to the maze.

"Doctor Lewis, this is Sergeant Armstrong from Kensington Police Station."

"Sergeant." She nodded to the pale, sandy-haired officer.

"Margot Miller's body is just inside the maze," Tennant said.

Armstrong and the inspector followed Julia into the green corridor. Margot's body lay ten feet inside the hedges. She was crumpled on her left side, her face in profile, with one arm extended above her head. Her bonnet had come off, spilling auburn hair into a pool of blood. A wound, dark with congealed gore, had sliced into the side of her neck. Margot's facial muscles had frozen into the stiff grimace of death; little of the beautiful woman Julia had glimpsed was visible.

The doctor removed a black, vulcanized glove from her bag and pulled it on, covering the sleeve of her coat to just below the elbow. She knelt, raised the bottom of the victim's skirts, and felt her calf muscles.

"Rigor mortis is just easing off."

"Time of death?" Tennant said.

"In this cold weather, it's difficult to pinpoint, but eighteen hours. Possibly longer."

"So, yesterday, late in the afternoon. Roughly?" Sergeant Armstrong asked.

She nodded. "I'll know more when I complete my examination."

Gently, Julia pushed Margot's hair away to get a better look at the wound. Then her eyes dropped to the victim's waist. She rested her hand on Margot's mounded stomach and winced.

"I think she was with child." Julia sat back on her heels and stripped off her rubber glove. "Many months into her pregnancy, I'd guess."

"That's consistent with our information." Tennant slipped his hand under her elbow to help her rise.

"A possible motive," Armstrong said. "A married lover, maybe?" He waved to a pair of constables to bring the stretcher forward.

Julia and Tennant stood aside to allow the policemen through. The officers shifted the remains of Margot Miller to the pallet, covered her body, and carried her out.

Julia asked Tennant, "Where are they taking her?"

"Kensington Police Station."

"Will I conduct the postmortem there?"

"Yes."

Julia recalled the many times she'd found the inspector hard to read. That morning wasn't one of them.

"You sound angry."

"I am. Witnesses have been lying to me. Or withholding evidence, which amounts to the same thing. Threats, vandalism, anonymous letters, disappearances, blackmail, a suicide . . ."

"And two murders," Armstrong said.

"Sir?" O'Malley held up a black, blood-spattered, vulcanized glove by its cuff end. "A constable found it shoved into a laurel bush by the southwest entrance."

Sergeant Armstrong looked at Julia's glove. "Blimey."

It was identical to the one O'Malley held.

Julia cut away Margot Miller's fur-collared cape and her emerald dress. She laid her undergarments aside and thought, *Good quality.*

The doctor started the postmortem from the top. She combed through the victim's hair, sponging away the dried blood and loosening leaves and twigs consistent with the debris on the maze pathway. She examined Margot's scalp but found no evidence of a blow inflicted before the fatal wound.

Sergeant O'Malley's description of the neck wound hadn't been accurate. It wasn't a slash. It was a deep, penetrating jab to the neck that had severed her jugular. The position suggested a right-handed assailant who stood behind the victim and plunged the weapon deep into her flesh. The blood would have spurted away from the attacker. And the gory, discarded gauntlet probably allowed the killer to walk away without much blood on him.

The cause of Margot's death was a severed jugular that had led to exsanguination. Julia probed the deep, narrow gash. Then she glanced at the instruments on the table. *A lancet? Some sort of stiletto?*

Julia found no other wounds on the victim's body. She finished her examination, drew a sheet over Margot Miller, and washed her hands at the sink. She looked up when Tennant came in carrying a parcel.

"Any surprises?"

"None relating to the cause of death." Julia shook droplets from her hands and finished the job with a towel. "Whoever stabbed her used a thin, sharp instrument that cut clean and deep. Margot was pregnant, but you knew that. I'd estimate she was about six months gone. A boy."

"Two lives taken swiftly and brutally," Tennant said.

"One thing surprised me." Julia held up the pieces of Margot's clothing one by one. "These look new, and the quality is excellent."

"More expensive than one would expect in a shopgirl."

"Yes," Julia said. "Even one who supplemented her income by modeling. Mary told me the going rate is a shilling or two an hour."

"And you found nothing in her pockets? No key to her flat or a change purse?"

Julia shook her head.

Tennant sighed. "Old Josiah Miller may have disowned Margot, but he's still her next of kin."

"You'll bring him in for the identification?"

"Sergeant O'Malley is on his way to Poplar to inform the Millers. Given her stepbrother's habit of stalking, he's someone at the top of our list. I'd like to know his whereabouts at the time of death."

"What about male admirers? She was a beautiful woman."

"There's a disgruntled lover. A merchant seaman, Arnie Stackpole by name. But he's not the father. The timing isn't right."

"So, two men, since the father is someone else. The plot thickens." Julia eyed Tennant's package. "What do you have there?"

Tennant unwrapped the rubber glove found at the scene and placed it on the instruments table. "What do you make of it?"

"Clever. It minimizes the gore. If the attack came from behind, only the gauntlet would be spattered with blood, sparing the killer's arm and hand. Where did you say the officer found it?"

"In bushes by the southwest entrance. About fifty yards from where we discovered the body."

Julia picked it up. "It was a risk to carry the thing unless the killer had some means of concealing it until it was safe to discard. But why not strip it off and leave it with the body?"

Tennant shrugged. "In a hurry to get away after he did the deed?"

"And he rid himself of the glove at a safe distance. Yes, that sounds right."

"These gloves . . . who uses them?"

Julia pushed back her hair with the flat of her wrist and considered the question.

"Doctors. Those like me who perform autopsies, at any rate. One wouldn't use them for surgery. The gloves are thick and clumsy. I witnessed an embalming once, and the undertaker wore a pair. For mucking out sewers? Men who work with chemicals or use them for other industrial processes?"

"Someone working with paints?"

"That's a possibility," Julia said. "It mostly comes in tubes nowadays, but Mary mentioned mixing colors. I'm trying to remember if I noticed a pair in her studio."

"It's worth checking."

Julia raised the glove. "Would you consider allowing me to remove some of the blood to see what's underneath?"

"I don't usually like to tamper with evidence, but in this case . . ."

"Shall we start with the underside of the sleeve? I can leave the rest of the glove as you found it."

Tennant nodded.

Julia poured out a basin of warm water and unrolled a length of cotton wool. Carefully, she dabbed away the gore from the glove. A multicolored spattering of paint appeared.

"I think you have your answer, Inspector."

Julia returned the glove to its wrapper and handed it to him. They hadn't quite resumed their old rapport. Julia felt a lingering constraint between them.

"Well . . ." He hesitated. With a slight shrug, he said, "Now, to find the glove's mate." He headed to the door and stopped. "I suppose . . . you think it might have been Miss Allingham on the table if the blackmailer had turned up at the maze that day."

"The thought had occurred," Julia said. "Richard, we differed. Let that be the end of it. I don't expect you to agree with all my opinions."

"No? That's what people usually expect."

"That's not . . ." Julia smiled ruefully. "Fair enough. But don't expect me to hold back on my opinions."

"Only when the sun rises in the west."

"I say we call a truce."

"Agreed."

His expression softened, and a slow smile spread, reaching and warming his gray eyes. He extended his hand, and Julia took it. It felt warm in hers. He held on to her hand with subtly increasing pressure until he finally released it.

Tennant pushed through the double doors. Julia stared as they swung and settled closed. She looked at her palm, and her eyes widened. A smile played on her lips as she packed her scalpels and snapped the catch on her medical bag.

Two hours later, Sergeant O'Malley drew down a sheet to reveal Margaret Miller's face and shoulders. A granite-faced Josiah Miller identified his daughter with a single nod.

O'Malley had found several witnesses at the East Indiaman pub who had seen the cooper in his workshop around the time of Margot's death. The old man had paid the costs and fines for Micah Miller's vandalism. The stepson was out of jail and on the loose, and his whereabouts were hard to pin down. Josiah Miller had sent him to a ropewalk to purchase some barrel cording on the afternoon of Margot's murder.

"Bunked off for most of the day," O'Malley said. "Two hours missing at least. Walking is the lad's story. Stopped for a pint but couldn't remember where."

"And the seaman-boyfriend, Arnie Stackpole?" Tennant said. "Is he still in the wind?"

"I have two lads walking the docks and checking pubs and boardinghouses for him. Not a whisper so far. They'll go back tomorrow."

What was left to do was search the victim's flat. Tennant and O'Malley headed by hansom cab to Margot Miller's address in Chelsea. They drove the route she might have taken from Kensington, riding along Queen's Gate to Brompton Road, passing the gardens.

"I peeled away two coppers from the park search to check the cab and omnibus stands as you asked," O'Malley said.

"That should produce something."

"The cabbies and 'busmen wouldn't be forgetting her. She was a fine-looking woman, that Margot Miller."

"And what about Micah Miller?"

"The lads will be showing Miss Herford's likeness of him as well. Someone will recall the fella if he was hanging round about."

When the hansom crossed into Chelsea, O'Malley said, "The Harvey Nicols store is only a quarter mile from Margot's street. 'Tis just off Brompton Road."

"Interesting, given the doorman's evidence that Franny Riley walked in that direction."

The cab stopped at the last of five houses on a quiet, tree-lined street. *Turn of the century,* Tennant guessed by the look of the symmetrical windows that flanked a columned entryway.

At some point, a builder had divided the house into upstairs and downstairs flats; Margot had occupied the ground floor. Two Kensington constables waited at the front door. One enterprising officer had located the key under a stone near the front porch. He handed it to Sergeant O'Malley.

"Impressive address for a shopgirl, Paddy," Tennant said.

"Someone with a coin or two is footing the bill for this place."

"Let's see if our constables can find out who it is."

"All right, lads," O'Malley said. "Crack on with a neighborhood door-to-door. We want the landlord's name and a description of any recent male visitors."

The sergeant inserted the key, and the front door swung smoothly on its hinges.

"'Tis arctic inside," O'Malley said. "The coal burned down hours ago."

They entered the large, light-filled, and well-appointed main room of the flat. Creamy yellow-and-blue upholstery covered the parlor furniture in a style Tennant recognized as French provincial. Doors opened into a kitchen and a dining room; a hallway led to the flat's two bedrooms, the smaller of which was unfurnished.

A large, four-poster bed stood in the center of the occupied chamber. O'Malley opened a wardrobe filled with women's dresses. It also held a gentleman's smoking jacket and two shirts. A man's slippers sat on the cabinet floor next to pairs of women's boots and shoes. A shaving mirror, table, and bowl occupied the corner near the wardrobe. Women's intimate clothing and night things filled most of a bureau on the opposite wall, with one drawer reserved for a gentleman's use.

"Impressions, Sergeant?"

"All in all, a cozy setup. The furnishings look new. Top quality."

"All right, Paddy, go through everything in the bedroom. Check garment pockets, look under the mattress, and lift the carpet. You know the drill."

Tennant returned to the parlor, where an easel by the north-facing window caught his eye. A half-finished still life rested against the wooden panel. Tennant paged through a sheaf of discarded sketches; several showed signs of a second hand at work, suggesting changes of line and shading.

Someone was giving Margot drawing lessons.

Tennant moved to the opposite side of the room where a writing desk held a marble pen holder, an inkwell, and a supply of inexpensive writing paper. He picked up a sheet and held it to the light, looking for a watermark.

The inspector turned his attention to the first of the desk drawers. He found more writing paper that matched the sheets on the desk, a pile of envelopes, and a box of one-penny stamps. He jiggled the locked pulls on the middle and bottom drawers. Tennant was about to force one open when he spotted the edge of a key between the inkstand's legs. It slipped into the lock and turned.

The middle drawer held a brass-embellished teak box. Tennant's eyebrows shot up at the wad of five- and ten-pound notes he found inside. What he discovered underneath the bills was more surprising still.

"Paddy, come, please."

The sergeant appeared at the door. "Sir?"

Tennant placed the box on the desk. "Take a look."

"For the love of God." O'Malley shuffled through a stack of hand-printed envelopes. "They're addressed to all of them—to Miss Allingham and the rest. And five names we've not heard before."

"We've found our poison pen."

"What's in the bottom drawer?"

Tennant inched it out and found two wooden boxes carved with lotus leaf motifs. One held twelve stoppered bottles wrapped in tissue paper; the other had ten bottles and two empty slots. The inspector unwrapped a small blue flask, its label stamped at the top with a company's name and a lotus leaf crest.

"Laudanum," Tennant said. "Two dozen bottles of a preparation sold by S. Cooper of London."

"Two dozen? That'll leave you fluttered and your head in bits the next morning. She was something of a chancer, our Margot Miller. What was she doing with such a supply?"

"Well, there's nothing illegal about it, but it's far more than one would have on hand for personal use." Tennant replaced the bottle. "Anything to interest us in the bedroom?"

"Clean as a whistle."

Tennant stowed the boxes in the drawer, and they left the house, locking the door behind them. One of the coppers doing the rounds waited at the gate.

"What have you got for us, lad?" O'Malley said.

"The bloke next door gave us the name of the rent collector, so my partner's gone off to sort him out. His office is a quarter mile along Brompton Road."

Tennant asked, "And the door-to-door?"

"The upstairs flat is empty. Has been for the past year, according to the neighbor."

"What about the other addresses on the street?"

"The ladies at home answered a few questions. All of them had seen Mrs. Miller coming and going."

"Well, now . . . *Mrs.* Miller, was it," O'Malley said.

"A widow-lady, they thought. The sharp-eyed missus one house up sniffed and said she'd spotted a gentleman who arrived by hackney cab at all hours. Day and night."

"Could the lady identify the gentleman?"

"Rolled by with its shades drawn, she said. Bashful bugger."

O'Malley grunted. "Married bugger, most like."

The constable looked at Tennant. "Anything else, guv?"

"Just your final report. I need it by tomorrow morning. I especially want to know the name on the lease."

The following morning, O'Malley examined a late-day find from the park. A sharp-eyed constable spotted Margot Miller's handbag shortly before the search was suspended for the evening. He'd found it in a hedge near the northwest entrance to the park.

"Located it a distance from the maze," the sergeant said. "Looks like the killer walked north toward Kensington Road after doing the deed." O'Malley handed Tennant an inventory he'd made of the bag's contents. "It has a few surprises tucked inside."

Tennant scanned the list. "An empty change purse . . . a robbery gone wrong or meant to look like one? A wedding ring, and a note addressed to Miss Miller from . . ." He looked up, astonished. "From Louisa Allingham?"

O'Malley passed him the letter. "Asking Margot to tea on the day of the murder. That explains why the lass was in the neighborhood."

"The note mentions a three o'clock appointment."

"Fits the time of death."

"This invitation strikes me as odd, Paddy."

"I'll say. Margot Miller and the lady of the house, sipping tea and eating crumpets?"

Tennant folded the note and slipped it into his pocket. "I'd like to hear Mrs. Allingham's explanation."

"Will you drop me at Kensington station house on the way? Maybe one of those young coppers found the name on the lease."

*   *   *

An hour later, Tennant knocked on the door of Blenheim Lodge. While he waited for the footman, a newsboy trudged up the drive and walked around the house to the tradesmen's entrance.

The door opened, and Tennant asked the servant if Mrs. Allingham was at home.

"I'm afraid the mistress is— "

"Inspector?" Mary Allingham said from the morning room doorway. "Can I help you? My sister-in-law isn't down yet."

"I apologize for arriving so early, but I wanted to ask Mrs. Allingham about a note she sent."

"Louisa sent you a note?"

"No." Tennant drew the invitation from his inner pocket and gave it to Mary.

She looked up with a puzzled frown. "My sister-in-law didn't write this. It's nothing like her handwriting."

"You're certain, Miss Allingham?"

"Of course. But it explains something strange that happened a few days ago." She looked around for the servant. "Alfred?"

"Yes, Miss Mary?"

"Tell Inspector Tennant about Miss Miller's visit."

"Two days ago, it was. Showed up at the front door, asking to see Mrs. Allingham, bold as brass. I told her the mistress was out for the afternoon."

"What was her response?"

"Stamped her foot and stormed off in a huff."

"Thank you, Alfred," Mary said.

Tennant waited until the door closed behind the servant. "Was your sister-in-law out or simply not receiving visitors?"

"Louisa had gone to Garrard's, her jeweler, to inquire about a mourning brooch."

"What did Mrs. Allingham say about the incident?"

"She thought Alfred had misunderstood, that the girl had

asked for me. But Margot never knocks on the front door when she comes for a sitting. She walks around back to my studio."

"And you hadn't arranged to see her?"

"No. I don't understand. It's such a . . . pointless, heartless prank to pull on a widow and a household in mourning."

"Miss Allingham, I saw your morning paper arrive. You haven't heard the news. Yesterday, Margot Miller was found dead in the maze at the horticultural garden. She'd been murdered the day before."

"Good God! The afternoon she . . ."

"Yes. The day she called here. Miss Allingham, perhaps we could sit?"

"Of course." Tennant followed her into the drawing room. She dropped onto a chair. "Margot, murdered. This is some sort of . . ."

Tennant eyed her closely as she rubbed her temple. "First, a letter asking for money and sent to Louisa of all people. Now, a forged note and the maze again. I don't understand any of it."

"A search of Miss Miller's rooms produced a surprise. We found unsent, printed envelopes addressed to you and other artists."

Mary's eyes widened. "Margot? She was the letter writer? But why?"

"Money, most likely. We found a surprising number of pounds stashed away in her drawer. It's given us a few leads. Some victims who are new to us."

"She wrote accusations about herself in the letters to Annie." Mary shook her head. "Clever."

"Miss Allingham, I don't want to add to your sister-in-law's distress, but—"

"I doubt she can help you. Of all the unaccountable things, Louisa's entanglement is the strangest. She has little interest in the art world, and I doubt she ever saw Margot Miller except to glimpse her walking along the path to my studio."

"The forged note achieved the killer's end. It brought Margot to him. Miss Allingham, there is a way you can help me."

"I will if I can."

"You've painted Margot Miller. Do you have a sketch I could borrow? Something I could show to potential witnesses?"

"In my studio." Mary stood and rang for the servant. "Alfred will let you in. Ask him to add some coals to the fire. I'll look in on Louisa and fetch a wrap. I'll meet you in the studio in five minutes."

Mary, as good as her word, appeared a few minutes later. "Louisa is asleep."

"Forgive me, Miss Allingham, but who looks after you?"

Tears sprung to her eyes. "It's kind of you to ask. I have a few cousins and many dear friends, but Charles . . . Well, he was the link to the parents I never knew."

She turned away, sorted through some folders and sketch pads, and carried the stack to a table.

"Before we begin," Tennant said, "I have another question. Do you ever use vulcanized rubber gloves in your studio?"

"Yes, when I mix paints, although it's been a while since I've bothered. Oil paints come in tubes nowadays. I've become lazy about making my own colors."

"Do most artists use gloves?"

"I really couldn't say."

"All right, Miss Allingham. Now, for that picture of Margot Miller."

Mary opened the first sketch pad, turning over page after page. "Most of these are studies of poses, not faces." She picked up a second pad and flipped through it. "Better, but not detailed enough." She looked up. "I wonder . . ."

Mary pulled a portfolio from a shelf along the back wall and carried it to Tennant.

"My brother bought these from the artist and gave them to

me." Mary placed the folder on the table. Tennant opened it to a watercolor of Margot Miller's head and shoulders. "This is the one you want, I think. It's by a young Irishman."

It was no quick sketch; the artist had labored over it. "This is perfect for my purpose." Tennant picked it up. Underneath it was a second portrait of Margot Miller. "This artist," he said sharply. "Can you tell me his name?"

Mary looked at him curiously. "William Quain."

WQ was on the list he'd taken from Allingham's cabinet. *WQ—the initials on Franny's sketch.*

Tennant said, "I imagine this second portrait required many sittings."

"Weeks of work."

"Miss Allingham, you said your brother purchased these paintings and sketches directly from the artist. Might there be an address for Mister Quain amongst his papers?"

"Well . . . possibly. You'd like me to look?"

"I'd be grateful."

They returned to the house, and Tennant waited for Mary to find the information. When she handed him the artist's address, he read the question in her face, so he satisfied her curiosity with a part of the truth.

"We need to interview anyone who spent time with Margot Miller. Can you tell me the names of male artists who employed her as a model?"

Tennant wasn't an art connoisseur, but Mary rattled off a set of names so famous that he recognized them all. The inspector blew out his cheeks. "That's quite a list." He took out his pencil and notepad. "Can you write all the names down for me?"

Tennant left Blenheim Lodge with William Quain's address, the list of artists, and two pictures of Margot Miller. One was the sketch he'd use for identification. The other was a painting of Margot standing at her washstand, naked to the waist. The room, the bed, the green dressing gown tossed carelessly aside; it was the same setting as a picture of Margot he'd found locked away in Charles Allingham's cabinet.

The emerald wrap with its glittering moths thrown across the bed matched the one they found in the other painting and on Franny Riley's body.

CHAPTER 8

Tennant picked up a cab on Kensington Road and headed west to the police station. He spotted O'Malley waiting on the corner.

After the sergeant eased his bulk into the hansom, the inspector untied his folder's ribbon and held up the picture of Margot at her bath.

O'Malley whistled. "'Tis a match."

"Yes. And we have a name and address linked to a painting in Allingham's collection, thanks to Miss Allingham. He's William Quain, a countryman of yours who spent hours with Margot. Weeks of work, Miss Allingham said."

"Hours staring at the likes of Margot Miller? You'd be codding me to call that work."

"Not digging ditches, to be sure." Tennant slid the picture into its folder.

"And what did the lady of the house say about the note?"

"A clever ploy," Tennant said, and explained the ruse. "Any joy over that lease? Tell me the coppers turned up a name."

O'Malley rolled his eyes. "Fella named John Smith if you can believe it."

"Original. Did the officer get a description from the agent?"

"That he did not. Couldn't recall his face from a year ago, the copper said. The agent is saying the lady of the house paid the monthly rent."

"Visit the agent tomorrow, Paddy. Lean into him hard, if you must. See if he holds to his tale."

"Could it be our John Smith is William Quain?"

"Someone was giving Margot Miller drawing lessons." Tennant banged on the hansom's roof. "Scotland Yard," he called to the driver. "I want my hands on Allington's painting of Margot and that list of initials before we chat with Mister Quain."

Mary retreated to her studio after Tennant left Blenheim Lodge. Her paintbrush had always been her refuge, but she'd found it impossible to concentrate since her brother's death.

Her sister-in-law had chosen laudanum and fantasy, believing her husband's suicide was an accident. Gently, Mary had explained the verdict of the coroner's inquest, but Louisa refused to listen. Instead, she had turned away, her face a mask.

Mary indulged in no illusions. She'd watched the police remove her brother's covered corpse from the house. And while the housemaids had tried to be discreet, she'd caught them carrying slop buckets and brushes from his room to the back staircase. Mary accepted the reality of his death, but she struggled to understand it. Yes, Charles had been drinking too much. Yes, he had been troubled. But to kill himself? Yes, her shining brother had ended his life.

Tears welled, but so did anger, robbing her of the solace of memory.

Even joyful news failed to stir her. A day earlier, Mary had learned that the Royal Academy would include *Repose* in their "Annual Exhibition." Her acceptance envelope included an invitation "requesting the honor of your company" at the opening. A blue admission ticket had fluttered to the floor. Mary had picked it up and laid it aside, feeling hollow rather than triumphant.

She stared at her easel for twenty minutes with a dry paintbrush in her hand. Finally, she eyed the open sketch pads and the scattered drawings on the table and surrendered. If she couldn't manage a single brushstroke, she would tidy up.

Mary gathered William Quain's sketches into their folder. Then she changed her mind and took out his study of the Irish cottage. She put the rest away and returned to the watercolor, admiring it afresh.

Mary wondered why she'd been disingenuous with Tennant about Will Quain's address, pretending to search for it among her brother's papers. She knew perfectly well where the artist lived. A week before Charles's death, Mary had run into him, literally, in a Soho doorway. He'd stood back as she exited the shop where she purchased her paints.

"Miss Allingham." He'd touched the brim of his tweed cap. "The Fates had another meeting planned for us, buying as we do from the same supplier."

"Mister Quain." She'd nodded and brushed past him on the way to her carriage. He'd followed her and opened the door.

"My studio is just along the way. Number ten." He'd cocked his thumb at the corner house across the street. "Have you a moment to favor me with your opinion?" When she'd hesitated, he smiled. "I'm not the big bad wolf, you know. If you wish, I can ask my landlady to chaperone."

"Another time, perhaps."

"Ah, in a hurry, the curse of modern life. 'Tis living in hope I'll be," he'd said, exaggerating his Irish cadences. She'd noticed his accent faded in and out. When he closed the carriage door, he had an amused gleam in his eye.

Too good-looking, and he knows it. Mary shrugged away the memory and returned the picture to the folder.

Yet, Will Quain had left a kind condolence note at the house.

He wouldn't intrude on their grief but wanted to express his gratitude for Charles's help and his sorrow at his passing. Her brother had been generous to the artist when he needed assistance. It was a simple, heartfelt note.

Quain had enclosed a separate letter to Mary, telling her he'd seen the SFA exhibition and admired her work. He'd singled out *Down the Rushy Glen*, making several perceptive comments about its composition and praising her brushwork. She had yet to thank him, and Mary felt guilty about putting Tennant on his trail.

She thought, *A long list of artists painted Margot. It doesn't make them murderers.* And Louisa proved that an investigation's web could entangle an innocent person. But why had Tennant inquired about her rubber gloves, asking if other painters used them?

Impulsively, Mary pulled the bell cord to call the coachman. She'd placed Will Quain squarely in the inspector's sights and thought she should warn him. Then she changed her mind. *Too late. Tennant is probably on his way to Soho by now.*

Mary dropped into a chair and waited for the coachman to answer her summons. Sitting, she realized how tired she was and how badly she'd been sleeping. She dragged a sheet of paper forward and scratched out a note for the coachman to deliver to Doctor Lewis.

Mary's message had arrived just before Julia left Finsbury Circus for the clinic.

The girl asked for an appointment, but how urgent was the request? Julia thought she'd read agitation in the slapdash note, so she suggested that afternoon at her clinic or the following morning at her office. Margot Miller's death must have come as a shock to her. *Another one, on top of all the others.*

Mary appeared in Whitechapel just after midday. Julia closed her office door and invited her visitor to sit, noting the smudges under her eyes and the restless fingers that smoothed the fur of her sable muff.

"Thank you for seeing me so promptly, Doctor. I hope it's not inconvenient. It might have waited until tomorrow, but . . ."

Julia smiled and said, "No trouble at all, as it happens. You've come on a rare slow day."

"Doctor Scott has been our family physician, but I'm not ill often, so I've rarely consulted him. These last weeks . . ." Mary looked away, frowning.

"They've been more than anyone should bear, Mary. Sometimes, it's hard to reach out for the help we need."

"Dr. Scott barely listens to Louisa and just hands her a tonic. Now I realize it's how he's always treated her ailments. I just never thought about it before."

"You'd like to make a change?"

"Yes, I would." Mary put her muff aside and sat up straighter. "A doctor should listen to what a patient has to say. But Doctor Scott was her father's oldest friend, so his attitude is more paternal than professional."

Julia smiled and said, "I promise to listen. Always. So, tell me, what brings you here today?"

Mary described her sleeplessness. It didn't surprise Julia: the girl looked hollow-eyed and worn out.

"Louisa is having trouble sleeping as well," Mary said. "Doctor Scott prescribed laudanum for that and her headaches."

"I wouldn't recommend it," Julia said quickly. "Laudanum is a powerful drug and far more addictive than people realize. Parliament may take up the question of regulation this year, and not a moment too soon."

"Is there something else?"

"Were the mild bromide mixtures I gave you earlier effective?" When Mary nodded, Julia said, "Let's try them again."

Mary's shoulders relaxed. "Thank you, Doctor. Perhaps Louisa—"

"I need to tread carefully here. Your sister-in-law is not my patient. Still, you might talk to her about my suggestion for *your* treatment."

"She's steadfast in her confidence in Doctor Scott, but she's not herself these days, and no wonder." Mary sighed. "First Charles and now Margot Miller. You heard about her death?"

Julia nodded. "I performed the postmortem and will give evidence tomorrow at the coroner's inquest."

"Two deaths," Mary said. "I hadn't thought about the child until I saw your nurse with a mother and her baby."

"Margot's pregnancy was known, generally?"

"Oh, yes. I'd wondered how she would manage with no father coming forward."

"Had she continued to work as an artist's model?"

Mary nodded. "Most recently for Laura Herford. Just the finishing touches for her Royal Academy submission, so Laura was able to . . . paint around the problem."

"I'd wondered . . . had she posed for male artists in addition to the women painters in your circle?"

Mary's restless fingers went still. "Yes. For Rossetti and . . . and others."

Julia nodded. "The police will look closely at them."

"I . . . I imagine so." Mary's gaze dropped to her tightly knitted fingers. She stirred in her seat. "Well, I've kept you long enough, Doctor."

Julia said, "Stay a moment while I fetch that bottle of bromide." Julia wondered about her sudden change in mood. *Something about the artists.* When Julia returned from the medicine storeroom, she found Annie O'Neill waiting in the hallway.

Julia smiled and asked, "Are you here to have those stitches out?"

"Annie?" Mary crossed the corridor and gripped the girl's

hands. "Dear Annie, this terrible news about Margot. I'm so sorry. I know she was your friend."

The girl flinched. "Thank you, miss," she whispered. "And . . . and you, grieving as well. For your brother. 'Tis sorry I am that he passed." She glanced at the door.

To Julia, Annie looked like a creature caught in a trap. But Mary seemed not to notice and asked questions that Annie answered with nods.

When Mary finally stopped for breath, Annie looked at Julia. "I can't be staying to have those stitches out after all. Can I come back another day?"

"Of course, Annie."

"Thank you, Doctor. Good day, Miss Allingham."

Mary watched the front door swing behind Annie. "Poor girl."

Julia handed her a brown, corked bottle. "The directions are on the label."

"Thank you, Doctor." Mary stashed it inside the pocket of her muff. "I know your week is busy, but would you join us for tea some Sunday?"

"I'd like that."

"Oh" Mary said, biting her lip. "I should have offered to drive Annie home. Let me try to catch her up. Goodbye, Doctor." She hurried out the door.

Catch Annie up, indeed, Julia thought. Something ailed the girl, but what?

The cabbie dropped Inspector Tennant and Sergeant O'Malley in front of a bookshop at Oxford and Dean Streets in Soho.

A half century earlier, private houses in the once-residential neighborhood had given way to commercial properties. Tennant and O'Malley looked for Quain's address, passing furniture makers, drapers, and cobblers along the way. Finally, they spotted it, a three-story brick house whose portico sorely needed whitewash. Interior doors in a dim vestibule divided the bottom floor into two flats. Quain's rooms were on the right. O'Malley lifted a gloved fist the size of a coconut and rapped on the door. It creaked open.

"Be gone," someone shouted, "unless you've got a bottle of Kilbeggan's on you."

Tennant pushed the door wider. "Empty-handed, I'm afraid." He stepped over the threshold. "Mister Quain? Detective Inspector Tennant with Detective Sergeant O'Malley."

The artist peered around the edge of his easel. "The peelers, is it now?"

"That's right, sir. The Metropolitan Police. I'd like a word if I may."

Quain glanced at the windows and sighed. "The light's going on me anyway." He stowed his palette, wiped his hands on a rag, and crossed the sparsely furnished room.

His easel occupied the right-center of an ample, undivided space that had started life as a warehouse. Three six-foot windows in the side wall opened onto platforms whose swing-arm cranes still hung over the exterior windows like forgotten gibbets. That day, the only thing entering through the windows was the last of the soft, even daylight, ideal for an artist's studio.

Quain led them to a set of rickety chairs around a scarred table. "My rent is paid, and I've settled the tab at my pub, so I'm asking you to sit with a clear conscience on me."

"Thank you, Mister Quain." Tennant placed a folder on the tabletop and opened it to the pictures Mary had given him of Margot Miller. "I'm investigating the death of this young woman. Your work, I believe?"

Quain nodded. "She was a fine one, that Margot. A crime against nature it was to take her from this world."

"When did you see her last?"

"Not for donkey's years. I painted that two summers past."

"I believe you sketched this young woman in the park." Tennant showed him the picture of Franny Riley. "She's dead, too. Beaten to death—were you aware of that?"

Quain stared at the picture before saying, "I'd heard that news."

Tennant uncovered the picture of Margot on the bed and the girl with the paddle. "And this one?"

Quain's head jerked up. "Where did you . . . of course, you've been through Mister Allingham's effects. Stupid of me."

"When was the last time you painted Miss Miller?"

"I finished that one two years ago, and I haven't laid eyes on Margot in months."

"And Miss Riley? When did you see her last?"

"A year ago. I assure you, Inspector, as God is my witness, I know nothing about her death."

"The green dressing gown in this painting." Tennant tapped the picture of *Margot at Her Bath*. "It matches the one we found wrapped around Franny Riley's body. The moth design is distinctive. Have you an explanation?"

Quain licked his lips. "It was Margot's gown."

"I might have guessed," Tennant said. "Miss Miller is conveniently dead."

"What the hell do you mean by that!"

"Just a statement of fact."

Seconds ticked by. Then the artist leaned back. "Margot supplied all the props for the composition. I'd like to see you prove otherwise, Inspector."

O'Malley narrowed his eyes. "Where are you saying you hail from, sir? You're speaking the Queen's English now."

Tennant, too, had noticed the sudden change in the artist's accent. "Yes, Mister Quain. Why play the stage Irishman?"

The artist shrugged. "A bad habit, I'm afraid, my having some fun at the expense of the natives. I'm Irish, although your sergeant might dispute it. I'm not a left footer."

"Meaning?"

O'Malley said, "He's not a Catholic, he's saying. He's Anglo-Irish. A Protestant."

"That's right." The artist knitted his fingers behind his head and leaned back in his chair. "I'm a deanery brat from Waterford. My father is dean of Christ Church, the city's Anglican cathedral."

"For shame, boy-o." O'Malley picked up the painting of the naked, voluptuous Margot sprawled across her bed. "What would your daddy be making of this, now?"

Quain sat up straight and patted his pockets. He pulled a pipe from his painter's smock and struck a match. He took several draws until the tobacco in his bowl glowed red and tossed the match into the fireplace.

"Not a clue, Sergeant. But like so many hypocrites, the old boy would enjoy having it both ways. Public outrage, private ogling."

Tennant asked, "Did Charles Allingham commission these portraits?"

"Just the second one. *Margot at Her Bath* was part of a collection of watercolors Charles purchased from me when we first met."

"How do you explain the notations on this?" Tennant showed him the list taken from Allingham's cabinet. "The initials 'WQ' appear three times on this inventory of commissions."

"Well . . ." He hitched his shoulder uncomfortably. "I painted two others for him."

"Portraits of Margot Miller?"

"No. Yes. Not precisely, although she was part of the ensemble. You see . . ."

"I'm afraid I don't."

"Charles commissioned two Chinese scenes in the French style. Modeled on the work of Eugène Delacroix, but more—"

"Yes, more," Tennant said. "I've seen Mister Allingham's collection. Did he dictate the compositions?"

"Only in the most general terms. Charles paid for the paintings, but Margot . . . well, Margot managed it all."

"What do you mean by that?"

"She arranged for the models. Brought them to my studio and staged the poses."

"Who paid them?"

"Margot. The girls she brought . . . They were getting younger, and some didn't seem too keen. One dark-haired girl got as far as the door and then bolted. Others kept looking at the food and drink Margot had set up here." Quain smacked the tabletop.

"Why only three commissions? Other sets of initials appear many times on this list. Did you and Mister Allingham have a falling-out?"

"No." Quain stood abruptly. He knocked the tobacco into the fire and turned. "We parted friends, and I'll always be grateful to him. His introductions opened doors for me and led to several commissions. The excuse that I was too busy was a face-saving way to turn him down."

Tennant raised his brow. "Why did you need one?"

The artist combed his fingers through his dark, curly hair. "Look, Charles was a good bloke. I don't think he knew that Margot . . . he saw the fantasy I painted, not the truth behind it."

"And what was the truth, Mister Quain?"

"That Margot found poor girls desperate to do anything she asked." The artist dug his hands into his trouser pockets. "I'm not proud of my role in it."

"And Margot?"

"There was nothing she wouldn't do, come to that. Margot loved stripping off. She knew the power of her body, her allure, and who could blame her? In a world where men write the checks, she called the tune."

O'Malley said, "Did she ever whistle your way?"

"No such luck, Sergeant. Margot knew I couldn't afford her."

"Someone could," Tennant said. "She dressed in silks and satins and a fur-collared cape."

"Oh, Margot was sleek, all right. The girls she brought to my studio were awed by 'Miss Miller.' Her clothes, her manner, and the way she walked and talked. She learned those airs and graces from the lady artists who hired her to sit. Margot spent as much time studying them as they spent looking at her."

"We know a 'John Smith' leased the house she lived in," Tennant said. "Most likely, an assumed name."

"Not the most creative alias."

O'Malley asked, "Could Charles Allingham have paid for Margot's gaff?"

"Possibly . . . but the poor sod is the one person who couldn't have killed her. That's why you're here, isn't it? To find Margot's murderer."

"And where were you on the afternoon in question?" O'Malley said. "The day before yesterday and going on for dusk."

"I was here. Working in my studio."

"Not the most creative alibi," Tennant said. "Your model can corroborate your story?"

"I didn't use a model that day." Quain crossed to his easel and jerked it around. "I'm working on a landscape, as you can see." He pointed to a corkboard with sketches pinned to it. "Those sheep weren't here either."

"What about the last evening in January," Tennant said. "Sometime after midnight, someone tossed Franny Riley in the gutter."

"At a guess, I'd say I was heading home after a pint at my local."

Tennant spotted a self-portrait in charcoal and removed it from the board. "I'll take the liberty of borrowing this if you have no objection. You shouldn't . . . if you're as innocent as you contend."

"At least you didn't say 'pretend.'" Quain spread his hands. "Take it with my compliments, Inspector. Show it to whomever you please. It won't link me to Margot or Franny's murder."

Tennant added it to the folder. "Margot is turning out to be a woman of parts. I heard she was an aspiring artist. Taking drawing lessons."

"That's news to me. I'm surprised she bothered. Margot's most perfect work of art was herself."

"Meaning what?" O'Malley said.

"The best models are actresses. They telegraph whatever mood or emotion you're trying to express. Most will pose for a bob, but a skilled sitter more than repays her two shillings an hour. Margot was the best. Worth every penny."

Tennant eyed him levelly. "And you have nothing to add that may help us with our investigations?"

"Nothing." Quain watched the inspector gather the sketches. "Inspector . . ."

"Yes, Mister Quain?"

"Does Miss Allingham know about those paintings? She thinks little enough of me as it is, but her brother . . . Charles told me they were very close."

"Miss Allingham strikes me as a levelheaded young woman who can look after herself."

"That doesn't answer my question."

"Good day, Mister Quain."

"Wait."

The inspector turned.

"Wait just a minute. I . . ."

"Yes, Mister Quain?"

The artist pulled off his smock and tossed it on the chair by his easel. "I don't want to make trouble for myself . . . he's a powerful man in the art world."

"Who?"

"Frederic Leighton."

"What about him?"

"He and Margot . . . she had some sort of vendetta against him. At our last sitting, well, she hinted . . . No, damn it, she *said* she knew things about him, and he'd be sorry he crossed her."

The following morning, the jurymen and witnesses in the death of Margaret Miller gathered at the Campton Arms on Kensington Road. The jury would deliberate in the back room of the public house and reach a verdict on the cause of death. For the sake of the ratepayers who footed the bill, the coroner hoped to wrap things up by lunchtime: the publican's rates went up each hour they drifted past noon. The jury would hear first from the unfortunate parkkeeper who stumbled on the body, then from the police, and finally from the doctor who performed the postmortem.

When the coroner asked Doctor *Julia* Lewis to take the stand, a surprised murmur, like a humming vibration from an unseen engine, followed her across the room.

Julia gave her evidence in a firm voice. When she finished, the coroner invited the jury to withdraw and consider the testimony. Ten minutes later, they returned the obvious verdict: death by a person or persons unknown. The finding was signed and sealed on the tenth of March 1867. The coroner thanked them and noted the time with satisfaction. By ten thirty, he'd sent all on their way.

Outside the pub, the sun shone palely on a wintry Kensington Road. Neither the inquest nor Tennant's investigation had shed much light on the case. Everything about Margot's murder remained stubbornly in the shadows.

Tennant spotted a coffeehouse across the street. He touched Julia's elbow and pointed to it. "Have you time for a cup?"

"Hmm, that would be lovely. The coroner asked me to wait for him, so I'll meet you."

Tennant crossed to the café, slid into a street-side bench, and watched Julia from the window. One of her hands struggled to keep the wind from spinning her hat down Kensington Road. The other clutched her cape below a chin that bobbed in agreement with the coroner's comments. Whatever he was saying, he said it at length. Finally, after what looked like Julia's third attempt to break things off, the coroner bowed and walked away, freeing her to cross the street.

They'd met many times, but Tennant could count on one hand the occasions they'd spent in each other's company: times that hadn't involved a dead body.

One hand? Hell, three fingers.

They'd had coffee once, and Julia's grandfather had invited him to dinner at their town house. And they'd shared a walk around Finsbury Circus a few days after she returned home from the hospital. But even then, the conversation had turned to the shocking conclusion of their first case and other professional concerns.

None of that mattered. A long, solitary walk across the Kentish downs on a crisp Christmas afternoon had clarified his feelings for her. What Julia thought of him . . . *Some detective*, he thought, waving to her as she entered the coffeehouse.

Julia sat down, pulled off her tam-o'shanter, and fanned four coins across the tabletop. "My princely fee as prescribed by law. The two pounds, two bob from the coroner for my postmortem services."

"Riches, indeed." Tennant raised two fingers to the waiter.

Julia unbuttoned her cape and pulled off her gloves. "Given that I'm flush with pounds and shillings, I should offer to pay, but you invited me, so . . ." She brushed the coins into her palm. "I'll pocket them."

No other woman Tennant knew would make a breezy suggestion to foot the bill.

Then, as if reading his earlier thoughts by strange telegraphy, she said, "Speaking of invitations . . . Before I forget, Grandfather would like to invite you to dinner again. One of his Wednesday gatherings."

"I'd be delighted."

The waiter placed two cups of steaming coffee on the table. "Anything to eat, guv?"

"Julia?"

She shook her head. "Nothing else, thank you."

"Grandfather will send you a note." She cupped her coffee with two hands to warm them, then sipped. "He understands that you might have to beg off at the last moment."

"The policeman's lot."

Julia edged her cup and saucer to one side and leaned forward on her elbows. "I know you don't put all your cards on the table at an inquest, but has the investigation dealt you any?"

"It's too rich a hand. I'm unsure what to hold or discard." He ticked off his fingers. "There's the unknown father of Margot's child and the mystery man who pays her bills. She has a father and stepbrother, both of whom seem unstable, to put it mildly. There's an angry seaman-lover, Stackpole. He's somewhere in the wind. And she's modeled for all the male luminaries of the British art world. Landseer, Rossetti, Frederic Leighton, and other members of the Royal Academy, not to mention some lesser lights."

"Oh, dear." Julia's smile twitched. "Chief Inspector Clark won't like your stepping on those celebrated toes."

"And we've uncovered Margot Miller's role in procuring young women for the purpose of pornography."

"Good Lord. You and Sergeant O'Malley have been busy."

"It's one compelling motive for her murder. So is blackmail." Tennant explained the discovery of the envelopes in Margot Miller's desk.

Julia shook her head. "Surprising but not shocking, somehow. She's been knee-deep in everything about this case."

"And in the background is the disappearance of several shopgirls over the past year. At least one of them modeled for the artists. Yet the chief refuses to hand us the earlier cases."

"Why?"

"Partly because I asked for them. Partly because the chief always doubles down on a bad decision."

"Frustrating for you."

"An artist named Will Quain told us about Margot and the pornography scheme. Miss Allingham gave me his name."

"Mary is a good guide if the answer is somewhere in the art world."

Tennant nodded. "Louisa seems to hold it at a distance, so I needn't bother her, but Miss Allingham might recognize the style of some of the other paintings. I'm not eager to show her the kind of work her brother commissioned, but I'm afraid it must come to that."

"Well . . ."

Tennant waited as Julia hesitated. "What is it?"

"I don't know about Mrs. Allingham, but Mary is no Dresden figurine. She's less breakable than you think. Do you remember the newspaper story about a woman who paid twenty pounds to save one of the Regent's Park skaters?"

"Was that—"

"Mary."

Tennant blew out his cheeks. "The lady keeps a cool head in a crisis."

Julia stirred her cup, considering. "Perhaps it's best not to push Mary too hard just now. What about asking the artist? Show the pictures to Mister Quain. He'd probably be happy to cooperate if only to deflect suspicion from him."

"That's an excellent suggestion. I won't say you're wasted in the medical profession. Still . . ."

"Just doing my bit for Queen, country, and the Yard."

"Sergeant O'Malley wonders if a dark-haired girl Quain mentioned—a girl who fled his studio—might be Annie O'Neill."

"It's possible. Margot had pressured her to sit for more revealing poses. She refused. But for Margot to go from modeling to pornography?"

"It's a fine line under the statute. Eastlake, the family lawyer, rightly pointed out that a private art collection isn't illegal. If Allingham sold them to like-minded 'connoisseurs,' that would be trafficking and quite another matter."

Julia fiddled with her teaspoon. "Yesterday, Annie came to my clinic while Miss Allingham was there."

"With injuries again?"

"No. She came to have some stitches taken out. Instead, the girl took one look at Mary and bolted. It was obvious that she had something on her mind."

"I think it's time for another word with Miss O'Neill."

Julia sighed. "I know you must. Look, I'm seeing Annie tomorrow about removing those stitches. Let me try once more to win her confidence and persuade her to talk to you."

"Very well."

"Thank you, and . . ." Julia looked away.

"What is it?"

"I'm sorry. I was about to ask you to tread lightly with Annie. I know you will." Julia smiled. "You and that amiable bear of a sergeant."

"Of course." Tennant looked over his shoulder for the waiter. "Another cup?"

Julia shook her head. "When I'm flagging a few hours from now, I'll wish I'd taken the offer." She started to rise, then sat again. "I've remembered something. Margot paid Annie to hold her room. Perhaps she left something behind."

"Worth pursuing. Thank you."

Tennant left two coins on the table and stood to the side to allow Julia to pass. As she swung her cape around her shoulders and brushed by him, a scent of something warm and spicy like sandalwood drifted his way. He breathed it in and blinked when she looked up from hooking her collar, her eyes inches from his.

She put her hand on his sleeve. "Richard, I think Annie is quite frightened about something."

CHAPTER 9

Three reports waited for Inspector Tennant the following morning, beginning with O'Malley's account of his interview with Margot Miller's house agent.

"He's sticking to his story about remembering nothing. So, I leaned in and got my nose in his mug. Politely, I'm asking him to have another think." O'Malley grinned. "And doesn't he recall a familiar face?"

Tennant leaned back in his chair. "You have my attention, Sergeant."

"Tidy fella, John Smith, says the agent, and not bad-looking for a man trying to hide a gammy lip under his mustache."

"Rawlings. He of the harelip. Time for a chat with that gentleman's gentleman."

"Sorry, sir, but our bird has flown. I stopped at Blenheim Lodge on the way back from Chelsea. The valet handed in his notice. He's going to America to work for an uncle who owns a men's shop."

"Damnation. Get on to the steamship lines," Tennant said. "Perhaps we can cage Rawlings before he flies away."

Tennant drew two reports toward him. "What about the park search and the neighborhood canvass?"

"The omnibus conductor on the Cromwell-to-Brompton line remembers Margot well. Forgetting her would be the stranger thing."

"Did he see her on the day of the murder?"

"He's not certain of that," O'Malley said. "He recalls her riding the line often and recently. But he couldn't swear to a day."

"What about our elusive seaman? Do we have a line on Arnie Stackpole?"

"Ah, there we have an answer. A magistrate in Limehouse gave him thirty days in the nick for destruction of property. Blind drunk and brawling, he was, and leaving some patrons— and the pub—in bits. The creature's been inside all the past week."

"So not our man," Tennant said.

"The killing wasn't his style. A smash to the head or hands to the throat, more like. He wouldn't draw the lass into a trap by sending her a letter to tea."

"Useful to eliminate a distraction." Tennant swept the reports into his drawer. "We can't afford to lose time over those passenger ships, Paddy."

"I'll get on to it."

Tennant plucked his hat from its peg. "I'm off to see the artists of Kensington. I'm curious about the bad blood Quain mentioned between Frederic Leighton and Margot Miller."

Crossing artists off Mary's list proved easier than Tennant expected: all the leading lights of the British art world had made a pact to live in Kensington.

The inspector caught most of them working at home and racing against a deadline. "Send-in day" for the Royal Academy's Annual Exhibition was just weeks away, and the artists emerged from their studios paint-smeared and irked by the interruption. To a man, they said they hadn't seen Margot Miller in over a year, and none had employed Franny Riley.

Tennant's last stop was Holland House, the brick mansion built by Frederic Leighton on a wooded site off Kensington High Street. A servant wearing billowy cream trousers and an embroidered red jacket ushered the inspector into a vast, domed hall whose scale seemed designed to make a visitor feel small.

After a brief wait, a tall man with dark, curling hair and a graying beard appeared. He'd dressed as extravagantly as his servant in a flowing Turkish kaftan of crimson and gold.

"Inspector." Leighton extended his hand. "You're here about Margot Miller, I expect. A shocking end, but not surprising."

Tennant raised an eyebrow. "Will you explain that comment?"

"The woman was a menace. I had nothing to do with Margot's death, so I needn't hide my animus. I haven't employed her in nearly two years, with good reason."

"You have my attention, Mister Leighton."

"She tried a spot of blackmail on me for . . . improper behavior, let us say, with my models."

"What did you do?"

"I took a page out of the Duke of Wellington's book. I told her to accuse and be damned. Never hired her again."

"You had nothing to fear?"

Leighton smiled, white teeth gleaming between his dark beard and mustache. "The British public balks at a bohemian banker but accepts a free-spirited artist. And I have no outraged wife to begin divorce proceedings on the strength of Miller's lies."

"She was with child when she was murdered. Can you suggest a name for the father?"

"Alas, I cannot. Still, Margot knew her worth and wouldn't sell herself cheaply. If I were you, I'd look for someone who could afford her."

"One last question. Have you ever employed a model named Franny Riley?"

He shook his head.

Tennant retraced his steps to Kensington Road and thought, *These artists live in each other's pockets, but no one knows a thing.* He signaled a cabbie and hoped Sergeant O'Malley had better luck with the passenger ships.

At noon, Julia's omnibus stopped at Aldgate High Street and Blue Boar Lane. She looked up as the bells of nearby St. Katharine's Church rang the hour. Then Julia glanced at the Blue Boar Inn's window sign and read it regretfully. She started to walk away and thought, *Why not?*

Twenty minutes later, Annie cracked open her basement door.

Julia held up two steaming packets of fish and chips wrapped in newspaper sleeves. "I skipped breakfast, and the aroma from the Blue Boar was irresistible."

The door swung open, and a delighted Annie smiled, the first joyful one Julia recalled. "A doctor paying a house call with a meal in her hands? 'Tis service above and beyond." She stood back and let her in.

Julia had caught Annie in the middle of a project. The girl laid her scissors aside, reached for two plates and a pair of forks, and placed them on her tiny kitchen table. Then Annie peeled the newspaper away from her chips and breathed in.

"Ah . . . they have a lovely tang of vinegar on them. A grand meal they make of it at the Boar."

Julia sliced through the coated fillet and popped a piece of cod into her mouth. "Grand, indeed." She pointed her fork at the plate. "My American grandmother always said nothing in the States matched English fish and chips. That was quite an admission, coming from her."

They ate for a minute or two in silence. Then Annie said, "I haven't thanked you properly."

"For what?"

"For taking the time out of your day to, you know, to examine me in the police station. 'Twas kindness itself you were."

Here was her opening. *Would Annie take it?* "It's Inspector Tennant who most deserves your thanks. He persuaded the local inspector to call me in and drove to my house to fetch me."

Annie looked down at her plate. "I'd help him if I could, but I've little to tell. I've not seen much of Margot these last months. God rest her soul."

"You had a falling-out?"

Annie shook her head. "Nothing like that. But Margot said . . . I told her I'm happy as I am, trimming my hats and sitting for the ladies."

"Did Margot get on well with the women artists?"

"She . . ." Annie frowned. "Margot mocked them much of the time. Taking their money but resenting them all the same. Saying they paid her a pittance, but she'd be getting what she was worth in the end."

"Did she explain her meaning?"

Annie shook her head. The girl crumpled the newspapers, carried the plates to the washbowl, and returned to the table.

Julia moved her medical bag from the floor to the table. "Shall we have those sutures out?"

Annie sat, pushed up her sleeve, and extended her arm. Julia used tiny forceps to lift each knot. Then she cut away the threads with a lancet. "There. All done." She held on to the girl's wrist until she looked her in the eyes. "Annie, I don't want to frighten you, but you must understand the danger."

The girl stiffened and withdrew her arm.

"It's not only Margot Miller and Franny Riley. Several other girls who worked in Cheapside have disappeared. Are you aware of that?"

Annie nodded solemnly.

"Did you know any of them?"

Annie dropped her gaze. "No, but I was hearing the Bow Lane shopgirls talking about it."

Julia spoke gently. "Doctors know the difference between a fall and an attack."

Annie rolled down her sleeve, continuing to avoid Julia's eye.

"Annie, men are generally stronger than women. If they wish to do us bodily harm, there is little we can do to stop them. But there is something you *can* do. . . ."

Annie looked up from the tabletop and into Julia's eyes.

"Speak. Take back the power this man has to silence you. Speak to Inspector Tennant."

Annie sighed and got up. She walked to her worktable, picked up the scissors, and ran her finger along the blunt edge of the outside blade. "My Aunt Maggie gave me these. Made of the strongest Sheffield steel, she said. If she were here today, she'd tell me the same as you."

"May I ask Inspector Tennant to call on you?"

"Yes, and there are a few things that I'll be telling him."

As Julia climbed Annie's steps, a young constable opened the gate for her and touched his hand to his helmet. Julia smiled her thanks, relieved to find him by Annie's door. She turned left on the High Street and stopped to let a woman step in front of her. The lady had exited the dressmaker's shop with a hatbox in her hand. She wore a pleased look and one of Annie's decorated derby hats.

Julia thought, *Annie's going to be fine.*

*   *   *

At three o'clock, Tennant and O'Malley met back at the Yard.

"The artists were less than useless," the inspector said. "No one knows a thing. How did you fare at the docks?"

"There's no record of a Herbert Rawlings at the Cunard or Inman lines. And nothing from the smaller passenger lines or tramp steamers."

"I'm starting to wonder if he plans to leave England at all," Tennant said.

At a knock, O'Malley twisted around to face the young constable at Tennant's door. "What is it, lad?"

"A messenger delivered this note for the inspector."

"Thank you, Constable." Tennant read and looked up. "It's from Doctor Lewis. Annie O'Neill is ready to talk."

Tennant and Annie sat across from each other at her kitchen table with cups of tea.

"Tell me about the man who hurt you, Annie, and try to remember exactly what he said."

"His name is Arnie Stackpole, and he came here hoping to find Margot."

"I've heard of the man. You needn't fear him now that Margot is dead."

She raised her eyes from her cup. "I'm hoping that's true. Owing him money, Margot was, and giving him the slip. 'I'll have the other half of twenty pounds for them,' he shouted at me. 'I'll not deliver the goods until I'm paid.' "

"What goods? Had they been in business together?"

Annie shrugged. "I didn't want to know, and I wasn't asking."

"You haven't a guess?" Tennant took a sip and watched her over the rim of his cup.

Annie shook her head. "He wanted her address, but he'd not be having it off me."

"Refusing a man wielding a knife—that was brave of you, Annie."

"He has the look of an angel with his fair, curly hair. Until he opens his trap, that is. Then he looks like someone took a hammer to his teeth. But he's a devil, that one."

"Stackpole didn't murder Margot. He was in prison when it happened. What about other men in her life? Had you ever seen Margot in the company of Mister Allingham's manservant? Rawlings is his name."

Annie touched her mouth. "The one with the lip, you're meaning?"

Tennant nodded.

"Thick as thieves, they were, while Margot was living here. It puzzled me, him turning up with notes, left and right."

"Love letters?"

"Never. Not with the likes of him. Lists of dates and times and numbers, they were. Couldn't make head nor tail of them."

"I'd like to look at Margot's old room, if I may. Did she leave anything behind after she left?"

"You're welcome, but you'll not find anything." Annie opened a bedroom door. "Clean as a whistle, it was, and all her bags and boxes gone."

Tennant looked inside a bare cabinet and three equally empty bureau drawers.

Tennant crossed to Annie's front door to examine the two bolts that secured it. The bottom one looked new. He looked around the rest of the room. *Too many bloody windows.*

Tennant rattled the doorknob and said, "Best keep your door double-bolted and on the chain, even in the daytime."

"I'll not be opening up to anyone I don't know. Of that, you can be sure."

"The father of Margot's child . . . Can you tell me his name?"

Annie flushed. " 'Tis hard to speak ill of the dead. Margot

wasn't one for keeping her knees together, as my old aunt would say. Keeping her mouth shut? She was champion at that. I'm only guessing, but . . ."

"Yes?"

She sighed. "It can't matter now, seeing as they're both dead. I'm thinking Mister Allingham was Margot's man. I can't be certain, but it may have been so."

"Thank you."

"I felt bad about thinking it when I saw Miss Allingham the other day at the clinic. He was a married man and her big brother. She thought the world of him."

The following morning, Sergeant O'Malley said, "So Charles Allingham was Margot Miller's fancy man."

"Annie claims she's not certain, but I think she is," Tennant said. "But where does it get us? A married man with a strong motive who died before he could kill her."

O'Malley handed a slip to the inspector. "There's a note to you from the man's sister. Her coachman dropped it off late yesterday afternoon."

Tennant unfolded and read it. *Sergeant O'Malley asked about Rawlings. Louisa has no forwarding address, but I thought of something. Charles made small bequests to all the servants, his valet among them. Perhaps Mister Eastlake, our solicitor, knows his whereabouts.*

"A promising line of inquiry," Tennant said. "And Miss Allingham supplied the lawyer's address on Chancery Lane."

A cab carried Tennant and O'Malley as far as Lincoln's Inn gate. They dodged the congested street traffic by paying off the driver and continuing on foot. A choking, gray fog had settled in, so they had to take care as they walked the rest of the way. At the street's end, they found the offices of Eastlake and Hepburn.

Inside, a balding clerk dressed in sober black inclined his head when they asked for Eastlake. He retreated silently through an inner doorway.

O'Malley said, "His man couldn't be more buttoned-up if he'd been sewn into that suit."

The clerk reappeared as noiselessly as he had departed. "This way, gentlemen," he murmured, ushering them into the inner sanctum.

Cyril Eastlake stood behind a broad mahogany desk in a room that smelled of pipe tobacco and lemon polish. Papers littered much of the leather desk surface. Sets of legal volumes and stacks of black boxes filled the walls, each case fitted with a lock and surname lettered in gold.

The solicitor didn't offer his hand; instead, he gestured to two chairs whose seats bore wear marks from generations of clients. O'Malley stayed on his feet while Tennant settled into a chair.

"Thank you for seeing me, Mister Eastlake."

"What is it you want?"

Still smarting over the search of Allingham's rooms, Tennant thought. "We're investigating a young woman's murder and seeking a person of interest. Miss Allingham suggested you might know Herbert Rawlings's address. He was a beneficiary in Charles Allingham's will, I believe."

"That is correct."

Tennant waited, expecting a question about the murder victim's identity. None came. "What sum did Mister Allingham leave his valet?"

When Eastlake hesitated, O'Malley said, "Wills are a matter of public record. Will you be forcing the inspector to make the trip to Somerset House to look it up?"

"My sergeant makes a point. Must we do this the hard way?"

The lawyer cleared his throat. "The estate paid Herbert Rawlings the sum of fifteen hundred pounds."

"A sizable bequest," Tennant said. "Was Mister Allingham as generous with his other servants?"

"A hundred pounds each to the coachman and housekeeper. Fifty pounds to the other servants."

Tennant said, "You've informed Rawlings of his good fortune, I take it? At what address?"

"I corresponded with him at a coffeehouse that lets rooms, although he may be gone by now. He mentioned a desire to emigrate to America."

O'Malley took out his notebook. "I'm thinking the coffeehouse has a name and address. Making a meal of it, you are . . . sir."

Eastlake glared at the sergeant. "The Chapter Coffeehouse on Paternoster Row. My clerk can give you the street number on the way out."

"Paternoster Row?" O'Malley looked up from his pad. "That'll be just down the road from the offices of Allingham and Allen."

"Yes."

The inspector asked, "Did the will include other surprises?"

"Well . . ."

Tennant waited. "You may as well tell me. As Sergeant O'Malley observed, I can find the information I need at Somerset House."

"Charles left fifteen thousand pounds to Margaret Miller."

"Fifteen thousand quid," O'Malley whistled softly. "The devil he did."

"She was to receive only the interest on the sum, which amounted to about five hundred pounds a year, paid quarterly. The principal reverts to the estate as the legatee is now deceased."

"You knew about Margot Miller's death," Tennant said.

"From the newspapers."

"And you had no intention of telling me about the bequest until I dragged it out of you."

Eastlake cleared his throat. "Well, I—"

"By God, Mister Eastlake, I have a mind to charge you with obstructing a police investigation."

"I had a duty to—"

"You are a court officer," Tennant snapped. "And a servant of the queen. Your duty lies there, sir. What was Mrs. Allingham's reaction at the reading of the will?"

"Well . . ." The lawyer shifted uneasily. "I merely summarized the contents. Mrs. Allingham never asked me to name the persons or sums in question."

"That is highly unusual, is it not, Mister Eastlake?"

"The implications were painfully obvious, Inspector. I wanted to spare Louisa the knowledge of her husband's infidelity."

"Quarterly payments, is it?" O'Malley said. "That's a hundred and twenty-five quid four times a year. You'd not be handing it to her over your desk."

"Miss Miller gave me her banking particulars. The first quarterly deposit was made two weeks ago."

O'Malley waved his notebook. "You'll be giving us that information as well."

Eastlake opened an address book and scribbled on a slip of paper.

Tennant asked, "Did Margot Miller leave a will?"

"Our firm did not prepare one for her." He handed Tennant the address of the West London Bank on Sloane Square in Chelsea.

"Thank you." The inspector passed the information to O'Malley and stood.

Eastlake, scowling, rang the bell for his clerk.

Tennant eyed him for a moment. "You take a lot on yourself, Mister Eastlake. Mrs. Allingham is a grown woman, not a child." He nodded curtly. "Good day to you."

On the pavement, O'Malley said, "So, little Annie O'Neill was right. Charles Allingham was keeping Margot Miller."

"Let's head to the coffeehouse," Tennant said. "High time we ran the elusive Mister Rawlings to ground."

But the Chapter House clerk told them Rawlings had checked out four days before. The clerk provided one piece of pertinent news: Rawlings had received letters from the publishers Allingham and Allen.

Outside the coffeehouse, O'Malley said, "The fella is writing letters to Allingham and Allen and then he scarpers."

"I'll have another chat with Mister Sidney Allen." The inspector pulled out his watch. "It's nearly three. We've missed the Chelsea bank manager. He'll have to wait until tomorrow."

"Banker's hours," O'Malley grumbled, raising his arm for a cab. "Nice for some."

Without a court order, an inquiry about a depositor's account ordinarily elicited a starchy refusal to cooperate. But a murder investigation had wilted the Chelsea bank manager's resistance. Tennant returned to the Yard in the morning with the banking information he'd sought.

O'Malley looked up from the copy of Margot's account and blew out his cheeks. "Mother of God, nearly five thousand quid?"

"That's the sum, Paddy."

"That gives holy Joe and young Micah one hell of a motive. They're next of kin."

"They'd have to know about the money, and I'd wager Margot kept that information close to the vest. As to her inheritance, don't forget the principal reverts to the Allingham estate."

"Even without it, she's leaving five thousand pounds for them to pocket." O'Malley scanned the dates. "Deposits nearly every week. Micah was in the habit of following her around. He might have trailed her to the bank and guessed she had a pile on her."

"A sharp fellow would know that few shopgirls have bank accounts. But does Micah Miller seem bright to you?"

"Thick as a plank, I'm thinking."

Tennant tapped on a report. "What do you make of Micah's alibi for the day of Margot's murder? Picking up a coil from the ropemakers, walking about, and visiting some unnamed pub?"

" 'Tis thin. But it's got me wondering. . . ."

"About?"

"Remember that bawdy house guide we found under the bed?"

"You think Micah spent the afternoon and a few shillings in questionable company? Why not say so?"

"Old holy Joe would be praying and psalming over the lad all day and night, the poor sod."

"The coppers in Poplar will point you in the right direction."

O'Malley nodded. "If Micah has an alibi, we can cross the creature off our list."

Tennant pulled out his pocket watch. "While you head over to Poplar, I'll have a conversation with Mister Sidney Allen about these letters to Rawlings.

Sidney Allen was more wary at his second interview, and the pretense of cooperation had disappeared.

"I told you aught I know about Charlie. You and those Kensington coppers who came around. What is it now?"

Tennant took off his gloves and laid them across his knee. "I have a few questions about Rawlings, Mister Allingham's man-servant."

Allen stared while Tennant waited. Finally, the publisher said, "Well? What about him?"

"You wrote to Rawlings at his rooming house. About what, sir?"

"Who says so?"

"Is that a denial?"

"It's a question."

"Let me repeat mine," Tennant said. "What did you say to Rawlings in your letter?"

Allen scowled at his desktop. Then he snatched up a pencil and jammed it back into its holder.

"If you must know, Rawlings wrote and asked about a valet's position. But I don't employ a bloody manservant. Told him I can pull on my socks and trousers without help, thank you very much."

"I understood from Miss Allingham that Rawlings acted as a go-between for you and her brother. What exactly were his duties?"

"These valets are arrogant bastards, the lot of them. Rawlings was no different. But I agreed to write a reference for him, and doesn't the bugger send two lines back. No thanks, he says. He's come into some money, and he's emigrating to America."

Tennant held Allen's gaze. "That was the extent of your exchange?"

"Aye."

"Thank you, Mister Allen. That wasn't difficult." Tennant stood. "Good day."

After he exited, Tennant looked up at the window. Allen stared down; the inspector nodded.

You dodged my last question, Tennant thought. *What was Rawlings doing for Allingham and Allen?*

Back at the Yard, Tennant found a note from his sergeant.

Poplar has more bawdy houses than a year has Sundays. Finally found the one where the madam remembers Micah turning up with a coil of rope. Fella was otherwise occupied the afternoon Margot was killed.

"Hell and damnation." Tennant crushed the note in his fist. *Every avenue's a dead end.*

CHAPTER 10

A line of sleepy fishmongers queued up at the coffee stall at sunrise, waiting for Billingsgate Market to open. On a freezing March morning, the brazier's coals and the dark brew warmed and wakened the drowsy market men.

A thick mist blanketed the warehouse district. The Thames was only steps away, but the river was invisible behind a curtain of fog. Only the river's slapping at the waterline, creaking oak timbers, and the distant clang of a lonely bell reminded the fishmongers it was there. Wagons lined the street. Horses stamped, drivers hunched shoulders against the cold as men and beasts streamed steamy breath into the chill.

A speeding carriage with its shades drawn careened around the corner. As it passed the coffee stall, its door opened, and something tumbled from the cabin. Then the carriage flew down Lower Thames Street and made a sharp left turn. The incident was over in twenty seconds.

Two men with coffee mugs left the warmth of the stall to investigate the bundle. "Oy, mate, it looks like a . . ." The man handed his cup to his partner and dropped to one knee. When he tugged at the bundle, it opened.

"Bloody hell." The man leaped to his feet and shouted to the men on the coffee line, "Christ sake—somebody find the fecking rozzer on this beat!"

Sergeant O'Malley handed Inspector Tennant the police report from Billingsgate.

"Someone dumped a woman's body near the fish market. They're wanting to turn it over to the detective squad, and the chief has a mind to give us this one."

"Why? Any connection to our cases?"

"Someone tossed her from a moving carriage. Tied up in a sack, poor lass, just like Franny Riley and . . ."

"Something else, Paddy?"

"They're describing her as an Asian lady. Strange for these parts, I'm thinking."

"All right, Sergeant. Have a note delivered to Doctor Lewis at Finsbury Circus. Where are they holding the body?"

"At Tower Street Station."

"Send the doctor my compliments and ask her to meet us there."

Julia had begun her postmortem preparations in a narrow back room of the Billingsgate station house by the time Tennant arrived. Sergeant Smithson, the local officer who'd taken charge of the body, was there to observe as well.

Julia cut away the rope and removed the torn canvas sack that covered the corpse. "I doubt her heart was beating when they threw her from the carriage," she said. "One side of her face and upper body is severely abraded, but there should have been more blood."

Julia heaved aside a second sack that held four heavy stones.

Tennant said, "Probably heading for the Thames, intending to throw her in, but changed their minds."

Sergeant Smithson nodded. "You couldn't see an inch past your nose by the river's edge, so they dumped the girl and scarpered."

"It's similar to an earlier case of ours," Tennant said. "Someone dumped a girl in a sack near Lambeth Bridge."

Smithson wasn't listening closely. Instead, the young sergeant watched Julia work. She must have seemed as exotic to him as the Asian victim on the table. Tennant had grown used to working with a female medical examiner. What he'd never adjusted to was tight spaces, a legacy of his military service and the bombardment he'd survived during the Crimean War.

Tennant's eyes prickled, and droplets spread across his forehead. The gaslight seemed to shrink into a small circle and slowly expand, returning the room to its original brightness. He struggled to regulate his breathing and concentrate on the postmortem.

Julia held up the undergarment she'd cut away. "The chemise is lace-trimmed silk. Quite expensive, I'd say. French or Belgian, most likely. No corset."

Congealed blood covered one side of the girl's face. Before Julia sponged it away, she wiped the victim's other cheek and lips with a dry white cloth. Faint, reddish marks stained the fabric.

"Rouge and lip paint." The doctor picked up a scalpel and made a Y-shaped incision extending from her shoulders and down to the pubic bone.

Sergeant O'Malley rapped on the window and held something up. Tennant wasn't the only one relieved to leave the room. A pale, swaying Sergeant Smithers followed him out the door and headed for the loo.

"A cracked bottle rolled out of the bag when the coppers moved her." O'Malley handed it to Tennant. "The name and markings look the same as the laudanum we found in Miller's stash."

"*S. Cooper, London,*" Tennant read. "Yes, it looks identical to me."

O'Malley cocked his thumb. "The divisional inspector upstairs is telling me she's not the first foreign lass to turn up on his turf. Himself is asking to see you when the medical examination is done."

An hour later, Julia sat across from Tennant and O'Malley in a borrowed interrogation room.

"The girl had been ill, a well-established infection," she said. "Yellow mucus filled her bronchia, and her nails were blue from lack of oxygen. She almost certainly had a high fever before she died."

"So, not murder," Tennant said.

"Not directly, at any rate."

"A prostitute, do you think? The face paint and expensive undergarments point to a high end of the trade."

"I found the telltale genital signs of the occupation's risk—the ulcers of first-stage syphilis."

"Poor lass," O'Malley said. "They'd have no patience with a girl who's rotten with the pox. Wanting her off their hands, the bastards, and dumping her like she was week-old fish."

"Someone shackled her," Julia said. "Her wrists showed marks of bondage, and . . ." Julia bit her lip and looked away. "And she'd made an unsuccessful attempt to end her life. The marks are on her wrist."

Tennant heard the strain in her voice and observed Julia's tightly gripped hands and white knuckles.

She reached for her medical bag and stood. "The report will be on your desk tomorrow." Julia nodded and exited.

"Excuse me," Tennant said to O'Malley, and followed her. He caught up to her outside the street door and took her elbow.

"Let me hail a cab for you."

"Thank you."

"This postmortem . . . I know it was painful for you. A young girl, desperate to end her life. Difficult after—"

"After Helen's suicide."

"Yes." His heart twisted at her trembling attempt to smile. "Thoughts of my old friend will intrude," Julia said. "But you were kind the day you listened to me tell her story."

A hansom slowed and stopped at Tennant's signal, and he handed her into the cab and stepped back.

Julia settled in and looked at him. "It helps to share things that haunt you. To share one's nightmares with a friend." Her eyes flickered to his leg. "Perhaps one day you'll honor me by confiding yours."

He watched her cab roll away and thought of her word "friend."

Layers of guilt and shame wrapped their experiences. For Julia, it was an unmarried friend's pregnancy and the suicide she had failed to prevent. For Tennant, the Crimean War had left a shaming legacy of physical and mental weakness.

He still dreamed about the Russian bombardment and the dying sergeant entombed by his side. A rescue party had pulled Tennant out alive, but he'd led battles that left many men in graves far from home. Captain Tennant had followed orders to charge into withering fire, commands issued by aging generals using outdated tactics. Yet Russian aggression and their appetite for neighboring lands had to be checked. The irony wasn't lost on him: that a soldier of the British Empire should criticize imperial ambition.

Tennant knew that war and empire were messy and imperfect. So was police work. Justice and right were elusive.

"Is everything all right with the doctor?" O'Malley had appeared at his elbow.

"Yes. I'll find the divisional inspector and hear about this other girl. You head back to the Yard. See if any reports have come in from Limehouse or the docks about Rawlings."

"The man is somewhere. 'Tis only a matter of time and boot leather."

Divisional Inspector MacNair flicked a bony wrist from behind his scarred oak desk, inviting Tennant to sit. MacNair wore the black garb and sober expression of a Kirk of Scotland preacher. His brow's pronounced ridge made dark pools of his eyes, and they regarded Tennant gravely. MacNair began his story of a lost Chinese girl, speaking in a soft Scottish burr.

"Aye, it's strange, but long before we discovered this body, we found another such girl on the streets."

Tennant asked, "When was this, sir?"

"About ten months ago, and a frigid night it was for any of God's creatures to be out. My constable spied the wee lass slumped at the walls of the Tower."

"How was she dressed?"

"In knickers and underskirts," McNair said. "With a long, hooded cape thrown over it all. Only slippers on her feet. Torn to shreds by the time we found her."

"She must have come from someplace nearby. Were you able to track her movements?"

"First, we had to find someone who understood the lass. The folk at the London Missionary Society sent a parson who'd been ten years in Hong Kong. Mister Lloyd talked to her in Cantonese, he called it. Who'd have kenned there are dozens of tongues in China."

"What did she tell him?"

"Brokers shipped her out on a promise of marriage. A Chinaman was waiting to wed her in California, they told her. Instead, she ended up in a London brothel, drugged much of the time. It was how they controlled her and the other lasses in the house."

"How did she come to rest at the Tower of London?"

"They took her from the brothel to some grand house, a regular arrangement by her telling. On the drive back, her keeper fell asleep, drunk by the sound of it. She slipped out of the carriage and wandered along the riverfront."

"What steps did you take to locate the brothel and the house?"

"The parson volunteered to accompany us, so we drove Mister Lloyd and the lass along the quayside. But the devils had bundled her in and out in the dark of night with the shades of the carriage drawn. Aye, t'was hopeless."

"Where is the girl now?"

"Mister Lloyd took her in. He lives with his widowed sister and two nieces, and she looks after the wee bairns."

"I'd like to speak to him. Perhaps the girl has said something more in the time she's been with him."

MacNair scribbled an address and handed it to Tennant. "The London Missionary Society headquarters is on Carteret Street. You'll find Mister Lloyd there."

Tennant tucked it away and stood.

"The lass's name is Jin-Bou," MacNair said. "And to ken its meaning is to break your heart. In Cantonese, it means 'Beautiful Treasure.'"

At the headquarters of the London Missionary Society, the Reverend Mister Owen Lloyd spread his hands. "You find me a prisoner of my desk, Inspector Tennant."

Mr. Lloyd might have stepped out of the Elgin Marbles frieze in the British Museum. His classically perfect features looked as if some ancient Greek had chiseled them. He'd brushed his hair back in thick, dark waves, and his cobalt eyes were a dramatic contrast to his black brows and lashes. As with so many Welshmen, he had music in his voice. Lloyd spoke in a deep, sonorous baritone.

A world map covered the wall behind Lloyd with the possessions of the British Empire colored in standard pink. Two red-tipped pins marked Ceylon and Hong Kong.

"You miss your work in the East?"

"I do. Among other duties in Hong Kong, I served as chaplain in the colony's Anglican orphanage. When scarlet fever broke out amongst the children, it spread to the staff." Lloyd patted his chest. "It left me with a dicky heart, so the society shipped me home. That was two years ago, and here I am. Raising funds and giving speeches are the most strenuous tasks I'm allowed."

I'll wager you're good at it, Tennant thought.

"How can I help you, Inspector?"

"I have a few questions about a Chinese girl you shelter in your household."

"May I ask why?"

"This morning, someone dumped the body of an Asian girl near Billingsgate Market."

"I see. Another poor girl found on Inspector MacNair's patch."

Tennant nodded. "There are similarities to an earlier case under investigation, although the girl was Irish, not Asian. About the young woman who lives with you . . ."

"Jin-Bou."

"The inspector told me some of her story. In her time with you, has she spoken about her ordeal? I'm hoping there is more you can tell me."

"Oh, I can tell you many things, Inspector."

Lloyd swung his chair around and looked up at the map. The wall clock ticked loudly in the quiet room. He swiveled back.

"Jin is but a tiny dot on an atlas of degradation that we abet or simply ignore. Every year, thousands of Chinese are shipped around the world as coolie laborers. Men, for the most part, but countless women are sold as domestics and prostitutes."

"Sold, Mister Lloyd?"

"I believe the word is apt."

"Ten years at Scotland Yard . . . I thought I'd seen everything."

"Ten years after my ordination, I'm no longer surprised by the diabolical in human nature. Thank the Lord, I see much that is angelic as well."

"Was she alone on the voyage?"

"No. There was another girl. She was already aboard when Jin came on the ship. They kept her in a separate cabin, and she spoke a Chinese language Jin didn't understand."

"Did she know the vessel's name?"

"Jin didn't mention a name, but she described a three-masted ship."

"Sounds like one of the clippers that ply the China trade," Tennant said. "Has Jin spoken about what happened after she arrived in London?"

"Yes. After a long voyage, two beautiful ladies—one a European, the other Chinese—met them at the dock. The Chinese woman spoke to her in Cantonese and told Jin that she was in the great city of London. She would be taken to a beautiful house, given much to eat, and would serve a powerful prince. They forced Jin to service 'many princes,' she said."

Tennant winced. "The recruitment process never changes. Here, they entice shop assistants and servants, promising riches and comforts."

"Jin thought her destination was the *gam saan*—the gold mountain. It's a name for California that I often heard in Hong Kong. Thousands of Chinese men have gone to America to work on the railroads. Jin had been promised marriage to an honorable man when she arrived."

"I can guess what happened next."

"She confided the details to my sister. The following day, an older woman carrying a black bag examined her 'between her legs.' After that, she was bathed, dressed, and given something that made her drowsy. Then she was taken, half dreaming, to another place and fell asleep in a big bed. She awoke, crushed under a great weight with a searing pain 'down there,' she told my sister."

"Inspector MacNair said Jin couldn't pinpoint the location of the place. Has she remembered anything else?"

"She heard church bells from her room." Lloyd shrugged. "But where in London wouldn't one?" He narrowed his eyes. "I remember she called the European woman the *kong que*— the peacock lady for the feathers she wore in her hat. Again, not very helpful. One sees them on ladies' heads all over London."

"Could she describe this woman in more detail?"

"I can ask her."

"It's possible that Jin's traveling companion is the dead girl we found this morning. I'm afraid she will have to identify the body."

"Is that necessary, Inspector? Jin didn't know her."

"I must insist. Jin is a living witness, a link to this girl and those who held her captive. Perhaps you or your sister might accompany her?"

Lloyd considered. "I'll speak to them this evening."

"Tomorrow afternoon, then. At the police station on Tower Street."

The following morning, Chief Inspector Clark waylaid Tennant in the Yard's vestibule and ordered the inspector to follow him upstairs. After an unsatisfactory interview, Tennant arrived late at his office.

O'Malley met him outside his door. "The chief is hunting for you. Looking like thunder, he was."

"An apt description. He found me."

"Doctor Lewis and Mister Lloyd are waiting in your office."

Julia and the clergyman sat in the chairs by Tennant's desk. "The clinic is off Whitechapel Road on Fieldgate Street," she said. "Past the bell foundry. It's number twenty-three."

Lloyd scribbled the address in his agenda and stood when Tennant entered. "Ah, Inspector." He slipped a note from his coat pocket. "Jin provided this description if it's any help to you." He handed it to Tennant.

"And the identification of the body?"

"My sister will accompany her to Tower Street this afternoon at two o'clock."

"Thank you, sir. That's most helpful."

Lloyd turned to Julia. His face, weathered from years in the sun, wrinkled into an attractive smile. "Alas, I'm late, but I look forward to hearing more about your work in Whitechapel."

"And I about yours in Hong Kong, Mister Lloyd."

He offered his hand. "Is tomorrow a good day to visit your clinic?"

"Of course."

Lloyd nodded to O'Malley, who closed the door behind him. 'So, what does the handsome parson have for us?"

The inspector held up the note. "A possible witness—a Chinese girl named Jin-Bou who lives with Mister Lloyd and his sister."

"She knew the victim?" Julia asked.

"Perhaps. Jin escaped. Unlike the poor girl you examined yesterday."

Tennant read through the note. "Well, well. The girl says the 'tall sailorman with yellow hair' who brought her food gave her to . . ." He passed the letter to Julia. "Who does this sound like to you?"

She read, *"The beautiful peacock lady had hair the color of pomegranate seeds and dressed in green silk.*" Julia looked up. "Margot Miller." She handed the note to the sergeant.

"Miller to the life," O'Malley said.

Julia nodded. "I saw her outside Annie's flat in an emerald frock. So, Margot was enmeshed in this terrible business, too."

"Likely," Tennant said. "Do you have the medical results for us?"

Julia dug into her doctor's bag. "Nothing much beyond the summary I gave you yesterday. I also have that invitation from my grandfather." She handed over his note. "Tomorrow, if you are free."

"Delighted."

"He scribbled seven thirty, but his handwriting is execrable, like most doctors." She snapped her case and stood. "Margot Miller, a procuress . . . another card in the mysterious deck. I'll leave you gentlemen to sort out the complicated hand."

After the door closed, O'Malley grunted. "Complicated. That's one way of putting it. What was the chief wanting with you? Only to give us a tongue-lashing?"

"That, of course. Also, Sir Francis Grant wants a meeting at the beginning of next week."

"And who is he when he's at home?"

"Sir Francis is President of the Royal Academy of Art. The Annual Exhibition opens on the sixth of April, just over two weeks from now. He wants to discuss police protection for the event, given the recent events at art galleries."

"Manpower being no problem when the likes of Sir Francis come calling. The budget be damned, then."

"It's the way of the world, Paddy. And the Yard, I'm afraid."

O'Malley waved Mr. Lloyd's note. "This puts the peacock lady and a 'yellow-haired' seaman together. Miller and Arnie Stackpole. I'd be betting money on it."

"He's the likely candidate. Annie described him as fair-haired. What was the name of his ship?"

"The Flying something or other." O'Malley pulled out his notebook and flipped through his interviews. "The *Flying Spur*."

"Go down to the docks and dig up the name of the company that owns her and find out how long she's been trading between London and China. Ask if they take passengers."

"You're wanting me to go to the Billingsgate for the Chinese girl's identification?"

"No. I'll see to it. And there's something else . . . another possibility."

"What are you thinking?"

"When Stackpole threatened Annie O'Neill, he said Margot Miller owed him money 'for them.' We thought he was trading in goods."

" 'Tis women he's buying and selling, you're thinking?"

"Might he have another pair of girls like Jin and the girl who sailed with her? According to Annie, Stackpole was waiting for payment before he 'delivered the goods.' "

"Where is he keeping them now that he's in the nick?"

Tennant looked at the calendar and consulted his watch. "Stackpole is two weeks into his thirty-day stretch. Time to pay him a visit. I'll let him think we know more than we do—it may loosen his tongue."

Tennant's cab left Westminster and crossed the river into Southwark by London Bridge. It stopped in front of a brick-and-stone prison that was a place of incarceration and public execution with space for a gallows on its roof. A convict either walked out when he'd finished his sentence or swung for the entertainment of a gaping, hooting audience, leaving in a box.

Tennant raised the entry's clapper and dropped it with an iron bang. A slotted window scraped across metal, and the gatekeeper's face appeared in the void.

"Detective Inspector Tennant to see the warden."

Keys jangled, the door swung open, and the keeper directed Tennant to his chief's office. Twenty minutes later, a jailer escorted the gangly, shackled Arnie Stackpole into the waiting room. The yellow-haired sailorman needed a wash, but fair-haired fit the bill.

Stackpole's leg chains dragged along the stone floor, the sound rising to the rafters of the vaulted ceiling and echoing down again. His clanging journey ended at an oak bench, where the guard shoved him down by his shoulder. The jailor retreated a few yards and waited, tapping his truncheon against his palm.

Tennant took Will Quain's sketch of Margot Miller from its folder and held it up. "I assume you know she's dead," Tennant said.

Stackpole dug around the back of his ruined mouth with a grubby finger, dislodged a bit of breakfast from his broken teeth, and spat it on the floor. "Heard that rumor."

"Word on the docks says she owed you money, and you were looking for her."

"Wasn't me what killed her."

"Convince me."

He balled a fist and raised it. "I'd stop her mouth for her, but I have an iron rule. Never kill a slag who owes you money. Bad for business."

"What business are we talking about?"

Stackpole tapped his nose and winked. "Little of this. Little of that. Nothing to interest the Yard."

"You've got two weeks left in prison. Cooperate, and I can do something about that."

"Two weeks? Crikey. I can do that standing on me head."

"A bright fellow like you knows it pays to cooperate with the police."

"Nah. You got nothing to barter, and I got nothing to sell. Still, it was nice talking to you. A pleasant stretch of me legs." He rattled his leg irons. "More or less."

Tennant rolled the dice. "Now that Margot is dead, what will you do with the girls?"

Stackpole's smirk vanished. "Don't know what you're on about, mate."

"One of the girls escaped a few months ago, did you know? She has quite a tale to tell."

The seaman licked his lips.

"We're closing in, Stackpole. Don't leave yourself twisting in the wind. If you change your mind, a word to the warden will bring me back."

Tennant nodded to the guard. By the time Stackpole reached the door, he'd regained his equilibrium.

"Nice chatting with you, guvnor. But I'm thinking you got nothing."

The inspector hailed a cab and headed to Billingsgate to meet Jin and Mr. Lloyd's sister. At least Tennant had Stackpole under lock and key. After his release, he'd follow the man and see where he would lead.

Tennant returned late to the Yard but caught O'Malley on the landing.

"Any joy at the docks, Paddy?"

"Found the owners of Stackpole's ship, J. Robertson and Company. The *Flying Spur* plies the China trade, hauling tea from Canton and Hong Kong."

"Do they carry passengers?"

"At the shipmaster's discretion, so they're saying. I couldn't interview the captain because the *Flying Spur* sailed for China a week ago."

"Damnation."

"What about Arnie Stackpole?" O'Malley said. "Did you find him in a talkative mood?"

"I found an insolent sod who guessed I was bluffing."

"Any luck with the identification of the Chinese lass?"

Tennant shook his head. "Not the girl who traveled with Jin."

"That means she's still out there, and likely others. Did you show the girl Quain's sketch?"

"Yes. No surprise there. Margot Miller was the peacock lady."

CHAPTER 11

The following evening, Inspector Tennant's cab pulled up to number seventeen Finsbury Circus. It delivered him to the Lewis house narrowly in time for his dinner engagement.

Mrs. Ogilvie smiled a greeting and assured the inspector he hadn't delayed the evening's proceedings. The housekeeper handed a maid his top hat and cape and led him into the drawing room. Tennant followed, pulling at his cuffs and settling his white tie. When Mrs. Ogilvie opened the door, Tennant recognized the sonorous voice inside.

"The tragic chain begins with two generations of chaos," Mister Lloyd said. "The dislocations from opium wars with Britain, floods, famine, droughts, even swarms of locusts—there's something biblical about China's plagues."

Julia's Aunt Caroline said, "But to sell one's daughters, Mister Lloyd!"

"Lady Aldridge, it shocks you, I know."

Mrs. Ogilvie cleared her throat and announced Inspector Tennant.

"Richard, my boy." Julia's grandfather stood to greet him. "We'd almost given you up."

"My apologies, Doctor Lewis. I'd almost given up as well."

"You've met Mister Lloyd, but I don't think you know his sister, Mrs. Davies."

A woman in a widow's half-mourning mauve smiled and offered her hand. She was as darkly handsome as her brother and spoke with the same musical cadence.

"The inspector and I met yesterday, as it happens." Mrs. Davies added quietly, "I wasn't sure whether to be sorry or glad that Jin couldn't help you identify that poor girl."

"I felt the same, Mrs. Davies."

Tennant turned to greet Lady Aldridge. He had met Julia's Aunt Caroline several times and admired her as a shrewd and formidable woman.

She took his hand. "Richard, Mister Lloyd has been telling us about the selling of girls in China."

"A father doesn't think of it that way, Lady Aldridge," Lloyd said. "He is securing his child's future as a prospective wife, not selling her into domestic slavery. And families are compensated for losing a daughter."

"It seems a fine distinction to me," Lady Aldridge said.

Julia asked, "Are we so different, Aunt? Consider the dowries some families dangle to make advantageous matches for their daughters."

"My dear niece, it's hardly the same thing."

"Hmm...I wonder." Julia smiled at her grandfather. "What's my going rate would you say?"

"My dear, you are a pearl without price."

Tennant caught Lady Aldridge's eye and smiled. Then he crossed the room to join Julia. "I'm sorry I kept you all waiting."

"Never mind," she said. "I barely beat you here—for the last time, I hope. Gregory Barnes will switch his Thursday evenings at the clinic to Wednesdays."

"Are you happy with the young doctor?"

"Very. What delayed you? End-of-day developments?"

"I arrived directly from a command interview with my chief."

Julia eyed his evening clothes. "Did you change at the Yard?"

He nodded. "Clark caught me putting the last loop in this." Tennant patted his white tie.

She smiled and straightened it for him. "He must have enjoyed that."

Tennant's working-class chief resented his more polished junior. The inspector had been educated at Sandhurst, served in an elite regiment, and was the godson and namesake of the Yard's commissioner, Sir Richard Mayne. Clark loathed the whole list.

"Just one more nail in my coffin," Tennant said.

"Which does the old boy find more irritating? That white tie or your regimental striped one?"

"As ties go, it's probably a tie."

The door opened, and Mrs. Ogilvie announced, "Dinner is served."

Julia took his arm. "We made it just in the nick . . . both of us."

Tennant sat at Julia's left at the table, ceding the floor to Mister Lloyd at her right. The clergyman and his sister had visited Whitechapel that morning, and Lloyd was full of praise for the clinic and its doctor. The inspector couldn't fault anything he said, and Lloyd said it so well.

At the end of the meal, Julia replaced her napkin and looked around the table. "Will you all follow me to the drawing room?"

Mister Lloyd stood and offered Julia his arm.

Her grandfather drew back his dining partner's chair. "We're an eccentric household, Mrs. Davies, by English standards at any rate. The legacy of Julia's American grandmother, also named Julia."

She smiled. "Eccentric in what way?"

"No tea after dinner and no separation of the sexes." Doctor Lewis offered his arm. "We will enjoy our port, sherry, or barley water, if one prefers, in the drawing room together."

Julia's aunt took Tennant's arm. "You seem quiet this evening, Richard." She smiled faintly, glancing at Mister Lloyd and her niece. "And a little . . . watchful."

"And you, Lady Aldridge, see too much." He leaned in closer. "I would have you in the Yard if I could."

"Dear boy." She patted his hand. "Julia's been telling me about the case. She said you knew Louisa Allingham."

"The last time we met, I was her escort for an endless French opera. My reward was to make way for Charles Allingham."

"Never mind. I've lived long enough to know that life presents unexpected compensations."

"A hopeful thought," Tennant said as they followed Doctor Lewis and Mrs. Davies to the drawing room.

Mrs. Ogilvie offered drinks to the guests; Mrs. Davies accepted a sherry and Tennant a port. She smiled at him to invite conversation, so he followed her to the settee.

"Thank you for your assistance yesterday, Mrs. Davies."

"I was worried, but Jin proved strong enough for the ordeal."

Tennant said, "Sometimes, it's a fine line between pressing a witness and victimizing her again."

"You managed the delicate balance." A ripple of doubt crossed her face. "Now, I'm wondering if we've navigated equally well, Owen and I."

"What do you mean?"

"Perhaps our reticence with Jin was wrong, and we should have encouraged her to speak."

"As you say, it's a delicate balance," Tennant said. "As for the interview, you handled it admirably. May I ask how you came to be so proficient in Cantonese?"

"Our parents were missionaries in China."

"And we moved to Hong Kong as young children," Mr. Lloyd said.

He had joined them with Julia on his arm. Tennant stood to make room for her on the settee.

Mrs. Davies said, "Owen followed in the family's footsteps. Rather like you, Doctor Lewis."

"Yes, we have physicians galore in the clan," Julia said. "My grandfather, my father, and a rather famous American one on my grandmother's side, Doctor Benjamin Rush. He signed the Declaration of Independence."

"Headstrong and rebellious, just like my Julie," Doctor Lewis said. "Am I right, Richard?"

"I wouldn't contradict you, sir."

Julia's grandfather chuckled. "I blame it on the Rushes."

Tennant said to Julia, "Your middle initial . . . R for Rush?"

"We keep it quiet on this side of the Atlantic. Tell me, Mrs. Davies, was your husband also in the missions?"

"Gareth was an officer in the Royal Navy."

"And a sore disappointment he was," her brother said, smiling.

"Now Owen, just because he bested you regularly in chess . . ."

"I let him win so he'd keep coming back to see you."

"What nonsense."

"As a young lieutenant, my brother-in-law cut a fine figure. But as a Welshman . . ." Lloyd shook his head mournfully. "Gareth was sadly wanting. A tone-deaf Cardiff man—whoever heard of such a thing?"

Mrs. Davies laughed. "He would try. Do you remember him singing 'Bread of Heaven' in that tiny church in full voice and off-key?"

"And Father's pained expression," Lloyd said. "He forgave him. For that and for taking you away. My brother-in-law was a thoroughly good chap, and I miss him sorely."

Mrs. Davies looked at Julia. "The last thing I expected was to marry a navy man. Life with a husband in the missions is what I'd planned."

"That's natural," Julia said. "Common interests surely strengthen a matrimonial bond."

She nodded. "Especially for women who want to do more than—"

"Stay at home as wives and mothers?"

"Yes. I saw myself wedded to some good man like my father, working side by side, toiling together in God's vineyard." Mrs. Davies shook her head and smiled. "Having fixed ideas about one's straight path can be fatal. Life so often presents a corner to turn."

"Yes . . . I suppose that's true," Julia said slowly.

"Sometimes, we complicate things," Mrs. Davies said. "Things that are simple, especially in matters of the heart."

Lady Aldridge looked at Tennant, smiled faintly, and sipped her sherry.

Dr. Lewis trilled the piano's keys. "Do you play, Mrs. Davies?" When she nodded, he said, "Will you indulge us?"

"Delighted, if my brother accompanies me." She stood and offered Lloyd her hand. "Unlike my late husband, Owen is a fine baritone."

He led his sister to the instrument and pulled back a piano bench of gleaming, golden nutwood.

"What a handsome Bösendorfer." Mrs. Davies sat and ran her fingers over the keys. "It has a lovely tone."

Lloyd asked, "Have you made your choice, Sister?"

"'Simple Gifts,' I think." Mrs. Davies looked at Julia. "An American at our mission in Hong Kong taught it to us. It's become one of my favorites."

She began with a five-note, descending phrase that she played twice. Then Mr. Lloyd joined in.

*" 'Tis the gift to be simple, 'tis the gift to be free, 'tis the
gift to come down where we ought to be.
And when we find ourselves in the place just right, 'twill
be in the valley of love and delight.
When true simplicity is gained, to bow and to bend we
shan't be ashamed,
To turn, turn will be our delight, till by turning, turning
we come 'round right."*

Tennant stood to the side where he could see Julia's face and
watch the performers.

Mrs. Davies introduced the melody again. When her brother
joined in, she stopped playing, and he sang the lyrics a second
time unaccompanied. The effect was haunting, and Julia looked
rapt, her eyes shining with unshed tears. When Lloyd finished
and the company clapped, she looked away, blinking.

"Lovely, lovely." Dr. Lewis escorted Mrs. Davies back to
the settee and kissed her hand. "Thank you, my dear. Thank
you both."

"It's a pleasure to play such a fine instrument, Doctor."

"It's all the better for being played. Now . . ." Dr. Lewis
looked around. "Ladies and gentlemen, has everyone a glass?"
When the company murmured in the affirmative, he turned to
Owen Lloyd and lifted his port. "A toast: to the work of the
missions, sir, and to all who labor in them."

"Hear, hear, Brother," Lady Aldridge said. She and the doctor sipped, and the company followed suit.

"Now, Mister Lloyd." Dr. Lewis settled into his chair. "Will
you tell us more about the Chinese girl you and Mrs. Davies
shelter?"

The clergyman set down his glass and glanced at his sister.
She nodded.

"I only wish . . . I wish Jin's ordeal were unique, but such
girls are to be found all around our empire and beyond. They

are a smaller part of a larger problem we Britons choose to ignore, although numbers don't tell the whole story. Women suffer a particularly abject form of degradation."

Lady Aldridge asked, "What is the larger story, Mister Lloyd?"

"That a 'coolie' system has replaced enslaved labor. Even as we speak, ships that are little better than the slavers of a generation ago carry their human cargoes around the world."

"Good Lord," she said. "I thought such horrors were long past."

"Our mission in Hong Kong has tracked the trade for the last decade. Ten, perhaps as much as twenty percent die on the journey in a modern form of slavery. From disease, most often, but mutinies are frequent and savagely suppressed. Suicides add to the toll."

"This is appalling," Dr. Lewis said. "After all the efforts of the abolitionists?"

"Parliament needs another William Wilberforce," Tennant said.

Mr. Lloyd nodded. "Tens of thousands labor under sham contracts on sugar plantations in the Caribbean. And as for poor girls like Jin, brokers promise them marriage and a better life, but in the end . . ." Mister Lloyd's voice caught. "I'm sorry. This isn't a platform or my pulpit. Forgive me."

"Only one thing surprises me," Tennant said. "That my case involves girls so far from our shores. There is plenty of prey closer to home. Impoverished girls from the slums of St. Giles or Whitechapel. Shopgirls and servants, as well."

Tennant realized at once he'd put a foot wrong. The quality of the atmosphere changed. Mr. Lloyd and his sister wore polite expressions, but Doctor Lewis and Lady Aldridge looked stricken.

Julia said, "What is it, Grandfather . . . Aunt Caroline?"

After a pause, Lady Aldridge answered. "We're remembering Lizzie Sullivan, Julia. Your first nursery maid."

Doctor Lewis sighed. "Let me tell the story, Caroline, although Richard and Mister Lloyd know its general outlines all too well. It happened in the spring of that terrible year. . . ."

Lady Aldridge looked at the Lloyds. "My brother refers to the year his son and daughter-in-law, Julia's parents, were lost at sea. They were sailing home from America aboard the *President*."

"Lizzie Sullivan . . . she came to us from an agency that placed serving girls from Ireland in respectable households. After a few months, a woman enticed her with promised employment in a West End shop."

"Oh, she was clever, that woman," Lady Aldridge said. "She befriended the girl as she sat in the park with Julia in her pram. The woman told Lizzie she could earn three times as much as a dressmaker's assistant."

Dr. Lewis said, "A year later, Lizzie returned to us, pregnant. The shop was a fiction. She'd been taken to a house, drugged, and . . . they shamed the poor girl into continuing, saying who would believe a ruined girl."

"The whole procedure was diabolical, Andrew."

"Lizzie thought she had no choice but to stay. They turned her out when she became pregnant and was no longer useful."

Tennant asked, "Did you inform the police?"

Dr. Lewis nodded. "But they offered us little hope."

"The next part of the story is mine," Lady Aldridge said. "My sister-in-law and I went to Lizzie's priest for advice. He suggested a Catholic home run by nuns for unmarried mothers. When we took her there, we made it clear to the Mother Superior that we would welcome Lizzie back after the birth of her child."

"That was the last we saw of her," Dr. Lewis said. "We were told she went to a home for girls in Ireland. That she'd given birth there and worked in a convent as a laundress."

Lady Aldridge lifted her chin. "The Mother Superior rebuffed our request for more information because we were not Lizzie's family. A letter to Bishop Griffiths in London produced a polite but firm refusal to answer our questions."

"I had no idea," Julia said. "I don't even remember Lizzie."

"My dear niece, you were not yet three years old."

Tennant said, "I wish I could say that Lizzie's ordeal was a case of abduction, plain and simple. But so long as the age of consent in Britain is twelve years old—"

"Monstrous."

"I agree, Lady Aldridge. It becomes a war of accusations. A girl of twelve or older says she was taken by force. Her abductor claims she is a 'fallen woman' who came looking for work."

"A child of twelve . . . Lord, forgive us our sins." A brief silence followed Mr. Lloyd's prayer.

"This has ended as a somber evening," Dr. Lewis finally said. "As host, perhaps I should apologize."

"My dear brother, we are two doctors, a missionary, a policeman, and I daresay Mrs. Davies has seen a thing or two in this world. Mister Lloyd, Richard, I thank you for your candor. Now, I am not so young as I was. I will say good night and borrow my niece to take me to my carriage."

Julia smiled at her aunt and took her arm.

"My brother won't admit he tires easily," Mrs. Davies said, "so we'll also say our good nights. Thank you for a lovely evening."

"The music made it especially memorable," Julia said. "Such a poignant song. It *is* a gift to find oneself in the place just right."

Mrs. Davies smiled. "It helped me in a time of indecision. I had to bow and bend for things to come 'round right. Isn't that true, Owen?"

"Indeed," Lloyd said, opening the door for Julia and his sister. "And if he were here, my brother-in-law would agree."

When the door closed, Dr. Lewis asked, "One last drink, Richard? While we wait for Julia to return."

Tennant shook his head and lifted his glass. "I'll finish this and be on my way."

"My boy, I mean no criticism of the police. We had very little to tell them about Lizzie's ordeal."

"Jin's rescue is the rare happy ending." Tennant drank the last of his whiskey and stood just as Julia returned.

"It's late for hailing a cab, so I've asked Ogilvie to drive you home."

"That was kind of you, sir." Tennant lent his arm and helped Dr. Lewis to his feet and into the hallway. Julia and the inspector watched her grandfather climb slowly up the stairs. He waved good night from the landing.

Julia sighed. "I worry about him. But it's a relief to have a fierce Scotswoman on the watch while I'm not here. I believe Mrs. Ogilvie was a hawk in another life."

Julia took Tennant's arm and headed toward the front door. "I enjoyed tonight. They're an attractive pair, Mrs. Davies and her brother. I mean in every way. Good, kindly people who draw you to them."

"I agree."

"Mrs. Davies . . . I'd like to know her better." Julia opened the front door and stopped. "Richard . . ."

He turned and looked at her. Her back was to the hall lamplight, and her face shadowed so that he couldn't read the expression in her eyes.

"I was thinking about that song, 'Simple Gifts.' Do you ever think . . . do you wonder if it's possible to . . ." She shook her head.

"I think and wonder all the time. Perhaps things are simpler than you believe."

"Richard, I . . ."

Something unspoken seemed to tremble on her lips. He

wanted to trace his finger along their edges, take her in his arms in answer to her unfinished questions. He took a step closer.

Then the coach driven by Mister Ogilvie rattled to a stop. *Damnation.* So, instead of doing the thing he desired, he raised her hand to his lips and wished her good night.

Mary Allingham was late on the first Monday morning in April, and she'd kept Laura Herford waiting in her carriage for ten minutes.

Mary flew down the walkway of Blenheim Lodge, carrying her hat and muff. A footman trailed behind with her paint box.

She dropped onto the seat across from her friend. "I'm sorry, Laura." The servant handed Mary the box. "Oh, thank you, Alfred." He closed the door. "It took me ages to find the Royal Academy's invitation card. And now I've made us late!"

"No matter. Better, in fact. The first varnishing day is bedlam, and we'll miss the opening crush." Laura eyed Mary's box. "Are you planning on repainting?"

"I came prepared. I'm always one highlight short of perfection."

Laura said, "Leave your muff behind in the carriage. Some oaf with a careless brush might streak paint on it."

"You're probably right. The calendar says it's the first of April, but it feels like winter."

Mary pulled off her muff and stroked its sable before laying it aside. It had been her brother's last Christmas gift. He'd bought a pair, and both she and Louisa cherished them.

Charles. If only he were here to share the day.

Thirty minutes later, Laura's coachman avoided the Monday morning traffic and let them out on the far side of Trafalgar Square. They walked across the plaza and mounted the four wide steps of the National Gallery. Mary felt dwarfed by the portico's soaring Corinthian columns.

Porters in the foyer handed out Royal Academy catalogs and answered questions. Mary decided the guides came in two varieties: twinkling ones and grave. She had drawn the former, while the man assisting Laura had the funereal mien of an undertaker.

Mary gave her name to her smiling porter. He consulted the list at the back of his catalog and said, "Here you are, miss. You're hanging in the East Room." He pointed the way.

Mary flipped through her book, thrilled to find her entry on page fifteen. They'd hung her painting as one of the last in the largest of the exhibition's chambers. There it was: *Repose,* and her name, Miss M. Allingham.

Laura looked up from her catalog. "My *Margaret* is in the Middle Room." She took Mary by the arm. "Come, my dear. Take a deep breath and brace yourself."

They passed through a columned archway and into the crowded East Room. Mary had visited the annual art show as a spectator, but this was her first varnishing day as an exhibiting painter.

She stopped inside the gallery and gaped. "Good Lord."

Over two hundred paintings crammed the East Room's walls from floor to ceiling. One gilt-framed picture after another hung inches from the next. Scores of men and a scattering of women hovered near paintings or stood on ladders. Mary and Laura crossed the space as quickly as traffic allowed and found *Repose* hanging near the entrance to the Middle Room.

"A doorway location isn't ideal," Laura said, "but look. You're only one row up from hanging 'on the line,' just above eye level."

Mary said, "Not bad for a first-time exhibitor."

Laura pointed to the ceiling. "I was in the rafters my first time out."

They stood for a few moments admiring the painting. Then Mary hooked elbows with Laura. "Come. Let's find your *Margaret.*"

"The Middle Room is just through here."

They found Laura's painting hanging in the center of the left wall. *Margaret*, like Mary's picture, was one level above the line.

Mary touched the red star fixed to the frame. "Laura, you've sold it. Congratulations."

"And I'm hanging above August Burke, a Royal Academician. The RA after his name will draw crowds and some reflected glory."

A voice behind them said, "And there I am in the East Room, languishing high above Miss Obbard's *Apple Blossoms.*"

Mary turned, and William Quain shrugged. "Well, what can I expect, placed above a woman?" He quoted in a high-pitched, affected tone, "'Fruits and flowers are by divine appointment the property of ladies.' Or so the *Art Journal* said this month."

"This is Mister Quain. Miss Laura Herford."

Laura offered her hand. "Do you agree with the author's sentiment?"

Quain grinned. "The man's a condescending twit and should open his eyes and look at your *Margaret*. Miss Herford, many artists have tried, but few have caught Margot Miller's resplendence. You've placed her in a garden, but she's its most vivid presence."

Surprised, Mary looked at him appraisingly.

"Thank you, Mister Quain," Laura said. "Few models radiated her vitality. A tragic loss."

"Ladies, I'll let you get on with the day's business, as shall I. Some of my Irish sheep need a shadow or two."

Laura followed his dark head as he threaded his way through the crowd. "Quite good-looking, don't you think?"

Mary made a noncommittal noise. "Well, he's right about your *Margaret*. I may have misjudged him. But he needs a haircut."

"Oh, I don't know about that," Laura said. "He's a bit roguish, but in an attractive way. Well, shall we get on with our varnishing? I'll finish up and meet you."

Mary reentered the East Room and spotted Quain. He hadn't

gone far. The artist stood, gaping at a picture to her left. Then he turned abruptly.

"Excuse me." He grinned, brushed past her, and bobbed across the room and out the door. He looked as if he'd placed a winning bet at the Derby.

Mary opened her catalog and flipped to the picture. It was number 233 by JA Whistler: *Symphony in White, No. 3.*

Quain jiggled the coins in his pocket and considered. Instead of a cab, he'd save a few bob and take an omnibus to Scotland Yard.

The day was cold but sunny, so he settled into a bench at the top of the 'bus.

Whistler? Painting smutty pictures for a few quid? When he laughed, a gentleman in the seat opposite gave him a curious look and angled his shoulders away.

Tennant had asked him to go through Allingham's folders, and he'd spotted a match in the East Room. The exhibition's version of Whistler's *Symphony* showed two girls dressed in white. One lounged on a creamy sofa; the other sat on the floor, reaching for a fan. But in Allingham's copy, the two girls were naked. The girl on the carpet stretched to grasp a paddle. Her other hand rested on the thigh of a copper-haired beauty sprawled across the couch, gazing open-legged at the viewer. The lounging model in the Allingham version was Margot Miller.

Inspector Tennant had hoped Quain would recognize the hand of other artists in the collection. But many of the works were paintings like his Delacroix imitation: erotic images executed in the style of the great masters. Some were dark and disturbing. In the original *Rape of the Sabine Women,* the Roman soldiers carried their "prizes" away to a fate Rubens hadn't painted. In Allingham's version, someone had rendered the acts of sexual assault in brutal detail.

Any competent artist could have viewed those old masters in galleries or books and copied them. But Whistler's painting was new. Whoever painted Allingham's version must have spent hours studying the original and recently.

Quain flipped to the back of his exposition catalog and found the alphabetic list of artists and their addresses. *Tennant will have to sort it out.*

The inspector had asked for names. *I'll give him a famous one and get him off my back.*

An hour after his interview with William Quain, Inspector Tennant hailed a cab and headed to Chelsea. The driver slowed as he passed Battersea Bridge and stopped at number two Lindsey Row.

Whistler occupied one of four residences carved out of a three-story stone house that faced the river. The afternoon sunlight glittered and caught the white sail of a small boat as it slipped between Battersea's curving piers. The tide flowed out, exposing an expanse of the strand where bootless mud larks braved the cold, wading in search of river treasure.

Whistler needn't roam far for a picturesque subject, Tennant thought. He could set up his easel twenty yards from his door.

The inspector wasn't surprised when his knock went unanswered. Number two Lindsey Row had the shades-drawn look of a house whose resident was absent. A white-haired lady with a yappy terrier said the artist was in Paris. Tennant scribbled a note on his card and slipped it into the brass letter slot, hoping Whistler planned to return in time for the exhibition's opening on Saturday.

Tennant would be there, heading up the plainclothes police presence. Given the recent attacks on art studios and galleries, Sir Francis Grant had asked for the Yard's protection on opening day. Tennant had proposed stationing twenty of the tallest bobbies they could muster. He had argued that their helmets, visible above the crowds, would be a deterrent. But the RA president refused to dampen the day's festive spirit by filling the National Gallery with uniformed coppers.

The inspector doubted anything untoward would happen. O'Malley had warned off Josiah and Micah Miller, and Tennant planned to post two coppers at the entrance should they appear. Still, it wouldn't be a wasted day.

Tennant had sent tickets to Julia and Dr. Lewis as a thank-you for their dinner invitation.

CHAPTER 12

The Saturday edition of the *Illustrated London News* boldly predicted that the Royal Academy's Annual Exhibition would sell over ten thousand tickets in the first week.

Julia eyed the crowds in the East Room and believed it. She studied the throng, knowing Inspector Tennant had assigned constables to police the Academy's galleries, and she thought she'd spotted one. A man had his eyes on the spectators and his back to the paintings. Sergeant O'Malley, on the other hand, seemed intent on the art. He circled the room, inspected each painting, and stopped near the entrance to the Middle Room, joining Inspector Tennant at Mary Allingham's *Repose*.

Julia and her grandfather caught up with them. She asked, "What do you think, Sergeant? If you could take a picture home, which would it be?"

O'Malley smoothed his bushy mustache and considered. "This one by Miss Allingham is Margot Miller to the life, but as for hanging it on my wall . . ."

A man behind him said, "Come now, Sergeant, show a little fellow feeling. We Irishmen should stick together."

"Well, now, if it isn't Mister Quain."

The artist pointed up. "One row down from heaven is catalog number 249, *Galway Pastoral* by that budding genius, William Quain."

O'Malley eyed Quain in his rumpled tweeds. "They'll be letting the likes of you into the Royal Academy?"

"Not usually, Sergeant, not usually." He made a two-fingered salute and strolled away.

Julia watched the artist head straight for Mary Allingham and her sister-in-law. When Quain offered his arm, Mary took it, smiling.

A line of Byron's poetry came to Julia. " 'All that's best of dark and bright.' "

Dr. Lewis followed her gaze. "The fair Mary 'walks in beauty,' indeed."

"As for the dark," Julia said, "I was thinking of him. I've framed them in my mind's eye. His dark good looks are a foil to her golden loveliness."

Her grandfather raised his eyebrow. "Matchmaking, my dear?"

Julia laughed. "Miss Allingham invited me to tea tomorrow. Perhaps I'll steer the conversation around to him."

When Mary and Quain walked off arm in arm, Tennant said, "I believe you're on to something."

Mrs. Allingham remained where she was, flanked by two attentive gentlemen. One took Louisa's arm and directed her eye to a painting's detail.

Julia said, "I wonder if this is Mrs. Allingham's first social outing since her husband's death."

Louisa looked around and caught Julia's eye. She said something to the gentleman on her arm, and he withdrew his support, bowing.

Julia crossed to Louisa, meeting her halfway. "Mrs. Allingham, it's a pleasure to see you here."

"My first foray into society. I thought it would be difficult, but now . . ." She looked over her shoulder, then leaned in. "Now, I find it's merely tedious. I've just had a lesson in glazing . . . until my eyes glazed over."

There's no denying it, Julia thought. *Louisa Allingham is charming.* "Miss Allingham never mentioned that process, but she told me all about *Repose*. It's wonderful to see it on display."

Louisa waved around the room. "But so crammed among the multitudes—viewers and canvases alike."

"Yes, I've always found it difficult to see any single work."

"You've come before?"

Julia nodded. "But not lately."

"I never did—until I married Charles, of course. My father had no interest in art, and I'm afraid it rubbed off. Yet here I am, every year for the past ten." Louisa looked away. "It's strange. A father's indifference, a husband's career . . . odd, how circumstance hands us our lives. Had I married someone else, it would be altogether different."

"Yes. That's true."

"Ah, but it's not true of you, Doctor. You made your life. How I admire that." She roused herself and smiled. "I must go. My guide is waiting to resume my tutorial. Will I see you tomorrow for tea?"

"I'm looking forward to it."

Heads swiveled as Louisa walked through a corridor of admiring glances. Julia turned and saw Tennant watching Louisa's retreat as well. Julia weaved through the crowd and rejoined her party.

"Mrs. Allingham is an exceptionally lovely woman," she said.

"And in exceptional company," Tennant said. "On Louisa's left is Sir Francis Grant, the RA's president. And that's the celebrated Sir Edwin Landseer, pointing at something in the painting. Two knights vying for her attention."

Competing for the beautiful widow? Julia looked at Tennant. "You're very knowledgeable about the art world. I'm impressed."

Tennant offered his arm. "I've had dealings with both gentlemen over security measures."

"It's no wonder, after the gallery attacks."

"More specifically, someone sent a threatening letter to Sir Edwin after he unveiled a portrait at his studio called *Her Majesty at Osborne*. It's hanging here and has created a storm."

Julia said, "A picture of the queen? Why on earth?"

"Landseer painted the widowed Victoria in a private setting, looking despondent. Some viewers see an insult to both Her Majesty and the monarchy." Tennant shrugged. "Why, I can't fathom. And then there are the whispers . . . the painting has added fuel to the rumors."

Julia said, "What rumors?"

"About the queen's, ah . . . relationship with the other figure in the painting, her Scots servant, John Brown."

"Oh, surely not," Dr. Lewis said.

"As you say, sir. It seems unlikely, but tongues wag about it."

Dr. Lewis flipped to the catalog's index. "Landseer, Landseer . . . catalog number 72." He looked up, smiling. "Excuse me, my dear. I must inspect this artistic outrage before we leave." He patted his granddaughter's hand and walked off.

O'Malley asked, "Have you spotted Mister Whistler about the place, sir?"

"Not yet. Any other candidates?"

The sergeant opened his catalog. "Number 113—*Bacchus* by Simeon Solomon." O'Malley cocked his thumb. "Middle of the far wall, you'll find it. I'll see what turns up in the other rooms."

Julia eyed Tennant curiously. "What are you and the sergeant looking for?"

"The originals of pictures in Allingham's collection."

"And you've found a few?"

"At least two are altered versions of paintings on display, including this one." Tennant moved to a canvas at the right of the door. "*Symphony in White.* It's curious because the RA bars artwork from earlier shows. How, then, could a copyist know them so intimately? It's a puzzle."

Julia squinted at the signature in the lower corner and straightened abruptly. "JA Whistler? You suspect *him*?"

"His initials don't match any on Allingham's list, but I'd like to hear his explanation. He's in Paris at present but expected back any day."

Julia looked closer at the two figures in the painting. "That copper-haired girl on the sofa. She isn't . . ."

"Margot Miller? No. But there's no doubt about the Allingham copy. She's the girl in that version."

Julia shook her head. "All the secrets she took to her grave." She turned to him and smiled. "Thank you for today. You know, I haven't visited since I returned from Philadelphia. I used to come every year with my grandmother."

"And I with mine. She bought several of the exhibition's paintings over the years. They hang in the house she left me, including a late-career Turner, the prize of her collection."

"A Turner? Good Lord, what a treasure!"

"It's an unusual picture . . . a hazy seascape, more fog and clouds than water, and just the suggestion of a mast lost in the mist."

"Unusual but beautiful?"

"Yes . . . I find they often go together."

Julia looked up at something in his voice and saw a hint of a smile playing around his mouth. The room felt suddenly warm, and so did her cheeks. His gray eyes held her gaze. Eyes she'd thought of as granite shone as if lit from within. She drew a breath to reply, but her mind was blank.

She blinked and looked away. "Where is my grandfather . . . ?"

Tennant leaned in and gestured. "There he is, standing next to Johnny Osborne."

As if he had heard him, the reporter from the *Illustrated London News* looked up and made an exaggerated bow in their direction.

"As insufferable as ever," Julia muttered. "I hoped I'd seen the last of him."

"Wishful thinking, I'm afraid. The man's a human limpet."

"More like a rash with an annoying itch. No amount of scratching will get rid of him." Julia sighed and offered her hand. "Thank you again."

My pleasure, he thought, smiling to himself as she walked away. Tennant watched her deftly fend off the reporter, extricate her grandfather, and thread her way through the crowd. He lost her and crossed the floor to look at Mary Allingham's *Repose.*

He couldn't see the sitter's full face or the expression in her eyes. Margot Miller looked away from the viewer, her gaze fixed on the scene outside the window. Still, Tennant knew her thoughts. Mary had painted the woman's longing for something beyond her reach, a subject he understood all too well. Tennant wondered how much of the picture's effect was Margot's contribution. Quain had said the best models were actresses who channeled the painter's intentions.

Margot Miller . . . how many parts did you play?

On Sunday, five women gathered in the drawing room of Blenheim Lodge.

The Allinghams' invitation to tea included Julia, Laura Herford, and her niece, Helen Paterson. Mary passed around plates of crumpets and cucumber sandwiches, but Julia noticed that her sister-in-law ate nothing. At first, Louisa sat quietly with her gloved hands on her lap. Then, gradually, she roused herself to take her share in the conversation.

The discussion turned to art, and Mary congratulated Helen Paterson on her recent admission to the Royal Academy's art school.

"I'm following in my aunt's footsteps," Helen said. "Doctor Lewis, did you know Aunt Laura was the first woman admitted?"

"No, I did not."

"You and she are fellow pioneers," Helen said.

"My niece stays with me while she studies," Laura said, "although it gives her mother pause. My sister imagines that artists consort with all manner of disreputable people. Aesthetes, bohemians, opium smokers, and the like."

Helen laughed. "That only slightly exaggerates my mother's attitude."

Julia tried and failed to imagine Miss Herford as a denizen of London's darker corners. Middle-aged, wearing a black dress with a prim, white collar, she looked like someone's governess.

Laura said, "I see you've hung *Down the Rushy Glen*. It looks wonderful on that wall."

Helen Paterson looked at the painting over her shoulder. "From the poem? *Up the airy mountain, down the rushy glen. We dare not go a hunting*—oh." A smile spread. "Allingham, of course."

"William is a cousin," Louisa said. "He'd be flattered that you know his verses by heart. The next time he's in London, we'll introduce you."

Mary said, "He's our one poetic relative in a family of painters, so Louisa cherishes him."

Julia asked, "What did you think of the Annual Exhibition, Miss Paterson?"

"Overwhelming. One could hardly take it in, but . . ." Helen smiled. "As a watercolorist, I must lament the Academy's preference for oils."

"Oh, I agree," Mary said. "Watercolors are such a demanding medium. With oils, you can scrape away mistakes and paint over them."

Louisa put down her cup. "And tinker endlessly. I've watched you fiddle with canvases I thought were long finished. And as for varnishing day . . . after months of work, is it necessary?"

Mary waved a teaspoon airily. "Art is never done."

"Literature is," Louisa said. "Once it's in print, that's that."

"What about new prefaces?" Laura said. "They're filled with second thoughts. And even Mister Dickens, genius that he is, doubted, changed his mind, and altered the ending of *Great Expectations.*"

"I like his happier version better," Mary said. "It leaves open the possibility that Pip and Estella marry in the end."

"My dear, you are a romantic," Louisa said.

"Not at all. I'm a realist. What rational person wants to plow through eight hundred pages of a three-volume novel only to be left heart-sore and depressed by a sad ending?"

"As much as painting and literature feed the spirit, the healing arts most ennoble," Louisa said. "Did you see the recent edition of *The Lancet*, Doctor Lewis? On hospital outpatient treatment?"

"It had much to commend it. Sensible proposals to improve care," Julia said. "I remember seeing a February copy of the journal on your reading table the last time I visited Blenheim Lodge."

"I've always had an interest in medicine," Louisa said. "If it wouldn't be an intrusion, may I visit your clinic one day?"

"Of course. I'd be happy to take you on a tour. I'll give you the address before I leave."

Louisa said a little sadly, "How I admire your career . . . that you let no obstacle stand in your way. Had I your courage, I might have been a nurse."

"Obstacles, indeed," Mary said. "An artist friend I met in

Paris once said that the highest hurdle to a woman's professional success is that she can never have a wife. Someone to darn the stockings and keep the house clean. Someone to do all the other disagreeable things, so she has time to paint."

Helen said, "I imagine female physicians could use a wife to do the darning, too."

"I see a look in my sister-in-law's eye," Mary said. "Louisa longs to say that I've never darned a stocking in my life, so I hardly need a wife."

"I've said nothing, my dear, but now that you mention it . . ."

"After ten years together, my sister-in-law knows me too well."

"Indeed, I do." Louisa stood and smiled around the room. "This has been a delightful afternoon, but I'm a little tired now. Will you ladies excuse me?"

The company murmured farewells, and Louisa closed the sitting room door behind her.

Mary sighed. "I'm glad she came down and happy she stayed as long as she did."

"I spoke to her at the exhibition yesterday," Julia said.

"It was her first real outing." Mary frowned. "If only . . . well, I'm betraying no secrets. If only Louisa had the children she always wanted. Perhaps she wouldn't be so adrift in the world. So many disappointments. It broke my heart to witness her grief."

"She's still young," Laura said, "and so beautiful. Has she ever been painted?"

"Charles tried, but he was never satisfied with the results."

Laura nodded. "Perhaps life has happiness in store for her yet."

"Perhaps."

"And for you, my dear?" Laura said. "I saw Mister Quain squiring you around the East Room. He's attractive, in a rakish sort of way."

Mary shook her head. "Are you and Louisa conspiring to find me a husband?"

"Perhaps Mister Quain might be willing to darn your stockings."

Mary laughed. "You met him, Laura. Does he look like a man who mends his own?"

"I am in earnest," she said. "Marriage between professional partners is one solution to the challenge of matrimony for working women. Sharing life and labor, as it were."

"If my friend in Paris is correct, *he* shares the life. You do the labor." Mary waved in dismissal. "He's amusing company, that is all."

"Aha," Laura said. "Sharing laughter. You're well on your way."

"Quite a few painting couples have made it work," Helen said. "Henrietta and Edward Ward. Joanna and Henry Wells. You're a professional woman, Doctor Lewis. What do you say?"

Julia smiled, shaking her head. "I say it sounds like the conversations I have with my great-aunt all the time. But shared work might increase the chance for success."

Mary waggled her teaspoon. "I'm remembering. You are a medical examiner for Scotland Yard . . . and the policeman you work with, Inspector Tennant. *Very* attractive, and *not* in a rakish sort of way."

Julia laughed. "Now *you* sound conspiratorial—in league with my Aunt Caroline."

It was getting late. Cups were set aside, wraps and hats gathered, and coachmen signaled. Julia hung back at the front door and handed Mary a card.

"For Mrs. Allingham. It's the address of my clinic in Whitechapel. I assume Doctor Scott is still treating her, but if she ever wishes to make a change, please tell her I would be happy to see her."

"Thank you, Julia. I hope she will. About Inspector Tennant . . . Forgive me. I only brought him up to divert the conversation from Will Quain." Mary smiled impishly. "But there's no denying it. The man *is* handsome. It's no wonder he was one of Louisa's old beaux."

"No wonder."

Mary took Julia's arm and walked her to the front door. "About the case . . . is there anything new? The inspector seems focused on painters. I only wondered . . ."

"We mostly discuss the medical side of things. Still, I wouldn't worry too much about the artists. The investigation is heading in many directions." Julia offered her hand. "I'm sorry. I'm afraid there isn't more I can tell you."

Mr. Ogilvie nosed the carriage into the Kensington Road traffic. Lost in thought, Julia noticed none of it.

They made good points, she thought. But the married women artists they mentioned combined domesticity with their profession. Julia guessed that many, like Mary, painted from studios in their homes. *My case is different.* She left the house every day for her clinic in Whitechapel.

Even if her private practice were to thrive, *about as likely as my becoming head of the medical board,* it wasn't enough. Her important work happened at the clinic. *What husband wants an absentee wife?* What about children, what then? How would a doctor-mother balance their needs with her medical commitments?

Aunt Caroline often reminded her that life involved risk and reconsideration. After the dinner party with Mister Lloyd and his sister, her aunt had said, "My dear, that hymn might have been written for you."

"I know you believe things are simple, Aunt. I'm not as certain."

She'd kissed her niece's cheek and climbed into her carriage. Before the coach rolled away, her aunt let down the window to have the last word. "You have many gifts, but it *is* a gift to be simple. Stop analyzing and listen to your heart."

Heart, mind, and senses . . . and taking a chance. Julia closed her eyes in the rocking carriage. She pictured a summer morning at the pond, her grandfather in water up to his chest, arms outstretched, and her ten-year-old self hesitating. He'd said, "Jump, Julie," and she'd vaulted from her perch. She recalled the rush of air, the weightlessness of the water, and her grandfather's strong arms encircling her. Julia remembered the fear of that leap. She also recalled its thrill.

At ten, she had hurled herself into the void. Nearly twenty years later, she stood on another brink, hesitating.

Monday, the second week of April, opened at the Yard with two promising lines of inquiry.

Arnie Stackpole's imminent release from prison offered them a potential trail. The seaman would finish his sentence in three days, and plans were in place to follow him.

Stackpole and Margot Miller were confederates in a criminal cabal linked to prostitution and pornography. At least, that was the inspector's theory. *And God knows what else,* Tennant thought. Somehow, it had led to her murder. And he believed Rawlings, still in the wind, was deep in the scheme.

Chief Inspector Clark was less convinced of the linkages, and he'd made that clear in their meeting that morning. It had been weeks since Margot Miller's murder and longer since the body of Franny Riley was found. Clark wanted arrests, not a Byzantine conspiracy. For Tennant, the connections held. He had murder victims linked to two criminal enterprises; either one could have led to Margot's death.

More immediately, there were the pictures to explore. How had salacious versions of recently painted works ended up in Allingham's collection?

While Clark grilled Tennant about the investigation's lack of progress, O'Malley tracked down Simeon Solomon to question him about *Bacchus.* The sergeant's contented smile had spread when he'd found the artist's address at the back of the RA catalog.

"Gower Street, is it?" he'd said. "The station is on the underground line. I'll get on at Farringdon and see what this Solomon fella has to say for himself."

Have at it, the inspector had thought. A belching steam engine pulling a line of cars through a dark, buried tunnel? It was Tennant's idea of hell. On any day, he'd take horses and the stench of dung over the reek of billowing smoke trapped inside a black hole. But O'Malley was an enthusiast, and in the four years since the underground opened, he'd ridden the subterranean railway countless times. For the sergeant, the experience was evergreen.

"'Tis a marvel of the age," O'Malley said when he returned from Gower Street. "The stations are like palaces, and the railbeds curve through great iron archways buried under the streets."

"I prefer an arching sky over my head."

"Old-fashioned you are, sir, and no mistake."

"Perhaps. So, what did Solomon have to say?"

"He can't be found. He's been in Italy these last six months." When Tennant groaned, O'Malley grinned. "But the sister was at home. Miss R. Solomon as she's listed in the catalog, Rebecca by name. The lass has two paintings in the exhibit to her brother's one."

"Since you're smiling, I assume Miss Solomon told you something."

"Before he left, her brother sold the reproduction rights to *Bacchus* and handed it over so an engraver could get busy with it. Small world. It's Allingham and Allen that's owning the permission to publish."

"Well, well. Perhaps Sidney Allen is up to his ears in it after all."

"Sir?" a constable said from Tennant's door. "Chap's here to see you, a Mister Whistler."

"Show the gentleman up."

"Now, there's timing for you," O'Malley said. "Always the way with an investigation. When at last the sky opens after a drought, the rain comes bucketing down."

A monocled gentleman in a caped inverness coat and carrying a silver-handled cane followed the constable into the office. A white streak split his shock of dark hair, and a drooping, dolorous mustache gave his expression a melancholy cast.

"Mister Whistler, sir."

The artist held his wide-brimmed hat at his chest and bowed. "Inspector, here I am," he said in a nasal Yankee twang. "Your summons intrigued me. How can I help the Metropolitan Police?"

Tennant gestured to a chair. "Sergeant O'Malley and I have some questions about your painting in the Annual Exhibition."

"Oh?" He unwound a yellow scarf and draped it across his knee. "Which one? The RA had the good taste to hang three this year."

"*Symphony in White, Number Three.*"

"What about it?"

"Did you show it to the public before the exhibition? In your studio, perhaps?"

"No." He flicked a speck of lint from his sleeve. "Next question."

"Did you sell the reproduction rights in advance of the exhibition?"

"Yes."

"May I ask to whom?"

"To Allingham and Allen. Well, Inspector? I guess you'll tell me sooner or later why you're asking these questions."

"We'll show you."

Tennant nodded to O'Malley. The sergeant slipped a painting from its portfolio and handed it to the artist.

Whistler's monocle popped. "Christ Almighty!" The copy shook in his hands. "I'll sue the bastards."

"For now, I'll ask you to do nothing," Tennant said. "This is a police investigation involving several deaths, including murder. From your reaction, I take it you've never seen this version before?"

"No. You have my word on it, Inspector."

"May we also count on a promise of your discretion?"

The smoldering artist considered. "Yes." He passed the picture back to O'Malley and eyed the bulky portfolio. "Is that all?"

"For the moment, sir," Tennant said.

Whistler screwed his monocle under his eyebrow ridge and stood. "Get the son-of-a-bitch who did this." He left trailing his yellow scarf.

"Nothing we'd like better," O'Malley muttered.

"Our next order of business is Allingham and Allen." Tennant tucked the Whistler and Solomon copies into a folder and plucked his hat from its peg. "But we'll go by omnibus or hansom. Sorry to disappoint, Sergeant."

Sergeant O'Malley made a show of his role as a notetaker for Sidney Allen's benefit.

He settled his bulk into a chair, patted his pockets for his police pad, and flipped through it until he came to a blank page. He gave the tip of his pencil a lick and set the point at the top. Then he cleared his throat and looked up.

"Ready, I am, sir, to take Mister Allen's testimony."

The publisher blinked. "Testimony?"

"Just a few questions connected to official inquiries," Tennant said.

"Again?"

"Yes, Mister Allen." The inspector looked around the room, in no hurry to begin. Allen shifted in his chair and drummed his fingers on the armrest. But his eyes were watchful and still.

"Questions have arisen about the reproduction rights of several paintings."

"Oh, aye. What about them?"

"Our information is that you purchased the rights for works by JA Whistler and Simeon Solomon."

"Whistler and Solomon . . . let me think." Allen leaned back and tilted his head at the ceiling. "Poor old Charlie dealt mostly with the artists, but I reckon you're right, although I'd have to consult our records."

Tennant had expected that gambit. A dead partner was a convenient scapegoat.

"Let me help your memory, Mister Allen, although they were recent purchases. The engraving rights are for two paintings. *Bacchus*, by Mister Solomon, and *Symphony in White, Number Three*, by JA Whistler."

"Oh, aye. They're ringing a bell with me now. Charlie thought they'd get a lot of play in the press. Worth the brass we'd fork out, he said."

"I'd like to speak to the engraver."

"I don't rightly know. Charlie kept the originals for a while, and he brought in an outsider to work on—"

"Mister Allen, you told me earlier that you ran the business side of the partnership. Failure to assist the police in an official inquiry and the publication of pornographic materials are criminal offenses."

"Pornography?" The publisher shifted uneasily in his chair. "Don't know what you're on about. You're losing me, mate."

Tennant held up Allingham's *Bacchus*.

Allen sprang to his feet. "It's bollocks, I tell you."

"We found this 'bollocks' in your partner's study. Sit down, Mister Allen."

The man dropped heavily into his chair. "I know now't about the mangy thing."

"And this one?" Tennant held up the Whistler. "Come, sir, cooperation is in your best interest. Surely, an old firm like Allingham and Allen wants to avoid the scandal of a charge?"

"'Tis the way of it," O'Malley said mournfully. "Reporters always turn up at magistrate's court when something dodgy is on the docket." He tapped his pencil to his temple. "Don't know how they find out, but they do."

"Yes," Tennant said. "I imagine Johnny Osborne of the *Illustrated* would be curious. He takes a keen interest in the worlds of art and scandal. This case is an enticing mixture of the two."

Allen stuck out his chin. "You wouldn't be threatening me, Inspector?"

"Not at all, but I suggest you find the name and address of this outside contractor. And while you're at it, my sergeant will look around the premises—with your permission."

Allen glared. "I give sweet feck-all for what he looks at. He can park his arse on the factory floor for all the good it'll do him." He considered for a moment. "Arthur Griffiths was the engraver." He snatched the bell from his desk and rang for his secretary.

"I'm glad your memory hasn't deserted you after all," Tennant said.

The door opened, and Allen said to his assistant, "Take the sergeant along to see the foreman and bring me Arthur Griffiths's file."

"Yes, sir. Typesetting has a question for you."

"Bloody hell! Does now't get done around here unless I do it?" The publisher pushed past his secretary. "Find the address for Griffiths and give it to the inspector."

The file and the sergeant's tour unearthed treasures: a Soho address for the engraver and a book. O'Malley found copies of *Pleasure Gardens: The Art of the Ming Dynasty* on the loading dock, awaiting delivery to the South Kensington Museum. Allingham had written *Pleasure Gardens* on one folder of erotic paintings.

The sergeant said, "We found the motherlode for the man's naughty Chinese paintings."

The engraver lived in a seedy Soho neighborhood not far from William Quain's address. Once, the town houses of the well-to-do had lined the streets around Soho Square. Arthur Griffiths's building hadn't retained a trace of fading elegance. The engraver lived in the rear flat at the end of a dank alleyway.

Tennant led O'Malley to the back entrance and knocked. A thin man opened the door. Dark, close-set eyes buried beneath a jutting brow gave him the aspect of a bird of prey.

"Mister Griffiths?"

The man swallowed hard when Tennant identified himself as a detective inspector from Scotland Yard. The bump of his Adam's apple jumped above the loose collar of his shirt.

"We have a few questions, sir. May we come in?"

Griffiths stood back, and Tennant and his sergeant entered. The room held the fusty smell of unwashed linen, spoiled food, and disappointment. An empty easel stood near the back window where inadequate light slanted through cracked panes, catching motes that drifted through the air. A settled gloom had fallen over everything like dust.

Tennant said, "Mister Griffiths, we've come from the office of Allingham and Allen. The firm hired you to make several engravings that interest us."

Griffiths's expression shifted from wary to frightened. He licked his lips. "What about them?"

"We're interested in . . . let's call them the 'special' versions you made for Mister Allingham."

Griffiths's face turned white when O'Malley held up the copies.

"We have his records," Tennant said. "We know you painted these, so don't lie to us. By assisting, you might avoid charges of fraud and forgery."

Griffiths's story tumbled out. Charles Allingham had approached him, explained his wants, and given him the paintings. After that, Margot Miller ran the show. She brought in the girls he needed to paint the lewd versions of the originals and, for *Bacchus*, the boys.

Griffiths completed four works in all. When the artist described two additional pictures he'd painted—harem scenes—Tennant recognized them from Allingham's collection. Griffiths said they were copies of original works by John Frederick Lewis.

"After I finished the paintings, I completed the engravings at Allingham and Allen. I don't have the equipment here, so I engraved my versions after the others left for the day. Allingham gave me a key, and I let myself out."

Tennant held the artist's eyes. "Let me get this straight. You're saying you also engraved the pictures *you* painted?"

Griffiths nodded.

O'Malley said, "Are we right in thinking the only purpose of an engraving is to print multiple copies of a painting?"

Griffiths nodded again.

Tennant said, "What was Charles Allingham doing with the engravings of your work? Think carefully before you answer, sir."

Griffiths replied without hesitation. "I didn't ask, and he didn't say. I just collected my five quid for each job from Allen's secretary."

Tennant said, "So Mister Allen, not Mister Allingham, paid you for your services?"

Griffiths nodded.

"Have you anything else to tell us?"

Griffiths chewed at his lip, considering. "One odd thing happened. I'd finished my version of *A Slave for the Harem* when one of the girls walked around the easel. She said it reminded her of the Topkapi. When Margot looked daggers at her, the girl shut up."

O'Malley asked, "Why would she do that, now?"

The artist shrugged. "But she was right. The sultan's harem was at the Topkapi Palace. But they were shopgirls earning a few extra quid. How could a girl like that have visited Turkey and seen the palace? It didn't make sense."

Outside, Tennant said, "The model didn't mean the Ottoman palace in Asia Minor. She meant Allingham's club on East Pall Mall."

CHAPTER 13

Julia was late for the clinic.

Snarled Monday traffic at Whitechapel and Commercial Street had forced her out of the cab, so she crossed the last quarter mile on foot. It was well past noon when Julia finally pushed through the doors; her head nurse and three patients awaited her.

Annie O'Neill whispered to a wan, slumping girl at her side, "'Tis Doctor Lewis, Kath."

Nurse Clemmie took Julia's cape. "Annie's friend is waiting to see you. Kathleen Morris. But may I have a word with you first, Doctor?"

Julia smiled at the girls. "I'll be with you in a few minutes." She followed her head nurse into the office and closed the door. "What is it, Clemmie?"

"Yesterday afternoon, Annie found Kathleen huddled on her doorstep in a pitiable state—exhausted and feverish and complaining of body aches. The girl was no better this morning, so Annie brought her here."

Her head nurse dealt efficiently with all routine cases, so

Julia knew something more was coming. "So . . . she needs more than just a few days' bedrest?"

"It's the girl's hands. She has a blistering rash on her palms. When I asked her about the soles of her feet, the poor child said they were also red and spotted."

Julia closed her eyes. "Syphilis, most likely."

"And not yet twenty, by the look of her. What would you like me to do?"

"Is our fever room still unoccupied?"

Clemmie nodded.

"Settle her there while I talk to Annie."

The young milliner knew only part of Kathleen's story, but she understood enough. "She made hats for Wheatlands' shop, like me, before disappearing."

Julia asked, "Where had she gone?"

"Ireland, I thought. That's what I'd been told."

Then, on Sunday, Kathleen found her way to Annie's flat and waited for her friend to return from Mass.

"But I made a day of it, walking from Saint Anne's to the Sunday market on Chester Street. When I got home, Kathleen was huddling at my basement door."

Julia smiled. "So, like a good friend, you took her in."

"Ten months she was away. She was knackered, the poor lass. I wasn't wanting to plague her with questions, so I put her to bed. This morning . . . Doctor, she told me it wasn't to Ireland she'd gone."

"I see," Julia said. "We'll keep her overnight. After that—"

"She can stop with me. I'll let her have Margot's old bedroom for as long as she wants."

"That's kind of you."

"I got Kath the job with Wheatlands'. And didn't I introduce her to that devil, Margot Miller?"

"Annie, what happened to Kathleen wasn't your fault."

"I wasn't brought up to speak ill of the dead, but you can be certain of it. Margot brought the lass low."

"Why do you say that?"

"She talked Kath into sitting for the artists—the men, I'm saying. And I know what that means. And wasn't it Margot who put it 'round that she was homesick for Ireland? Lying was as natural as breathing to that one."

"Lying about what, Annie?"

"All I know is what I was hearing. Whispering, they were, the shopgirls who worked around Wheatlands', saying Margot got some of the models to do worse than sit and have their pictures painted."

"I see."

Annie looked at Julia gravely. "Can you help her, Doctor?"

"I'll do what I can. Come back tomorrow, Annie. We'll look after her tonight."

Julia sat at Kathleen's bedside at the end of a long afternoon. After telling her story, the girl slept. Julia pulled the blanket to Kathleen's chin and thought about Lizzie Sullivan, her old nursery maid.

Nothing changes—a quarter century ago, today, or a hundred years hence. Girls were ever exploitable, with poverty on one side and selfishness, appetite, and money on the other.

That evening, Julia waited in the library for her grandfather's return and Inspector Tennant's arrival. She reached for the sherry, changed her mind, and poured herself a whiskey.

Hours earlier, the damaged girl had given her account slowly, haltingly, abashed. But the disgrace was not hers. It belonged to others. At first, her story trickled; then, the words spilled in a torrent.

Kathleen's ordeal had shaken Julia in a way the narrative about her nursery maid had not. That girl's tragedy was long past and involved someone Julia couldn't recall. She hadn't thought about Lizzie Sullivan once since the evening of the dinner party.

Two nights earlier, Julia had passed near Fenchurch Station. That was where they'd dumped Kathleen. Julia had rolled past St. Katharine's Church, where the girl had huddled for the night. Julia saw—or rather hadn't seen—the church as her coach rattled along. Why should she have noticed it? It wasn't memorable. Its stubby stone tower was a nondescript landmark she passed nearly every day. Tired, late for dinner on a Saturday night, comfortable in her carriage, she'd rolled by the church on her way home, unseeing.

We walk past tragedies every day with our eyes on our shopping lists.

It wasn't an original thought about the ocean-deep troubles all around her. But when needs stretched like pebbles on an endless strand, sometimes her services seemed nothing more than specks of sand. Julia wondered if policemen felt the same way as they walked the beats of their blighted neighborhoods, sifted the debris of blasted lives, and tried to sort the innocent from the guilty. *As if most people are one or the other.*

She heard the doorknocker and the voices of her grandfather and Inspector Tennant in the hallway. Julia had sent him a note promising links to his case.

After some commonplace conversation about the drive over, her grandfather poured two more whiskies. At Julia's nod, he added a splash to her glass. Then they settled into chairs around the fireplace to hear Julia tell Kathleen's story.

"I felt I was back in our drawing room the night of our dinner party," she said. "Kathleen's experience was the twin of my nursery maid's ordeal twenty-five years ago."

Haltingly, Kathleen had explained that Margot Miller had recruited her to pose "the way Annie did." But unlike Annie, she had been tempted to remove her clothes for "life studies," lured by the extra money Margot dangled.

"Then, on the last day of the sitting, Margot invited Kathleen to a party for the models. She would collect the girl that evening. Kathleen said she rolled up in a 'great black coach dressed like a queen.'"

"Poor child," Dr. Lewis muttered. "Swept away."

"Margot gave her a drink in the carriage. The next thing Kathleen remembered was waking in the morning in a different room with Margot standing over her. Miller laughed and pointed at the tangled bed linen. 'Those stains were worth the other half of twenty quid.' Margot called her 'ruined' and told her to make the best of it."

"Twenty pounds," Tennant said. "That's the rumored price for a girl without sexual experience. One guaranteed to be free of disease."

"Dear God." Julia shuddered.

Dr. Lewis held up a match, struck it, and tossed it into the fireplace. "Used once. Then, discarded."

"But not before they're handed off to others," Tennant said. "Men with smaller purses and a greater willingness to risk their health."

Dr. Lewis said, "Continue, my dear."

"Kathleen said they forced her to make that carriage ride repeatedly. Gin laced with laudanum made it bearable." Julia shook her head. "At first, they kept her for the exclusive use of the same man. Then they stopped taking her to the second location and brought a string of other men to her room."

Her grandfather asked, "How did the poor child finally escape?"

"They discarded her once she showed symptoms of syphilis. She made her way to Aldgate High Street and turned up at Annie's flat."

Julia crossed the room and gave the fire a few hard thrusts with her poker. "I think Kathleen may have overheard Franny Riley's murder."

Tennant asked, "What makes you think that?"

"Kathleen said they brought in a girl who refused to go along. She never saw her. They locked the girl away in a room for several weeks until, one night, Kathleen heard screams followed by silence."

"Did she say when this was?"

"After the New Year. Sometime in January." Julia leaned on the mantel, staring into the yellow and orange flames flickering above the pile. The fire glowed white-hot in the crevices deep within the coals.

"They probably drugged Franny like Kathleen," Tennant said. "Then took her to be raped the night she disappeared."

"And held her for weeks," Julia said. "Trying to break her will."

"It's a terrible story, but the links are no longer speculation." Tennant lifted his glass. "Kathleen's evidence supports Jin's story and connects Margot Miller to an abduction and prostitution ring. If only she were alive to be charged."

"Someone you know *is* alive and well," Julia said. "A few weeks ago, someone new turned up to guard the girls on the carriage ride . . . a man with a cleft lip."

"Rawlings," Tennant said.

"He guarded Kathleen on her last carriage ride. Two Chinese girls were with her, and a third was a child, ten years old at most. Kathleen said the little girl . . ." Julia's voice caught. "She whimpered in the coach the whole way back to the house."

"By God, it's utterly revolting." Dr. Lewis reached for his whiskey, hands shaking.

"Allow me, sir." Tennant took hold of the decanter and poured. "Can Kathleen remember anything about the house where she was taken?"

"Not much." Julia brushed at her cheeks. "It wasn't a long ride, but the shades were drawn tight. Gates opened, and they entered a courtyard, stopping at a doorway under a canopy.

Then they walked down a long hallway to the rooms. Her usual escort for the last few weeks was the man with the lip."

"I think Stackpole is up to his neck in it as well." Tennant nodded. "Margot Miller told Kathleen that her bloodstains were worth 'the other half of twenty quid.' And Stackpole shouted that phrase at Annie O'Neill when he came looking for Margot weeks ago. He said Miller owed him 'the other half' of twenty pounds for 'the goods.' "

"The goods," Dr. Lewis spat out. "Trading and trafficking the bodies of young girls. The law makes men the guardians of female interests, but we do a terrible job."

"That's the hole in the suffrage argument, isn't it, Grandfather? That it's enough for husbands and brothers to legislate for their wives and sisters. But if women had the power to decide, would we set the age of consent at twelve? Never."

"My dear, if I had the power, I would herd the gentlemen of Parliament into a surgical theater. Force them to witness the ravages of childbirth on an immature mother's body. The tearing, the fistulas that leave a girl permanently incontinent—if she survives the attendant infections and lives."

Julia looked at Tennant. "Just now, only one of us has the power to do anything."

She thought of their many disputes about men, women, and their place in the world and the times she'd thought him deaf to rational argument. How often her judgments about him had been wrong.

He looked surprised when she said, "I'm glad it's you in charge of this case."

Julia hooked her arm around her grandfather's elbow, and they walked to the door. Mrs. Ogilvie waited with Tennant's overcoat.

As the inspector shrugged it on, he asked, "What do you know about the Topkapi, sir? It's the new club on Pall Mall."

"Not so new anymore. It must be ten years since it opened those extraordinary front doors." Dr. Lewis chuckled. "Many of my fellow clubmen are happy they face Whitcomb Street off *East* Pall Mall."

Tennant smiled. "Yes, the façade is something of an Ottoman fantasy. What sort of members do they admit?"

"Retired diplomats, East India Company men, Indian Army officers. Men who served the Empire." Doctor Lewis laughed. "One fusty old boy at my club said, 'They might as well let in a pack of Johnny Foreigners from the bloody abroad.'"

Julia handed Tennant his hat. "What's your interest in the Topkapi Club?"

"I'm not sure. Just a secondhand comment passed along to me."

"And?"

"Strangely, its name keeps cropping up."

The following day, Tennant hailed a cab and headed to the South Kensington Museum with Allingham and Allen's printed copy of the *Pleasure Gardens* catalog and the matching folder of erotic art.

The hansom dropped him off at the North Cloister gardens, still dormant in early April but showing signs of life. A guard directed him to the offices of the museum's director, Henry Cole.

A rumpled figure with a bristly thatch of white hair and a fringed, snowy beard invited Tennant to sit. "Should I be anxious about our treasures?"

"Not at all, Mister Cole. I have some questions about this book." Tennant held up *Pleasure Gardens.* "And about your collection of Chinese art."

"You have an advantage over me, Inspector. I've only seen the galley pages, not the finished product. What is your interest, if I may ask?"

"I'll get to that, sir. But first, am I right that the museum produced this book to coincide with an exhibit?"

"That is correct. *Pleasure Gardens: The Art of the Ming Dynasty* opens Saturday, the twentieth of April."

"How did Allingham and Allen acquire the publication rights?"

"Well, they are a well-regarded house—in the forefront of fine arts publishing, as it happens. And Charles Allingham was the moving force behind the exhibit."

"In what way?"

"Allingham acted as the broker for several pieces. We've been expanding our collection of Far Eastern art these last ten years, and Charles secured the loan of works that will be on display." Cole shook his head. "His death was a great loss. His connoisseurship of Chinese art was unmatched in Britain."

"May I view the works in the exhibition?"

"Yes, I suppose so, although it's not fully hung. See here, Inspector, what is this all about?"

"Forgery, of a sort, and murder."

Cole stared. "But I thought . . . well, I thought Charles Allingham took his own life. Didn't he?"

"I refer to the murder of another person." Tennant stood. "Shall we proceed to the gallery?"

Cole looked shaken. As Tennant strode the long hallway, their footsteps echoing, the director hurried to keep up, peering at the inspector as if trying to parse his expression.

Tennant said, "Chinese art seems an exotic interest. How did Mister Allingham develop his expertise?"

"He has friends who've spent time in the East," Cole wheezed, catching his breath. "Men who have a good eye, based on the quality of the work they've lent for this exhibition."

"Is interest in Chinese art increasing?"

"Oh yes. But a lot of inferior pieces are churned out for the export market. One needs to be discerning." They came to a stairwell. "This way, Inspector."

They climbed to the upper gallery, passing a sign that read THE RAPHAEL CARTOONS.

"A gift to the museum from Her Majesty. One of the great gems of our collection. They are Raphael's original color sketches for a series of tapestries."

Tennant glanced through the doorway. Two artists had set up side-by-side camp chairs. The woman leaned forward, intent on her sketchbook. Over her bowed head, William Quain locked eyes with the inspector and nodded.

"A lovely girl, Miss Allingham," Mister Cole murmured as they walked by. "I feel for her and Charles's widow. Such a beautiful woman, Louisa Allingham, and so young. A tragedy."

"Yes. I've met them," Tennant said.

"Of course, indeed. In the course of your duties."

Cole flipped through a ring of keys at the door to the Chinese gallery and unlocked the door. After a quick count, Tennant identified eight pictures in his folder that matched paintings labeled "On Loan to the Collection" without listing the lenders' names.

"Who provided the artwork without an owner's attribution?"

"Charles's friends and fellow clubmen."

"Members of the Topkapi Club?"

The director cleared his throat. "The gentlemen are anonymous under the terms of our arrangement, I'm afraid."

"Mister Cole, *I'm* afraid murder tosses anonymity out the window. I will know who they are, sir."

The director scowled and named three men. One the inspector knew: Dr. Preston Scott.

Mary Allingham and Will Quain had spent the morning sketching in companionable absorption. At noon, they folded their camp chairs, packed their sketchbooks, and headed out the exit.

"Is that Inspector Tennant?" Mary nodded at a receding figure.

Quain glanced over his shoulder. "It looks like him."

They walked the length of the museum's carriage drive. Quain glanced down at the silent Mary. She'd folded in her lower lip, a habitual tick. Her eyes flickered up and away. *Making up her mind about something,* Will thought.

"I . . ." She flushed. "I owe you an apology . . . or at least, an explanation. Quite by accident, I drew the inspector's attention to you. He asked for your address, and I gave it to him." She added in a rush, "You see, Charles had given me your folder and—"

"What folder?" *Good God,* he thought, *he couldn't have shown her . . .*

"Your Irish watercolors and the sketches of Margot Miller."

"Oh. Those."

"The inspector wanted a sketch, and I had none that showed her full face. Then I remembered yours, so Tennant took Margot's pictures away. He . . . it was only then he said he wanted to track down all the artists who had painted her. I should have warned you."

In a heavy brogue, he said, " 'Tis a kindness to be worrying yourself over the likes of me. Why were you thinking I'd be needing a warning, Miss Mary Allingham?"

"How should I know?" she snapped. "And I'll thank you to stop your Irish nonsense when I'm being serious."

"I'm sorry."

"And you haven't been forthcoming with me. Neither has Inspector Tennant. Or Charles, for that matter, and he took his secrets to the grave, whatever they were. That very first day, the day Charles . . . the inspector said something about black-mail."

Quain said nothing. How could he be candid with her without tarnishing her brother's memory? *And I don't come off very well, either.*

Mary stopped at a four-wheeler parked at the end of the carriage drive. She said stiffly, "It looks like rain. May I drop you on Kensington Road?"

"Thank you."

Quain climbed into the seat across from her. "Mary . . ."

"Yes?" she said, sounding coolly polite.

"I know only a small part of the story. It involves copies made of other artists' works and Margot Miller's role in the scheme. I recognized one of the originals of the copied paintings and told the inspector." He leaned forward, his forearms on his knees, trying to draw her gaze. "Tennant doesn't tell me very much."

Mary looked out the window. "We'd better be on our way." She tapped the carriage roof with her umbrella.

Bruised clouds had massed in the south. They billowed toward them, erasing the sun and throwing the carriage into twilight. The wind shifted, and a pelleting rain caught the carriage as it turned right on Cromwell Road.

Mary's husky voice came from the shadows. "I don't know what's wrong with me. Sometimes, I think I'm turning into Louisa, unable to face reality." She drew a long breath. "Charles is dead and by his hand. It's still inconceivable to me, but nothing will change that."

One thing likely to change was a sister's memory. Quain wondered how Mary would react if she found out the truth. *But what was the truth?*

He, too, had been surprised by Allingham's suicide. Charles had seemed a sunny sort of chap. Someone who took life as it came. *Not a brooder.* Still, Mary had hinted he'd grown secretive and morose. And Quain had seen enough of the world to know that hidden sorrows beat in other hearts, buried and unfathomed.

At first, Quain had dismissed the pictures Charles commissioned as an odd but harmless obsession. That was before disgust with the rotten enterprise took root. Still, it seemed unlikely that someone had killed Margot Miller over a collection of lewd paintings.

Were the pictures only the surface, like the scraps scavenged by mud larks at the water's edge? Was there something else in the murky depths? Quain could only guess how far Charles Allingham had waded into the mire.

In the late afternoon, a maid showed Inspector Tennant into Dr. Scott's waiting room. It had the stale, dated feel of an older medical practice winding down. The lumpy horsehair chairs needed upholstering, and the Turkish carpet bore the wear marks of many years' usage.

The doctor's office may have been worn and tired, but the man who extended his hand was shipshape. A well-tailored, still vigorous man in his late sixties with gray hair and a neat mustache offered the inspector a seat.

The doctor's medical diploma and a nautical picture held pride of place on the wall behind his desk. The print of a naval engagement showed a fleet of smoking and sinking Chinese junks succumbing to a British naval bombardment. The caption read, "HMS *Volage*."

Tennant bent and leaned the folder of Allingham's paintings against the side of his chair. When he straightened up, he saw that Scott's eyes had followed his movements.

The inspector nodded to the diploma. "I see you're a University of Edinburgh man. Do you know Doctor Andrew Lewis?"

"Not in Scotland. He was a few years my senior, but we are slightly acquainted as doctors in London often are."

"And you were a Royal Navy man, I believe. That's a dramatic print on the wall. Did you see action in the first war with China?"

"Yes. I served as the ship's surgeon on the *Volage*. That was before they converted her into a survey vessel."

"Not a very taxing assignment?" When Scott scowled, Tennant added, "I only meant that the battle in the picture looks like a lopsided victory. There can't have been many British casualties."

"Oh. Quite." He leaned back in his chair and ran his index finger across his upper lip, smoothing his mustache. "Mind you, sickness and accidents at sea kept me busy enough."

Tennant nodded and let the silence play out. He glanced around the room, his gaze lingering on three rectangles where the wallpaper was darker than the rest.

Scott cleared his throat. "I'm surprised to see you, Inspector. Surely, there are no lingering questions about Charles Allingham's suicide?"

"Yes and no. As often happens, an investigation can go far afield."

"Indeed?"

"In this case, it led me to the South Kensington Museum. And then back to you." Tennant looked to his right. "Your three Ming Dynasty paintings hung there, perhaps?

Scott blinked. "Yes. What of it?"

"May I ask where you acquired them?"

"If you must know, I bought them in Canton. We dropped anchor there for several months."

"If you bear with me, my questions will become clear. Can you tell me the times and circumstances when they were out of your possession?"

"Well . . . until recently, they hung here, as you guessed. But last December, I was persuaded to part with them, temporarily, as part of an exhibition."

"At the South Kensington's exhibition called *Pleasure Gardens*?

"That is correct."

"Other than the museum director, did anyone else have access to the paintings?"

"Well, first, they went to Charles's firm, the art publishers Allingham and Allen. The company is printing the exhibition catalog."

"Did Mister Allingham take charge of your paintings personally? I mean, did he collect them from you himself?"

Scott considered. "No . . . his manservant took them away."

"Rawlings?"

"I believe that's the fellow's name. Look here, Inspector, what is this all about?"

Tennant bent for the folder and extracted Allingham's versions of Scott's original paintings. He set them side by side on the desk. The doctor licked his lips and stared at the pictures. The ticks of the grandfather clock sounded loud, as did Scott's labored breaths.

"Where did you . . . I mean to say, who is responsible for these abominations?"

"It looks very much like Charles Allingham arranged for these copies. For his or others' . . . perusal. You knew nothing of this?"

Scott purpled. "I have no knowledge . . . I have never seen . . . Your suggestion is an outrage."

Tennant nodded. "The late Mister Allingham was responsible, then. Unfortunately for the police, he isn't available for questioning."

"I cannot speak to anything Charles might or might not have done with them."

"Versions of Chinese paintings owned by others are included in . . . shall we call it an eclectic collection of pornography? A compilation not merely for the private entertainment of a connoisseur with exotic tastes."

"How do you conclude that?"

"We have evidence that someone engraved them. The only purpose would be to print multiple copies of the salacious works for distribution. That, of course, is an offense under the Obscene Publications Act."

Scott's eyes widened. His cheeks held their high color, but he'd gathered his wits enough to say, "Your remarks mystify me, Inspector. I know nothing of these . . . works."

"What about these?" Tennant removed four other pictures. "Someone copied these from paintings lent along with yours to the museum. Friends of Mister Allingham's, the museum director said. Do you know a Mister Lionel Bruce or a Colonel Cedric Hamilton?"

"Yes."

"How do you know them, sir?"

"We're members of the same club."

"Oh? Which one is that?"

"The Topkapi."

"Charles Allingham's club."

"That's right." Scott stood, jamming the fingers of his shaking hand between the buttons of his waistcoat. "Look, I've told you all I know, and I have patients arriving. I'll bid you good day unless there's something else."

"Thank you, Doctor. I may return with other queries as our investigation moves forward. We are at work on several fronts."

As Tennant gathered the pictures, he knocked Scott's Chinese porcelain pencil holder out of place. The doctor reached across the desk to return it to its original position.

"A lovely piece," Tennant said. "So many beautiful . . . things . . . come from China these days."

The inspector closed the street door behind him, walked to the corner, and waited. A few minutes passed, and Scott hurried down the steps and waved his walking stick at a cabbie.

Rattled the old boy. Tennant smiled. *That's when blackguards fall out.*

The inspector hailed another cab and followed the doctor to the corner of East Pall Mall and Whitcomb Street. Scott mounted the steps of the Topkapi Club and disappeared through its exotic doors.

Tennant paid off the cabbie. An interview with the club's secretary could wait, and the short walk would ease the cramp in his leg, so he headed back to the Yard on foot. The rain had passed, and the London air felt cool and cleansed. *Only a temporary respite,* Tennant thought, *and a good thing, too.*

Stackpole would be released in the morning, and a little fog and mist would make trailing him easier.

CHAPTER 14

Inspector Tennant, Sergeant O'Malley, and two constables dressed as dockmen waited for the prisoner's release.

They counted eight bells from a nearby church tower. Then the iron doors swung open, and Stackpole emerged. He headed straight to Blackman Street at a rapid clip and turned right. The two coppers on opposite sides of the pavement followed while the inspector and his sergeant trailed behind.

"Heading for London Bridge, I'm thinking," O'Malley said. "Thirty minutes on foot, give or take."

The congestion made their task easy. Nothing—neither beast, 'bus, nor cart—moved quickly in the midmorning crush. Stackpole crossed the bridge and hopped on an omnibus heading east. Tennant and company followed in a hackney cab, stopping when their quarry jumped off at the West India Dock Road.

The police arrived at the most exposed part of the enterprise when their quarry turned into a narrow lane with little foot traffic. Tennant and O'Malley hung back, keeping the constables in sight.

The air was dense with the stench of tar and offloaded coal. Screeching gulls signaled that the riverfront was close. Their calls vanished when Tennant and O'Malley entered the dark tunnel of the London and Blackwall line, its railway cars thundering overhead. Tennant's forehead beaded with sweat. He sucked air between clenched teeth and focused on the light ahead. When they broke free of the tunnel, he turned away from O'Malley and drew a steadying breath. Ahead, one of the constables waited, and they caught up to him outside a cooperage on the corner of Limehouse Causeway.

Everywhere, a foreign presence was evident. A grocer and a laundry displayed signage in English and Chinese. Men wearing seamen's trousers and jackets had tied their hair in long, black braids: sailors who hailed from Hong Kong, not Hammersmith.

Tennant caught up with the constable on the corner. "Where is Stackpole?"

"He ducked into a pub three doors down. My partner gave it a minute and followed him in."

"Walk by the door," Tennant said. "Cross over and come back with the name."

The constable pulled down his cap and ambled off. He finished his circuit and returned.

"It's a pub and boardinghouse called China Sal's."

They watched the comings and goings for about ten minutes. Then the pub's door banged open, and Stackpole staggered across the pavement and tripped into the street. A stocky Asian followed. He grabbed two fists of the lanky seaman's jacket and hauled him to his feet. He growled something into Stackpole's ear, shoved him stumbling down the street, and returned to the pub. Tennant and his companions ducked behind the cooper's barrels as the seaman passed them, cursing.

"Go after him," Tennant told the constable. "The sergeant will trail you at a distance."

A minute later, the copper who'd followed Stackpole into the pub joined Tennant.

"What happened, Constable?"

"The blighter headed for the back room, so I ordered a pint and waited. After some back and forth that I couldn't hear, a man shouted, 'Those effing coolie girls belonged to me. You had no right.' A woman cut him off, saying, 'She's dead' and 'He had the papers to take them.' Then he calls her a liar and a thieving bitch, and she shouts, 'Yee, Yee.' A scuffle breaks out behind the door, and the next thing you know, it slams open. A thuggish Chinaman frog-marches Stackpole to the exit and into the street."

"We saw the rest. Sergeant O'Malley and your partner are trailing him now."

"Looks like this Yee bloke is China Sal's muscleman."

"A first-rate job, Constable. I'll take over from here. I'd rather not have anyone spot you as a copper in civvies."

"Right, guv. You'll find a pub room, an office, and a back room. Saw some groggy Chinamen wander out of it."

Inside China Sal's, a sweet, faintly floral odor replaced the usual pub-reek of ale and tobacco. The scent drifted between the strands of a beaded curtain that covered an inner doorway. *Opium*, Tennant thought, not surprised. The drug was legal in Britain, and opium had its tentacles around many of Sal's customers, merchant seamen from the East. China Sal could offer them a beer, a bed, and a pipe while they waited for an outbound clipper ship to hire a crew.

The pub room was empty save for a few idled seamen who had started drinking early. Coughs came from behind the curtain. Between the stringed beads, Tennant spotted the on-and-off glow of opium pipes.

A barman with rolled sleeves and forearms tattooed with sets of Chinese characters polished a pint glass and eyed the inspector.

"Please inform the proprietress that Detective Inspector Tennant of Scotland Yard is here to see her." When the man turned his back and picked up a second glass, Tennant said, "I know she's in the back room. If you prefer, my constables can close the premises to carry out a search for several missing persons."

A slight, dark-haired European woman in Asian dress opened the inner door. She wore a gold-colored robe in a dragon-and-phoenix pattern. Whitecapped waves lapped across the gown's hem and along the edges of the sleeves.

"Come in, Inspector."

Tennant followed China Sal into an exotic inner chamber. A low platform in the middle of the room supported three chairs and a tea table. Walnut columns etched with a lotus design rose from the corners and held up a canopy of emerald silk. A three-paneled screen painted with a landscape of mountains, clouds, and lakes divided the room. Brass-fitted cabinets lined the far wall, and he spotted the end of a table stacked with boxes stamped with a lotus motif.

China Sal nodded to a pair of rattan seats under the canopy. "Park yourself in one of 'em."

She sat opposite him, a tiny figure dwarfed by a wicker chair whose back fanned like a throne. A low rosewood table separated them. On it, a silver tray etched with palm trees held tea for one.

China Sal may have been clothed and cosseted by goods from the exotic East, but she was an East Ender, born and bred. In a Cockney accent, she asked, "Fancy a cuppa?" Without waiting for his answer, she shouted, "Yee. Another teacup."

The man carried a delicate, bowl-like cup without handles in his square fist. His broken knuckles reminded Tennant of O'Malley's, except this man's right hand had three dots tattooed in a triangle above his thumb and index finger. Yee poured, bowed, and withdrew.

China Sal palmed her cup and sipped, eyeing Tennant over the rim. She assumed a candid expression, gazing at him with violet-blue eyes fringed with dark lashes.

"So . . . a missing person at my pub. Someone's lost a Chinaman?"

Tennant settled back in his chair. "To save time and pointless evasion, I'll tell you that I know Arnie Stackpole left you in charge of his Chinese girls. They were meant for Margot Miller, and you handed them off to Herbert Rawlings."

"You know it all, luv. Nothing left to tell."

"I want to know where he took the girls. And I want Rawlings. Indeed, I do."

"Can't help you there. And I don't know the girls' whereabouts. Never asked."

"Why do I find that difficult to believe?"

"Stackpole said Margot would collect them and pay me for their room and board. Then Rawlings turns up with papers, pays me, and takes them away." Sal shrugged. "With her dead and gone, what was I to do? Right sorry I was that somebody offed her. She was a good customer and a friend."

"Customer?"

"Bought laudanum off me."

"Marked S. Cooper, London?"

"That's right, my own formula."

"I found your boxes in Margot's flat."

She tapped the side of her nose and winked. "Honey, sherry, some spices of the East, and ten percent opium. Arnie Stackpole keeps me supplied with the stuff." She cocked her thumb at the door. "And smoking it is the only thing that keeps those poor, idle buggers happy until they ship out."

"You knew why Stackpole brought those girls to London. Or you guessed."

China Sal shifted in her chair. "They were models for Margot's painting lark."

"You don't believe that. As a woman, have you no fellow feeling, no pity for—"

"Can't afford it, mate," she snapped. "And what do you know about it anyway? What women the likes of me and Margot do to survive."

Tennant looked around the room. "You look snug enough."

"You think so? You know nothing, sonny boy."

"Enlighten me."

"When my Jack hauled me off to Hong Kong, he promised a fortune. Instead, cholera got him and left me on my own with a mountain of debt. Clawed my way back, and Margot was the same. Peas in a pod, she once told me."

"For your sake, I hope not. Your friend came to a bad end. Nor was she frank with you about her activities."

"I knew the story about the girls was bollocks, but I did it to help a mate." She folded her arms into her sleeves and muttered, "Doesn't mean I liked doing it."

"What did she tell you about her 'painting lark'?"

"Gents with an itch for the East. Some blokes like 'em dusky. Fancy a 'touch of the tar brush,' as they say."

"Who? Did she mention these gentlemen's names?"

"No, but she always said they were all the same with their trousers off . . . more or less." Sal cackled. "Margot laughed at the toffs with their airs and graces and gentlemen's club."

"What club was she talking about?"

"No idea. Margot never said too much. She was nobody's fool."

"Someone got the better of her." Sal's gaze held steady. She didn't flinch when he added, "The last time I saw her, she was stretched on a slab with her throat cut."

"You think you can frighten me? Think I don't know the world's a dangerous place? Ask any woman on her own. And it's no use depending on husbands or lovers or the law to see you through." She balled her fist and rapped her chest. "China Sal looks after herself."

Tennant let a few seconds tick by. "Margot Miller thought so, too."

Sal glared at him, then shouted, "Yee! The inspector's leaving."

Tennant stood and scanned the man up and down. The inspector stood a head taller, but he wouldn't want to tangle with Yee on a foggy night.

Tennant looked back at China Sal. "A few words of advice. Women are dying, so keep this fellow close."

Yee escorted Tennant to the door and watched until he turned off the Causeway. The inspector retraced his steps to the West India Dock Road and looked for the blue lamp of Limehouse Police Station. He spotted it at number twenty-nine.

Tennant asked the duty sergeant if he'd heard any talk on the street about Chinese girls brought into the country for prostitution.

"You'd need two sets of ears for two lines of talk, sir."

"Meaning?"

"Chinamen over on Ming Street haven't a clue what they're saying down on the Causeway. Different parts of China, different languages. Still, I haven't heard a squeak about the thing you're talking about."

"I've just come from China Sal's. She claims to know nothing either."

"You think she's involved?"

"I suspect Sal's establishment is a way station only."

The sergeant grinned. "Did you meet that thug of hers, Yee?"

"Yes . . . What's the significance of that triangular tattoo on his fist? Anything?"

"Means he belongs to one of the triads, one of the Hong Kong gangs with fingers in a dozen illegal pies." He paused. "So far, Sal seems mostly on the up-and-up."

Tennant asked the duty sergeant to keep an eye on China Sal and keep him informed.

*   *   *

Sergeant O'Malley eased his bulk into Tennant's office chair, stretched his legs, and winced. "I'm knackered and mad to be out of these boots."

"And Stackpole?"

"He legged it straight for the Bunch of Grapes on Narrow Lane. Got drunk as a lord and staggered off to a rooming house three doors down after asking everyone in sight if they knew of a ship taking on a crew."

"Sounds as if he's packing it in."

"I'm thinking he hasn't a clue about Rawlings's whereabouts or what's happened to the Chinese lasses. He's cutting his losses."

"Damn it, Paddy. Without the girls, we have no reason to hold him."

"What was China Sal saying for herself?"

"Would you care to guess? She knows nothing, of course. And she's about as Chinese as I am. Born in Poplar, I'd wager, not Peking."

"Trading everything but information for the police."

"Sal gave me one thing," Tennant said, smiling grimly. "Another reason to pay a call at the Topkapi Club."

"She knows of the place?"

"Not by name, but she said Margot had dealings with 'the toffs' at a gentleman's club."

"You don't say, now."

"I think we can guess which club."

The exotic began at the Topkapi Club's entrance. The doorman might have served an Ottoman sultan. His conical red fez made the towering man look taller still. The ruby lining of his cream-colored cape gleamed in the morning sunlight when he reached to open the carved bronze door for Tennant. Polished black boots and a stiff, red-and-gold collar gave the man a military air as if he were an adjutant to some foreign potentate.

Tennant asked for the club secretary and followed the doorman down a corridor, his steps cushioned by a russet-and-gold runner on the tiled floor. It led to a domed hall whose iron-and-glass ceiling arched overhead. Three wings joined the entrance hallway, boxing in the central rotunda. When the doorman left to find the club secretary, Tennant walked to the middle of the space and took in his surroundings. Outside, the morning was cloudless, and the room flooded with light. A series of columns with geometric capitals defined the square area beneath the dome. Tiles covered in a floral arabesque of blue, cream, and gold ran around the room from the floor to about shoulder height. A horseshoe arch along the far wall opened into a hallway. A walnut bench with a filigreed back sat next to the entryway.

Tennant opened his folder to the picture on top, Griffiths's erotic version of *A Slave for the Harem*. He smiled and closed the cover. *Spot-on.*

The inspector turned at the sound of a tentative cough and faced a slight, bespectacled man. His pink-rimmed eyes and twitching nose gave him a hare-like aspect that added to the inspector's sense that he'd tumbled down a rabbit hole into Wonderland.

"Marvelous, isn't it?" the man said. "From where you're standing, 'every prospect pleases.'"

Tennant finished the quotation, "'And only man is vile?' You are the club secretary, I presume?"

"That is correct. Arthur Stewart."

"Detective Inspector Tennant of Scotland Yard. I have questions about an ongoing investigation. May I have a few moments of your time?"

"Er . . . of course." He hesitated and glanced around the hall as if he'd forgotten his way. Finally, he said, "Come to my office."

"Through here?" Tennant extended his hand toward the

horseshoe arch. It led to what Tennant guessed was the back wing of the building.

Stewart shook his head. "This way." He led the inspector in the opposite direction along a carpeted, paneled hallway.

The Topkapi's exotic impression proved only skin deep. Stewart named the interior chambers in a clipped staccato. They were rooms typical of most gentlemen's clubs: hushed, plush, and well-upholstered. Wide doorways opened into a lounge, billiards room, and library furnished with familiar Western comforts. Oil lamps lighted thick carpets, deep leather chairs, and polished mahogany tables.

Tennant asked, "Have you followed the fashion of the Reform Club? Do you have chambers and suites available for your members?"

"Yes . . . some clubmen . . . they have rooms . . . ah, residential premises . . . in the opposite wing."

Stewart's phrases darted and halted as if he wanted to consider, and possibly retract, each utterance before he chanced another.

The beginnings of a portrait gallery lined the wall opposite the library door.

"Our chairmen," Stewart said. "Two to date. Mister John Aubrey and Mister Reginald Bruce. He heads the club today."

Bruce, a Scotsman, had been painted in resplendent tartan evening wear. He wore a red-and-green kilt crisscrossed with white and yellow lines, a snowy lace neckcloth, and a black jacket with gold buttons running up the cuffs and chest. His attire overwhelmed the man: gray eyes, thinning brown hair, and doughy features formed a forgettable face.

The club secretary opened the door at the corridor's end. "After you, Inspector," Stewart said. "Please take a seat." The secretary sat behind his desk, blinking rapidly. "Now, how can I help you?"

Tennant settled in and smiled. "I won't take up too much of your time. The Yard is investigating a case that involves art . . .

well, forgery, for lack of a better word. And I'm afraid we've uncovered a range of other crimes."

"Heavens."

"Do many club members have connections to China?"

"China? Odd question." Stewart cleared his throat. "Well . . ."

"I've spoken with one of them, Doctor Preston Scott. I know of two others who collect art from the East. Indeed, they have all lent items to the exhibit at the South Kensington Museum."

"Yes. Mister Bruce, our chairman, and Colonel Cedric Hamilton. I organized the handing off."

"Directly to the museum?"

"To a publishing house for the museum catalog."

"Allingham and Allen?"

"That is correct, but . . . is there some question? Do you doubt their authenticity?"

"Not precisely. I know Doctor Scott served in the First China War. What about the others?"

The secretary shrugged. "I can't fathom the relevance, but I believe Colonel Hamilton fought in the Second."

"And Mister Bruce?

The secretary's pale, pink-rimmed eyes flickered. "He was the late Lord Elgin's great-nephew."

"And the late Lord Elgin was—"

"Appointed by Her Majesty's government as High Commissioner for China. Mister Bruce traveled there and served as his secretary."

"What is Mister Bruce's London address?"

"Here, actually. The chairman of the club has a suite of rooms."

"Tell me, is the artist John Frederick Lewis a member here?"

"No, but . . ." He narrowed his eyes as if straining to remember. "He made some sketches for a painting in our rotunda. Seven or eight years ago if memory serves."

"This one—*A Slave in the Harem?*" Tennant held up Griffiths's version.

Stewart's eyes widened, and he pointed a wavering finger. "That's not the painting the artist showed us. Lewis painted his wife fully clothed, not . . . not that naked creature. Mrs. Lewis was here when the artist displayed the finished picture in our hall."

"How puzzling. Would it also surprise you that the model who posed for this picture said it looked like the Topkapi?"

He blinked. "The Topkapi? Why I—"

"Are women—other than kitchen and cleaning staff—allowed in the club?"

He hitched his shoulders. "Certainly not. She . . . this woman . . . a model, you say? Perhaps she saw illustrations of the Topkapi *Palace*. In Constantinople. At the artist's studio."

"That's where the sultan housed his harem of sex slaves. And yet the background of this picture—the russet carpet, the arch, the tiles, the decorative bench—they're not in a Turkish palace. They're in your rotunda. That's the scene she recognized."

Stewart's hand shook as he poured water from a carafe and drank. Then his shoulders relaxed. He looked up with a rictus of a smile.

"This female must have worked on the cleaning staff. It's the only possible explanation."

"Yes." Tennant nodded. "Undoubtedly, you're right. Still, my chief wanted me to follow up. Several artists who suffered parodies of their work made a fuss."

Stewart said, "Not . . . not the artist who painted here?"

"No. And I see no point in telling him. Well, it's a tempest in a paint pot, in my opinion. Especially when I have more important matters on my plate."

"Yes. Of course. I am sure you do. Well . . ." The secretary cleared his throat. "Is there anything else, Inspector?"

"I think that's all." He took a last look at the painting before tucking it away. "A slave in a harem. Nice arrangement, for some."

Tennant exited the club and turned right. He followed the club's eight-foot brick wall and stopped at a carriage gate near the end of the property. A pair of bolted oak doors guarded the entrance. *For tradesmen?* No. He'd noticed that entry to the right of the front door.

Gates that opened into a courtyard. It matched Kathleen Morris's recollections of where they'd taken her. Tennant crossed the street. From there, he could see the top of a portico over the wall. *A covered entrance to the back of the club?* She'd described that to Julia as well.

Tennant spotted a constable near the corner of St. Martin Street. The inspector approached him, pleased that the man looked like a seasoned copper.

Tennant identified himself and showed the officer his warrant card. "Have you walked this beat long, Constable?"

"Fourteen years, sir. Give or take a few months."

"What can you tell me about the club on the corner? The Topkapi."

The copper scratched at grizzled, graying side whiskers and considered the question.

"They pulled the building to bits about ten years ago and rebuilt it. Queer sort of place with all those arches, turrets, and blokes out of the *Arabian Nights* standing out front."

"Those oak doors leading to the rear of the building . . . that entrance doesn't seem to have a purpose."

"That's what I'd have said, guvnor. Nothing much in and out. Still, back in the day, I'd spot the odd carriage or two coming and going late at night, but it's been a while since I've walked the graveyard shift." He tapped his temple. "That's a lark for young lads with sharp eyes, not old blokes like me. I'm nodding over me fire by nine o'clock these nights."

"Who's on night duty now?"

"Gordie Havers. Bright lad."

"All right, Constable. I'll clear it with your divisional chief, but I'd like you and Havers to keep a sharp eye on the place. Note any unusual activity—any uncharacteristic comings and goings. But keep your interest quiet."

"Can I know what it's about, guv?"

"So far, there are only suspicions, but we may be looking at abduction and the trafficking of young girls for prostitution. And possibly the murder of a woman who procured them and the death of another."

His face hardened. "I take great exception to that happening on my watch, sir. I have three daughters at home." He nodded. "You can rely on me."

"Thank you, Constable. Keep your eyes peeled for the next few days."

An hour later, Tennant concluded an interview with the local chief inspector and left the station house with his full co-operation.

The inspector hoped his interview with the club secretary had achieved its goal. After rattling Stewart, the inspector wanted him to believe he was satisfied with the secretary's explanations. Tennant sought to ruffle the fellow's feathers, not pluck them. He didn't want the cats inside the coop prematurely, only prowling nearby.

Can't have our pigeons flying off.

CHAPTER 15

A stretch of warm weather brought spring to the South Kensington Museum's grounds.

The sun had coaxed shy buds into bloom, and color-drenched beds bounded the carriage drive. Waves of yellow and purple crocuses surged to meet swaths of creamy primroses like foam at a tide's edge. Overhead, the fleeting green of early spring filled the trees, a hue that would soon give way to darker shades as the season matured.

On an afternoon in late April, Julia breathed the scented air, grateful Dr. Barnes was on duty at the clinic. She'd awakened that morning feeling buoyant, eager for the day. Her Saturday off was lovely, and it was a shame to go inside. But Mrs. Davies and Mister Lloyd had invited her to attend the *Pleasure Gardens* opening, and she was curious to view the collection of Chinese art. The invitation had included her grandfather and great-aunt.

The walk and unaccustomed warmth had fatigued Dr. Lewis, so he and Aunt Caroline availed themselves of a South Kensington innovation: a museum tearoom. They would join

Julia at the gallery for the exhibit's opening. She hadn't spotted Mary or Louisa Allingham, but they would surely be there. The exhibition's program included a warm tribute to Charles Allingham and his role in assembling the collection.

Julia expected to see someone else as well, and she looked around for him. Inspector Tennant planned to attend the opening to observe. When he said he'd be less conspicuous among a party, Julia suggested he write to Mister Lloyd asking to join them. She leaned forward on her bench, scanning the garden's new arrivals, wondering if he'd taken her advice.

Fifteen minutes before the gallery show's opening, Inspector Tennant strode up the carriage pathway. Julia followed the progress of his head above the crowd, his polite sidestep and tip-of-his-hat to a pair of ladies. One glanced back as she passed him. *Why not?* Julia was aware of his dark good looks, aware, too, about how glad she was to see him. Words from the Sunday service sprung to mind: *Lift up your hearts.* The invitation had always seemed a figure of speech, not a physical state. She was changing her mind about that. Perhaps her heart hadn't shifted, but its beat sped up.

When he reached the end of the main walkway, Julia rose from her bench, smiling a greeting, thinking he'd spotted her.

But he turned left and touched his hat to Mary and Louisa. "Have I arrived too late?" Julia heard him say.

Louisa Allingham smiled, dimpling. "Not at all, Richard." She took his arm. "Shall we go in?"

Julia hung back. Then she followed, feeling like the sun had passed behind the clouds.

An arch of hothouse flowers entwined with greenery curved over the closed doors of the *Pleasure Gardens* gallery. A lectern and three chairs waited at the entrance for the ceremony to begin. Julia's grandfather, her Aunt Caroline, and Mrs. Davies had found a bench along the wall. Mr. Lloyd caught her eye and nodded an invitation to join them.

At two o'clock, doors at the opposite end of the hall opened, and two gentlemen escorted Louisa and Mary into the room and handed them to their seats. William Quain and Inspector Tennant followed the party and stood behind the ladies' chairs.

Mr. Lloyd leaned in. "The older gentleman is the museum director, Mister Cole. I don't know the stout fellow next to him."

Mister Cole adjusted his glasses at the lectern and cleared his throat. "Mrs. Allingham asked me to thank you all for attending and say a few words about the exhibit." He smiled. "And not wanting to delay your enjoyment, my remarks will be brief. Charles Allingham created this collection. It exists because of his vision and his passionate conviction that a great civilization's art deserves space in British galleries. An afternoon wandering through this garden of pleasure will prove how right he was. Now, Mrs. Allingham, will you do the honors?"

Louisa stood, and the director presented a key to the widow. With Tennant's assistance, Mrs. Allingham opened the doors to the patter of polite applause.

As the gathering shuffled into the gallery, Tennant spotted Julia and walked over.

"I see you procured an invitation after all," she said.

"Miss Allingham and Louisa kindly included me."

"Front row seats, to be sure. But what are you expecting to find?"

"I'm not sure. . . . Sometimes police work is just turning up at the right time and place."

"Who is the fellow bursting his buttons? The twitchy gentleman who came in with you."

"Mister Sidney Allen."

"Charles's partner?"

"Yes." Tennant looked around. "I asked the director to be

on the lookout for members of the Topkapi Club who lent works to the exhibit. I'll ask Cole when I get him on his own."

"Here's your chance. Mary and Louisa just left his side and are heading our way, followed by Mister Quain."

Tennant excused himself, and Julia introduced the ladies and the artist to her grandfather and aunt.

"This is a fine exhibit," Lady Aldridge said. "Mister Allingham had a discerning eye."

"They're glorious pictures, aren't they?" Mary said. "I adore that first landscape with its ghostly mountains in the misty distance. It's a miniature world, marvelous and magical, hidden on the craggy cliff amid the twisty pines. I only wish..." Her voice caught. "I wish Charles were here to share the day with us." Her eyes shone, and Quain took her arm protectively.

Julia's grandfather said, "Mister Allingham shared a gift with the nation. A wonderful legacy."

"Thank you, Doctor," a composed Louisa said gravely. "Many of the paintings are new to me. My husband's last surprise."

Louisa made "widow's weeds" look exquisite, and Julia noted the perfect harmony of hat and frock. It gave her an idea. She would pursue it on Monday morning, enlisting her Aunt Caroline in the scheme.

"Thank you all for coming," Louisa said. "If you'll excuse us?"

William Quain escorted the ladies back to the pictures.

Mrs. Davies touched Julia's elbow. "May I speak with you and the inspector? It's about Jin. Yesterday, something happened that jogged her memory."

Tennant had finished his conversation with the museum director, but Julia tried and failed to catch his eye. He walked across the gallery and joined the Allingham party where Will Quain held forth. When he pointed to a detail in the picture, Louisa turned, commented to Inspector Tennant, and the company laughed.

"Come with me," Julia said to Mrs. Davies. They caught up with him as Mary and Louisa moved on to another picture.

Mrs. Davies said, "Inspector, I have something to tell you about Jin."

"She's remembered something?"

She nodded. "Yesterday, my brother took Jin and my daughters to see the changing of the guard at Buckingham Palace. The Coldstream Guards' band played that day in their kilts. Jin became agitated, but when Owen asked her what was wrong, she shook her head and refused to say. He cut the outing short and took her home."

"Where she confided in you?" Tennant said.

"Yes. About the man who raped her. A man who continued his assaults for the first weeks of her captivity. She remembered his kilt and the colors. Red and green with thin yellow and white crisscross stripes."

"Thank you, Mrs. Davies. Could she describe the man—his face?"

"I asked her about that. We were having tea, and she touched the jug. She said the man's face was like milk, and his eyes had no color. His hair, she said, was the shade of a bamboo mat."

"Thank you," Tennant said. "Anything she remembers helps the investigation."

"I'll continue to encourage her, but . . ."

"Without pressing her," Tennant said. "I understand."

"I know you do, Inspector. And we're grateful." She looked around. "Now, where is that brother of mine?" She spotted him and excused herself.

Julia said, "Your expression tells me that Jin's information is helpful."

Tennant nodded. "I saw a portrait of the Topkapi's chairman in full Highland dress, wearing a kilt of exactly those colors."

"Did her description of him fit as well?"

"Spot-on. The chairman's costume was far more colorful than the man."

Julia tilted her head, considering. "The Topkapi Club . . . Its member list must be stocked with the wealthy and powerful."

"Its chairman is particularly well connected, the cousin of an earl," Tennant said. "We're thinking along the same lines— perhaps Margot Miller extorted the Topkapi members to feather her nest."

"And paid the price."

On Monday morning, Julia and her Aunt Caroline pulled up in a carriage to Annie O'Neill's house on Aldgate High Street. But instead of descending to her flat, they walked upstairs to the dress shop above it.

A lean gentleman with thinning white hair, pince-nez clipped to his nose, and a buttonhole sprig of lily-of-the-valley hurried to meet them at the door.

"Good morning, ladies. A beautiful spring morning it is. I am the proprietor, Mister Smythe." He made a slight blow.

Julia smiled. "Good morning, sir. My name is Julia Lewis, and this is Lady Aldridge, my aunt."

His eyes popped behind his lenses. "Delighted, madame. Delighted, my lady." He bowed a little deeper the second time. "How may I assist you today, Mrs. Lewis?"

Julia let the form of address pass. "You have a delightful shop, Mister Smythe."

"You are too kind,' he said, beaming.

Lady Aldridge removed Annie's bowler from its countertop hat stand. "Charming. But a little too youthful for me, I think." She put it aside. "This paisley shawl is lovely. Will you wrap it up, Mister Smythe?"

He unfurled tissue paper with a flourish and folded it around the shawl.

Meanwhile, Julia eyed the shop floor, happy to see plenty of room for her plan.

"Mister Smythe, would you think it terribly impertinent if I asked what you pay annually in rent?" Julia smiled at his startled expression. "I have a particular reason to ask."

He coughed discreetly and murmured a sum.

"If I wrote a check for that amount, would you rent a quarter of your floor space to me for . . . say . . . two years? With an option to renew the arrangement indefinitely if we both agree. The far end of your shop is perfect for what I have in mind."

"Why . . . that is to say . . ." He adjusted his spectacles, looked at Lady Aldridge, and back at Julia. "But for what purpose, Mrs. Lewis?"

"Hats."

Twenty minutes later, a smiling Mister Smythe bowed Lady Aldridge into her carriage and watched the coach rattle down the high street. Julia stayed behind.

"Now, sir." She took his arm and walked him to the foot of the stairs. "All I must do is persuade Miss O'Neill. I will return to write that check if I succeed."

Downstairs in Annie's flat, Julia said, "I preached a marriage of frocks and hats to Mister Smythe and converted him to something more than just a solitary bowler or two."

"Hats in a dress shop?" Annie and Kathleen Morris looked at each other across the table.

"Yes, and like most converts, he is now an enthusiast. The idea is to match your hat designs with his frocks and fabrics." Julia smiled. "Don't look so surprised. Stores that carry a variety of merchandise are popping up in America and London. Soon, you and Mister Smythe could rival the likes of Harvey Nicols in Knightsbridge."

"Think of that, now, Annie," Kathleen said.

Julia nodded. "The Harvey half of the partnership is a woman, by the way."

"There will be plenty of work for the two of us, Kath."

"Between Wheatlands' and Mister Smythe, you'll be busy," Julia said. "May I tell him yes?"

When Annie nodded vigorously, Julia raised her cup and said, "Here's to new paths forward," and they clinked teacups.

"I'm wishing my Aunt Maggie was here to see it," Annie said, her eyes shining. "Her dream was to own a shop, and this is a step along the way."

"That's right, Annie," Julia said. "The first in a journey."

"And I'm wishing she was here to know you, a lady doctor. A grand thing, she'd be thinking."

"Thank you, Annie. I wish I'd known her, too."

When Annie refused her offer of help to clear the table, Julia settled back and smiled at Kathleen. "How are you feeling . . . better?"

"At first, I was knackered every afternoon, but I'm stronger now."

"And you're sleeping through the night?"

"I am that. Thank you, Doctor."

Annie called from the sink. "She's been remembering things, as well. Some of what happened to her early on with that first devil." She looked at Kathleen. "I'll crack on with the washing up while you talk to the doctor. Maybe she'll be telling the inspector so he can catch the creature."

While Annie busied herself with the dishes, Julia said, "Tell me about him, Kathleen. Anything you remember, in your own good time."

She looked down. "An old fella, he was," she whispered. "Straining at it, and not always able to . . . finish his business." She colored, and her eyes flicked to Annie. "Keeping his shirt on all the time and falling exhausted on his back with his arms up over his head. And I'm seeing his strange cuff links staring me in the face."

"What did they look like?"

"They were circles of gold with a blackish background and a strange symbol stamped into them. A pair of wings at the top of a stick, they were, with two things curling around it. Like snakes."

Julia blinked. Then she pulled out her prescription pad and pointed to the symbol at the top of a page. "Did it look like this?"

Kathleen looked up in wonder. "That's the one. 'Tis just the same."

"It's called a caduceus, Kathleen. It's an ancient medical symbol, and it's not uncommon for physicians to wear such cuff links."

"Think of that, now."

Julia colored in fury and disgust. *First, do no harm,* she thought bitterly. *The doctor's dictum.* "It was a terrible betrayal, Kathleen. I'm sorry."

Annie dried her hands and picked up Julia's pad. "He was a doctor, then, was he?"

"Most likely."

Kathleen tapped her left wrist. "They had letters on them as well."

"Can you remember them?"

"I'll not be forgetting, ever. They had a P and an S sitting on either side of the stick."

Julia stood. "Thank you, Kathleen. I'll tell Inspector Tennant."

"You'll be off, Doctor?" Annie said.

"Yes, but I'll see Mister Smythe on the way. He'll want to talk to you about the arrangements before closing shop."

"I'll never be thanking you enough for all you're doing."

Julia waved away the girl's thanks. "My Aunt Caroline and I

will know where to go for wonderful hats." She smiled. "She's Lady Aldridge, as it happens, and Mister Smythe was a bit fluttered by the title."

Julia closed the door to Annie's basement flat and headed up the stairs.

P and S—for Doctor Preston Scott?

"The duty sergeant sent this up." Sergeant O'Malley handed Inspector Tennant a note. "A porter brought it over from Doctor Lewis."

Tennant scanned it. "Well, well. Kathleen Morris has given us something interesting indeed. Look at this, Sergeant."

O'Malley read it and whistled. "The old bastard. There may be others on the medical registrar with his initials." The sergeant screwed up his face. "I'm not remembering the man's cuff links."

"I do. I'd knocked something on the man's desk. Sent a porcelain pencil dish askew, and Scott reached across to straighten it." Tennant smiled grimly. "At the time, I thought the cuff links were a harmless affectation."

"Harmful for him, I'm thinking, if we can get the lass's identification."

Tennant leaned back in his chair and contemplated the web of cracks in the ceiling plaster. "So, where are we, Paddy?"

"Two witnesses—a hatmaker and a Chinese lass—are after giving us a gammy lip, a kilt, and a set of cuff links."

"Hmm . . . when you put it that way. Still, they link Rawlings, Mister Bruce of the Topkapi, and Doctor Scott to a forced prostitution ring. But is it enough to justify a raid on a Pall Mall gentleman's club? Or to arrest a Harley Street physician?"

"Thin, I'm thinking. And the chief will be asking us how it leads to Franny Riley's or Margot Miller's killer."

"The logic is irresistible," Tennant said. "But is it proof?"

"And Stackpole, the creature. He'll be wriggling out of it,

claiming ignorance about the fate of the Chinese lasses. And as for Scott, I'm guessing he's not the only Harley Street doctor with a taste for harlots. 'Tis a long way to a murder charge."

"True. But have a word with the coppers on the doctor's beat. Ask them to note Scott's movements."

The inspector could hear Chief Inspector Clark. *You're sodding kidding me, Tennant. Cuff links and a kilt? Evidence from a hatmaker turned whore and some Chinese slag?*

"We've got to catch them in the act." Tennant opened a folder and tapped the top sheet. "This report from the local coppers . . . the Topkapi Club has been quieter than I'd like."

"Young Havers on the night beat has sharp eyes on him, so his sergeant is telling me."

Tennant ran his hand through his hair. "I hope my Topkapi visit hasn't put the wind up in that quarter. Frightened them into cautiousness."

"Something will be happening soon—Friday or Saturday, I'll wager. Promising nights for entertaining, and there's church coming up on Sunday for contemplating your sins."

"This foul trade . . ." Tennant set his jaw. "They're bringing girls into the club by carriage. I'm sure of it."

"Likely, you're right, sir."

"We'll follow the coach when it leaves the Topkapi. If we can trace it to the house where they keep the girls, we can pounce on both addresses and arrest everyone we find. Catch them all—"

O'Malley grinned. "With their trousers 'round their ankles. We'll be needing reinforcements."

The inspector nodded. "A little night duty is in order at the end of the week, and I'll talk to the chief about assigning additional constables."

"The A Division coppers will be wanting an invitation to the party. The club is on their turf."

"Sir?" A constable at the door held up a slip of paper. "A message came in from the Limehouse station."

"I'll take it, lad." O'Malley opened and read it. "Only a line from China Sal, but she's ready to talk."

Tennant swung out of his chair. "Let's hear what the lady has to say."

China Sal invited the inspector and his sergeant to sit underneath the canopy in her exotic lair.

O'Malley eyed the rattan chairs warily. "T'will be a pile of matchsticks with me in the middle if I park myself on that."

Sal cackled. "Give it a go, Sarge, it's sturdier than it looks."

O'Malley lowered himself by inches and perched on the edge as if ready to bolt.

China Sal had exchanged her golden phoenix-and-dragon robe for a tangerine version covered with butterflies and lilies. She poured three handle-less cups of tea from a blue-and-white service and handed one to O'Malley. He cradled it gingerly in his sizable fist.

"No fears, luv." She winked. "It's easily replaced. Made in Staffordshire, not Shanghai. Drink up."

Tennant took a sip and eyed Sal over the rim. She fiddled with the tie that secured the flap of her robe and tapped a silk-slippered foot on the platform's carpet. China Sal no longer seemed the indomitable empress, secure on her wicker throne.

The inspector let the silence play out. Finally, he said, "Our Limehouse colleagues say you have something to tell us." He sounded only mildly interested.

She crossed her arms. "I don't want trouble . . . but I don't want you rozzers thinking China Sal's not helpful to the police. It's about that bugger. The one that's got the gammy lip."

"Rawlings."

"I know you're looking for him. You said so last time you

was here." She tilted her head. "How much is the sod worth to you?"

Tennant considered. "What's your asking price?"

"Ten quid."

"What does that buy?"

"The name of a street. The backcourt where he's holed up."

"And you know this . . . how?"

"The bleeder came in here yesterday. Looking for Stackpole. So don't I send for my man, and Yee follows him."

Tennant eyed her levelly. He reached into his breast pocket and pulled out his money clip. He removed three notes and fanned them across the tea table.

"Three pounds now. Two more if your information proves accurate."

Sal scowled. "Five quid's not—"

"You realize I can have you arrested for withholding evidence? Come now, Sal." Tennant tsked. "Don't be greedy."

She smoldered for a bit, then snatched up the bills. "Rawlings took the Blackwall 'bus clear across the Commercial Road to Charing Cross. Then he footed it to Denmark Street."

"In St. Giles?"

"That's right. The bloke slipped through an alley into the pokey lane behind it. Denmark Court."

O'Malley said, "And you'll be telling us the house number?"

Sal shook her head. "Yee wasn't quick enough. But Denmark Court is a dead end with a handful of houses. Rawlings went into one of them." She waved the notes at the sergeant. "For three lousy quid and two more only promised, you don't get it on a silver plate."

They left Sal's and returned to the Commercial Road, where O'Malley spotted the blue sign of the Blackwall omnibus stop.

Tennant raised his hand. "A hansom will be quicker."

After they settled into the cab, O'Malley said, "Are we

thinking Rawlings has the girls stashed in a house in St. Giles and takes them on to the club?"

"It's a convenient distance." Tennant rapped for the cabbie's attention and said, "Pall Mall." When O'Malley looked at him, the inspector said, "We'll test the route from the Topkapi to St. Giles."

When they reached the club, Tennant asked the cabbie, "What's the most efficient route from here to Denmark Street in St. Giles?"

The man scratched under his brim with his whip handle, considering. "Haymarket to Shaftsbury to Charing Cross Road, and Bob's your uncle, guvnor. You're there."

"Take us."

Tennant paid off the driver when they reached their destination in St. Giles.

The neighborhood was one of London's worst rookeries, where disease and delinquency ran rampant. Terraced brick houses leaned into each other along narrow streets. Tennant and O'Malley passed secondhand clothing stalls, gin shops, and reeking fishmongers' barrows, glistening with herring for a half-penny each. Ragged, soot-smeared children flogged limp cabbages and bits of kindling from curbside baskets.

"Sweet, suffering Jesus," O'Malley muttered. "St. Giles is bleaker than the worst of Dublin's slums."

They found the alley to Denmark Court, but Tennant walked on. "Let's not go blundering in," he said. "Not just yet, Paddy."

"The lane's just wide enough for a four-wheeler to transport the girls."

Tennant spotted a sign that read, FIRST FLOOR OFFICES TO LET, WAREHOUSING IN THE REAR.

"I wonder. . . . Give me a name, Sergeant. Someone with a keen eye and an iron backside who can sit all day in a records' office."

O'Malley grinned. "That's Williams to the life. He always

prefers parking it to legging it, and the man's a human ferret. He'll winkle it out if there's something to be found."

"Let's get him on the property conveyance records for St. Giles. Give him a list of names. Rawlings, Sidney Allen, Charles Allingham, Doctor Scott, and Lionel Bruce."

"You're thinking someone owns that house on Denmark Court."

Tennant looked around. "Have you spotted a constable on this beat?"

"We could use some eyes on the place." O'Malley glanced over his shoulder and made a sharp intake of breath. "Mother of God. There's the creature, now."

Rawlings stood at the entrance to Denmark Court. He had his head down and his hands cupped, concentrating on lighting his cigar in the whipping wind. He took three long draws and flicked his match into the gutter. Then he turned right and walked away from them.

"Well, well," Tennant said. "The man hasn't emigrated to America after all."

"Heading for Charing Cross Road." O'Malley made to go after him.

Tennant grabbed his elbow. "I don't want him to spot you. We've run our man to ground, and that's enough for now. We'll flush him out when we're ready."

"Rawlings is in our sights, at last," O'Malley said. "You owe China Sal another two quid, I'm thinking."

At the Yard the following morning, a livid Chief Inspector Clark laid into Tennant for not arresting Rawlings on the spot.

"Let me get this straight. You had the bleeding valet on a plate and let him go? By God, Tennant, the time you've wasted looking for the bugger, and he's still in the wind?"

"Sir, when I brief you on our plan, I think you'll agree to hold off on Rawlings."

"You think so, do you?" Clark pulled out his pocket watch. "You have two minutes to convince me."

"The plan is to bag all our birds at once. We have coppers on the spot, watching the Topkapi Club, Doctor Scott's office on Harley Street, and the comings and goings from Denmark Court. In addition, Constable Williams is with the local clerk-of-the-peace, searching through the conveyance records for St. Giles."

"For what purpose?"

"To identify a property transfer on Denmark Court, a deed that ties one of our suspects to the prostitution ring."

"Explain how this helps us catch the sod who murdered the Riley girl and the Miller woman."

"Thieves fall out. Once we've arrested them for prostitution—"

"The threat of a few months in the nick for running a brothel, and you think someone will turn Queen's evidence and finger the killer? You're dreaming, Tennant," Clark sneered.

"With respect, sir, he'd face more than that. We have witnesses to kidnapping, trafficking girls from abroad, and procuring minors for prostitution. And Margot Miller's death must be tied to these dark deeds."

"All right, all right. Get on with it. But remember: a bird in the hand, Tennant. Don't leave Rawlings hanging too long." Clark snatched up some papers and waved the inspector out of his office.

Or I'll be twisting in the breeze, Tennant thought. He hated to admit how much of his case was supposition.

But that afternoon, Constable Williams struck gold in a dusty office. Twice.

Williams unfolded two documents and spread them on Tennant's desk.

"A beady-eyed little bugger in specs huffed and puffed about releasing the records," the constable said. "Told him to hop it. They were wanted at the Yard."

O'Malley leaned over the documents and whistled when he spotted the same buyer's name on both deeds. "Our old friend Sidney Allen is after buying number two on Denmark Court. And he's up to no good at an address across the way, at St. Giles Passage."

Tennant picked up the second deed. "Number twenty-nine . . . it's described as a warehousing and factory site."

"St. Giles Passage," O'Malley said. "Sounds like a nice, secluded spot for getting up to wickedness. And we'll need eyes on Allen's company on Paternoster Row."

"And his house in Chelsea. I'll see to it," the inspector said. "Let's talk to some of the local bobbies about the warehouse. Discreetly, for the moment."

The St. Giles copper told Tennant, "It's a printing business, guv. Been here six or seven years, I'd say."

O'Malley said, "Anything dodgy about it?"

"Never been any trouble, as far as I know. Still, I've heard some grumbling along the street."

"About what?" Tennant asked.

"They don't employ local lads, and they keep themselves to themselves. Makes for bad feeling." The constable grinned. "Not enough drinking in the neighborhood establishments to keep the publicans happy."

"Anyone around these parts who might be wise about the place?" O'Malley asked.

The constable considered. "You might try the Swan. Slip the barman five shillings. Ted, by name. He knows most of the local chatter."

They took his advice. O'Malley sank a Guinness at the pub,

and Tennant bought an ale for the barman, pushing a crown in Ted's direction. It bought him a story about the man's brother.

"Dan's a plumber," he said. "They called him in to fix a leak in the printshop's warehouse. Maybe a year ago." The barman tapped his nose. "My brother saw a few things and told me about 'em."

"What things?" Tennant asked.

The barman leaned in on his elbow. "You've heard of French postcards? Well, Dan said they're nothing compared to what they're printing in there."

O'Malley made a two-note whistle. "You don't say, now."

Ted winked at the sergeant. "Singe off your eyelashes just looking at 'em, says Dan."

On Friday morning, Tennant read the night report about the surveillance of the Topkapi with satisfaction. Gordie Havers from the local division had observed the club from his usual beat. At the same time, a plainclothes constable from the Yard got closer, keeping to the shadows near the Topkapi's back gates, listening for movement. A third copper had idled on Pall Mall with a hansom at the ready. Around nine o'clock, a carriage turned at the entrance and clattered up to the club; the wooden doors swung closed behind it. When it left, the hansom had orders to follow it.

A few minutes past twelve, the detective constable stepped from the shadows, struck a match to light his cigar, and walked away. Constable Havers at the corner of Pall Mall spotted the sign and signaled the copper in the cab.

A few minutes later, a coach rolled by Havers. The following hansom kept its distance, but it had been easy to trail. As Inspector Tennant had predicted, the coachman drove directly from Haymarket to Denmark Court.

A St. Giles constable had noted the time the carriage passed him. And a copper who looked more like a bundle of rags than a man stirred at the curb and lifted his head. He'd watched the carriage stop at the first house on the north side—number two—and discharge its passengers. The coachman and a guard had bundled three girls down the side of the house. Then a door slammed.

Tennant looked up from a second scanning of the report when a constable interrupted with stunning news.

Doctor Preston Scott had been found dead at his house.

CHAPTER 16

Tennant looked around the doctor's study.

For the second time, the shabbiness of Scott's furnishings surprised him. That, and the nautical touches, reminded the inspector of the man's seedy medical office. Odd because suits from a storied Savile Row tailor filled the bedroom wardrobe, and Tennant had unearthed Scott's financial documents from a desk drawer. The doctor had over ninety thousand pounds invested in securities, and his liquid resources amounted to another ten thousand.

A well-dressed miser. Tennant was never surprised by the contradictions in human nature.

The inspector circled an upended chair. Scott had fallen from it to the floor and died in agony. He'd clawed away his cravat, torn off his collar, and crawled a few feet before collapsing. Tennant crouched and retrieved a shirt stud from the middle of the carpet.

The doctor who had pronounced Scott dead looked at his contorted frame and twisted face, frozen in the grimace of death. "Strychnine poisoning, I'd say."

Tennant had asked, "Suicide?"

"Doubtful. It's a horrible death. No sane physician would use it when he had a chemist's shop of poisons at his disposal. There are easier ways to exit this world."

Tennant had asked the doctor to look through Scott's medications cabinet. On a middle shelf, he found a half-empty bottle of strychnine tablets.

"More than enough to do the job," the doctor had said. "But so would a half dozen other pills and potions."

Two bottles of expensive whiskey stood on the side table: two bottles of the same eighteen-year-old single malt, Royal Lochnagar. *Scott drank as well as he dressed.* One was empty; the other was missing about an inch of liquid. They would send them for analysis along with the glass from the floor. The D Division coppers had removed the body to the police station on Marylebone Lane, and Tennant had sent for Julia to perform the postmortem.

O'Malley returned from his reconnoiter of the house, waving a book. "From the doctor's bedside drawer." He passed it to the inspector.

Tennant opened to the title page. "Well, well. *Pleasure Gardens,*" he said, then flipped through the rest of the book. "Pleasures indeed. All the altered Chinese paintings gathered between two covers." Tennant returned it to O'Malley. "It's evidence that Allingham's collection was published."

"An easy guess who printed them, I'm thinking."

"Did the servants have anything useful to say?"

"The doctor wasn't one for keeping a large staff. There's no cook. The man was eating his meals at the Topkapi most nights. The housekeeper would leave a sandwich on the evenings he stayed home."

"Is she a reliable witness?"

"Ancient and deaf as a post. Heard nothing in the night and didn't go downstairs after eight o'clock."

"Other servants?"

"A young housemaid. She's the one who found him, poor lass."

"And the front door?"

"Locked but not on the chain. They'd fastened the windows and bolted the back door." O'Malley circled the stained carpet. "Are we thinking the creature knew we were closing in and took the easy way out?"

"Not a painless death, according to the doctor. Perhaps someone removed a weak link in the chain."

"There's the single glass and no evidence he had company."

"There are three others on the shelf. Someone might have replaced their glass and slipped away, leaving the door unchained."

" 'Tis possible."

"Still, we don't want to get ahead of ourselves, Paddy."

"Sir?" A young constable with an empty crate came into the room.

"Pack up the bottles and the glass," Tennant said. "And take the three clean ones as well. Have them tested for traces."

Tennant ran his finger along a line of navy-blue, leather-bound casebooks. He stopped at the end of the row and slipped two volumes from the shelf, the record of Scott's patients for the past two years. He looked around a final time and opened the door for the officer with the crate.

"We're finished here, Paddy. Let's hear what Doctor Lewis has to say."

Julia stood at the head of the autopsy table. Her gaze flicked to Inspector Tennant and back to Dr. Scott's corpse.

The room was small, and the bulbous glass shades of two oil lamps glowed brightly over the examining table. Julia had nearly reached the end of the procedure. She listened to Tennant struggle to control his breathing. He didn't have to stand over her while she worked, but he did it time and again as if testing himself in a trial by ordeal. *Why?* Julia wanted to ask him. She looked at his strained, pale face, and her heart ached. *Who shares your burdens? No one*, she suspected. She wanted to cross the room and take his hands. Draw him close and whisper, *Tell me.*

"Richard . . ." Her voice sounded strained to her ears.

He dragged his gaze from the body and looked at her. "Yes?"

"I . . ." She turned away to look in her medical bag. "I'm nearly finished. I'll meet you outside, shall I?"

"Very well."

She heard the doors swing shut. *What a coward I am.* Then, she drew a needle from her bag, threaded it, and sutured the Y-shaped opening she'd cut into Scott's cadaver.

Twenty minutes later, a pale but collected Tennant asked, "Have you any reason to doubt strychnine poisoning?"

"No. That twisted jaw is a telltale, and the body shows signs of asphyxia. There is no other obvious cause of death, although we'll wait for the analysis of the whiskey and stomach contents to be sure."

"Do you agree that suicide is unlikely?"

"I've never witnessed a strychnine death, but descriptions in the medical literature are harrowing. The victim suffers violent convulsions and suffocation as the drug paralyzes breathing.

"A horrible death."

"Doctor Scott would have known what he faced. It seems an unthinkable choice."

"Murder, then." Color had crept back into Tennant's face, and his expression darkened. "We've drawn our net carefully, but if someone killed Scott to silence him . . ."

"Could his murder be unrelated?"

"A fantastic coincidence, but I must consider it. Perhaps an angry patient?" He smiled. "Which leads me to beg a favor—a task outside your role as a medical examiner."

"You intrigue me, Inspector."

"I have Scott's casebooks for the past two years. I've looked at last week's entries, but nothing stands out. And some of the medical terms and abbreviations defeat me."

"You'd like me to review them?"

"Yes."

"A homicidal patient with a grudge? As a doctor, I confess, it's an uncomfortable thought." She held out her hands for the books. "I'll take a look."

"Thank you," he said, passing them to her. "I may be wasting your time. I still think it's Rawlings or Allen. Someone else tied to their foul business."

"Seems likely, given all that has happened."

"A request to carry out raids went up the Met's chain of command. Yesterday, it was approved. We hope to drop the net tonight and bag the scoundrels."

"Thank God. Finally, a measure of justice for Jin and Kathleen and all the other girls."

"It comes in many forms." Tennant's eyes glinted. "I'm on my way to Fleet Street to see an old friend of yours. Someone who will mete out justice in his inimitable way."

"Fleet Street? Not Johnny Osborne?"

"None other. God's gift to journalism."

"I suppose you know what you're doing."

"Watch me."

Julia had an hour before she had to be back at the clinic. She wanted fresh air, exercise, and time to think about Richard.

She knew he'd been injured in the Crimea. He mentioned recovering in the military hospital at Scutari. Julia remembered from childhood her grandfather's friend who barely survived an artillery barrage at Waterloo. Forty years later, shaking still gripped him during thunderstorms.

She knew there were no ready cures for such injuries. *Still, to bottle it up* . . . She had to find the right time and place to coax him to confide in her.

Julia heard her name and looked up, surprised to find herself on Harley Street. A familiar figure descended a set of steps she knew well. Mister Lloyd had exited her Uncle Max's offices.

He raised his hat and smiled. "Are you here to see Doctor Franklin?"

She shook her head. "Just hunting for a cab to take me to Whitechapel."

Lloyd looked over her shoulder and raised his walking stick. "Shall we share this one? It can drop me at Carteret Street and take you to the clinic."

"With pleasure."

When they'd settled into the hansom, Lloyd said, "I had a note from Inspector Tennant. He asked if I'd make myself available tomorrow. He may need someone who can interpret Cantonese."

"I was with him this past hour. He called me in to perform a postmortem on a doctor."

"And I just spent an hour with a live one. Doctor Franklin. He performed some tests, but I'm afraid the results aren't good." He shrugged. "I was hardly surprised, but I consulted him at my sister's insistence and on your grandfather's recommendation."

"I'm sorry."

"Scarlet fever leaves its damage behind. In my case, it's severe. Still, I'll depart this world knowing my brother-in-law left his family well-provided."

"That is a comfort, I'm sure."

The carriage trundled along. Lloyd broke a silence stretch.

"The source of his family's wealth always troubled Gareth. They made their fortune in the sugar trade. Tainted money earned off Black backs and the sweat of enslaved labor. That's why the trafficking of girls like Jin has a tragic resonance for my sister and me."

"I understand all too well. The Lewis fortune has murky origins. It goes back several generations to a soldier-adventurer in India, so we've tried to put some of the money to good use."

"Well, I hope I can do some good for Inspector Tennant tomorrow." He touched her forearm to draw her gaze. "My dear, if I weren't such an old crock with a dicky heart, I'd give your inspector a run for his money."

Julia smiled with a slight shake of her head.

He took his hand away. "Now, don't tell me it's not a race. I have eyes in my head."

The cab had pulled up to the address on Carteret. Lloyd got out, handed the cabbie a few coins, and directed him to Fieldgate Street.

Before the hansom rattled away, Lloyd leaned into the cab. "He's a good man, the inspector." He stepped back and raised his hat in farewell.

That night, Tennant, O'Malley, and ten officers waited in the shadows.

"The crawling clock," the sergeant said. " 'Tis the worst of it now."

The inspector dared not risk a light to check his pocket watch. But within a quarter hour, he heard the chimes and counted nine bells from the clock tower at Westminster.

"Damn it to hell. Where are they?" he muttered to O'Malley.

The sergeant touched his sleeve. "Look."

A carriage had turned left from East Pall Mall, and the lights from its dual coach lamps drew nearer.

"All right, lads," O'Malley said in a low voice. "Hold your places and get ready."

The four-wheeler clattered and stopped at the back entrance of the Topkapi Club. In under a minute, someone drew the bolts, the doors swung inward, the carriage rolled forward, and the gates banged shut behind it.

O'Malley clapped a constable's shoulder. "Go, lad." The young policeman sped to the wall with his partner. One officer braced himself against the brickwork and gave a leg up to the other copper, who inched his eyes over the top. After a short wait, he held up three fingers.

Three girls had exited the carriage.

Tennant struck a match and drew it in a line. A copper at the corner relayed the signal to three officers in separate hansoms. They sped to St. Giles, Limehouse, and Chelsea. There, coppers waited to raid the brothel, arrest Arnie Stackpole at his rooming house, and take Sidney Allen into custody.

The constable at the wall dropped down. "Two blokes smoking at the entrance. And the driver's up in the coachman's seat."

"Let's give it a few minutes," Tennant said.

O'Malley said grimly, "We'll let the party get started."

Five minutes later, Tennant sent the pair of constables back to the wall. At O'Malley's signal, one man got up and over, hung by his hands, and dropped. O'Malley called, "Now, lads," and eight coppers with drawn truncheons massed outside the gates and waited for the doors to swing open.

At that point, they abandoned all attempts at stealth. Bolts screeched, gates banged, and boots pounded up the drive.

The doorman's head jerked up. "What the bleeding—"

An officer knocked the man's pipe from his teeth, and his partner seized the doorman by the shoulders. Two others dragged the coachman from his seat while Tennant, O'Malley, and a third constable cornered a gaping man with a cleft lip. The sergeant clapped him on the shoulder.

"Good evening, Mister Rawlings," Tennant said.

O'Malley twisted the man's arm behind his back. "Sure, we've been searching for donkey's years, and here you are at last."

"Hand him off to the constables, Sergeant. Mister Rawlings can sit in the police wagon, contemplate his many sins, and meditate on the virtue of cooperation."

The acrobatic duo who had scaled the wall frog-marched Rawlings to the police wagon.

"And now you, boy-o," O'Malley said to the doorman. "You'll be directing us to the girls inside if you know what's good for you."

The man swallowed hard. Then he led them through the back entrance and down a carpeted hallway, where he pointed to three doors.

Tennant asked, "Are they locked?" The doorman shook his head. "Which room belongs to the club chairman, Mister Bruce?"

The man pointed a shaking finger at a fourth door. "Bruce isn't here tonight."

"Hell and damnation," Tennant muttered. He waved O'Malley and three pairs of constables forward. "All right, Sergeant."

"Now, lads," O'Malley ordered, and the lead constable threw open the doors.

Ten minutes later, constables escorted three stunned girls from the rear of the Topkapi Club and into a second police wagon. They'd found two young women in stages of undress, so the officers told them to gather up their clothes and wrap themselves with blankets. The third girl told O'Malley she was thirteen, but he doubted she was that old. He found her alone in her room, dressed and waiting on the bed.

The cooperative doorman said, "Her gent never turned up. Surprising, since he ordered the girl for tonight." The man lowered his voice. "He's a member of Parliament and likes 'em young. He's always here on Fridays and Saturdays when the House of Commons sits."

They arrested the two men they found with the girls. Since sex with a prostitute wasn't against the law, the charge would be kidnapping. They'd appear in magistrate's court and be held overnight for further questioning.

The men, braces hanging, trouser bands clutched in one fist and shoes in the other, shuffled into the police wagon in stocking feet. Rawlings and the coachman waited inside. Tennant had sent a pair of constables to the club's front office to arrest the chairman's secretary. They marched him handcuffed, looking like a terrified rabbit cornered by yapping hounds, his round, staring eyes magnified by fear and his spectacles.

O'Malley slammed the wagon door. "Are we thinking they'll face the music or walk free?"

"We'll do everything in our power, Paddy," Tennant said. "And, more immediately, they'll face a tune of a different sort."

"And what would that be?"

"At lunchtime, I ran into Johnny Osborne at his local on Fleet Street, so I stood him a pint. I wouldn't be surprised if our newspaper friend appears in magistrate's court tonight."

"The buggers will be roasting on the grill of public opinion before long." O'Malley grinned. "Never thought I'd be saying it, but God bless Johnny Osborne and the free press."

On Saturday morning, the raid on Sidney Allen's printshop and warehouse proceeded as planned. Allingham's lewd artbooks proved to be a tiny province within an expansive pornographic empire. Constables seized and carted off boxes of books, prints, and picture postcards of the "French" variety. Then the police arrested the manager and padlocked the premises.

Later in the afternoon, Tennant returned to the Yard to report the operation's many successes. But Chief Inspector Clark was livid about a pair of failures.

"What about that Parliament sod who slipped through the net at the Topkapi?"

"The Honorable Alistair Gathorne-Hardy," Tennant said. "The doorman expected him, but he failed to show up. Interesting that Gathorne-Hardy shares his unusual surname with the government's home secretary."

"They're bloody cousins, damn it, and the Yard reports to the blighter." Clark clenched his jaw. "I hate this shite, this old boy's bollocks." He looked Tennant up and down. "All right for some," he said, and threw himself into his chair.

Tennant said, "There's no way to prove he warned his cousin."

"And if we make an unsupported accusation against the home secretary . . ." The chief slammed his fist on his desk, rattling everything on it. "It will mean our heads."

"I believe someone alerted Sidney Allen, as well."

The publisher was their second failure. Allen had slipped out the servants' entrance of his house, emptied his bank account at a Chelsea branch, and vanished.

"We've sent word to all the ports," Tennant said. "My bet is on Dover."

"Doing a moonlight flit to the Continent? Likely, I'd say." Clark scowled at his junior. "Do you think Allen killed those women and Doctor Scott?"

"That is the question."

"I want a sodding answer, damn it," Clark shouted. "Lean into Rawlings and Stackpole. Put the squeeze on all the little fish you netted with them." Clark waved him to the door. "Get on with it, man."

*   *   *

Late Saturday evening, Julia regarded a bleary-eyed Inspector Tennant as he sat across from her grandfather in their library.

"It doesn't take a medical degree to prescribe a good eight hours of sleep. What do you say, Grandfather?"

"I concur. That's two doctors telling you what you already know, Richard."

The corner of the inspector's mouth ticked up. "I haven't managed that over the past three days together."

Mrs. Ogilvie brought in a tray with sandwiches and a pitcher of beer and placed it on the table next to Tennant.

"I bet you've eaten as little as you've slept," Julia said.

"You'd win that wager." Tennant reached for a sandwich. "Thank you, Mrs. Ogilvie."

Julia had never seen him so hollow-eyed and exhausted. He looked as if he'd aged ten years. Frustration had added to the toll: Sidney Allen was still at large, and Herbert Rawlings had been cooperative only up to a point.

"The man stumbled over himself to tell us all he knew about Allen's prostitution scheme," Tennant said. "Bringing in girls from China, tricking and drugging locals, trolling the streets of the East End looking for pretty children because one of the gentlemen preferred the very young."

Dr. Lewis said, "And all this was happening at the Topkapi?"

"There was a club within the club, conceived and orchestrated by Allen with the club chairman's connivance, Reginald Bruce. Seven members had rooms along the back corridor with a convenient separate entrance. Among themselves, they called it the Harem."

Julia said, "How utterly revolting."

"Allen catered to their tastes. The very young. Asians— whatever the members' predilections, Sidney Allen supplied it.

Two girls were artists' models, groomed the way they'd ensnared Kathleen Morris and the other shopgirls who went missing."

"So Chief Inspector Clark should have combined the cases from the beginning," Julia said.

Tennant nodded. "All the girls shared one characteristic: they were virgins. Freedom from venereal infection was the paramount concern. That and . . ."

"And what?"

"According to Rawlings, several gentlemen enjoyed the fear and pain a forced deflowering inflicted."

"Barbarous," Dr. Lewis said. "I've met Reginald Bruce. Dined in his company at the Athenaeum. Did you take the brute into custody?"

"He was in Scotland during the raid. Still, I'm confident I can make a case against him. I've recommended that the Scottish police arrest him. It's gone up the chain of command."

"Recommended?" Julia said. "Surely, Rawlings's evidence and that of the girls removes all doubt."

Tennant's head dropped against the chair back and he said, tiredly, "We shall see."

Julia asked, "What about Franny Riley and Margot Miller? What has Rawlings said about their deaths?"

"Nothing. Nothing to the purpose, that is."

"Not even a denial?" Julia said.

"At first, my questions shocked the fellow. That he was under suspicion of murder stunned him. Struck him near dumb, in fact. Then he was volubly terrified. He stuttered and babbled and cried like a baby."

"Well, he would deny it, wouldn't he?" Dr. Lewis said. "Facing the hangman's noose."

"My judgment isn't infallible, but if Rawlings lied, he's a consummate actor and should go on the stage."

Julia topped up his glass of beer. "What about the girls?"

"They held seven at a time to . . . serve the gentlemen of the

Topkapi harem. If the men tired of them, they were prostituted to others at the St. Giles house. Constables freed four girls from that hell. Mister Lloyd has been of immense help dealing with the young women from China."

Julia said, "I ran into him yesterday on Harley Street."

Tennant caught her eye and smiled faintly. "Yes . . . so he told me."

Julia thought of his parting words in the cab and wondered what he said.

"Of the two Chinese girls they had in their claws, only one spoke Cantonese. Mister Lloyd brought in a colleague who is fluent in Mandarin. They and the other girls tell a consistent story of deception, drugs, imprisonment, and rape."

"What will happen to the girls?" Julia asked. "Surely, the authorities won't charge them with prostitution."

"No. But their testimony will form the core of kidnapping and enslavement charges. If they come to trial—"

"If?" she said, startled.

"No doubt, the gentlemen in custody will mount a vigorous defense, pleading ignorance of the girls' origins."

"Damnable," Doctor Lewis muttered.

"Still, there will be a rough sort of justice, even if they manage to evade the law." Tennant sat forward in his chair. "Do you have the *Sunday Telegraph* delivered? If not, you may want to send out for it tomorrow. Johnny Osborne has promised to splash the story and the men's names across its pages."

Julia said, "The *Telegraph*? Osborne no longer writes for the *Illustrated London News*?"

"He told me the weekly *Illustrated* offered insufficient scope for his genius."

"I'll let that remark pass," Julia said. "Where will the poor girls go?"

"There, again, it's Mister Lloyd to the rescue. He and his fellow clergyman-interpreter will take in the Chinese girls."

"And the others? What will happen to them?"

"Mister Lloyd knows of a home for the others called Mercy Cottage. It's a refuge for 'fallen women' that minimizes moralizing and maximizes sympathy and practical help."

"Thank goodness for his kindness."

"Mister Lloyd attends Mercy Cottage twice weekly for prayer and counseling. And singing." Tennant smiled. "He said the girls prefer it over preaching."

Dr. Lewis said, "The man and his mission are well matched."

"About Charles Allingham . . ." Julia looked into the fire. "Was he involved in—"

"Rawlings says the pornography scheme was the extent of Allingham's entanglement. Sidney Allen recruited Margot Miller to procure the girls for 'the Harem.' Allingham was a club member but hadn't a room in the Harem."

"Do you believe Rawlings?"

The inspector shrugged. "I see no reason the fellow would lie to protect a dead man."

"I'm glad for Mary and Louisa," Julia said. "Although what he did was sordid enough."

"The 'artistic' collections made a tidy profit, according to Rawlings. They turned things around for Allingham's foundering firm. The books sold for thirty pounds each. We found shipping details for their domestic and international clientele at the factory. It included some eye-popping names."

"What about the murder of Franny Riley," Julia said. "Could it have been Rawlings?"

Tennant shook his head. "According to the girls, he showed up later. The timing places him at the brothel *after* Franny's death. And none of them ever saw the girl who was locked away. I'm convinced it was Franny, but I can't prove it."

They sat for a few moments, listening to the fire crackle. Then, Julia clapped her hands to her skirts, pushed herself up, and stood before Tennant's chair. She extended both her hands. "Up," she said, and he allowed her to help him to his feet. 'You must be longing to go to bed."

A corner of his lips turned up. "Longing . . . indeed."

His slight smile, the flicker in his eyes, and his tone of voice made his meaning plain. Julia felt a flush rise. He held on to her hands, and she wondered if he could feel her beating pulse. Finally, he released his grip, and she turned.

"Come, Grandfather, you're next."

At the door, Dr. Lewis patted the inspector on the arm. "Richard, my boy, you've done fine work these past weeks."

"It's back to the beginning for the murders, I'm afraid. I've missed something." He sighed. "I'll take Sunday morning off, go for a long walk, and clear my head. Then I'll start again."

Julia retrieved Tennant's hat and handed it to him. "I've started on Doctor Scott's journals. Nothing so far, only that he was mean about money. Gloating over pennies and farthings saved."

"People are unaccountable. The fellow was rich."

"He was also incredibly vain. He recorded every little compliment, especially if it came from Lady So-and-So or the Honorable Mrs. Whatsis." Julia shrugged. "But I'll soldier on with it. Something might turn up."

"Thank you." Tennant glanced over his shoulder at the waiting carriage. "And thank you, sir, for the services of Mister Ogilvie."

"My pleasure, my boy."

Julia smiled. "As your sergeant would say, 'It's knackered you are,' and you'll be glad of a ride."

After a long night's sleep, Inspector Tennant hiked through Hyde Park to Green Park and back again.

He'd pushed his leg to the limit and looked around for a pub with a Sunday license. He ate a ploughman's lunch and then took a cab to Dr. Scott's address on Harley Street. He wanted another look at the doctor's checkbook. Earlier, Tennant had noted the considerable balance, but a thorough examination of the entries was in order, so he settled behind Scott's desk and started reading.

Tennant flipped through the counterfoils. The doctor had been a meticulous creature of habit, writing predictable checks for identical amounts, month after month until . . .

Starting in October, Scott had written a monthly check for twenty pounds in cash. He'd issued the last one in February.

The inspector inched out the stiff bottom drawer. There, he found stacks of canceled checks returned by the bank. Tennant sorted and found the ones made out for twenty pounds; Margot Miller had countersigned them all. The payments stopped the month of her murder.

Blackmail? But how could she have threatened Scott without endangering herself? *Twenty pounds is the going rate. . . .* Perhaps she was supplying inexperienced girls for the doctor, getting around Allen, and keeping both halves of the fee. Both theories provided a motive for killing Margot Miller. *But who murdered Scott?*

Bloody hell. Tennant shoved the materials back in their drawers. He locked up and left for Russell Square, where he asked his housekeeper for dinner on a tray in the library. After he finished, he poured himself a whiskey and stared into his fireplace.

Sidney Allen? Maybe Scott told him about Miller's blackmail, and the publisher decided to eliminate both loose cannons.

Damn it, Allen is still in the wind.

Tennant sat all evening in his chair, thinking about a poisoning, a stab wound to the neck, and a second poisoning. . . .

＊ ＊ ＊

Mary and Louisa returned to Kensington on Sunday evening. They'd spent ten days on the Isle of Wight, Mary sketching and her sister-in-law reading in the sun.

Louisa handed her hat and wrap to the housemaid and went upstairs to rest before dinner. Alfred, who'd opened the door for them, drew Mary aside and asked if she'd heard the news about Dr. Scott.

She gasped. "He was poisoned?"

Alfred nodded.

"By his own hand?"

"This morning's papers said the police hadn't ruled out foul play."

"Good God." Mary wondered how she would tell Louisa.

"And there is something else," Alfred said. "About Rawlings and Mister Allen. But it might be best to read it for yourself. Shall I bring the newspapers to the library? Your letters are there."

"Thank you. And Alfred . . . please keep the papers away from Mrs. Allingham unless she asks for them."

While she waited for Alfred, Mary picked up her post and sat by the garden window. She shuffled inattentively through a stack of envelopes until one with a Soho return address stopped her. Mary opened a letter from Will Quain.

Would you care to join me for a day of plein air painting? Monday, I thought, after your return from the Isle of Wight. I know a perfect spot at the edge of Hampstead Heath. I'll hire a carriage for the day and provide luncheon. Bring a maid to chaperone if you must, but I assure you, my intentions are honorable— more or less.

Mary smiled. *Cheeky, but irresistible.* Not only the invitation but also the man. She'd missed him. The ten days she'd been away had crawled like a month.

Will's invitation added something else she'd rather keep from her sister-in-law. Mary sighed, knowing she had to tackle two tricky subjects: Dr. Scott's death and an unchaperoned outing with Will Quain.

Then Alfred handed her the Sunday newspapers.

CHAPTER 17

On Monday morning, Julia ignored the newspaper and absorbed herself in Dr. Scott's casebook. She looked up when her grandfather joined her for breakfast.

"Interesting reading . . . or at least legible?"

"Murder victims haven't a right to privacy, but this case cracks open the personal lives of the doctor's patients." Julia closed the book. "I came across a notation about someone I know. Louisa Allingham."

"Inevitable if you're to do a thorough review."

"Sad, because Doctor Scott notes a pregnancy that will end in a miscarriage. He shaded his entry with foreboding. And his desire to conceal his pessimism."

"Does he say why?"

"No, but Mary mentioned Louisa's several failed pregnancies."

Julia took a last sip of tea, dropped her napkin on the table, and gathered up the book.

"Busy morning, my dear?"

"Not enough to fill it. Two patients, then I'm off to White-chapel. I'll read a little more before they arrive."

By the time Julia left for the clinic, she'd reached Scott's notes for the end of September. She found a terse entry recording Louisa's miscarriage.

The likely outcome, he'd written. *Tragic.*

Then, in late October—only weeks after Louisa lost her baby—Scott saw a patient who surprised Julia, although his diagnosis did not. "Mrs. Margaret Miller" was pregnant but showed "no sign of vaginal chancres, although that is inconclusive." Julia looked up from the page. *He suspected syphilis.*

Julia scribbled a note to Inspector Tennant. *I'm halfway through the casebooks and have found no medical motives for his death. But I thought you should know this: two of your murder victims knew one another. Margot Miller was Doctor Scott's patient.*

Julia resumed her reading and came across a November entry about Charles Allingham.

Good Lord. She closed the casebook. According to Dr. Scott, Allingham had begun to show the early signs of third-stage syphilis.

His disease, Louisa's miscarriages, and Scott's looking for early symptoms in Margot Miller all fell into place. She arrived at the clinic just before twelve, having read the last entries for 1866.

By the time Sergeant O'Malley arrived at the Yard, the inspector had come and gone. Tennant had dumped and spread all the printed envelopes they'd removed from Margot Miller's desk. Next to them, he'd placed the letter written to draw Mrs. Allingham to the maze and the scrap of paper found near Charles Allingham's fireplace.

The inspector had left a note for the sergeant. *Checking on two things. Will be back this afternoon. Keep abreast of the search for Allen.*

"He's onto something," O'Malley muttered. "But what?"

The duty sergeant sent up messages that arrived from Southampton, Portsmouth, Liverpool, and Bristol. There was no sign of Sidney Allen at any of the ports. Then a message came in from Dover.

A sharp-eyed copper had spotted a gentleman boarding the midnight ferry to Calais. A gent with one suitcase in the dead of night? Making a flit, the officer guessed. They exchanged pleasantries, but the constable let him travel on. He had no reason to stop him: the message to arrest Sidney Allen arrived two hours later. But he'd noted the time, the man's appearance, and his destination.

O'Malley read through the report. The officer described him as square-built but running to fat, middle-aged, and with a pronounced north-of-England accent.

Skipping off to the Continent, the creature. And speaking of skipping off . . .

O'Malley looked up at the clock. Where was the inspector?

Around noon, Mary stood atop a hill on Hampstead Heath, looking down at a spot where rock, knoll, and stream met. She was happy to steal away for an afternoon of painting with Will, leaving newspapers, half-formed questions, and Louisa's fears behind. Cyril Eastlake was coming to lunch, so her sister-in-law had manly shoulders to lean on. Mary could take hers away without a twinge of guilt.

"Cyril will soothe her," Mary said to Will's question about Louisa. "He'll explain the state of things at Allingham and Allen and advise her. It's not good, I'm guessing."

"Let's forget about Louisa, the business, and everything else and focus on painting. Are you ready?"

"Oh, yes. Lead on."

Will navigated the slope with easels and camp chairs strapped to his back, lugging a basket that held their picnic lunch. Mary carried their paint boxes. At the bottom, Will deposited his loads and stretched his back. "Shall we eat first? Paint later?"

"Luncheon sounds lovely."

Will unfurled a plaid blanket and moved the wicker basket to its center. Then he extracted a camp brazier from a canvas sack, set it up on a flat rock, and struck a match to light the paraffin.

He bowed. "Tea in ten minutes, madam. The sandwiches are cheese-and-pickle, but I'm sorry that the rock cakes deserve their name."

"No matter," Mary said, spreading her skirts on the blanket. "How domestic you are."

He grinned. "I was hoping you'd notice."

Will picked up the teapot and headed toward the stream. He inched sideways down the bank's slope, lost his footing, and plunged his left boot into the water.

He sloshed across the grass to the blanket. After setting the pot on the brazier, Will pulled off his boot, turned it upside down, and shook. Then he flopped on the blanket and wiggled his wet toes in the sun. Mary noticed a repair to his sock. Someone had mended it with red yarn instead of matching black. She wondered who had darned it for him.

Will passed Mary a sandwich, and they munched for a while in companionable silence. Then he tossed the rock cakes like a juggler and cocked a questioning eyebrow. Mary shook her head, leaned back on her elbow, and looked at the sky.

"Do you know Shelley's poem, 'The Cloud'?"

"No." Will rolled on his side and looked at her. "Tell me."

"*I am the daughter of Earth and Water, And the nursling of the Sky; I pass through the pores of the ocean and shores; I change, but I cannot die.*" Mary smiled. "I think a painting is like that."

"In what way?"

"It's made up of the elements of one's experience. Eternal once it's fixed on canvas, but changeable, too, because each viewer sees something different."

Will moved to sit beside her. He put his arm around her shoulder and lay back on the blanket, taking Mary with him. With his free hand, he brushed her cheek. They watched the drifting clouds for several minutes, listening to the humming meadow.

She murmured, "Tell me . . . who darned your sock?"

He lifted his head, puzzled. "I did."

"That's good." After a while, Mary said, "I suppose we should paint something, or I'll have some explaining to do."

Will turned on his side, propping his head on his hand. "Give me a minute. Let me think . . . gypsies stole your canvas?"

"That's the best you can do? And you an Irishman?"

"I'm distracted today." After seeming to mull, he said, "I've been thinking about Louisa's problems. . . . I suppose she could move into my house."

Mary sat up abruptly. "Move in with you?"

"If the firm goes bust, as you fear, and Louisa loses the house, she can live with us . . . after we're married."

"Married?"

"My flat's a bit pokey, but I expect we can all make do."

He was on his knees in a fluid movement, facing her, cupping her face, his eyes inches away. "Marry me, Mary Allingham." He kissed her lips lightly, then lingeringly. "Say yes." He kissed her mouth's corner, tracing his lips along her cheek. He breathed in her ear, "Please say yes."

When he pulled back, Mary looked into eyes that were green and gold-flecked and fringed with dark lashes. She felt lightheaded, felt something thrumming inside her. It was her beating pulse. She started to speak, but her voice caught, so it took her a moment to say the word.

"Yes."

Sometime later, Will rolled on his back and stretched like a cat. "I suppose we should get on with some painting while there's still light in the sky."

Mary sat up and raked dark curls away from his forehead. She traced a finger along the curve of his cheek and the groove of his upper lip. She heard his breath catch and then felt its warmth. Mary leaned over and touched her lips to his. She lifted her head and smiled. "I suppose we can paint . . . if we must."

He took her in his arms again.

Still later, they packed their luncheon things, letting the brazier cool. Then they set up their easels, unfolded their camp chairs, and set to work.

Before she began, Mary looked at him. "You're wrong about all of us needing to move into your flat. The house belongs to me, not Louisa. And my fortune has always been independent of the publishing firm."

Will smiled. "If I'd known that, Mary Allingham, I'd have asked you to marry me a month ago." He reached for his tube of Paris Green and squeezed a generous disk of emerald in the corner of his palette.

He looked over at her quick intake of breath. "Mary . . . my love. I was joking."

She pointed her brush. "That color . . . I just realized. I hadn't thought of it until now, but I've avoided using it."

He looked at the tube. "Paris Green?"

"Ever since . . ."

"Since when?"

"Since my brother died." She took a deep breath. "Since Charles killed himself." She still had trouble saying the words. Mary saw Will's confusion. "It's loaded with arsenic."

"Are you saying—"

"Charles broke some off the block in my studio, ground it up, poured it into his whiskey, and drank it."

"Good God. Mary . . . my dearest girl."

She looked down at her hands, gripping them so tightly that her knuckles shone white in her flesh.

"I don't understand. How . . ." Will's jaw tightened. "How could he do that to you?"

"Most of the time, I ask, how could he throw his life away? My fun-loving brother." In a low voice, she said, "But he did."

He reached across and gripped her clasped hands. Then he looked up at the sky. "We could pack up and call it a day."

"No, let's paint. Let's at least rough out ideas and return another time."

Mary sorted through her box, choosing and then rejecting several tubes. After a while, she glanced over at Will. He'd squirted a round of Flake White and had scooped up a daub. He was staring at the paint-smeared palette knife.

"Mary . . . why did they conclude it was suicide?"

"He'd been moody. Morose. He died brooding over that painting of a suicide, *Chatterton*. The coroner made much of that as . . . as revealing his state of mind. And there were blackmail letters."

"Do you know what they said?"

Mary shook her head. "And there was the Paris Green paint in his whiskey. I saw the emerald powder spilled across his desk. It couldn't have been an accident. He drank it deliberately."

Will looked again at the daub on his palette. "But why would he use your paint? Every kitchen has rodent killer in a cupboard. Every carriage house has it on a shelf somewhere. With a signature, any chemist will sell you arsenic. Could your brother be so cruel?"

"Will, what are you saying?"

He held up the palette knife with its daub of Flake White. "Begin with arsenic in another form." Then he scraped it into the circle of Paris Green. "And mix the two later." He swirled the paints with the tip of the knife.

"But—"

"Who was with him the night he died?"

Mary bit her lip. "Doctor Scott was there. He came to play chess, but he's dead, too. Poisoned. Did you know that?"

"Yes. Who else?"

Mary's eyes widened. "Sidney Allen. And there are all these things in the newspapers about him. And Rawlings. Rawlings was there, Charles's manservant. Inspector Tennant has been searching for him for weeks. Good God, is it possible? Have we been wrong all this time?"

"Yes. I think it's possible."

Mary bundled her tubes into her paint box. "We must go back. I must tell Louisa. All along, she doubted—and she was right. Inspector Tennant . . . perhaps he suspects, too. Maybe that's part of it. The reason he arrested Rawlings and is looking for Sidney Allen."

They packed everything and made their way up the hill. Almost at the top, Mary stopped.

"Will?"

He was a little ahead of her. He put the basket down and waited for her to catch up.

"The newspapers wrote about unspeakable crimes. Kidnapping and prostitution. Does that mean Charles . . ."

Will turned away. "Come along, Mary. We're nearly at the top."

They covered the last few yards to the carriage. "Will, why would Rawlings or Sidney Allen want to murder Charles and Margot Miller? Why would anyone?"

Will stowed their equipment and looked at her. "I'll tell you what I know . . . and my part in the story."

* * *

Julia's early afternoon filled with problems and patients. At two o'clock, a lull brought time and tea. Julia opened the casebook, scanning the entries for January, reading on into February, and arriving in mid-March.

She stopped dead. "Good God."

Julia scrambled to the door and looked left and right for the clinic's orderly. She called to Clemmie, "Is Jackie back from the chemist?" When the nurse nodded, Julia said, "Ask him to find me a cab—as quick as he can."

She packed her medical bag and Doctor Scott's case notes. Jackie Archer and a hansom waited at the door.

"Where to?" Jackie asked.

"Scotland Yard," Julia said, climbing in. "Driver, take the fastest route you know."

On the ride back to Kensington, Will said, "It was a low point, Mary. I was stony broke and grateful to have any commission at all, so I agreed to do the paintings."

"I see."

"And if Charles enjoyed looking at . . . well, it seemed a harmless pleasure. Still, I can see how a sister—a young lady— might be shocked."

"These last few months . . . nothing seems to shock me anymore."

"More and more, Margot made my skin crawl. The way she used the bribe of bread—and the lure of drink—to make those penniless girls she'd rounded up do her bidding. One girl she'd recruited for my last commission seemed little more than a child."

"So, you stopped?"

He shrugged. "By then, it was easy to quit. I'd sold a few paintings and had a new commission." He looked at her. "If

I'm honest, it was no grand gesture. I could survive and flourish without him."

They rocked along in silence for a while.

"What about the rest of it, Will? Charles and his entanglement with Allen and Rawlings?"

"I think Allen may have sought out your brother to exploit his reputation and his old, established firm. Charles may have been in the dark about most of it."

"And Margot Miller? What of her?"

He turned his head, and Mary waited. Then she touched his arm. "Please, Will."

He sighed and looked at her. "Your brother's connection with Margot had nothing to do with this business in the newspapers. It was something she said at our last session. Charles was . . . keeping her. Margot was his mistress."

Tiny brushstrokes, subtle halftones, and highlights all cohered and formed a picture. Margot in the studio, buttoning her sable collar, pointing out the likeness of the fur to Mary's muff, telling her it had been a gift. Charles, standing in the gallery, gazing at the Margot she'd painted as a Grace, saying she could strike a man dead.

"I've been a fool."

"I'm sorry."

Mary's hand flew to her mouth. "Good God!" She shifted in her seat and clutched Will's arm. "Margot's unborn child . . . Louisa must never hear about it. The horror and despair . . . it would drive her mad."

"But can you keep it from her? Should you?"

"I don't know," Mary said, shaking her head. "And I still don't understand. Who would want to kill my brother—and Margot?"

Mary felt more composed an hour later when the carriage turned into the Blenheim Lodge drive. Will had been quiet for a while.

"Mary, is it possible . . . ?"

"Is what possible?"

He shook his head. "Nothing."

They passed a little man in a bowler carrying a hatbox. "It's Mister Petrie," Mary said, "the furrier from Harvey Nicols."

The carriage pulled up, and Mary lowered the window. "No cab, Mister Petrie? Did you come all this way by omnibus for your delivery?"

He touched his hat. "I'm on my way home to Soho. I thought I'd deliver this personally to Mrs. Allingham."

"Soho. Will, can you . . . ?" When he nodded, she said, "Mister Quain can take you on. That's where he's heading."

"I'll just ring the bell, shall I?" Mr. Petrie said. "And be back in a jiffy."

Mary nodded. "I'll catch up with you."

"Very good, Miss Allingham."

She turned to Will and smiled. "It's been quite a day."

"Shall I come in?"

Mary shook her head. "It's best that I speak to Louisa alone."

"Very well." He took her hand and raised it to his lips.

Mary caught up with the little man at the front portico. Will watched them chat while they waited for the footman, with Petrie doing most of the talking. Then Mary took the box as the door swung open. The furrier touched his hat, hurried to the cab, and climbed in.

"That's a job well done," he said. "It pays to go the extra mile for a good customer, I always say."

Mr. Petrie prattled away. Will, frowning and hardly listening, thought, *It can't be . . . it's too fantastic.*

By the time they'd reached Knightsbridge Road, Petrie had concluded his disquisition on retail's problems and moved on to the challenges of cleaning fur.

"Blood is the worst, Mister Quain, as I just explained to Miss Allingham. Still, her sister-in-law was lucky. The stains marked

the inside of the pelt but didn't damage the sable. We didn't realize the blotches were blood until we sponged the inside, and
it came away pink." He lowered his voice. "The muff was a
Christmas present from her late husband, and thus quite—"

"What's that, Mister Petrie? You returned a bloodstained
muff to Mrs. Allingham?"

"Why, yes. She asked us to replace the lining as she'd torn it
badly." He tut-tutted. "I don't know why Mrs. Allingham removed it herself. We would have done that for her. The lady
must have had a sizable gash on her hand to produce those
bloodstains."

Will's mind raced. When Mary had asked who would want
to kill Charles and Margot Miller, it had flashed into his mind.
The wronged wife.

Will pounded on the carriage roof until the coachman
pulled up.

"I must let you out here, Mister Petrie. I'm sorry." The startled little man gaped from the curb as Will shouted to the driver,
"Take me back to Blenheim Lodge. Quick as you can!"

"Read this." Julia opened Dr. Scott's casebook on Inspector
Tennant's desk and pointed to an entry from March 14.

Sergeant O'Malley leaned over and read. *Louisa Allingham
was here about her headaches and rashes. Gave her laudanum
for her pain and a tube of mercury salve (unlabeled, of course)
for her skin. The dear girl made a gift of a bottle of Royal
Lochnagar, knowing it to be a favorite of mine and her late father's.*

"Louisa Allingham? You're saying Louisa Allingham poisoned Doctor Scott's whiskey before giving him the bottle as a
gift?"

"It doesn't surprise me," Tennant said from the door. "Julia,
will you accompany us to Kensington? I have a hackney waiting downstairs. I'll explain in the cab."

Julia grabbed her medical bag and the casebook and followed Tennant and O'Malley down the stairs and out the door. Tennant gave the cabbie the Allinghams' address.

"I spoke to her jeweler this morning," the inspector said as they drove off. "Louisa lied. She wasn't at his shop on the day Margot Miller was murdered. He hasn't seen her in over a year. Then I made the rounds of all the chemists along Kensington and Knightsbridge roads. Finally, I found the one where she'd signed the poisons register as Mrs. Alice Upton. Her middle and maiden names."

O'Malley said, "Signed for strychnine?"

"No. For arsenic, a week before Charles's death."

"Then . . . you're saying Louisa Allingham killed them all?"

"Yes, Paddy."

"I understand she'd be wanting her husband and his mistress dead, but why kill the doctor?"

"It's all there in the entry," Julia said, tapping the casebook. "Headaches and rashes and the reference to mercury. Louisa had syphilis. And I think she only recognized the truth lately and realized Doctor Scott had kept the knowledge from her for years. The doctor had been treating Charles Allingham for his late-stage disease."

"Then her husband was . . . sweet Jesus," O'Malley said.

Julia nodded. "The most likely source of her infection."

"She killed all three of them," Tennant said. Julia heard the bitterness in his voice. "Her husband, his mistress, and their doctor."

Julia touched his arm. "Richard . . . Louisa Allingham. You couldn't have known. Not without the doctor's case notes."

"No?" he said, stony-eyed. "It seems all too obvious now."

Julia said, "I missed so many signs. . . . Louisa's miscarriages and how she always wears gloves. Mary mentioned her brother's headaches and recent need for spectacles. And after the skating disaster, he was reluctant to take off his nightshirt when I examined him."

Tennant asked, "What would you have found?"

"Syphilis lesions, most likely. I thought nothing about his reticence at the time. It was typical. Men hate to take off their clothes for me." When O'Malley looked at her, she waved impatiently. "You know what I mean."

"Go on," Tennant said.

"Some doctors give their patients the false hope that mercury can stave off the disease indefinitely. But a diagnosis of late-stage syphilis is a death sentence."

"You're saying the so-called 'lifetime with mercury" is a short one, and treatment is bollocks," O'Malley said.

"Yes. Hope for Charles was gone, and concealment was difficult. The case notes show there was a conspiracy to keep the truth from Louisa."

"Mother of God," O'Malley muttered. "But to send Doctor Scott a poisoned bottle? He might share a glass of the stuff with someone else. Would she take such a risk?"

"Oh, I think Louisa knew her man," Julia said. "The miserly Scott would have kept that expensive whiskey all for himself."

"She was past caring," Tennant said.

"Poisoned alcohol . . . Charles joked that Louisa might add Paris Green to his absinthe," Julia said.

"Yes," Tennant said. "He handed her the method for murdering both men."

Julia asked, "What made you suspect her?"

"Last night, I started thinking, poison, twice in one case? I woke up convinced that both poisonings were murders. The imminent raid on the Topkapi distracted me from the obvious. A feeble excuse, I'm afraid."

"The signs were in front of us all," Julia said.

"It was the second poisoning that cast doubt on Allingham's

death as a suicide. But how to prove it? I thought the envelopes and letters might be a start."

O'Malley said, "I saw them scattered on your desk."

"Two hands *were* at work: Margot, the blackmailer; and the murderer. You had to look closely to see it."

"You've a good pair of eyes in your head," O'Malley said.

"That left three questions." Tennant ticked them off his fingers. "Who wanted to use suicide to cover up a murder, who had access to Allingham's whiskey bottle to add the Paris Green, and who wanted Charles Allingham and Margot Miller dead?"

"The betrayed wife," Julia said.

"A wife who bought arsenic and lied about her whereabouts. And you, Doctor Lewis, discovered why Doctor Scott had to die, too."

Mary stood at the door, waiting for the footman to open it. She held a box that contained Louisa's sable muff, the one with the bloodstains sponged away. "That was quite a cut on her hand," Mr. Petrie had said before he tipped his hat and walked away.

"My dear?"

Mary jumped at Louisa's voice. She was standing in the doorway with Alfred.

Louisa looked over Mary's shoulder. "Is that Mister Petrie getting into the carriage?"

"Yes." Mary felt a catch and cleared her throat. "He returned your muff."

"I see." Louisa took her arm. "Come inside. You look all in."

Mary looked over her shoulder at the departing carriage and followed her sister-in-law into the house.

In the hall, Louisa said, "Give Alfred the box and your painting things. There's tea in the drawing room. Come and join me."

Mary obeyed her in a trance.

Louisa had taken the seat at the head of the table with her back to the door. She was seated with her hands in her lap, and a second cup was on the table across from her. Mary sat and eyed the tea her sister-in-law had already poured. Close to Louisa's right hand, a gleaming knife balanced on the edge of a cake plate.

Mary stared into the amber liquid in her cup. *It cannot be. I must be mad.* Then she thought, *Is Louisa?*

"I added the sugar." When Mary didn't answer, Louisa said, "You're not drinking, my dear."

Mary lifted her eyes and found her sister-in-law staring at her.

Louisa sighed. "It's a pity you and Mister Petrie arrived together." Louisa smiled tightly. "I told him I would collect the muff, but tradesmen will always curry favor when they can." She shook her head. "We might have rubbed along together at least for a while, you and I. But now . . ."

Mary measured the distance from her chair to the door. She stiffened when Louisa picked up the knife. If what Mary was thinking were true, then her sister-in-law had used one before. Louisa held it suspended for a moment. Then she sliced the seedcake.

Still gripping the handle, she said, "Now, I'm afraid it's impossible."

When Mary opened her mouth, Louisa said, "Don't. I must think a little."

She turned the knife to look at the sharpened blade. Sounding meditative, she said, "It was surprisingly easy . . . although I made a mess of my muff when I hid the scalpel inside."

Mary felt as if she'd swallowed sand. She rasped, "Why, Louisa?"

"Why?" Louisa frowned, considering. "Do you mean why Margot Miller? Or why Doctor Scott?" She looked into Mary's eyes. "Or why Charles?"

Mary gasped. "You don't mean . . ."

"Death for death, Mary. Three dead babies, and I've had my death sentence, too."

Still holding the knife, Louisa opened her clenched left fist. For once, she wasn't wearing her knit gloves. Red sores dotted her palm.

"I don't understand. . . ."

"Syphilis. Charles knew he was diseased, and he infected us with his foulness. He murdered my children with the connivance of Doctor Scott. They made me think the miscarriages were my fault. My failure. My lost babies are little angels now. In heaven."

"How did you realize—"

"I found out the night I nursed Charles after his skating accident. Lesions covered his back and chest. Blistered and hideous like marks of Cain. Then I understood why he hadn't shared my bed in months."

Louisa held up her palm again. She turned her hand to look at it.

"This 'rash,' as Doctor Scott called it, is only the beginning. I know what comes next. Miss Nightingale took us through the hospital wards in training for the Crimea. So many soldiers were infected, you see. She had to prepare us. Still, I was blind to my early symptoms. In the dark, like other wives before me. And Charles . . . well. He could hide it no longer."

"But Louisa, how could you—"

"How could *I*? How could *they*? And that blackmailing harlot, that creature . . . that she should carry a child and not I."

"How long had you known about them?"

"A week after Charles's death, she wrote to me of their affair, demanding money, threatening to reveal the liaison. I'd lived for years, blind to his secrets." She struck her chest with the knife flat in her hand. "I would not live my last years with her and her threats. No. It was intolerable."

Mary willed herself to speak slowly and calmly. "Louisa, you suffered terribly. I see that now. But my dear, you cannot mean to kill me."

Louisa dropped her gaze and frowned, drumming the end of the knife on the table. The staccato taps cut through the silent room.

"It wasn't part of my plan." She stopped and looked up. "Not you."

Suddenly, pounding and shouting at the front door shattered the quiet.

"Mary, Mary—for God's sake, someone open this door!"

It was Will.

In a flash, Louisa was up and out. Mary followed her through the door, staring as her sister-in-law fled across the entrance hall and up the staircase, passing an astonished Alfred. Something crashed through the front door's stained-glass side panel. An arm thrust through the gap, feeling around for the handle. When the servant yanked the door open, Will staggered in.

He shouted, "Mary," and seized Alfred by the upper arms. "Where is Miss Allingham?"

"Will." Mary ran across the hall and flung herself at him.

"Thank God," he said, his voice ragged, repeating the words into her hair.

She pulled away, still clutching his coat. "Louisa ran upstairs. To her room, I think. She has a knife."

Will and Alfred took the stairs two at a time, with Mary trailing them. When they tried Louisa's door, they found it locked.

Mary knocked and called, "Louisa. Lou, my dear, open the door."

She stood aside while Will and Alfred took turns ramming their shoulders into the door and kicking it. But three inches of solid oak refused to budge. The scullery maid and the bootboy came running upstairs from the kitchen. Louisa's lady's maid and the housekeeper followed from the servants' quarters.

"Billy, go to the stables," Mary shouted. "Find an ax." The bootboy turned on his heels and ran.

Louisa's maid said, "Try the door in Mister Allingham's dressing room."

Mary moaned, "Oh God, I didn't think . . . through here, Will." Mary led them through her brother's study and into his dressing room.

Louisa had locked the communicating door, but it looked more vulnerable to attack.

Will said to Alfred, "Brace me," and the servant buttressed him as he pounded the door with the heel of his boot. After six kicks, it splintered away from the frame and crashed open.

Louisa was on the floor, doubled backward in agony, the soles of her feet curving toward her head. She gasped, choked, wrenched at the collar of her dress, frothing at the mouth.

Mary turned away in horror, leaving Will and Alfred to witness Louisa's last spasms.

And then it was over.

Their cab was halfway up the drive when O'Malley said, "Something's wrong. The front door is standing open." Then a man with an ax, followed by a boy, ran from the back of the house.

The cabbie reined in the horses, and O'Malley leaped from the carriage while it was still rolling. Tennant and Julia scrambled after him.

The side panel by the front door was shattered; a stone cherub sat amid the broken glass. They crunched across a rainbow field of shards as Will Quain came down the staircase supporting Mary.

Quain said, "Louisa is upstairs in her room. She's dead."

Tennant looked up the staircase and then at Julia. "Doctor?"

"I'll follow in a minute."

Tennant nodded and headed upstairs with O'Malley.

Julia looked around for the servant. "Let's take her to a room with a fire." They followed Alfred into a sitting room. "Fetch some brandy for Miss Allingham and ask her lady's maid to bring a wrap."

"I don't have a lady's maid," Mary said dully. "Lou's maid . . ." She closed her eyes.

"Ask Mrs. Allingham's maid to bring down a shawl or blanket."

Mary looked at Julia. "Why are you here . . . you and Inspector Tennant?"

"We know, my dear. I'm sorry." She took Mary's wrist and counted the beats. Then, she said to Will, "Keep her warm and give her brandy by the spoon. I must . . ." Julia's eyes flicked toward the ceiling.

"Of course, Doctor. I'll look after her."

Sergeant O'Malley arranged the removal of Louisa Allingham's mortal remains. Under his direction, constables carried her body on a stretcher from Blenheim Lodge to a waiting wagon. Julia would perform the postmortem at Kensington station.

She would likely conclude that self-administered strychnine had caused Louisa's death. Confirmation would wait for the chemical analysis, but there was little doubt. Will and Alfred had described the classic death contortions visited on the body by that deadly poison. And on Louisa's night table, O'Malley found a hundred-tablet bottle of strychnine sulfate with only a few pills left.

Julia looked around and thought, *All the tragedy's elements are in this room.* The marriage bed, a symbol of the betrayal and disappointment that drove Louisa to murder. *Her father's medical bag.* It stood open on its shrine-like stand, the likely source of the strychnine pills. Julia found a set of lancets inside the bag. Any of them could have inflicted Margot Miller's neck wound. When Julia examined the gash, she'd thought of a lancet first. The case also held several old syringes. Julia guessed that a closer examination of Scott's whiskey cork might reveal a tiny perforation. She would mention it to Richard.

Julia moved to the portrait of Louisa's father. He and Doctor Scott had been old friends, and she wondered if he'd been a party to the deception in its early stages. She thought, *Betrayal was in the man's nature*, remembering Louisa's thwarted ambition to nurse in the Crimea. *All the men in her life failed her, starting with him.*

Father, husband, doctor, all were trusted figures. All were authorities over their daughters and wives, or so the moralists preached. None of their actions justified Louisa's crimes, but they explained what she had done. Louisa must have looked at her father's portrait every day, along with the preserved remnants of his medical career. Julia felt a wave of pity, then a tide of love and gratitude for the doctor who'd played the role of parent in her life.

"So much went terribly wrong for poor Louisa." Tennant had come up quietly behind her. "So many betrayals."

At the word "betrayal," Julia looked at him. He read her thoughts uncannily at times.

"Miss Allingham confirmed your conclusions," Tennant said. "Louisa confessed most of it to her. The night he died, Charles escorted Scott and Allen downstairs." He nodded to the communicating door. "Easy for Louisa to wait for them to leave the room, slip into her husband's study, and add the arsenic she purchased to his whiskey. She returned later to stage the scene by adding the green paint."

"And what of Will Quain's intervention? How did he—"

"An amateur sleuth's flash of inspiration. He had an epiphany triggered by two daubs of paint and a conversation with a furrier. I'll tell you about it on the way to the station house."

Julia picked up her medical bag. "I wonder if Mary will forgive Louisa for her brother's death." She and Tennant stopped at the top of the landing. "Forgive his failures, too, and find peace."

Downstairs, the broken glass had been swept away, and Will helped Mary's coachman fit a wooden panel into the empty window.

"Unless my detecting powers have deserted me utterly," Tennant said, "that gentleman intends to help her try."

CHAPTER 18

The following morning, Julia nodded to the glazier fitting replacement glass into the front door panel at Blenheim Lodge.

"A temporary fix," he said of the frosted pane, "until Miss Allingham orders another stained-glass window."

Julia wondered what he knew. The morning newspapers had reported the death of Louisa, the widow of Charles Allingham. No other details had leaked to the press. At some point, the whole story would be part of the public record, but not yet.

The door was open, so Julia went inside. The silent house displayed none of the conventional marks of a household in mourning. Its window curtains stood open, and no black crepe shrouded the door knocker or the hall mirror. Julia supposed the ghastly circumstances of Louisa's death rendered those practices false.

Alfred appeared. The footman looked at Julia as if she were a fellow shipwreck survivor. The servant extended his hand and snatched it to his chest, remembering his place. Julia shifted her medical bag and grasped it.

"Did you sleep? You look to me as if you didn't."

He shook his head.

Julia had left a sleeping draught for Mary and wished she'd thought of him. Alfred had seen the worst of it, along with Mary and Will.

"I'll leave you something, although you may not need it by tonight."

"Thank you, Doctor."

"Is Miss Allingham awake?"

He nodded. "Miss Mary is in the morning room."

Julia followed him into a bright, south-facing room. Mary had abandoned her coffee and plate of eggs and sat at the desk by the window. She had pen and paper to hand and an address book held open by a paperweight. But the page was blank, and she was staring into the back garden.

Alfred cleared his throat. "Doctor Lewis, Miss Mary."

"Julia." She seemed to shake herself awake and stood. "How kind. Alfred, will you bring Doctor Lewis a fresh pot and a cup?"

They moved across to the breakfast table and sat. "How did you sleep?"

"Deeply . . . and dreamlessly, thank God. But I'm having some difficulty focusing this morning."

"An aftereffect of the sleeping draught. Another coffee and it will wear off." Julia eyed the plate. "Not eating as well as you slept?"

Mary shook her head.

"You should try, but not this." Julia carried the congealing eggs to the sideboard.

"Charles and I always ate here in the morning. The dining room is too formal and filled with mahogany."

"A room with happy associations."

"My . . . Louisa rarely joined us. She usually breakfasted in bed. But that desk was hers. She wrote all her letters and organized the household from it."

"You were sitting there when I came in."

"Yes . . . I must get over the idea that certain objects and rooms were hers if I'm to live here happily." She considered and said, "I never liked the desk. All that Louis Quinze gilt and filigreed inlay."

"Get rid of it. Buy something that is yours."

"Yes."

Julia nodded at the abandoned address book. "What task had you attempted?"

"Funeral arrangements. I was looking for . . ." Mary's voice caught. "It seems too hideous to bury her with Charles."

The servant returned with coffee. Mary said, "Thank you, Alfred," in a steadier voice. After he closed the door, she poured and said, "I thought burial with her father at Highgate Cemetery would be best."

"That sounds right."

Mary replaced the pot and folded her arms. She stared down at her untouched cup. Julia let the silence stretch out.

"I wonder . . . I wonder if we'd talked about it more. Louisa's miscarriages. I tried, but not hard enough. My brother was useless when it came to such things. And Charles was the one . . ." Mary bit her lip. "Louisa's pain, her bitter disappointments . . . they must have festered like an infection of the soul."

"I know a little about what you're feeling, Mary. About the ache of not having aided someone you loved. I speak from experience. It takes time, and it helps to speak of it with someone you trust."

"I'm lucky in my friendships. And Will. He's upstairs, sleeping in my bedroom chair." Mary waved impatiently. "I couldn't care less about appearances. Such nonsense. But he . . ." She smiled. "Silly man, there was plenty of room in my bed. But my last waking awareness was of him, sitting in the chair. And when I woke up, there he was. I tucked a blanket around him and came downstairs. Anyway, we are to be married soon."

"That is happy news. Best wishes, and I congratulate Mister Quain."

"I'm just glad that he asked—and I said yes—before Louisa . . ." Then Mary said in a rush, "I wouldn't want him to think I was marrying him out of loneliness or gratitude or anything else. I love him and want to be his wife. That's the simple truth."

Julia smiled and said, "Simple. Now, tell me, what are your plans?"

"Last night, we talked it through. We'll marry by special license. His father is an Anglican dean, so Will knows the Archbishop of Canterbury." Mary laughed and said, "Isn't that unlikely?"

Julia smiled. "A little."

"With a special license from the archbishop, we won't have to post the banns for three weeks and wait. We can leave for Paris almost immediately. We're not running away. We'll slip away and start over."

Julia raised her coffee cup. "Here's to simple truths—and to traveling new paths."

At six o'clock on Wednesday evening, Julia and her Aunt Caroline were the first down to the drawing room. Her grandfather would follow soon, and they expected Dr. and Mrs. Franklin, her grandparents' oldest friends, to arrive at seven thirty for their weekly dinner party.

That evening was the first time Julia had seen her aunt since Louisa's death two days earlier.

"Mary Allingham, that poor child," Lady Aldridge said. "But at least she's found . . ." She roused herself. "How is that young assistant of yours faring? Doctor Barnes."

"Very well, Aunt."

"So, you don't have to spend every waking minute at the clinic?"

"Well, I—"

"I lunched yesterday with the widows' club."

Her aunt's changes of conversational direction were head-snapping, and Julia smiled at her nickname for the surviving wives of her late husband's law colleagues.

"I can't remember how," her aunt said, "but that business involving Richard's father came up. He was the lawyer in that financial scandal back in the fifties. The guilty banker absconded, but William Tennant remained to face the music, although the authorities exonerated him in the end."

"I remember the story."

"The ladies agreed. It was high time that nice man, his son, had a little luck with the women in his life."

"Oh?"

"His mother was a . . . well, I won't use that word, although ladies of a certain age who are old friends sometimes do. Let us say that Mrs. Tennant was not an amiable woman. Nor was Isobel."

"Isobel?"

"Richard's fiancée. Someone said she tossed him away in the middle of the scandal like a bad penny."

"Aunt Caroline, I think—"

"You think too much, Julia. That is your trouble. You grew up amongst ancient relatives, and it's given you an old head. Try feeling for a change, my dear." She sighed. "My interference will not set you against him. You are too intelligent for such nonsense."

Julia smiled. "You know I value your opinion, Aunt."

"Well, listen to me now and think if you must. Think of it as fact-gathering and adding to your case notes. Observe the symptoms and reach the diagnosis that is obvious to me: Richard loves you."

"You sound very sure."

"I am. The only question is this: What do you feel for him?"

"Aunt, you've hardly given me a chance to speak. I—" Julia broke off at the sound of a knock and looked at the clock. "It's a little early for the Franklins."

"Simple gifts, Julia," her aunt said before the visitors arrived. "I shall ask Andrew to invite Mrs. Davies to play it once a week until its message sinks in."

But Paddy O'Malley, and not the guests they expected, walked in with her grandfather.

"Sergeant, you know my sister, Lady Aldridge."

"Sergeant O'Malley and I are old friends. Will you join me?" She lifted her glass. "It's not Irish, I'm afraid, but it's a lovely single malt from Scotland."

"Thank you, Lady Aldridge. That's grand."

Julia poured and invited him to sit, so the sergeant eased into a chair.

"I have news, and the first is from the Yard." O'Malley looked into his glass, and his jaw tightened. "The decision's come down from on high. All the big fish will be slipping the net."

Dr. Lewis gasped. "I can't believe it. No prosecutions for the clubmen? After what they've done? It's damnable."

"No one's paying any piper except the two fellas we caught in the act, thanks to Johnny Osborne. After his article, at least they'll be explaining themselves to their wives and sweethearts. Doctor Scott, I'm thinking, is explaining to his Maker. But that's all."

"It's not enough," Julia said. "The chairman, this Reginald Bruce, surely—"

"Claiming ignorance, he is. Rawlings is a liar, and Allen has scarpered. It helps when your cousin is the ninth Earl of Elgin and your friend is the Prince of Wales."

Lady Aldridge said, "Surely His Royal Highness had no part in this."

"He dines at the Topkapi," O'Malley said, "and runs with a fast crowd, but not as fast as the Harem."

Julia asked, "What about Sidney Allen?"

"The Yard won't exhaust itself over the chase. The creature would be shouting all the big names if they tried to prosecute."

"And the little fish?" Lady Aldridge asked. "What happens to them?"

"Ah . . . interesting, that is. Yesterday, I'm hearing the Crown will dangle transportation to Australia. Seven years instead of a longer stretch in an English nick. Rawlings, Stackpole, and a few others we arrested will be jumping at the chance."

"But I thought the government had halted transportations," Dr. Lewis said.

"There's one last convict ship sailing for the Antipodes. All the little fish will be on the *Hougoumont* when it leaves for Western Australia. They'll be far from our shores, swimming in southern waters before anyone's the wiser for it."

Julia set her glass aside. "Inspector Tennant must be furious."

"Spitting mad he was last night. 'Tis the second reason I'm here. After tying together some loose ends, I got back to the Yard late this morning and found his desk cleared out. All he left behind was a note."

"I don't like the sound of that," Andrew Lewis said.

"It said he's seeing the commissioner for a brief leave of absence, but that empty desk tells the tale." O'Malley shook his head. "Chief Inspector Clark will be hoping he'll never come back."

"I'll bet," Julia said, frowning. "But surely Richard won't give Clark the satisfaction."

"I thought I'd catch the inspector at Russell Square, but his housekeeper said he took the 12:10 from Victoria Station to his house in Kent."

"What do you think, Sergeant?" Dr. Lewis said. "Will a little time away in the country soften his disgust?"

"His note had a finality about it. Apologizing for not seeing me, saying some nice words, and thanking me. And that was that. I think he's planning to resign from the Yard."

"No," Lady Aldridge said. "That cannot be. Someone must go after the dear boy and change his mind before he makes it up."

Julia had the first-class carriage to herself, and the 12:10 to Dover gave her two hours to think before it arrived at Richard's village of Adisham.

That morning, she'd scrambled to install her grandfather at the clinic for the day and arrange the services of Dr. Barnes through Sunday. A note delivered by hand to Tennant's housekeeper had secured his country address and the information that Julia could hire a pony trap from the blacksmith near the railway station. The smithy's boy would drive her the last two miles to Tennant's house.

Aunt Caroline had urged her to go to him, but in the morning, concern for the proprieties sunk in. "Does Richard have a housekeeper in Kent?" Her aunt had eyed the bag Julia's maid packed for several nights away from home. Then Lady Aldridge left to telegraph for a room at a Dover hotel.

The train sped through Surrey and crossed into Kent. Julia closed her eyes and thought about her trip to Dover with her grandparents. *Nearly ten years ago . . .*

There had been no railway line beyond Canterbury. Instead, they'd traveled by carriage, sharing the road to the coast with the omnibus traffic from Canterbury. She and her grandfather had walked from Shepherd's Wall to Dover, the last miles of the Pilgrims' Way. Her grandmother hadn't felt up to it. It had been a bittersweet holiday, the summer before Julia left for medical school. The summer before her grandmother's death.

Julia's next journey took her across the ocean. She remembered the flutter of excitement and unease the night before she boarded the ship at Southampton. She felt similar sensations on the ride to Adisham. As the train chugged out of Canterbury station and the cathedral's towers receded into the distance, Julia rehearsed her arguments.

She'd begin by reminding Richard about the start of the case and how he'd asked her to bury her qualms and get on with the job. Wouldn't he heed his advice and do the same? And then there was his career, the over ten years he'd invested in the Metropolitan Police. Would he waste his time, talent, and the commissioner's confidence by throwing it all away? As for the squalid decision not to prosecute . . . wasn't that an argument for hanging on? The Yard needed police officers with Tennant's integrity and sense of justice. And last, Julia would tell him that acting on one's white-hot rage was a mistake. He should let his anger cool and reconsider.

What of her reconsiderations?

Julia sighed and looked at the spring landscape, the yellow-green countryside framed fleetingly by her window. Houses, fields, and villages flashed by and vanished in an instant. She thought, *The path I've taken . . . it's as if I've hurtled down a track.* She'd thought it hadn't mattered because she'd headed in a straight line, knowing what she wanted, sure of her destination.

But lately . . . Lately, she'd wondered about changing course, taking the turning, and walking through the open gate. Not lately. Since she met Richard.

Perhaps it's simple, after all. Still . . .

What if she couldn't persuade Richard to return to the Yard? What if the journey was an ending, not a turning? It was if she'd removed a stopper and felt her spirits drain.

With Canterbury and Bekesbourne behind her, Julia thought, *One more stop.* As the train neared Adisham, it curved along a high embankment, crossing a double-arched bridge before braking to a screeching halt at the sleepy village station. Julia asked the stationmaster about the pony trap and when the last train left for Dover.

He pointed out the blacksmith's workshop and said, "Last run from Adisham to Dover is the 4:50."

Julia left her overnight case with him and started across the road. Then she stopped. She retrieved her bag, hired the pony trap, and set off on the two-mile journey to Richard's house.

Orchards of white-blossomed apple trees stretched along the road. The spring breeze sent their petals afloat, settling on the grass like a dusting of snow. *How lovely*, she thought, and her heart lifted. They rounded a bend, and the pony trap slowed as they approached a house with an iron gate. Julia eyed the carpet bag at her feet.

To hell with Dover. She grasped the handle and stood.

A slight, older woman with salt-and-pepper hair opened the cottage door. She'd turned back her white cuffs and covered her black dress with a duster. The caller had interrupted her housekeeping.

Julia smiled. "Good afternoon. Is Inspector Tennant in?"

"I'm afraid you've missed him. He left this morning for Dover to catch the noon steamer to France, Miss . . ."

"Julia Lewis."

"*Doctor* Lewis?"

When she nodded, the housekeeper smiled and stepped back. "Won't you come in? I've been waiting for the postman. I have a letter for you. Richard asked me to send it off this afternoon."

In the morning in Dover, Julia ignored the waiting cabs at her hotel, passed the omnibus stand, and started the climb to the white cliffs on foot.

The morning was warm, so Julia peeled off her wool jumper

halfway up the path. At the summit, she crossed a field gilded with buttercups and stopped ten yards from the cliffs' edge. She spread her jumper and sat amid the humming grass, looking across the sea. The morning fog had burned away hours earlier, and the sun shone high in the cloudless azure sky. She ignored her vigilant watch for once and surrendered to the sunshine and the rippling breeze.

Julia leaned on her elbow and listened to the shorebirds' counterpoint. Soaring gulls wheeled and cawed, wings spread to the wind, dipping low beneath the cliffs. Skylarks shot heavenward, their piercing chirps and trills adding to the morning concert.

She slid Richard's letter from her pocket and read it again.

Dear Julia,

As you open this in London, I am in France. Sir Richard kindly granted me a six-month leave of absence. In my present state of mind, I am no good to anyone—not to the Yard, myself, and, least of all, my friends.

I am happy to write that my godfather didn't let the club-men slip the noose. The home secretary decided not to prosecute. While Sir Richard's disgust matches mine, his hands are tied. He has issued an open warrant for Sidney Allen's arrest, but it is an empty gesture without the resources to back it up.

I believe Sir Richard knows what I intend, although we said nothing at our meeting. If the Yard will not pursue Allen in earnest, I must, as a measure of justice for Franny and Jin and all the others.

I hope it won't be long before I return, restored in mind and heart.

Richard

Julia looked up from the letter. She stood and walked to the chalky edge, the wind streaming strands of hair that she dragged from her face. The blue-green sea stretched before her, restless and rippling. In the far distance, she made out the hazy cliffs of France and the white strand at their base. Then they dissolved in a blur of tears.

"Godspeed," she whispered, and walked back to the path.

AUTHOR'S NOTE

Two plotlines in the novel merit a few words. The first is the Victorian art world and who's real in the novel and who's not. The second is the trafficking of girls in Queen Victoria's England.

Artists Mary Allingham and Will Quain are fictitious, but the other painters mentioned in the book were prominent artists of the era. Some are famous: James Abbott McNeill Whistler, for example. Others, like Frederic Leighton—later Lord Leighton—may be less familiar to readers.

At the nineteenth century's end, Lord Leighton was the "grand old man" of Victorian painting and president of the Royal Academy. His work points to the divergent paths of British and French art. Not long ago, I visited New York's Metropolitan Museum to view Leighton's *Flaming June*, on loan to the museum. It's one of his greatest works. The often-reproduced image of a lounging woman asleep in her diaphanous, tangerine gown may be more familiar to readers than the painting's title. "Impressionist" it certainly is not. In *A Slash of Emerald*, Mary Allingham alludes to the contrast between London and Paris in discussing *Down the Rushy Glen*, her fictional painting. The artists agree: the painting's loose brushwork would baffle Britain's Royal Academy, and they would advise Mary to submit it later "when it's finished."

The painting's title references the only real-life Allingham in the novel: the poet William. It's a line from Allingham's best-known poem, "The Fairies." I had a little fun writing the scene where the artist Helen Paterson comes to tea. When she notices *Down the Rushy Glen* on the wall and quotes from the poem, Louisa Allingham is impressed and offers to introduce Helen to "Cousin William." The real-life Helen Paterson married William Allingham and painted under her married name.

Among the female artists in the novel, all except the fictional Mary were recognized in their day. Helen Allingham's aunt, Laura Herford, became the first female student admitted to the Royal Academy's art schools. In 1860, she submitted her work signed A. L. Herford. Although the ruse embarrassed the Academy, it allowed her acceptance to stand. In the ten years before her death in 1870, Herford exhibited twelve works in the Royal Academy's annual exhibitions. Her niece, Helen Allingham, worked as a book and journal illustrator, later turning to watercolors. Van Gogh admired Allingham's work, and she became the first woman admitted as a full member of the Royal Watercolor Society. The artist Barbara Bodichon is better known as a leading feminist and founder of Girton College, Cambridge. In 1869, Girton opened its doors, opening university education to women.

In 2019, the Royal Academy celebrated 250 years of annual art shows, now known as the Summer Exhibition. Since 1769, the RA hasn't skipped a year. Even COVID-19 only delayed the event from summer to fall. Each season, artists still line up for "varnishing day," just as Mary Allingham and Laura Herford did in 1867.

A digital copy of the Royal Academy's 1867 catalog is online. It lists the paintings mentioned in *A Slash of Emerald*, numbered and in the rooms where they hung. Of course, *Repose* and *Galway Pastorale* by the fictional Mary Allingham and Will Quain are missing. Laura Herford's lost portrait, *Margaret* (number 309 in the Middle Room), inspired the fictional Margot's name: Margaret Miller.

There is an irony in women's struggles with Royal Academy recognition. Two of its founding members in 1768 were women: Angelica Kauffman and Mary Moser. Yet, in Johan Zoffany's 1772 group portrait, *The Academicians of the Royal Academy*, Kauffman and Moser are absent from the assembled company. Instead, the artist painted their framed portraits on the wall.

The problem? Zoffany set *The Academicians* in the "life studies" studio where nude models posed for painters. Women, including the two founders, were banned. For decades, female art students tried and failed to win entry into life studies classes. Nearly 170 years after its founding, the Royal Academy elected a third woman as a full member. In 1936, Academician Laura Knight won the right to add the initials "RA" to her signature.

For much of the twentieth century, Victorian art lost favor with critics and the public. Leighton's *Flaming June* sold in the 1960s for a mere two thousand pounds. Exhibitions in the late 1960s and early '70s revived it. Victorian art reentered the popular consciousness in 1987 when Rosamunde Pilcher published her bestselling novel, *The Shell Seekers*. In it, the daughter of a fictional Victorian artist deals with family friction arising over her father's newly valuable painting. Since then, interest has waxed and waned. Perhaps Victorian art is due for another revival. Visit www.patricemcdonough1789.com for links to the artists and paintings mentioned in the novel.

Readers won't be shocked by the book's other storyline: human trafficking. It's a horrendous practice that continues to this day, familiar as the crimes of Jeffrey Epstein and Ghislaine Maxwell.

In the 1880s, the crusading journalist WT Stead exposed the sordid entrapment of young girls in a series of sensational articles in the *Pall Mall Gazette*. When some questioned Stead's claims about child prostitution and virgins sold for twenty pounds, he arranged the "purchase" of a thirteen-year-old and published the story. He was arrested, tried, and convicted for abduction, spending three months in Holloway Prison. The brevity of the sentence is as shocking as Stead's arrest. In the end, his work led to the "Stead Act," which raised the age of consent in Britain to sixteen. *A Slash of Emerald* is set in 1867 when the age of consent was twelve.

In 1912, WT Stead received an invitation to attend a peace conference in New York. In April, he boarded the *Titanic* and did not survive the voyage.

What might be more surprising to readers than sexual trafficking is the "semi-slavery" that continued after its official abolition. In the 1830s, Parliament finally outlawed slavery in the British Empire, freeing the enslaved but voting to compensate slaveholders. The man granted the largest payment was John Gladstone, father of the reforming Liberal prime minister William Gladstone. After John Gladstone pocketed his check, he petitioned the British government to allow the transportation of Indian indentured servants to his sugar estates in the Caribbean, so-called "coolie" labor. The Chinese, too, were caught up in the pernicious scheme. John Gladstone's role in the practice was so pivotal that the workers were known by the disparaging term "Gladstone coolies."

In *A Slash of Emerald*, the fictional Owen Lloyd accurately describes the suffering endured by indentured laborers. Modern-day Guyana reveals the scope of this "slavery by another name." While thirty percent of the population is of African descent, forty percent trace their ancestry to India.

I love hearing from readers. If you enjoyed *A Slash of Emerald*, please send an email through my website at www.patricemc donough1789.com You can sign up for my newsletter there. Its focus is on historical mysteries and classic films of suspense. It includes an occasional short story featuring Dr. Julia Lewis and information on book releases.

You'll also find me on Facebook and Instagram.

ACKNOWLEDGMENTS

The debts I owe to so many have stayed the same with the publication of my second book. My sister, Carol McDonough, and readers Kathy Sandt and Ginny Quain read the manuscript multiple times. Their patience with the process and insights into language, plot, and character helped shape *A Slash of Emerald*. Their greatest gift was their honesty. It sent me back to the drawing board many times to do better.

Kensington Books is the best home a new writer could find. Wendy McCurdy's sensitive reading of the manuscript and suggestions for changes shaped *A Slash of Emerald* into a much better book. Thank you, Wendy. Seth Lerner hit another home run with his cover design. I'm grateful for the efforts of production editor Robin Cook, editorial assistant Sarah Selim, and publicists Jesse Cruz and Larissa Ackerman. Publishing a book is a team sport: thank you to the stellar Kensington crew.

To the early readers who left reviews for my first book, *Murder by Lamplight*, I thank you sincerely. You provided insights that gave me much to ponder. I'm grateful to the many readers who found the book after its publication in a bookstore, library, or through a reading group. This literary world we're all a part of flourishes only when there are engaged and passionate readers who pick up a writer's book. It's a leap of faith to give a debut novel a chance. Reading this far means you've come back for a second Dr. Julia Lewis Mystery. Thank you.

Finally, to my literary agent, Jim Donovan of Jim Donovan Literary: none of this would have been possible without you.

Don't miss the first Dr. Julia Lewis mystery . . .

MURDER BY LAMPLIGHT

"Enthralling debut. . . . Mystery, pulse-pounding suspense, and a budding romance. More, please!"
—Mary Jane Clark, *New York Times* Bestselling Author

"Engrossing characters, a gritty, gaslit setting, and a compellingly twisty mystery.
Fans of *Miss Scarlet and the Duke* will devour this book!"
—Colleen Cambridge, Bestselling Author of *Mastering the Art of French Murder* and *Murder by Invitation Only*

"A riveting mystery that brings the gritty world of the Victorian era roaring to life."
—Andrea Penrose, Nationally Bestselling Author of *The Diamond of London*

Julia shifted her umbrella and extended her right hand to Detective Inspector Tennant, nodding to Sergeant Graves beside him. "Julia Lewis. You sent for my grandfather, Andrew Lewis, but I'm afraid he's unavailable. I assist him in his practice."

"Are you a nurse, Miss Lewis? Because we need a—"

"It's Doctor Lewis." Julia smiled. "I've thought about carrying my medical diploma with me. But even rolled up, it won't fit into my bag."

Reactions like his still galled her, but four years after qualifying, she usually managed to hide her irritation. The sergeant returned her smile, but Tennant did not. She sighed. *No sense of humor.*

"Is the victim over there, Inspector?" She nodded to the line of policemen's helmets and shoulders visible over the edge of a ditch.

Tennant nodded. "But I'm afraid it's not a sight for . . . Doctor Lewis, I don't think—"

"Inspector Tennant, you sent for my grandfather, and I am standing in for him while he convalesces. I am a fully qualified doctor listed on the medical register. Now, shall I proceed with the examination? Full-blown rigor may set in if we dither much longer."

Tennant stepped aside. "Of course, Doctor."

Julia picked up her bag and brushed past him. "I've seen my share of dead bodies."

Sergeant Graves called after her. "Not like this one, you haven't, M-miss—Doctor."

—from *Murder by Lamplight*